Buried
Too Deep

Jane Finnis

Poisoned Pen Press

Library of Congress Catalog Card Number: 2007940715

ISBN: 9781590583999   Hardcover
      9781590597249   Trade Paperback
      9781615950683   Epub

Poisoned Pen Press
6962 E. First Ave., Ste. 103
Scottsdale, AZ 85251
www.poisonedpenpress.com
info@poisonedpenpress.com

Printed in the United States of America

For Rhys Bowen
to celebrate our very long and happy friendship

Part of the province of Britannia in 98 AD

OCEANUS
GERMANICUS
(NORTH SEA)

GABRANTOVICUM
SINVS
(BRIDLINGTON BAY)

The Headland
(Flamborough Head)

OCELI PROMONTORIVM
(SPURN HEAD)

ABVS FLVVIVS
(RIVER HUMBER)

10 ROMAN MILES

PETVARIA
(BROUGH)

DERVENTIO
(MALTON)

Oak Tree
Mansio

DERVENTIO FLVVIVS
(River Derwent)

ABVS FLVVIVS
(River Ouse/Humber)

N

River Ouse

EBVRACVM
(YORK)

CALCARIA
(TADCASTER)

River Wharfe

to ISVRIVM
(ALDBOROUGH)

Chapter I

He lay sprawled in the farm cart, as still as a statue. His flushed face and the bloodstains on his cloak grew lurid in the red sunset. He looked half dead, and I said to myself, I doubt if he'll live to see the dawn.

Out loud I was more cautious. "I wonder who this is?"

I was standing on the paved forecourt in front of my mansio. I'd been out there for some time, trying to snatch a bit of peace and quiet after a busy afternoon in the bar-room. Trying, but not succeeding, because a customer had come outside for a breather too, and he was in the mood to chat. He was one of our overnight guests, which meant I couldn't just ignore him, and I couldn't think of a polite way to ask him to push off and leave me in peace. So I said "yes" and "no" and "really?" now and then as he rattled on, while thinking my own thoughts. It's a skill all innkeepers learn, otherwise we'd go mad having to listen to our customers' ramblings.

This talkative fellow was Curtius, a short fat Gaul with brown hair turning to grey at the sides. He was already reasonably drunk, but quite amiable. He was a private trader on his way north to do business with the natives across the frontier, which made him different from our normal run of guests. Being an official mansio, we mostly get travellers on imperial business, soldiers and government officers and army contractors, even the occasional spy. A private trader was unusual, and I'd made the mistake of saying so. Now he was convinced I wanted his life story. Oh, me and my big mouth!

"Yes, Aurelia, I see a lot of the world in my job. I travel all over Northern Britannia, selling Roman goods to the barbarians, and buying up native arts and crafts..."

"Really?" I could imagine his stock-in-trade: flashy knives that broke if they cut anything stiffer than cheese, gaudy mugs with not-quite-perfect glazes, imitation-gold trinkets, in fact all the usual cheap tat that Romans hope will impress barbarians. It does impress them, but nothing like as much as in the old days when our legions first conquered Britannia. Even here on the Empire's edge, the northern tribes are developing some semblance of taste. They mostly can't afford luxury items, but they are insisting on a better class of cheap tat.

"The tribes beyond the frontier are only too happy to trade, and you'd be amazed at some of the high quality goods they have to sell..."

"Really?" Actually I wouldn't be in the least amazed, but it was too much trouble to say so. I've lived in the province of Britannia for nearly twenty years, and I've long since realised that the natives here, still barbarians in so many ways, can also be fine craftsmen.

"...Beautiful gold jewellery, silver and bronze as well, wool cloaks and rugs. And then the novelty items, carved antlers, wolf-pelts, beaver-skins...Really good stuff, and dirt cheap. You know the sort of thing I mean?"

"Yes." I thanked the gods that he was on his outward trip, otherwise I felt sure he'd insist on trying to sell me some of his "really good stuff."

"...And there's always a market for anything a bit different, especially among the soldier-boys in the forts. I say to them, if you want an unusual present for the little woman, or even the wife," he gave an exaggerated leer, "just ask old Curtius, he'll always see you right. It was one of the lads from the Ninth Hispana who suggested I should stay here, you know. He said to me, 'If you're travelling east, stop a night at the Oak Tree, it's not a bad little place at all.' So here I am."

Thanks, soldier, I thought. I'd have preferred your recommendation to be a bit more enthusiastic. "The Oak Tree is the best mansio and posting-station north of the River Humber," is what I usually say myself. But it was a compliment of sorts, so I gave him a smile.

"…And you wouldn't believe what this lad wants me to get for him this trip? For his wife's birthday! You'll never guess in a hundred years…"

"No." And not much point trying, if it's going to take that long.

"Oh, go on, have a guess! Shall I give you a clue?"

But that was when the farm cart came into view on the main road, and turned down our track onto the forecourt. Until it came close, I thought it might be yet more thirsty customers. Our bar-room had been busy since well before noon, and no fewer than five guests were staying with us overnight, including this non-stop talker.

But as the cart rolled towards us, I realised its occupant was in no state for drinking. He lay flat out with his eyes closed, breathing loudly through his mouth. His tattered cloak was thick with blood, not all of it dry, and crawling with flies. He looked a typical native, tall and fair, and he was strong and sunburned, a farmer probably.

I said, "I wonder who this is?"

The cart's driver was another native, barely more than a boy with only the beginnings of a beard. He pulled his mules to a stop and spoke to us in broken Latin. "Which way is doctor, please? They said he live near mansio. I need hurry. Belinus has leg hurt bad."

I pointed to a narrow road leading off to the left, and replied in his own British language. "It's not far. Follow that track about hundred paces, till you come to a group of three farm buildings. The biggest one is a house, newly painted, with a shrine to Apollo outside it. That's the doctor's."

"Thank you, lady." He relaxed a little, relieved not to have to struggle with Latin. He raised his whip, then lowered it again.

"I nearly forgot. Belinus said he wants to talk to someone called Aurelia Marcella. Do you know her?"

"Yes, I'm Aurelia Marcella. I'm the innkeeper here. I'm afraid I don't recognise your friend though. What's it about?"

"I don't know. Could you talk to Belinus when he wakes up? Please? He made me promise to find this Aurelius. If you can talk to him…"

"Of course I can, whenever he likes. But I don't suppose he'll wake up till the doctor's seen to him. Get him along there as quickly as you can."

"I will. You won't forget? He said it's important."

"I won't forget, I promise. The doctor's a good man, he'll do everything possible. I'll come over to his house very soon, and make sure to see Belinus when he wakes up." *If* he wakes up, I thought, as the boy drove off.

Curtius the trader had been following our conversation. "You employ a doctor here? What's this, the latest in mansio services for your customers?"

"I'd like to say yes, but the truth is I don't employ him, he just lives close by. He's married to my housekeeper, as it happens. He's got a good reputation, and people come from miles around."

"Aha! So if you serve your customers bad wine or dodgy meat, you've got someone handy to put them on their feet again!" He laughed loudly at this, but when I didn't crack a smile, he subsided. "Sorry, don't mind me. Only joking."

That sort of joke I can do without. But you can't pick and choose your guests. We get all sorts staying at the Oak Tree, and we do our best to look after them, but there's no law that says we have to like every last one.

"You must admit it's unusual," he persisted, "a doctor in the wilds of the country like this, miles from anywhere. It's not as if you're near a town. Eburacum's the closest bit of civilisation, and that's sixteen miles away." He rubbed his backside. "I should know. I've ridden from there today, and got the saddle-sores to prove it."

"I wouldn't call Eburacum particularly civilised, though," I answered. "It's just a provincial dump, full of legionaries getting drunk and crooks trying to rip everybody off." Actually that was rather unfair on a perfectly ordinary garrison town, but he was beginning to annoy me.

"You reckon the countryside is better, do you? Well, so do I. Better for my sort of trade, anyhow. I'm heading east to the coast tomorrow, then I go north to the frontier zone. I haven't been across the wolds for a while. Natives still friendly, are they?"

"Yes, they are." I've always liked the wold country, it's gentle and peaceful, and I've got to know it quite well since my sister and her husband bought a farm there.

The bar-room door behind us swung open and my housekeeper Margarita came hurrying out. She looked, as always, calm and unruffled, but her fair hair was flopping untidily over her face, a sure sign she'd been busy. She pushed it out of her eyes. "Aurelia! I wondered where you were."

"Sorry, I didn't mean to leave you holding the fort for so long. Is everything all right?"

"Everything's fine, don't worry. I just thought I'd warn you…" She stopped as she saw the retreating cart. "Is that *another* patient for Timaeus?"

"Yes. He has an injured leg, so his friend said. He didn't look good—unconscious, and there was quite a lot of blood."

"Blood everywhere," the joker beside me agreed. "Makes you see red, doesn't it?"

Margarita ignored him. "They always look bad when they first arrive. But Timaeus can work wonders, if the gods are with him."

"That's what I told the lad who brought him. I didn't recognise him, or the patient either, and I think I know all the natives in the Oak Bridges area. They must have come a fair distance."

She smiled proudly. Her husband was a fine doctor, and not, like most of them, employed to care for a single rich family. He was prepared to treat anyone who could pay him, (and, I suspected, some who couldn't, but that was his affair.) "That makes three men who've come for treatment since this morning. He's had a busy day."

"He's not the only one. We seem to have been going non-stop today. We haven't had so many customers for ages. It must be the good spring weather, and the market in Oak Bridges. Not that I'm complaining, of course. Are you managing all right?" That was a silly question really. Margarita was brilliant at running the mansio, and could cope with the whole Ninth Legion on manoeuvres, or the Imperial court if Caesar decided to drop by.

"It's not over yet, that's what I came to tell you. One of the overnight guests has just decided he's giving a party."

The comedian beside me looked interested. "Really? Which one? I bet it's one of those soldier-boys."

Margarita smiled at him. "You'd win your bet. It's the tall lanky one, dark hair, who came in riding a good grey horse. It's his birthday apparently, and he intends to celebrate. He's started already, and now he's inviting everyone in sight to have a drink with him, and even telling all the natives to bring their friends along."

"I love a good party," the trader said. "Count me in. And if we all drink too much and make ourselves ill, it's nice to know we shan't have to go far to find a doctor." He chuckled as he headed into the bar.

"The gods preserve us from customers who think they have comic talents. I assume the birthday boy can afford to buy drinks for half the province?"

She touched her belt-pouch. "He can. I insisted he give me some money now, to keep the wine and beer flowing for a good while. We're keeping a slate for him, so we'll know when it runs out."

"Good. I'll come in and give you a hand as soon as I can. I'm just going over to Timaeus' to take a look at the latest patient. His friend says he was asking for me, though I've no idea why. He's in no state to talk now, but if he comes round, Timaeus can send one of the lads over to fetch me."

She went back inside, and I set off along the narrow road that led past my private garden, past one of the vegetable plots, till it reached the cluster of old farm buildings. Most of them were hardly used now, except for the big square house that Timaeus had built for himself, his family, and his patients.

Before I'd reached it, I met the young native driving his empty farm cart back.

"Are you waiting to take Belinus home again tonight?" I called out to him. "If you are, take your mules round to the stables and the boys there will see to them while you have a bite to eat."

"Waiting?" he said, in a mixture of surprise and irritation. "No, I'm not waiting, I haven't time. The doctor says he'll care for Belinus overnight and send a message tomorrow or next day. I can't hang about here."

"Have you far to go?"

"About fifteen miles east, up the Long Hill and into the wolds. Good road most of the way, but slower in the dark, which it will be soon. And the mules are tired." He stood up in the cart and stretched his shoulders and arms. "Can't be helped. I've got to get home as soon as I can."

"That's a pity. One of our guests is throwing a birthday party, everyone invited. I'm sure you deserve some refreshment, after bringing Belinus all this way. Are you a relative of his? Where shall we send to, when he's ready to come home?"

"Just a neighbour. I've told the doctor where his farm is. White Rocks it's called, there's a pile of them by his turning off the main road. Anyone'll give directions. I'll try and come down again in a couple of days to find out how he is. I'm sorry I can't do more for him, but the way things are now, I don't like to be gone from the farm for long, especially at night. You never know what's going to go wrong, when your back's turned."

"Oh? Have you had trouble?"

He shrugged and sighed. "Life seems to be one long trouble these days. Well, I'll bid you good-night." He cracked his whip, and the tired mules set off for home.

I paused as usual at the little shrine outside Timaeus' door, with the fresh flowers and beaker of wine he always placed there for Apollo the healer. I offered a short prayer to the god and his sister Diana, my own guardian goddess. Timaeus always said it isn't the gods alone that heal mortals, it's medical skill as well. Perhaps, but as my grandmother used to say, a prayer doesn't hurt, and it makes whoever's praying feel better, even if nobody else does. Poor Belinus needed all the help he could get.

I found the doctor in the large, light room he used for diagnosing and treating his patients. He was bending over Belinus, who lay on a high bed in the centre. There was a wide table alongside it, and his two assistants watched from the bed's foot, waiting for instructions.

"What do you think, Timaeus?" I asked. "He isn't too good, is he?"

He didn't raise his head, but grunted, "Wait while I finish examining him, Aurelia. Come and look for yourself, if you like."

I stepped forward cautiously. I'm not unduly squeamish, but doctors tend to forget how gruesome their work can appear to the rest of us. Belinus was still unconscious, still flushed, and now I could hear that his breathing was ragged, and catch an unpleasant smell that I couldn't identify. His stained cloak was gone, and he was naked. His chest was badly bruised and some of his ribs looked lop-sided even to my untrained eye, but there was no blood there. That had come from his left thigh, which had a deep gash near the top, right down to the bone at its upper end. It was caked with dried blood, was still bleeding, and the leg was swollen to below his knee.

One glance at all this was more than enough for me. I stepped back and waited for Timaeus to speak.

He straightened up and shook his head. "This leg wound's a mess. His neighbour said there'd been some sort of accident with a sickle, but if that cut was made by any kind of sickle my name's Hippocrates. It's completely the wrong shape. It's a sword cut, if you ask me. Look, boys, you can see it was made by a straight blade."

The two lads looked eagerly where the doctor pointed.

"Nobody's tried to clean him up at all," Timaeus went on sadly. "They've just covered the cut with that dirty old cloak. So the wound's inflamed, and from the smell of it, there's gangrene there. And the thigh-bone may be damaged."

"He's got some broken ribs too, Master," the elder of his two assistants put in. "And the jolting about on the journey here will have made them worse, won't it?"

Timaeus nodded. "Yes, Phokas, it will. Of course it's flattering that people are coming to see me from so far away, but usually it would be better for the sick folk to get help nearer home."

Well perhaps, but I didn't blame people for beating a path to Timaeus' door. There wasn't another healer like him for many miles around. "Can you do anything for him?"

"We'll do what we can." He turned to his two assistants, who were both young, but as different in appearance as chalk from cheese. The elder, Phokas, was a slave whom Timaeus was training, about eighteen, stocky and strong, with broad shoulders, powerful hands, and intelligent brown eyes which missed nothing. The younger boy was Timaeus' son Gaius, a slim, handsome lad of only eight. With his fair curls and fine-cut features, he looked too delicate for the hard physical work of a doctor, but he was determined to follow his father's profession, and had a child's callous lack of squeamishness concerning blood and gore.

"Well, boys," Timaeus said, "this is the second bad wound I've had to treat today, and it's serious because the patient is unconscious, and has clearly lost a lot of blood already. Let's see how much you've learned. Phokas, what's the first thing we need to do?"

"Find out if the bone is broken," the dark lad answered promptly, "because how you treat the wound will be different if you're dealing with a fracture at the same time."

"Quite right. And then?"

"Wash the cut with vinegar, to get rid of dirt and dried blood." The thought of how painful that would be made my stomach tighten, and I was glad Belinus wasn't conscious.

"Good," Timaeus agreed. "What next?"

Gaius said, "Cut away any of his leg that's in—in…"

"Inflamed," Phokas supplied. "Especially any flesh that's dried up, which might mean gangrene."

"Yes, inflamed," the boy agreed. "Inflamed flesh is bad and will stop the good flesh healing up. Clean it all again, then stitch the edges of the cut together with wool thread, like you did that man's arm this morning."

"No, not stitch," Phokas objected, "the cut's too big. We must use some of the little metal clamps to fasten it. But I don't think we should clamp the wound tonight. It's sure to need cleaning again in the morning, and there might be more gangrene. We should make a temporary dressing of lint, then bandage it but not too tightly. And bandage those ribs too, and try to make him drink something to give him calm sleep. Look, he's started tossing about like a ship in a storm."

Timaeus smiled. "That last suggestion will be easier said than done, but otherwise you're quite right. If we fasten up a bad wound permanently straight away, we run the risk that there may be tiny pieces of dirt, or even bone, or perhaps a blood clot left in there still, which will fester overnight and poison his whole body."

Gaius asked, "Papa, do you really think that's a sword cut? How did he get it?"

"Let's not worry about that now. Get busy, both of you, fetch everything I need onto the table. A bowl of vinegar, a sponge, clean cloth, lint, bandages, a small hook, a knife…and what do I rub into the bandages? Gaius?"

"Honey. And you want a spatula to spread it."

Timaeus turned to me, smiling. "See what a useful pair of apprentices I've got, Aurelia? Soon they won't need me at all."

I smiled back, trying hard not to show how queasy all this was making me feel. Yet at the same time, a part of me was fascinated by the doctor's skill. I knew he wasn't callous about his patient, just detached and professional. I also knew that if anyone could save Belinus, Timaeus could.

I watched as the boys collected what they needed. All the instruments and medicines were neatly ranged on stout wooden shelves around two walls of the room. There were the medicines themselves, clay flasks of liquid and alabaster jars of ointments and powders, each one neatly labelled, along with a variety of cups, bowls, dishes, spoons and small jugs. There were rolls of bandage and pieces of lint, balls of wool, piles of cloths, and trays of small instruments, clean and ready for use. The larger tools, mostly fearsome in appearance, hung on the third wall. I recognised knives, hooks, forceps, a bone-saw and a drill. I couldn't identify all of them, and preferred not to try.

"Timaeus, I don't want to be under your feet while you're working, but there's something I need to tell you. The young man who brought him in said his name's Belinus, and before he lost his senses, he asked to speak to me. Made quite a point of it apparently, although I can't think why, because I'm sure I've never seen him before. But I promised I'll talk to him, so if and when he wakes up, could you let me know, and I'll come straight here."

"Of course. The lad said much the same to me, so it must be something important. But I don't see Belinus regaining his wits any time soon. What if it's in the middle of the night when he wakes?"

"Send for me anyway. I don't want to miss…I mean if there's only one chance to talk."

"I will, I promise."

"Will you watch by his bedside?"

"Probably, if his fever doesn't improve. Phokas and I will take turns. Ah, good, you've got everything ready, boys. Then we'll begin."

They began. I left.

Back in the bar-room I helped myself to a beaker of red wine without adding any water, to quieten my quaking stomach. The party was now cheerfully noisy, with toasts to the birthday boy, and to practically everyone else in the room. As the night wore on, they even drank to me, so of course I had to return the compliment, but by then I was adding water, and plenty of it. It was all very respectable really. Here in the wilds of Britannia we don't go in for the exotic orgies they claim to have in Rome. They spent enough, and drank enough, to make it a good birthday, and about midnight we shepherded the locals off home, and our own guests across the courtyard into the guest wing.

There was still no message from the doctor, and as I got ready for bed, I sent a quick prayer to Apollo to give Belinus a restful night's sleep.

Chapter II

He must have had a reasonable one, because nobody came to summon me to his bedside. I rose at dawn as usual, and I strolled outside as I always do to savour the peaceful early morning. As I went to stand under the oak tree in the forecourt, I noticed with pleasure how it was coming into leaf. Oaks are always among the last trees to wake after the dead months of winter, but once they do, you can be sure that spring is here to stay.

I looked in at Timaeus' house and found him on watch beside Belinus' bed.

"No change in our patient, Aurelia," he greeted me. "He's slept the night through, if you can call it sleep, but it doesn't seem to have done him much good. He's still very feverish."

I looked down at him, as he tossed and turned on the bed. "That wounded leg looks more swollen than before. Is the bone broken?"

"I'm afraid so," Timaeus sighed. "We found the beginnings of gangrene last night. There'll be more diseased flesh by now, I expect. I hope I don't have to amputate, but it may come to that. When Phokas wakes up, what I'll do..."

"Thanks, I'm happy to leave the details to you and Phokas. I haven't had my breakfast yet."

He grinned. "Sorry. Nor have I, now you mention it. Could you tell Margarita I'll be over for something to eat as soon as Phokas relieves me here?"

"Better still, why don't I ask her to send you something on a tray? I'm sure you could do with it."

His face lit up. "Thank you, yes, I could. But won't she be busy with all the guests?"

"I doubt if they've surfaced yet, after the amount they all put away last night."

I was right there. Margarita was in the kitchen as usual, and the breakfasts were ready, but nobody had appeared to eat them yet. She was brisk and cheerful as always, but there were dark circles under her eyes. Perhaps she had helped her husband nurse Belinus? I really couldn't object to that, as long as she didn't become so tired it affected her work as housekeeper. All the same, it made me slightly uneasy.

"Good morning, Margarita. You know, I could have sworn we had some overnight guests staying. Don't say they've left without their food?"

"Still sleeping off their hangovers. It was a good evening, wasn't it?"

"It was. I've just looked in on Belinus, and Timaeus asks if you can send him over a bite of breakfast, so he doesn't have to leave the bedside."

"I will. I'm afraid it's touch-and-go for poor Belinus."

"He's in the best possible hands. Now, can I do anything to help?"

"Yes please, if you've time. There's a fair bit of clearing up to do in the bar-room after the party last night. If you'll keep an eye on things in here and the dining-room, I can be getting on with that. Everything's ready to go, I think. Plenty of fresh bread, goat's cheese, cold sausage, and the usual Rhodian wine."

The bread was still warm from the bakehouse, and the smell of it made me hungry, so I took the chance to snatch a bite or two myself. I'd just finished the last mouthful of cheese when footsteps and voices in the dining-room next door announced that it was time to serve breakfast.

I went to bid them good morning while the maids brought in the food. They looked remarkably fresh, all things considered, apart from the birthday boy. He refused food and wine and asked for a beaker of water, but with a smile. "Good wine you serve here. I just wish I hadn't had quite so much of it."

I said I hoped they'd all slept well, and everyone nodded, except the joker Curtius. "I'd have slept better," he answered, "if it hadn't been for the bed bugs."

"The *bed bugs?*" I almost dropped the jug of wine I was handing round.

"That's right. There weren't any. I felt so lonely, I'd a job to sleep at all!"

We all laughed, though I privately hoped the next bed he slept in would contain bugs the size of mice. But he became serious when they started comparing their travel plans, and soon one of the others mentioned rumours of trouble on the roads further east, towards the coast. There were raiders, he'd heard, based near the shore and picking off travellers who hadn't got enough men to protect themselves.

I couldn't help thinking that any raiders who robbed Curtius of his cheap merchandise might feel they'd wasted their time. But it seemed unlikely they'd try, because he assured everyone he was well prepared, with four strapping bodyguards to protect him and his mules. All the same I noticed he became thoughtful and didn't crack any more jokes till the meal was over. Of course I don't approve of raiders on the roads, but it just shows they can occasionally be good for something.

The younger of the soldiers, the one who hadn't celebrated his birthday, turned to me. "You're the one with the local knowledge, Aurelia. What do you think, should we be worried, or are these just rumours?"

Yesterday, I'd have said bluntly that I thought the stories were just the kind of over-embroidered tales that seasoned travellers use to scare one another, like children in the night telling stories of horrible giants and monsters. But for a heartbeat, I heard in my head the young carter's words of the evening before: "The way things are now, I don't like to be gone from the farm for long, especially at night. You never know what's going to go wrong when your back's turned."

"I've heard some very vague rumours too," I admitted, "but nothing substantial, and none of our customers have reported any problem on the roads. It never hurts to take care, but I'm sure you'll have no trouble. I visit the wolds quite often, and it's quiet country, peaceful and safe."

Which just shows how easy it is to give wrong information even though you're trying your best to be helpful.

The guests went their various ways, and I strolled outside and did my morning rounds. This is an old habit of mine, because I like to keep a personal eye on the outside work. The stables hardly need it, because my stable-master Secundus is an ex-soldier and likes to keep everything "fair and square and cavalry fashion." But there's our farm as well, and my farm manager Ursulus is competent, but sometimes inclined to cut corners. And, well, I just wouldn't feel the day had started properly if I hadn't had a walk round outside.

The stable yard was as busy as a beehive. The horse-boys were hard at work feeding and mucking-out the animals that we kept in the stables at night, except for two who were cleaning tack, and one who was taking grain out to the big paddock, where several of the brood mares were receiving extra rations. Secundus was in the smaller paddock, examining a mule's hoof. He let it drop as I approached, and stepped smartly back as the animal aimed a kick at him before trotting away, limping slightly.

"Pesky brute," he grunted. "It's a bit lame, which has made it even worse tempered than usual."

"Anything serious?"

He shook his head. "Just a bruise. I've had me eye on it since it came in yesterday. I'll see to it."

"Good. All the others look in good shape."

He smiled. "They are. We should have a grand crop of foals this year." Our herd of good black riding-horses is my pride and joy, my own special contribution to the farm. We've gained quite a reputation in the district, particularly among settlers, who want to ride something a bit livelier than the little native ponies.

"That reminds me, Secundus. Isn't it today that one of the new settlers from the wolds is coming over to buy a couple of yearlings?"

He nodded. "Ostorius Magnus. He's due sometime before noon. Do you want to show him what we've got for sale, or shall I do it?"

"I'll give him a beaker of wine and have a chat with him, then hand him over to you. It's always useful to meet other Romans in the area. I gather he's just taken over a place near my sister and her husband. You're clear on the prices, aren't you?"

"I am. But before you go, I had some news yesterday about our Victor."

"Good. How is the lad?" His son Victor, known to all of us as Titch, was a favourite with everyone. He was in the army, a cavalryman as Secundus had been, so we only heard from him now and then. "Has he got his posting to Germania? I know he's anxious to see service outside Britannia."

"No. He's coming home."

"Really? He's done well to get leave at this time of year. Mostly they're all out on manoeuvres if they're not actually fighting. When's he arriving?"

"I don't rightly know." He sighed. "Could be any day."

There was something wrong here. I expected Secundus to be overjoyed at the prospect of seeing his son, yet his expression was strained and unhappy.

"What is it, Secundus? Is it bad news?"

"Aye, very bad. The letter I got was from Victor's commanding officer, saying the boy's taken a serious wound in his left arm. A real bad one. The doctors have patched him up, and he's well in himself, but he's lost the use of his hand. He's going to have to leave the army."

"Oh, Secundus, *no!* That's terrible. I'm so sorry."

We looked at one another, sharing the sadness of it. Ever since Titch first came to work for me years ago as a young horse-boy, his ambition had always been to join the cavalry. He'd enlisted as soon as he was old enough, and by all accounts had made an excellent trooper, quick-thinking and brave. He'd been commended on a battlefield by a general, and had already been rewarded with promotion beyond most young men of his age. He'd done, in fact, just what we'd all expected of him. If he had to leave his chosen career, it didn't bear thinking about.

I searched for something helpful to say. "Maybe Timaeus can find the right treatment for him."

"I doubt it, if the army doctors can't. They're the best medics in the Empire."

"They are, but none of them are better than Timaeus. We mustn't give up hope. Was he wounded in battle?"

"Aye, in a scrap with some barbarians north of the frontier. Apparently his unit was ambushed, and the standard-bearer was killed by an arrow. Victor saw the standard fall on the ground. He galloped over to it, and had to dismount and drop his shield to pick it up, and while he was down two native horsemen came at him. He's been trained to fight on foot of course, we all are. But you're easy meat for mounted men when that happens, especially with no shield. He was knocked unconscious, still hanging onto the standard though, and two of his mates came and got him away, standard and all. Only by that time someone's horse had trampled on his shield-arm, above the elbow."

"Broke it, presumably?"

"Well and truly. And damaged the nerves, they think, because although the bone's mended nicely, he's got no use in his left hand now. He can't hardly move the fingers of it. That's what his commander says."

"If he saved the standard, he's a real hero. You must be proud of him."

"I am, very proud. But sad too, mind."

"So am I. Well, you know there's a job for Victor here, for as long as he likes. It won't be what he wants, I realise that, but perhaps it'll give him a breathing-space while he…" I trailed off. While he what? Got better? Or didn't get better, but came to terms with being a civilian? "…while he finds something else," I finished lamely.

"Thanks, that's a start, I suppose. But you're right, it won't be what he really wants. I hate to think what this'll do to him. His officer says he's taken it hard."

"He's tough, though. Tough and smart."

"Often it's worse for the strong ones." Secundus had a faraway look, perhaps remembering injured comrades from his own army days. "Well, we must all do what we can to help."

"You can count on it."

I finished my rounds and went into my study to do some paperwork, but I found I was restless and couldn't settle to it. In all truth it doesn't take much to distract me from dealing with bills and orders, but the bad news about Titch, and the odd request by Timaeus' patient to talk to me, gave me food for thought. I was relieved when a knock at my door gave me an excuse to put down my stylus.

Young Gaius stood there, slightly out of breath. "Please, Mistress, Father says can you come at once? The man with the bad leg has woken up."

I hurried over to the doctor's house. In front of it a small carriage was drawn up, and the driver was helping down a young man with his right arm in a makeshift sling. From his appearance he was a native, but a well-to-do one wearing good Roman-style clothing, and a lovely tooled leather sword-belt, but no sword of course. From his white face and clenched mouth, his arm was hurting him badly.

Gaius opened the door for him. "The doctor is this way. I'll tell him you're here." He led the way in, and called out, "Father! Another patient!"

Timaeus appeared and greeted the new arrival. "Timaeus is my name. I'm the doctor. Come through into my work-room."

"Thank you. My name's Coriu. I'm guard captain to Chief Bodvocos. I'm sorry I can't shake hands." He managed a thin smile. "I've broken my arm, or rather had it broken for me. I hear you're the best bone-setter in these parts, so I hope you can patch me up."

I'd never met Coriu, but I'd heard of Chief Bodvocos. He was a powerful native chieftain of the Parisi tribe, and he lived on the coast, so this guard captain, one of his senior men presumably, had travelled quite a distance.

"I'll do my best. When was it broken?"

"Yesterday."

"Good, you haven't wasted any time in coming to see me. Some sort of accident, was it?"

"Not really. A Gaul attacked me with an axe. I think he was aiming for my head, so I suppose I should be thanking the gods that it's no worse."

"I'll take a look, and we'll see. If it's a straightforward fracture it should heal up as good as new. If the ends of the broken bones overlap, we'll probably need to stretch it, to make sure the arm doesn't shorten." He looked round and seemed to notice me for the first time. "I'll be with you in a heartbeat, Aurelia. Now, Coriu, will you just climb onto this bed and make yourself as comfortable as you can. Phokas here will take off that sling and clean the wound, then we can see the damage. If you'll forgive me, I must just have a quick word with Aurelia about Belinus. Come with me, Aurelia, he's in the side-room."

Phokas moved forward to help Coriu onto the high bed, but the injured man waved him away. "Belinus? From White Rocks Farm? Is he one of your patients?"

Timaeus nodded. "He was brought in last night. He's quite badly hurt, I'm afraid. You know him?"

"Yes, I know all Chief Bodvocos' people, and Belinus is a good young farmer. What's happened to him? Was it the sea-raiders?"

"I don't know. He's been unconscious nearly all the time since he got here. His injury looks like a sword-wound, but the neighbour who brought him here said it was a farm accident."

"No accident, I'd stake my life on it." He paced across the room and back again, frowning. "Gods, this is serious. Belinus has had trouble from Voltacos' raiders before, but I didn't realise things had got as bad as this." He paced the room again. "The Chief will need me now more than ever. I think I ought to go straight home. If you can put this arm in a decent sling for me and give me something to dull the pain, I'll take a chance that it'll mend by itself."

"It won't," Timaeus said sternly. "You must know that, or you wouldn't have come all this way to have it treated. Do you want a deformed right arm the rest of your life?"

Coriu hesitated. "That's really what will happen? It won't just heal itself?"

"Oh, it'll heal after a fashion, but there's a big risk you won't have full use of it. Now I can see you're worried about Belinus, but the only way you can help him is to get well and strong again as quickly as you can."

Coriu shrugged, and the gesture made him wince. "I suppose you're right. Let's get on with it then." He eased himself onto the bed, waving away Phokas' help. "You say he's badly hurt? He'll be all right, won't he?"

Timaeus adopted his most professional manner. "We're doing everything we can for him, but these things take time. Now, let's concentrate on you. Phokas, you know what to do. Aurelia, if you'll just come with me to Belinus' room…"

We entered the little side-room that was used by any of Timaeus' patients who needed to stay in bed. I was disappointed to find that Belinus was unconscious. "Gaius said he'd woken up. I was expecting to be able to talk to him."

Timaeus shook his head sadly. "He was only conscious for a very short time. He asked for your brother. I said he wasn't here and I would fetch you, but he said that would take too long. He made me promise to give you this message: 'Please send for Lucius urgently, there are lives depending on it.' He repeated it two or three times and got quite worked up, and then he felt dizzy and passed out."

"Send for Lucius?" Suddenly I began to see a possible reason why this stranger had wanted to see me: it was my brother, not me, he really wanted. Lucius was an investigator on the staff of the Governor. Could this Belinus be one of his informers?

Timaeus must have been thinking the same. "If he's working for Lucius, that could explain why he was attacked, perhaps?"

"It certainly could, if whoever he was informing on found out."

"Can you reach Lucius? Are you in touch with him?"

I never know how to answer that. A definite "yes and no" is the best I can usually manage. My brother is sent on assignments all over Britannia, but I rarely know the details. All I have is the name of a contact who'll take messages for him, but he can't guarantee how long they'll take to arrive.

"I'll have to send to the garrison at Eburacum. There's a centurion there called Petreius who takes messages for Lucius. But how easily Petreius can get hold of Lucius to deliver them… anyone's guess is as good as mine. I'll do what I can. I'll send a note today."

He nodded. "Right. Now I must look after Coriu. It's quite an honour, being asked to treat one of Bodvocos' captains."

"You're treating quite a few natives now, aren't you? When you first came here, apart from people in Oak Bridges who knew you, it was mostly settlers who consulted you, wasn't it?"

"I suppose it was. I don't really think about what tribe or country they come from. If they're sick or hurt, I treat them. That's what I was taught, and that's what I do."

It didn't take me long to write a short note to my brother, simply saying "the man from White Rocks" had met with a serious accident, and wanted to see him urgently. I wrote it on papyrus rather than a note-tablet, partly so I could tie it securely and seal it, but mainly because that made it appear somehow more important. I didn't want some clerk at headquarters thinking it was just a party invitation.

I went to the stables, and asked Secundus to send someone to deliver it as fast as he could.

"It's for my brother, and it's urgent. I could wait for an official courier to come through, but I don't want to risk a long delay. It'd be just my luck if all the couriers today were heading east instead of west. So I'd rather one of our own lads rode over with it. It's to be delivered to a centurion named Petreius at garrison headquarters in Eburacum."

"Right. The lads'll be fighting over who goes, they always enjoy a visit to town."

"It needs someone sensible, though. It's not easy finding your way round a big fortress, and I want this delivered personally, preferably into Petreius' hands, not just left lying about."

"Understood. Malchus can go. He's got cousins in the army, so he knows his way round a military base."

"Fine, a good choice." Malchus was an experienced rider and had a calm head on his shoulders. "Make sure he knows it's urgent, and I don't want him fobbed off by some officious pest at the fortress gates if Petreius isn't there. In that case he's to leave the scroll with the duty gate commander, and get a receipt for it."

Secundus grinned. "Aye, so you said. It's something important. I've got the message."

"Sorry, Secundus. You of all people know what the army's like, it's just that I'm worried. One of the injured men who was brought in yesterday has information for my brother. He says it's life or death."

I'd wandered back to the forecourt, my steps slowing as I gloomily contemplated the paperwork still waiting on my desk, when a party of four rode in, two well-dressed Romans with a couple of muscular bodyguards in attendance, Gauls to judge by their haircuts. They were all well mounted, and though the Romans wore civilian travelling cloaks, they looked like soldiers, or possibly ex-soldiers. I stopped, wondering if these were the men who'd come to buy horses.

Sure enough, as they dismounted, the older Roman said, "I'm Ostorius Magnus. Will you tell Aurelia Marcella we're here?"

"I'm Aurelia Marcella. Welcome to the Oak Tree."

"Thank you. Let me present my eldest nephew Vividus."

I hardly needed to be told they were related, the family likeness was so marked. They were a handsome pair, tall and sandy-haired, though Magnus' hair had touches of grey. Their faces were similar, with bushy eyebrows and high cheekbones. Only one thing marred Vividus' appearance. His left cheek was badly swollen, and when both men smiled pleasantly at me, Vividus' smile was noticeably lop-sided.

Magnus held out his hand. "Pleasure to make your acquaintance. I've heard plenty about you."

I made the stock response. "Not all bad, I hope?"

"Quite the reverse." Now Vividus took my hand, and he wasn't in a hurry to let it go. "Your sister and brother-in-law have sung your praises." He had an odd lisp to his speech, presumably caused by his swollen cheek. "Their farm is quite close to ours. But I have to say, now that I've met you, their descriptions haven't done you justice." He gave my hand a final squeeze and smiled into my eyes.

Well well, I thought, this one fancies himself as a ladies' man, doesn't he? He's certainly attractive, if you like military good looks, which I do, or he will be when his face isn't swollen. But is he trying a bit too hard? Charm, as my grandmother used to say, should be sprinkled about like a rare spice, not ladled on like fish sauce.

I suggested we share a jug of wine before we started our horse-trading, but to my surprise they both shook their heads.

Magnus said, "Thank you, in due course, but business before pleasure, eh? And I think Vividus is anxious to see your doctor first, aren't you?"

Vividus nodded and smiled his uneven smile. He gestured towards his cheek, but didn't touch it. "It's quite painful, and seems to be getting worse. I think the tooth needs to come out."

"Bad luck. But you'll be in good hands with Timaeus, he's an excellent doctor. You're sure you wouldn't like a beaker of wine first?"

"It's tempting, but no, I'll wait till he's done his worst. It'll give me something to look forward to afterwards. As well as the pleasure of your company, of course." He gave me another oh-so-charming lop-sided smile. "Where will I find the medico?"

I pointed the way. "He's having a busy time at present. Several men have come down from the wold country to have wounds treated. I don't know if you've come across Chief Bodvocos yet? His guard captain Coriu is the latest patient, he came to see Timaeus this morning to have a broken arm set. He's probably still here."

Vividus scowled. "I hope I can avoid him. That would be worse than the toothache."

"You could break his other arm," Magnus suggested, and they both laughed.

Magnus said thoughtfully, "So there have been wounded natives, as well as wounded Romans? That's interesting."

"Some of each. Timaeus doesn't make any distinction. He treats anyone who needs him, as long as they can pay him something."

Vividus grimaced. "I'll pay all right, if he can cure this pain. Well, here goes. Save me plenty of wine." And he strode smartly off towards Timaeus' house.

Chapter III

Secundus was waiting for us in the stable yard, and I made the introductions.

"The four yearlings we're selling are in the small paddock there," he said, pointing. "The four black ones wearing halters."

Magnus looked surprised. "Still running loose? I thought you'd have had them tied up here by the railings. Don't they stand well?"

The stable-master grinned, recognising the start of a hard bargaining session. "They do, and I could have tied them up here ready. But then you might have wondered how easy they are to catch, mightn't you? And the answer is, very easy, as I'll show you."

"They're all used to halter work then?"

"Aye, they are, and they've all had some training carrying blankets on their backs, but we haven't saddled any of them yet. A year's on the young side for that."

"Good. I've my own horse-trainer on the estate, and he'll break them in. Well now, catch them please, and I'll have a close look."

Secundus beckoned Castor, one of the older horse-boys, and together they fetched the young black horses out and tied them to the paddock railings. All four came easily and stood quietly, looking good. They continued to behave beautifully while Magnus first walked all round them, then examined them carefully, looked in their mouths, and finally checked their feet.

"Not bad so far," he said. "Now can I see them in action?"

We went to an empty paddock, where Secundus put a long leading-rope on each in turn and made them circle round showing their paces. They worked well, and I was proud of them.

There followed some interesting bargaining. Magnus began by assuming that the innkeeper and stable-master of a country mansio would be easy to bully or persuade, and would naturally give a powerful estate owner a very advantageous deal. He soon discovered his mistake. I'm never short of customers for my horses, and I don't sell them cheaply. After protracted haggling he ended by buying all four, and for exactly the price Secundus and I had agreed beforehand.

We shook hands on the deal and went into the bar-room, where I produced a jug of our best Gaulish red, and ordered a big plate of bread, olives, and cheese to go with it. We sat down to wait for Vividus.

"You mentioned that Vividus is your eldest nephew," I said, pouring out the wine. "Have you other nephews and nieces here in Britannia with you?"

"I've three altogether, and yes, they're all here with me. They're my sister's boys, I took them on when she died. Ferox is next oldest, there's only a year between him and Vividus. He's our estate manager. He's a natural organiser and has a feel for farm work, and doesn't take any nonsense from the slaves. He's ex-army, finished up second-in-command of an auxiliary squadron, discharged just last summer."

"And your youngest?"

"Ah, Aquilo. Not a soldier, I'm afraid, and I doubt if he'll ever make much of a fist of being a farmer. He's more of a—a scholar, I suppose. He plays the lyre, and studies music. And writes poetry." It was clear from his tone that he didn't think much of these occupations.

"How interesting. I like both musicians and poets, and they're pretty thin on the ground in Britannia. I hope I'll meet him some day."

"Come and visit whenever you like. But Aquilo may not be here much longer. He's talking about going off to study in Italia, or even Greece. Leave the running of the estate to those of us that are good at it. I'll probably let him, but I don't believe in giving children everything they want straight away."

I'd like to have asked more, but Vividus strode in just then. He was pale, but his face was much less swollen, and his smile was symmetrical.

"Business all done, Uncle?" His lisp had gone. "Did you buy any?"

"Four yearlings."

"*Four?*" He laughed as he sat down. "Aurelia, he spent the whole journey here telling me that he definitely wasn't going to buy more than two today. You must have a silver tongue."

"Just some good horses," I smiled, and poured him a beaker. "How's the toothache?"

He took the wine, drank a good half of it, and sighed contentedly. "That's better! My mouth's still sore. Timaeus pulled the whole tooth out, roots and all. It hurt worse than a kick in the balls, but he said if he left it there the poison would spread all over my body. He's given me some ointment to rub into my gum, and he says it'll heal up clean." He drank the rest of his mug. "By Mars, this wine's excellent."

Magnus nodded. "It is. From Italia?"

"No, from the south of Gaul." I poured Vividus a refill.

"It's good to know we'll be able to get a decent tipple in the back of beyond. Sometimes I wonder why we've come to Britannia, you know. It's one thing fighting barbarians when you're in the army, quite another living among them, so far away from everything civilised."

"Now Uncle, that's hardly tactful, sitting here in Aurelia's excellent bar-room. At the Oak Tree at least there is civilisation."

"Sorry," Magnus said gruffly. "Didn't mean to be rude. Forgive an old soldier."

"We saw your sister and her husband quite recently." Vividus went on smoothly. "We're only about five miles from their farm.

What a nice couple, and they've a good place there. Albia told me she used to work for you here, before she was married."

"She was my housekeeper for many years. But she's very happy with Candidus. Farming life suits her."

"You're unusual, aren't you?" Magnus remarked. "I mean it's uncommon to find a woman innkeeper. Normally a man's in charge at an official mansio. But I expect the rules are slacker out here near the frontier."

I ignored the implication that a woman couldn't make as good an innkeeper as a man. It isn't true, and I've heard it too many times to let it upset me. "My brother Lucius and I are joint proprietors, but he's on the provincial Governor's staff, so the day-to-day running of the place is my responsibility."

"We look forward to meeting him when he's next in the area." Vividus smiled at me. "Does he look like you?"

I was taken aback by such directness, even though I could guess what lay behind his question. "Yes, there's a strong resemblance. Hardly surprising really. We're twins."

He nodded. "It's just that…I hope you won't mind if I say this, but you don't look in the least like Albia. I'd never have guessed you were sisters."

I stifled a sigh. It's what everyone says. Albia is small and dark and brown-eyed, while Lucius and I are tall and fair and have green eyes like our mother. Still, as our grandmother used to say, the fact that something is blindingly obvious never stops people assuming they're the first to notice it.

"Albia and I are half-sisters. Same father, different mothers, and we've each of us got our mother's looks." The food came, and I passed round the plate, but Vividus shook his head and helped himself to more wine instead.

I thought, if he can be direct, so can I. "Father was a centurion. You're both ex-army too, if I'm not mistaken."

Magnus said, "Quite correct. I've been retired some time, and Vividus finished his service last winter. We both made centurion too."

Vividus raised his beaker. "And I think I'm going to like it here in the north. Let's drink to a long and fruitful friendship between the Ostorius family and the Aurelius family."

We drank the toast, and I returned the compliment by wishing them prosperity on their new estate.

"Thank you," Magnus said. "We're going to make it the best-run estate in Britannia, aren't we, nephew?"

Vividus nodded. "A modest little goal, Aurelia, as you see."

"Only in Britannia? Why not in the whole Empire?"

"You can mock," Magnus said, "but we'll do it. We need more land though, to build up a really large property, like the farms in Italia. That's the way agriculture's going these days, you know. Consolidate the land into large holdings. So much more efficient. I'm trying to persuade some of the small farmers in our area to sell to me, but I'm sorry to say it isn't proving as easy as I expected." He sighed and hesitated, as if making up his mind about something. "Aurelia, you've been here some time, so you'll give me a straight answer, I hope. How do you get on with the natives in these parts? Friendly to settlers, are they?"

"They are, especially in your area. You know they're mostly from the Parisi tribe there."

"I've difficulty telling one tribe from another. A barbarian's a barbarian, when all's said and done. I suppose I'll learn the differences eventually."

"I'd advise it, yes, because they're important to the tribesmen themselves, as well as to us. Whether they're friendly to Rome is a case in point. The Parisi always have been, ever since before the conquest. People say it's because their ancestors came over from Gaul, but then not all Gauls are well-disposed to Rome, even now." I helped myself to olives. "Here in Brigantia it's different."

"So I've heard. Brigantians are all anti-Roman, aren't they?"

"Not all. It's not so simple." I felt myself losing patience, not because he was ignorant but because he didn't seem to want to lessen his ignorance by learning a few facts. When you set up home in a province, it seems to me you should make an effort to find out *something* about it. "Most Brigantians have accepted

Roman rule, with good grace or with bad. But there have always been a few who resent us, and have to be kept in order now and then. Mostly they're the ones that live west of here, in the Pennines."

He frowned. "I think Brigantian influence may be spreading. We've had some trouble with the local people."

"That's bad. What sort of trouble?"

"Well first, there's a gang of Gauls based on the coast who are plaguing everyone just now."

"Gods," I interrupted, "I keep on hearing about these sea-raiders. What are they, pirates of some sort?"

"Not exactly, although I suppose that's how they started. These days they spend far more time ashore than at sea, and they're a confounded nuisance—more than a nuisance, a danger. But it seems to be mostly the Roman landowners they're attacking, not the Parisi, which is why I was surprised when you mentioned about Bodvocos' man being injured. You're sure it wasn't just one of the usual mishaps, on the farm, or out hunting?"

"Quite sure. Corium said someone had gone for him with an axe."

"Bodvocos has land on the Headland, as we do. I suppose we have to expect them to plague us. But they're prepared to go miles inland to harass the smaller farms. They steal, they extort money, they occasionally rob travellers. And Bodvocos and his people don't seem to be making any attempt to control them. In fact..." he lowered his voice. "We think they're deliberately turning a blind eye to what the Gauls are doing, or even making use of them to harass Roman settlers."

"That's a serious allegation," I said. "Especially against Bodvocos, he's always been a good friend to Romans. I must be honest, it doesn't seem very likely to me. He's influential in his area, and the provincial authorities have left him with quite a lot of power among his own tribe. He'd be mad to antagonise the settlers, he'd lose everything."

"Fair point. Perhaps it's not Bodvocos himself. He's quite an old man now, isn't he? Could be some of his people acting on their own. This fellow Coriu, perhaps. They're giving us all sorts of petty aggravations. Our boundary markers get moved, or our fences are damaged so the sheep escape, that sort of thing. You may be right, the old chief knows nothing about it. I've reported it to Londinium, anyway."

"Really? Have you had any reply?"

"Not yet. But I intend to get it stopped, with or without help from the Governor."

"By the way," Vividus poured himself a fourth beaker of wine, or was it a fifth? "What's your Oak Bridges Chief Councillor like? We thought we'd call in on him today, introduce ourselves to him. He's quite a power in the land round here, isn't he?"

"Silvanius Clarus? Ah, you should have arranged to have your midday meal with him. He's got the best chef north of Londinium."

Magnus smiled. "I'll remember that. These natives never cease to amaze me."

"Clarus is a Roman citizen," I pointed out.

"But born here in province, I'm told. Related to Chief Bodvocos, so perhaps he can help me deal with him." He flashed me his charming smile. "I say, could we have some more of this excellent wine?"

They stayed for another jug, and very good company they were. They were intelligent and well-travelled, and we talked about everything from snail farming to the temples of Egypt. Vividus was quick-witted and charming, and Magnus had a dry sense of humour which compensated for his somewhat grumpy manner. By the time they left, they seemed like old friends I'd known for years instead of just a few hours.

After they'd gone, I went to congratulate Secundus on the sale, and asked what he thought of Magnus.

"A tough one, that," was all he'd say. "I'd not like to get on the wrong side of him."

Later I wandered over to see Timaeus, but he was taking a nap, and I told Phokas and Gaius not to wake him. "He's having a busy time, let him sleep when he can. I suppose that means there's no change in Belinus?" I asked the apprentice.

"There is, Mistress, but it's for the worse, I'm afraid. The master says we'll definitely have to amputate the left leg tomorrow if things don't improve."

"I'm sorry to hear that. You had a case of toothache this morning, I gather?"

He grinned. "We did, yes, one of the new settlers. Fancied himself a hard man, and said he didn't need anyone to hold him steady while the master pulled the tooth out."

"He was very brave," Gaius put in. "He never made a sound. Mostly they yell, or at least swear a bit. But he said afterwards it was the worst pain he'd ever had. He gave father a gold piece, and us each a copper one. So he must have been pleased really."

"How about Coriu? Did Timaeus set the broken arm all right?"

Phokas nodded. "It was quite a bad break, but it'll heal properly. It took two of us to stretch his arm out straight. If you don't do that it'll set crooked. We splinted it, and he'll have to keep it straight by his side for a month or so, which he wasn't too pleased about. He's gone home already, he said he had to get straight back to Chief Bodvocos."

"And was he brave too?" I couldn't help asking Gaius.

"He didn't yell, but he swore like anything." The boy giggled. "I'd never heard some of the words before. I expect they're *very* bad."

"Don't let the Master catch you using them," Phokas warned.

By late afternoon it was raining, and the bar-room was almost empty. The horse-boy Malchus rode in, soaking wet but pleased with himself, having delivered my message for Lucius safely into the hands of Petreius. I gave him a beaker of wine and a small tip, and listened to him enthuse about the fortress at Eburacum, and how wonderful a soldier's life must be. He'd watched a batch of new recruits practising throwing their javelins, and then battering at fence-posts with sticks as part of their sword training. It sounded pretty dull to me. If I've got to watch soldiers training, I prefer cavalry exercises, at least there's the occasional good laugh when somebody falls off. But Malchus had been thrilled, and I made a mental note that yet another of our lads might be off into the army soon.

We had just two overnight guests, a lead mining engineer, who had a bona fide government travel permit, and his lady companion, who didn't, but we take private travellers too, and they were no trouble. They weren't looking for company, being wrapped up in one another, and they retired as soon as they'd eaten.

The bar was very quiet, and I was tired, so I took the chance to have an early night.

Chapter IV

A loud hammering on my bedroom door woke me up when it was barely light.

I called, "Who is it?" But I knew the answer, and was already out of bed, sleepily reaching for my day-tunic and sandals.

"It's Phokas. My master says please hurry if you want to talk to Belinus. He's awake, but he's very poorly."

"I'm on my way." I dressed quickly, still only half awake, and went out through the side door into our private garden. The cool dawn air roused me like a splash of cold water in my face. I broke into a run along the path to Timaeus' house. My prayer at Apollo's shrine was extremely short, but none the less heartfelt.

Even before I went in, I could hear shouting, and I hurried to Belinus' room. The wounded man was not only awake, but sitting on the edge of his bed. He was dressed in nothing but heavy bandages round his left leg, which was swollen like a tree trunk from ankle to hip. His body glistened with sweat as if he'd just run a race, and he panted noisily. His eyes were too bright in his flushed face. Timaeus and Phokas were struggling to hold him still, while he fought to shake them off, shouting "Let me go! I've got to find Aurelia Marcella! I'm going to the mansio, so *let me go!*"

"Here she is now," Timaeus said loudly, and his relief was palpable. "I told you she'd come. This is Aurelia Marcella. Aurelia, Belinus is very anxious to…"

"You're Aurelia Marcella?" The sick man tried to get up, but his injured leg made him stumble and cry out. Timaeus and Phokas still held him fast. I was glad they did, because he looked more than half mad.

"I am. I came as soon as I could. It's good to see you awake. How are you feeling?"

"I hurt all over, especially my leg, and I can't breathe right. But never mind that. I need to talk to your brother Lucius Aurelius. Can you send for him please? I've got important information for him. He wanted me to find out something. But it's for his ears only. How quickly can you get him here?" He stared at me hard, as if he was trying to see into my mind. It was unnerving, but at least he wasn't shouting, although his voice was strained with effort.

"I've already sent him a message. The doctor said yesterday that you were asking for him, and I realised the matter was urgent."

He relaxed a little. "Thank you. When will he be here?"

"I don't know, Belinus, I'm afraid. I don't know where my brother is at present, so I can't say how quickly he can get here."

"You don't *know?*" He was shouting again. "But surely you must have some idea." With an obvious effort he lowered his voice. "I'm sorry. It's just that…well, this is important. I'm one of his informers, and he'll want to hear my report. He told me you'd be able to contact him."

"I've sent him one message," I answered, "and when we've had our talk I'll send him another. I'm afraid that's the best I can do. As you know, if you're one of his agents, he works for the provincial Governor, and that means he gets sent all over Britannia. But if the gods are with us, he'll be here soon. Meanwhile you can make your report to me, then if—if Lucius arrives while you're asleep, I can pass it on to him."

"I don't know. Do you help him in his work?"

"Oh yes, often." Occasionally would have been more truthful, but less reassuring.

"I suppose that'll have to do." He sighed and then coughed, and wiped the sweat from his forehead with his hand. "I'll tell you. Just you. Send these two away."

"You can trust them, I'll vouch for that. They're doctors."

"Send them away! I'm not having Lucius say I blabbed our business all over the province."

Timaeus shook his head. "We can't leave you without a doctor, the state you're in. But we'll both take an oath…"

"*Go away, I tell you!* Or I'm saying nothing."

I wasn't keen on being alone with him, but it was clear he wouldn't say what he wanted to say otherwise, and this might be his last chance to report to anyone.

"It'll be all right, Timaeus. Stay outside in the corridor and I can call if I need you. Now Belinus, before I send them away, will you please lie down on the bed? I'm sure it's not good for you to be struggling to use that bad leg. I'll sit here on this stool next to you. Then you can tell me quietly—*quietly and secretly*—what it is I must pass on to Lucius."

It worked. He lay down on the bed, I took the stool. Phokas propped pillows under his head and shoulders, then he and Timaeus went out. "And no eavesdropping," I called after them, in case they hadn't thought of it.

As soon as they'd shut the door, Belinus began talking, quickly but quite lucidly. "There's trouble in the wolds, over towards the coast. Not just for me, several other farmers, maybe even your sister and her husband, but they've got enough men to defend themselves. Which is more than I have."

"Albia?" I looked at him sharply. I was in regular touch with Albia and Candidus, but they'd made no mention of any trouble. "Do you live near her?"

"We're neighbours. She and Candidus have been good friends to us. Albia said you and your brother would help us, but we haven't wanted to call in any outsiders. Only now I think we need to."

"What sort of trouble is it?"

"Sea-raiders, thieving and making mischief. They've set up a camp on the Headland and they say they're looking for gold, but all they ever do is plague the small farmers. That's what your brother needs to know about. They're not local lads, they're mostly from Gaul. Their captain, don't know what his real name is, but everyone calls him Voltacos."

"Voltacos? He has long hair then?"

"That's right. A big tall man with a mane of brown hair. They say he wears it long because he only has one ear, so he cuts an ear off all the people he kills."

"Gods, that's disgusting. Does he kill many people?"

"If they get in his way. They'd have killed me, and young Cattos, he looks after my sheep, only they didn't have time. While they were attacking us some travellers came riding along the highway, and that scared them off. Otherwise…" He mimed cutting off his left ear, but the effort made him cough. I picked up a beaker of watered wine from a table nearby, but he shook his head. "They're a pest, always after money to let us alone. But it's more than that now. Much more, and we need Lucius to…" He broke off suddenly as a violent spasm of coughing seized him. He put his hands over his mouth, and phlegm oozed between his fingers. With horror I saw it was tinged red. I took a cloth from the table and held it to his mouth. He accepted it gratefully, but was still coughing too much to speak.

I said, "I'll get the doctor. He'll give you something to ease your chest. Then we'll talk again."

"No!" He seized my arm, and his grip was surprisingly strong. "Don't go. I must tell you this now, it may be my only chance."

"Timaeus!" I called. He was halfway through the door already. "He's coughing up blood."

"Phokas, fetch the strong cough syrup, the one with poppy seed in it." He took a clean cloth, dipped it in water, and gently wiped Belinus' face. His touch in itself was comforting, and the coughing fit subsided a little. "I was afraid of that. He has three broken ribs. They must have done damage inside him, and his blood is getting mixed with the phlegm somehow."

The apprentice handed him a small beaker of thick dark-gold liquid which smelt of garlic, and Timaeus held it to Belinus' mouth. "Drink this now, Belinus, and then rest for a little. Aurelia will wait till you can talk again, won't you, Aurelia?"

"Of course I will. This is important information. Take your time."

"But I haven't *got* any time." The words were no more than a soft moan. He drank the syrup, and the coughing became less continuous, but it still racked his body from time to time. As he held the cloth to his lips again, more red stains appeared on it.

"I'm for the Otherworld, doctor, aren't I?" he asked Timaeus.

"No, you're a strong lad, you'll pull through this. But you must rest, let these wounds heal."

"I know the truth, don't try to pretend. I haven't got long to talk. Go away please, so I can finish my report. *Please.*"

"Leave the syrup with me, Timaeus," I said. "I'll give him more if he needs it."

Timaeus and Phokas left the room, a sure sign that Timaeus too thought his patient hadn't got long to talk. But between bouts of coughing, Belinus managed to gasp out his words in short bursts.

"Make Lucius understand. . . the Gauls are working for someone else. Someone powerful, someone with a brain. There's someone wants our land. Trying to drive us out, drive all the small farmers out. Wants the land for himself. Keeps threatening us, making our lives miserable. We can't fight him on our own."

"Do you know who it is? There are laws to protect you."

"There are two it could be. Both rich, greedy, above the law." He coughed noisily, and I gave him more syrup. If it had poppy in it, it should make him drowsy, but that would take time.

"I'll tell Lucius all this. But if you even suspect who it is, you must give me the name. Lucius will expect it."

He tried to answer, but no words came out, only more coughing. I piled more pillows under his head, but that didn't seem to help. I waited, not sure what to do, only feeling I couldn't leave him now.

He took a deep breath and sat upright, as if gathering himself for a supreme effort.

"When I'm in the Otherworld, you and Lucius must help my family fight him off. Illiana, the children…." His breath was coming in rasping short bursts now, with agonising coughing in between. I opened my mouth to call Timaeus, but then he said clearly, "Keep them safe. Promise me."

"I will."

"Promise! Swear it!"

"I swear by Diana, and by Taranis and the Three Mothers." I hoped that invoking the native gods would reassure him, and it did.

"Thank you." He flopped back onto the pillows. "Now I've done all I can." His body jerked, then went slack, and his eyes closed. He let out a shuddering sigh, and lay quite still.

"Timaeus!" I called.

But even as he and Phokas hurried in, I knew there was nothing more they could do. Belinus had crossed to the Otherworld.

We stood round the bed, none of us willing to break the silence. I felt sad, for Belinus and for Timaeus too, because I knew how discouraged he felt when his medical skills weren't enough to save a patient.

Phokas looked suitably solemn, but he was young and resilient, and he was the first to stir himself. He walked over to the window and pushed the half-opened shutters right back, letting in more of the thin morning light and a cold breeze. He looked at Timaeus. "Master, I'll finish off here. You go and get something to eat. Mistress Margarita will have breakfast waiting for you."

"Good idea," I said. "I'll come too."

But Timaeus didn't seem to have heard. "I thought he had a chance. It was a terrible leg wound, and with the gangrene, and the broken ribs as well. But he was young and strong, and I've seen worse than that heal with barely a scar."

"If you couldn't save him, Timaeus, then nobody could. You've done the best any doctor could do. It was in the lap of the gods. If they didn't want Belinus to survive…"

He ran his hands through his chestnut hair. "I don't know about the gods. I just know I've been taught how to heal people, and when I fail, that must be my fault…Sorry, I don't mean to rant on. I'm just tired, and I hate losing a patient. I can't help wondering if there was something else I could have done for him."

"I'm sure there wasn't. You're a fine doctor." I touched his arm gently. I didn't like to see him so upset.

"I ought to have paid more attention to those broken ribs. Perhaps I should have opened up his chest to see what was wrong."

Phokas spoke up. "Master, that would have killed him for sure. He had a wound full of poison, and he was as hot as a furnace. He wouldn't have had the strength for that kind of surgery."

The apprentice was talking very good sense, and Timaeus seemed comforted. "I suppose not. Once the four humours get too far out of balance…"

"Try not to feel badly." I cut him short, not being in the mood for a medical lecture on the four humours. "You know my father was an army man. He told me what the military doctors say about medicine. I expect you've heard it?"

He shook his head. "Some hoary old saying of Julius Caesar, is it?"

"I shouldn't be surprised. 'Patients are like battles, you win some and you lose some. Just make sure you win more than you lose.'"

He smiled faintly. "You're right, Aurelia. I shouldn't let it upset me."

"I'm always right. It's a well-known fact. Now why not do as Phokas suggests, come to the mansio and we'll find you something to eat and drink. You look as if you need it."

As Timaeus and I walked out into the dawn, I felt my spirits lift in spite of everything. It's my favourite time of day, when the rising sun makes all the world seem fresh and clean.

But the doctor's mind was still on his patient. "I wonder how he came by those injuries. Obviously he'd been in a scrap, which is no big surprise, those young natives are always getting into fights. Not usually with swords though. Fists and cudgels, that's more their style."

"He mentioned the pirates, and some sort of threat to the small farmers. You heard it all, presumably?"

He nodded. "The wold country's so peaceful as a rule. But you know, I treated three more natives from near the coast yesterday, all fit enough to go home and not stay here the night. Three in one day—and normally I don't see three weapon-wounds in a month."

"I saw one of them, Bodvocos' man Coriu."

"Yes, his arm was broken, by an axe he said. Considering everything it wasn't too bad. Both of the others said they'd had accidents with tools in the fields, but both had sword wounds, I'd stake my reputation on it."

We'd reached the mansio, and he turned aside to head for the kitchen door at the back of the main building.

I stopped. "You go in and get breakfast, don't wait for me. Tell Margarita I'll be in soon, but first I'm going to get properly dressed for the day. By the way, that lad of yours is turning out pretty well, isn't he? How long have you had him now?"

"I bought him last June, so not even a year yet. I'm very pleased with him, though it doesn't do to say so every hour, or else he'll get too cocky. He's learning fast, and he's got a sensible calm head on his shoulders, which is half the battle in my trade. I've promised him his freedom as soon as he's competent to treat simple cases without me, so he's taking every chance he can to learn." He smiled. "I was the same at his age."

I stood a little while in the fresh air, mentally listing the various practical tasks for the morning. Another note for Lucius was top of my list. Next, I must make sure Timaeus remembered to send for one of the temple priests from Oak Bridges to perform the cleansing rituals needed to purify the room where Belinus had died. Though he denied that the gods had much influence on his patients' well-being, he still couldn't afford to take chances where divine favour was concerned. After that I must make arrangements to send Belinus' body home to his family.

As one of my brother's informers, it was the least he deserved, and I ought to write to his widow—Illiana, was it? And of course there were the usual chores of the day, because at a mansio life goes on, even with death close by.

Gloom settled over me as I considered the morning's tasks, and even the bright dawn light and the songs of the birds failed to dispel it. So I went inside, changed, and washed my face, which made me feel, if not happier, at least clean. Then I wrote to my brother, a short message as before, couched in words that wouldn't mean much to anyone else, except that the plea for him to visit us urgently was clear enough. I went straight out and asked Secundus to get Malchus to deliver it as soon as possible. The gods alone knew what good it might do.

Doing something practical made me start to feel better. I also felt hungry, so I went to the kitchen, where Margarita was having breakfast, and joined her. She'd already heard about Belinus' death, and lost no time in dispatching a messenger to the temple at Oak Bridges with a note and a purse of silver, asking one of the priests to visit us sometime today.

"Good. I'm sending Belinus' body home to his farm this morning. From what he said before he died, he was definitely one of Lucius' informers. I'll write a letter explaining what happened and expressing our condolences. I'll have to word it carefully, because it's possible his wife and family don't know he was working for my brother."

"Mistress, this letter's just come for you." One of the maids bustled in, waving a small package. "A farmer on his way to Oak Bridges brought it in. He said your relatives on the wolds asked him to deliver it on his way."

"From my sister? Thanks, Baca, I'll come through and thank him, but I'd better read it first. Gods, I hope there's nothing wrong."

"He said he should have brought it yesterday but he'd been delayed somehow, and he was in a tearing hurry and wouldn't even stop to see you. We gave him a drink on the house, but he just gulped it down and left again..."

I'd stopped listening. I quickly unwrapped the cloth around the package, and found inside a note written in ink on a flat wooden tablet. It wasn't from Albia, but from her husband Candidus.

"Candidus to Aurelia Marcella, greetings. We have some trouble near here, caused by a band of sea-raiders who are picking on small farms, stealing animals and extorting money. They haven't touched us so far, and we've enough farm boys to protect ourselves, but I can't help worrying because of Albia and the children. If things get worse, could Albia and the little ones come to stay with you at the Oak Tree for a while?

Do come and see us soon. You know you're always welcome, and I'd value your advice about what we can do to protect the farm. You're used to dealing with trouble.

Albia doesn't know I'm writing to you. I don't want to alarm her."

I stared at the note. It might or might not have alarmed Albia, who's a lot tougher than she looks, but it certainly alarmed *me*. The simple fact that Candidus had written it was worrying, and his comment, "You're used to dealing with trouble…" I was overwhelmed by a sudden strong desire to see my sister and make sure she and her family were well. Candidus had written that they were safe. But for how long?

"Margarita, I must ride over and see Albia today. Look at this." I passed her the note.

She read it and nodded. "Yes, I think you must. Candidus is normally such a calm man, and an optimist. If he's worried, you need to take it seriously."

"I do. I can ride with the carriage that's taking Belinus home, his farm's on the way. I can even call in and talk to his family. It won't be a very pleasant errand, but they'll appreciate my going personally I expect. Then I'll still have time to see Albia, and be back here tonight. Will you be able to cope without me during the day? If it gets busy again…"

She smiled. "Don't worry, I'll manage fine."

She would, too. I trusted her, and I knew she was more than capable of running the mansio in my absence. She'd been my housekeeper for two years now, and I suspected she enjoyed being in sole charge. She was looking thoughtful. "How far is it to Belinus' farm?"

"A bit more than twenty miles. Then it's another three or four to Albia's."

"And you'll be slow for those first twenty miles if you're with the raeda. So wouldn't you be better staying the night at Albia's, and coming home tomorrow? I don't like the thought of you riding back in the dark, if there's any chance of trouble."

"Yes, I will, if you're sure. Thanks."

"You'll want to take some food with you?"

That's one of the many reasons Margarita suits me as a housekeeper. She has a knack of knowing what I'm thinking, and she remembered I always like to take some provisions with me when I call in on my sister unannounced. "Yes, but I'll be riding, not driving in the raeda with the—with Belinus. So I'll be a bit limited in what I can carry. Some olives, I think, and sausage, and a piece of that goat's cheese."

"If those greedy gannets haven't eaten it all for breakfast. And Cook made some honey cakes yesterday."

"Ah, now that'll make me doubly welcome. As many as you can spare, please."

She began making me up a couple of saddlebags of food to take, while I walked outside to finish my morning rounds. I'd already seen Secundus, and when I went back to the stables he assured me my message for Lucius was on its way.

He was in one of the stalls now, smearing ointment on a horse's back where the saddle had rubbed its hide raw, and muttering curses on the careless courier who had ridden the poor animal in such a state.

"Could you tell someone to saddle Merula for me, and harness up a medium-sized raeda please? Make sure it looks smart and clean, because it's for one of Timaeus' patients who died this morning. I'm taking his body home to his family, then I'm going on to my sister's place."

He nodded. "I heard that poor young farmer died. A sorry business, but if Timaeus couldn't help, I doubt anyone else could. I'll put two drivers on the raeda with the body, just for once. Some of the boys aren't very happy about being too close to corpses, and they'll be company for each other on the way home."

"Good idea, yes, if you can spare two. I'm afraid I'm leaving you a bit short-handed."

"No bother, everything's well in hand. Now, there's this talk of trouble near the coast. Are you taking a guard?"

"Well…I don't know." Normally I'm happy to ride without an escort, especially on good Roman roads like the one I'd be taking today. But this morning, events were conspiring to make me nervous. I made up my mind. "Yes, I think I will. I'll take Taurus."

Taurus is my handyman, and I've often used him as a bodyguard when I needed someone strong and reassuring. Besides being tall and powerfully built, he's always been one of the most loyal of our slaves, more or less part of the family. And he loves children, so I knew he'd enjoy visiting Albia, and get a warm welcome there. I found him in the workshop, and he jumped at the chance of a trip into the wolds, even though it involved escorting a corpse part of the way, and possibly encountering trouble when we got there. "We'll have a brilliant time, Mistress Aurelia. Such a lovely day too. And I can take along those toys I made for the twins' birthday. And we'll be staying overnight? Oh, that's good!"

I wished I could share his simple happiness, but the more I thought about the day to come, the more apprehensive I felt.

I was almost back at the bar-room door when the sound of a horse cantering along the main road made me look up. A rider turned down our track, and as I recognised him, my gloom suddenly vanished. It was my brother Lucius, and he was waving joyfully.

Chapter V

"Lucius, this is wonderful!" I ran to him as he jumped down, and we hugged.

"Now that's what I call a proper welcome! Good to see you, too, Sis. You're looking well."

"I'm fine, sir. You don't look so bad yourself."

"I'm extremely well, Sis. Never better."

"But how did you manage this? I thought it might be a month before you got my message."

He laughed. "I've had no message from you, so it probably will be. When did you send it?"

"Yesterday, to Petreius. I've sent another this morning."

"I haven't been to headquarters for quite a few days. I'm based on the coast at present."

"You've ridden all the way from there this morning? You must have set off in the middle of the night."

"Nearly. But I've only come from Albia's. I went to see her yesterday as nothing much is happening by the sea, and decided I'd take today off to come and visit my favourite twin sister." He turned as one of the horse-boys came out to see who the new arrival was. "'Morning, Castor. How are you? Have you married that pretty girlfriend of yours yet?"

"'Morning, Master Lucius. No, I can't afford to get married, not on the wages I get here." He grinned. "That's what I tell her, anyway. It's good to see you again. Are you staying long?"

"Only a few hours, unfortunately. Long enough to sample some of Cook's food and have a beaker or two of wine, and maybe a hot bath." He patted his tall gelding. "Look after this old boy, he's had a hard ride this morning. And pick me out one of our good black horses to take me to the coast. I'll have to leave by noon."

He turned back to me, pushing his untidy mop of fair hair out of his eyes. "Well, what's all the to-do, Sis? Two messages in two days? Actually I can probably guess. Are they about Belinus?"

"You've heard he came here?"

"One of my other informers told me he'd been hurt. Is it serious?"

"Come inside and I'll find you some breakfast, then we can talk."

"That means it is," he said quietly, and followed me into the bar-room.

Everyone was pleased to see him, and he kept up a cheerful banter with Margarita, Cook, and the servants, while I collected a tray of bread and cheese and watered wine. We took it into my private sitting-room, where he dropped his cheerful mask.

"So what's happened, Aurelia? Tell me the worst."

I poured the wine. "It's bad news, I'm afraid. Belinus died this morning. Timaeus did his best, but the wounds were too serious."

Lucius sighed. "Poor lad. It's sad, and it's a blow, because I hoped he'd be one of my most useful sources of information on my present case. That's why the Governor sent me up here, because I have quite a few informers scattered about near the coast."

"Are you after the sea-raiders?"

He nodded. "My job is to find out about them, if possible locate their camp. Then either catch them if I can, or send for reinforcements if it's too big a job. I've only got six men, and we're camped near the Headland, because the raiders are supposed to be using the caves there as a hideout. Of course we haven't found any trace of it, or them. They can vanish like the morning mist, those boys. That's why local informers are so important. They can gather information slowly and quietly, and feed it to us." He took a long drink of his wine. "Well, I know the Oak Tree is as good a source of information as most. What have you heard about them?"

"Nothing at all till a couple of days ago. But if word's reached Londinium…"

"It has. They're causing real trouble to some of the settlers. And they're coming much further inland."

"You don't think they'll come as far in as Oak Bridges, do you?"

"No, you're safe enough here. The nearest bit of coast is thirty miles away, and they won't venture that far."

"But the Governor's taking them seriously, sending one of his bright young investigators all the way up from Londinium?"

"Thanks for the compliment, Sis, but sometimes I don't feel as bright or as young as I used to."

"Tell me about it."

"To be truthful, I wangled myself the assignment up here, because I've got—well let's just say some surprising family news."

"Gods alive, you're not getting married at long last?"

"No fear. I'm like young Caster, I enjoy my freedom."

"What then?"

"It's good news, and it's something you'd never guess. But I'd rather wait till the three of us are together. I said so to Albia, and I want to persuade you to come back with me today to her farm, so we can get together there. There's really no point telling you and then having to tell Albia all over again."

"Of course there is. If you keep me in suspense, I'll die of curiosity."

"Too bad. I haven't time to organise your funeral."

His words brought me up short. "We shouldn't joke about funerals, Lucius. Not today."

"You're right, sorry. Tell me about Belinus."

I told him all I could. He nodded at Belinus' comments on Voltacos' men, and frowned over his idea that someone rich and powerful was organising their raids.

"So," he said when I'd finished, "the raiders got to poor Belinus. I suppose they must have found out somehow that he was working for me. As far as we know, this is the first time they've killed anyone. A murder makes the whole business much more serious, and in this case, more personal."

"Do you think they're really looking for gold, as Belinus said? I don't know of any hoard of gold in these parts…"

He laughed. "I should hope you don't—at least if you did, I hope you'd tell me where to find it. There's King Caratacus' gold, of course, they could be hunting for that."

"You're not serious! You don't believe that old story?"

"Why not? I've always thought it was possible. Caratacus was a powerful warrior chief when Claudius Caesar conquered this province. He must have had plenty of gold…"

"I'm sure he did, but what I don't believe is that he hid some of it here in the north while he was running away from the Romans. It's too far-fetched for words."

"Plenty of people believe it."

"Oh certainly, and they've all spent the last forty-some years looking for the hiding-place and not found a single aureus. So even if there is any gold, a boatload of Gauls aren't going to discover it, are they?"

He shrugged. "I suppose not. And anyway, whatever they *say* they're up to, they're spending their time attacking innocent people, and that's got to be stopped."

"What worries me is that Albia and Candidus could be in danger."

"I know. Albia seemed happy enough yesterday, but Candidus told me he's concerned, only not wanting to show it for fear of frightening Albia. He said he'd written to you."

I handed him Candidus' note, and he scanned it quickly.

"Yes, this is worrying, Relia. Have you replied yet?"

"I've decided to visit them in person. I was all set to leave this morning when you got here."

"Really? Then we'll go together."

"And on the way I'm going to take Belinus' body home to his family. I thought I should, as he was working for you."

"Thanks, Sis. That was good of you."

"I wasn't looking forward to it. It'll be easier if you're there to offer your condolences in person."

He nodded. "I can do more than that. I'll make sure they're all right for money."

"Good. If there's nobody else on his farm who can do Belinus' share of the work, his wife and children will be struggling. And we can try to find out more about how he was killed. What do you make of his story of some rich landowner trying to drive him off his farm?"

"Unlikely, I'd say, though not completely impossible. There are only two landowners in that area who'd be powerful enough to try it. Ostorius Magnus, and the local chief, Bodvocos. I can't really imagine either of them conspiring with a gang of outlaws."

"Belinus was so sure, though. If you could have seen him…It's just a pity there wasn't time for him to tell me who he thought it was."

"I doubt if it's anything that sinister. My guess is he's fallen out with one of his neighbours, and they've been making trouble along with the raiders, so he's confusing the two. You know how these disputes go, they start small and get more and more bitter with every passing month."

"Maybe. It's something else we can ask his family about when we meet them. What are they like?"

"I hardly know them really. There's a pretty wife, an old lame father, a couple of children. I'll do what I can for them. And at least he managed to pass on one useful fact. The raiders are from Gaul—in other words not local criminals. And their captain's known as Voltacos."

I piled the breakfast things back onto their tray. "Voltacos could just be a nickname, though, because he's a long-haired Gaul."

He got to his feet. "There's only one way to find out, and that's to catch the bastard. Let's make a start, Relia. How soon can you be ready?"

As we walked through into the bar-room, the door to the forecourt opened and a soldier strode through. He was a cavalry-man in full military gear including a sword, but he carried no satchel of despatches. He glanced round the room and when he spotted Lucius, he saluted and came over to us.

"Ollius!" My brother exclaimed. "What in the gods' name are you doing here?"

"Sorry to disturb your day's leave, sir. There's been a development, and the decurion thought you ought to know about it straight away."

Lucius looked round, noticed that the first customers of the day were starting to drift in, and turned to me. "Can we use your study please, Aurelia?"

"Of course." I led the way.

"This had better be good, Ollius. I don't get much leave, and I don't appreciate having it interrupted. Make your report."

"There's been a shipwreck, sir, on the Headland. An important one, the decurion thinks."

"A *shipwreck?* You mean a boat that pirates have attacked?"

"No, sir, this was driven ashore in that bad storm we had late yesterday. It fetched up on the north side of the Headland—you know what a bad spot that is for wrecks."

I shivered. It was notorious, even to me, living well away from the coast.

"How did you hear about the wreck?"

"Two fishermen came along to the camp just after you'd gone, and they told us. They say they get a reward for reporting Roman wrecks."

Lucius nodded. "They do, as long as they stop the other natives from plundering the cargoes. But what makes Tertius think I need to know about this boat? What's the cargo?"

"Only one item, a big wooden chest, all nailed up and with Government seals on it. And it must be valuable, because there's a warship escorting the boat, a Liburnian of the Fleet. It's standing by just out to sea."

"Standing by?" Lucius looked at him sharply. "Are you sure it's not just sailing past?"

"Oh no, sir. Some of the sailors rowed ashore when they saw us, with a message from their captain. Apparently they've been following the ship, keeping an eye on it they said, and now they're under orders to stay and protect the cargo till someone in authority comes."

"Neptune's balls!" Lucius sprang to his feet excitedly. "What's this boat called, Ollius?"

"The *Sea Horse*, sir."

"Gods, it's our lucky day then."

"Sir?"

"Never mind. You were right to come and report this. The cargo that boat's carrying is extremely important, and I'll take charge of it as soon as I can." He stopped suddenly. "It's still intact, presumably?"

The soldier nodded. "As far as we can see. The boat's stuck on the rocks with some of its planks smashed in, so it's pretty well under water most of the time. We'll only be able to bring the chest ashore when the tide's low."

"You haven't moved it yet? Why not?"

"We didn't like to, sir, because the Liburian's captain said it wasn't to be touched."

"Fair enough. Anything else I need to know?"

"Tertius says to tell you he's moving our camp over to the north side of the Headland, to keep the wreck under continuous observation."

"That's right, don't leave that boat unguarded at any time. Now go and get something to eat, then ride back there as fast as you can. I'll be with you by dark at the latest. I've an important errand to do on the way, but I won't take longer than I have to. Off you go now. And Ollius..."

"Sir?"

"Guard that cargo well. There'll be a very handsome reward for everyone involved in recovering it."

Ollius grinned, saluted, and left. My brother began pacing round the room, as excited as a schoolboy going to his first gladiator show.

"This is the most amazing piece of luck, Relia. The *Sea Horse* wrecked, just when I'm here to deal with it."

"A shipwreck doesn't sound like good luck to me."

"No, but I mean if it had to be wrecked, it's lucky that I got to hear about it. I'm one of the few people who knows how important that box is." His green eyes sparkled. "Now, Sis, there's no time to lose. We must leave as soon as we can, and I'll fill in the details on the way. Oh, wait though—I'll need your help."

"What sort of help? I'm not getting onto any boat..."

"Nothing like that. This cargo's in a very large wooden box, too big for a horse to carry. I'll need transport to bring it back. So can you lend me an ox-wagon, please, and a couple of men? With food and bedding for them, in case they have to camp by the sea tonight. We may have to wait till tomorrow morning before the tide's gone out far enough...Don't worry, I'll requisition it all officially, with paperwork and everything. So you'll even get paid for the use of it."

"If I live long enough." But his excitement was irresistable. "Of course I'll lend you a wagon. But it's on one condition."

"Which is?"

"That I can come down to the coast with you and see this wreck for myself."

"Excellent!" He slapped me on the shoulder. "Then let's get moving."

Chapter VI

We were on the road within the hour. Lucius and I rode ahead, followed by the carriage, with its bodywork polished and its two mules smartly groomed, fit to carry Belinus home. Then came the wagon, drawn by a stout pair of oxen, with an experienced farm lad driving it, and Taurus riding alongside. Lucius had found a leather cover that could be put over it if need be at night, and Margarita and I had packed it with enough food, water and wine to feed a cohort, along with cooking pots and bedding. Taurus had brought a selection of his tools, some rope, and flint and steel for kindling a fire. By the time we'd finished, it looked as if we were on expedition to the wildest waste of Thule for at least a month.

To begin with we kept together, plodding up the Long Hill at the lumbering pace of the ox-wagon. Once we were safely at the top of the stiff mile-long climb, with the wide open spaces of the wolds ahead of us, the convoy split up. The raeda didn't need to travel at the wagon's tortoise pace, and neither did Lucius and I. We rode on ahead till we were well out of earshot of the carriage, but there was no point travelling so fast that we'd arrive far ahead of it and have to wait.

I like riding on horseback, though I know people say it isn't very seemly for a woman, especially as the only really suitable clothing for it is cavalry breeches and tunic. Well, let the great ladies of Rome or Londinium trundle around in carriages, or travel shoulder-high through the streets in litters. Give me a lively horse and pleasant countryside, and I'm content. Even today, though our visit to Belinus' family would be sad, it felt good to be on the road on a fine spring morning.

It was about twenty miles to Belinus' farm, but easy riding on a Roman road. It ran through gently rolling fields, most of them pasture for sheep and goats, and a few cultivated, with green shoots of grain well up in the chalky soil. Every now and then there were small native farms with their mud-walled roundhouses. Occasionally we passed new foursquare brick or stone buildings, announcing a Roman settler. Every time I travelled this way, which I admit wasn't often, I was aware how the number of Roman properties was increasing.

I smiled at Lucius. "I feel guilty for saying so, but I'm enjoying this ride. I don't get into the hills often enough."

Lucius smiled back. "I know. We should be feeling gloomy because of poor Belinus. Of course I'm sorry for him, but I must admit this shipwreck of the *Sea Horse* puts a different complexion on things."

"So it seems. You did promise to tell me the details, didn't you? You know I'll keep them secret if you want me to."

"I do, at least for now. I was involved in getting that ship ready to sail from Londinium. It's part of some sensitive diplomatic negotiations, and it's vital the cargo doesn't fall into the wrong hands."

"Is that why the Fleet are helping to guard it? That only happens with important ships, doesn't it?"

He nodded. "The *Sea Horse* is important all right, and extremely valuable. That box it's carrying is full of gold."

"Gold? Gods, then there'll be a reward for its recovery?"

"Bound to be. A hundred gold pieces for the cargo intact, or my name's Julius Caesar."

"That's a huge amount of money!"

"Isn't it? But then it's a huge amount of gold. We'll give some to the fishermen of course, and my men on the coast will expect a share, but most of it will come to me."

"To *us*," I corrected. "Don't forget I'm helping you with the transport."

He laughed. "I haven't forgotten, and if I do, I'm sure you'll remind me. The best part of a hundred gold pieces, just to pick up a box from a wrecked ship! Money for old rags, wouldn't you say? And thanks to you, I haven't had to waste a day organising army transport. By tomorrow night I'll have brought the gold back to the mansio, or even maybe all the way to headquarters at Eburacum."

"Who's it for? Some barbarian the Governor's trying to bribe?"

He put on a pained expression. "Bribe? What a horrible word! The Governor's simply sending a gift to an important tribal chieftain in Caledonia. A token of eternal friendship and esteem."

"A bribe, in plain Latin."

He laughed. "We don't use plain Latin much in this diplomatic game."

"I suppose it's a sweetener for some native chief who's supposed to be Rome's ally, but his loyalty is wavering a bit?"

"Exactly so. He's always been an ally, and helped to keep down some of the wilder tribes up there who prefer to be our enemies. We need to keep him on our side, so we give him expensive presents and lots of flowery compliments. It's a tried and tested policy, after all. If we don't want to conquer an area by force of arms, we can still control it for the Empire through its tribal rulers, if we make it worth their while. It's a cheaper option than sending in the legions. As for this particular barbarian, our agents have put a lot of time and effort into making sure he stays loyal to us, and the box of gold is all that's needed to seal the bargain. Then Caledonia won't be a problem, at least for a while."

"Assuming somebody eventually manages to deliver it. Didn't the Governor even consider the possibility of a shipwreck? Sailing's always risky, especially this early in the year. It beats me why he didn't send the gold by road in nice safe wagons."

"Actually I agree with you, and several of us tried to persuade him to use land transport. But he said it attracts less attention to send a cargo like this by water. And attention's what we don't want. When we give handouts to barbarians, we prefer to do it discreetly."

"So the chief's present is in a wrecked boat miles from where it's supposed to be. If *that* doesn't attract attention, I'm the Queen of Brigantia. Neptune's balls!" I had a sudden thought that was so shocking it made me jerk the mare's reins, and she looked round reproachfully. "Belinus said Voltacos' pirates were looking for gold. Could they have been trying to capture the *Sea Horse* on its way north? Trying to lure it ashore onto the rocks perhaps?"

"Absolutely not. That ship and cargo are top secret. Nobody knew about it outside the Governor's staff in Londinium, and not many inside."

"I know you, Lucius, and I know when you're not sure of something. Such as now."

He grunted. "Well…the thought had occurred to me too, of course it had. But look on the bright side. Even if the Gauls did bring about the wreck of the *Sea Horse,* they haven't gained anything by it. They haven't got their hands on the cargo."

We'd reached the top of a fairly steep rise, and got our first view of the sea. Lucius pulled up his horse. "Time for a short halt, I think. It's not far now, and we need to let the raeda catch up a bit. You did bring some wine, didn't you?"

"Wine, bread, cheese, sausage, and some of Cook's honey cakes. No, you're not having any food now, that's all for Albia. But I've plenty of wine." I detached a wine-skin and two beakers from my saddlebag and poured us each a drink. We sat gazing over the green fields that sloped down towards the German Ocean, which glinted in the warm sun. High above us among small white clouds a skylark was singing. I could have lingered all day, but Lucius was impatient to be moving.

"I can't dawdle," he said, "if I'm to have any time at all with Albia and Candidus before I push on to the coast. I want long enough to find out how things are with them."

"And to share your mysterious bit of family news," I reminded him. "Can't you give me just a hint of what it's about?"

"Not a chance. Change the subject. Let me work my plans out. If I leave Albia's with a couple of hours of daylight left, I'll easily get to the Headland before dark. With luck the tide will be low enough to let us bring the cargo on land tonight."

"But the wagon won't get to you much before nightfall," I pointed out, "so even if you've salvaged the box, you won't want to set off in the dark, surely?"

"No, we'll stay put till morning, whatever the tide's doing. Ollius said the wreck's under water most of the time, so I may have to wait till tomorrow anyway for a low enough tide."

"I don't think I'll ever get used to the huge tides here." I shivered in spite of the warm sun on my face. "The whole idea of waves rushing in and out and changing the appearance of the shore scares me. Our sea in Italia was so much less trouble. You knew where you were."

"I agree there, not to mention a lot warmer. Don't tell me you're changing your mind about coming to look at the wreck for yourself? If the sea scares you so much…"

"It's not the sea I'm coming to look at. It's this famous box of gold with its massive reward!"

We set off again and soon found the pile of white rocks that marked the turning to Belinus' farm. When the raeda had caught us up, Lucius and I led the way off the main road onto a rutted narrow track running between weed-infested pasture and fields of thin grass that was presumably being grown for hay.

The sound of our horses brought out a man carrying a huge cudgel. He came to stand just where the track entered the farmyard, barring our way. He looked very like Belinus, tall and square, with fair hair and beard.

He recognised Lucius and frowned.

"Oh, so it's you, Aurelius. If you're looking for Belinus, he's not here. He's gone to see the doctor down in Oak Bridges. He wouldn't have needed no doctor if he hadn't been working for you." Deliberately he spat at Lucius' feet. "So you can just clear off, or I'll set the dogs on you."

Lucius ignored the native's hostility. "Good day, Divico. I know that Belinus isn't here, but he's the reason we've come. I'm afraid we've some very sad news. He died this morning. The doctor did everything he could, but Belinus was too ill to be saved."

Divico swore at us, hurling a torrent of abuse that was like a blow in the chest. We stood there and waited. I wondered if he'd strike Lucius, but the violence was in words, not blows, and eventually it subsided a little.

"So your poxy Roman doctor couldn't save him? Couldn't be bothered, more like. What was the trouble, Belinus didn't pay him enough? Or he doesn't trouble himself to save Parisi men, is that it? Well listen, if I ever get my hands on that doctor..."

"No, *you* listen!" I was angry at the unfairness of this tirade. "He took a great deal of trouble, and he's a fine doctor. He treats everyone as well as he knows how, rich or poor, native or Roman. Belinus had a badly injured leg which poisoned his whole body, and broken ribs which damaged him inside. Timaeus tried his best, and he said that if Belinus had been brought to him a day earlier, he might have saved him. As it was, you left it too late, and Belinus has crossed to the Otherworld. Now we've brought him home where he belongs, because you'll want to perform his funeral rites." I indicated the raeda, which was waiting a few paces behind us. "He's in the carriage. We'll help you bring his body out, and then we'll be on our way."

There was a silence. Divico seemed stunned, and Lucius looked surprised by my outburst. Eventually Divico went to the raeda and looked inside. When he came back to us, his expression had softened from open rage to surly wariness. "Then I must thank you for bringing him home. Wait here, and I'll fetch Father. He's in the house."

As he walked off, Lucius whispered, "Well said, Sis! Mind you, I thought he was going to take his cudgel to us at one point."

"Is he Belinus' brother?"

"Wife's brother. Their father Esico owns the farm."

While we waited, we had a chance to gaze around us. The whole place had a sad, neglected air. The roundhouse, little more than a hut, was in bad repair, its walls uneven and flaking. The farm buildings were even worse, with cracks in their mud plaster and holes in their roofs. They'd let in water whenever it rained, and probably fall down flat in a really strong wind. The patch of garden we could glimpse to the left of the house was producing a fine crop of nettles and thistles, and half-a-dozen scrawny chickens and some scruffy ducks scratched listlessly among them.

"This looks bad," I said softly. "If the farm's got into such a miserable state with Belinus alive…"

Lucius nodded, but said nothing, because just then a young woman emerged, carrying a small baby about six weeks old.

"Illiana," Lucius whispered. "Belinus' widow."

She looked like her brother, but though her build and colouring were like Divico's, her manner was a wretched contrast. She was downcast and unkempt, shuffling along slowly with her head lowered. Her face, which could have been pretty, was pale and blotchy, and the baby was pale too, and dirty.

Behind her limped a grey-bearded old man, barely managing to put one foot in front of the other even though he leaned on a stick. But he held his head high and greeted us courteously. "I am Esico, father to Belinus' wife. You are welcome to our farm, even at this sad time."

"We're sorry to bring such tragic news," Lucius answered, and introduced me to the old man.

"The doctor couldn't save him then," Esico muttered.

"He did his very best," I repeated how hard Timaeus had tried to save his patient, and what were the causes of his death.

Esico sighed, and without another word, he and his daughter went to look inside the carriage. When they walked back to us, she was crying.

"Thank you for bringing him home," the old man said. "We're grateful, aren't we, Illiana?"

"Yes. Thank you for bringing him home," she echoed, so softly we could hardly hear.

"Poor lass, this is all too much for you, I reckon," her father said gently. "Take the baby back inside now. It isn't good for either of you to be out here. We'll manage this."

She headed for the house without giving us a second look.

Esico sighed again. "You must forgive her. She's been melancholy since the baby came. A hard birth it was, and she can't seem
to pick herself up. And now this. I don't know how she'll stand it,
she loved Belinus so much. But we'll see that he's properly buried.
His own father's dead, so it'll be me and Divico that'll take care of
things." He started to tell us about the ceremony: it seemed they
were going to bury him in the ground, with some of his favourite
tools which he'd need in the Otherworld. I know the natives here
often do this, not to mention folk in other parts of the Empire, like
Egypt, but I find the thought of burial unsettling. Also I couldn't
help thinking it would be a waste, on a farm as poor as this one,
to bury the farmer's tools along with the man himself. But I've
learned more sense than to argue with other people about their
religious beliefs, so I just listened, and eventually Lucius managed
to move the conversation to the attack on Belinus.

He started cautiously, with a question to which we knew
the answer already. "Belinus hadn't time to say much, and he
was fairly confused in his mind by the end. But he said he was
attacked. Is that what happened?"

The old man nodded. "For no reason, by strangers riding
out of nowhere. A terrible mess his leg was. Cut to the bone. I
was afraid it was too deep to be mended, even if we could have
got him to the doctor quicker. In the end we had to ask our
neighbour's boy to drive him."

"Father!" Divico interrupted sharply. "I'm sure these people don't
want to be wasting their time listening to our family business."

I said, "We don't want to pry, just to help if we can. Belinus
asked us to help you after he'd gone. I made him a promise that
I would, and I mean to keep it."

"We can manage without your help," Divico snapped.

"Be quiet, boy, and try not to be a fool for once in your life,"
Esico cut in, and despite his physical weakness, the anger and
authority in his voice silenced his son.

I looked directly at the old man. "Esico, we don't want to
interfere in your family's affairs. But somebody has murdered your

daughter's man, and surely you want justice for him. We can try to make sure you get it. Do you know who attacked him?"

Esico said "Yes," but Divico shook his head and growled, "This isn't the time for talking. We must move Belinus round the back, before my sister comes out again."

That, at least, was sensible. The poor girl was in a low enough state without having to look at her man's corpse when she came out of her front door. Divico fetched a hurdle, and he and Lucius carried the body round behind the house. For a brief while I had Esico to myself, and I said softly, "Belinus hadn't time to say much before he died, but I gave him my promise to try and protect you. So I feel honour bound to find out what I can." I shot an arrow in the dark. "He said you've been plagued by these sea-raiders, but he thought they were working for somebody else, not on their own account."

He scratched his beard. "Mebbe, mebbe not. The raiders are trouble enough on their own. They're mostly from Gaul, and they range up and down the coast, thieving and robbing, or getting paid for leaving us alone. But they don't usually kill. What's the point? They want all us farmers alive and well, with fat sheep to steal or full purses to pay them off. If they killed Belinus, it must have been for some other reason. Likely they found out he was passing information on to your brother."

I was glad the old man knew Belinus had worked as an informer. It made my next question easier. "Who could have told them that? Surely none of you?"

"'Course not. Divico didn't approve, but he'd never have put Belinus in danger. Anyhow, it hardly matters any more. We'll have to move off this land now. We four can't manage it alone."

"That's sad. Isn't there anyone who could help you?"

He shook his head. "And I don't know where we can go. By the Three Mothers, I don't! Belinus has no kin in these parts, he came from west of Eburacum. It's all bogs and mountains over that way. I suppose they'd take us in if we really can't find anywhere. But I don't want to go so far away. I was born here, in this farmhouse. It's where I belong…"

"Suppose you could find someone to buy the farm, but let you run it for them? Perhaps one of the new settlers. They're often glad to have local people to work the land."

"No." He almost shouted it, making me jump. "We'll have no Roman masters. We're used to being free. Begging your pardon," he added more quietly. "But it's the way we are. Either we work this land as free men, or we sell it. And we'll have to sell it, we've no choice. The young people can't manage it by themselves, and I'm not much use these days." He went to sit down on a low pile of logs near the door, and I sat beside him.

"I don't like to see Magnus get his way after all, but there's nothing we can do. And he'll give us a rock bottom price, being the man he is. Then what'll we live on? How'll we manage?"

"I've heard he's buying up land near here. He's offered to buy you out then?"

He nodded his grey head. "Twice he's offered. The first time he set a reasonable price, but we said no. The second time he came calling, the price was an insult. But even if it had been a good offer, we'd have said no. With Belinus here, we could manage well enough, and we wanted a future for the children. Now he's gone...He's trouble, that Magnus. I reckon a lot of our misfortunes are his responsibility. Between him and the raids from the coast, we're finished here now." He stopped as he saw Lucius and Divico returning, and the next thing he said was, "Let me bring you out a drink to set you on your road."

While he fetched it, I walked over to the raeda, where the two horse-boys were sitting demurely. (They'd usually be playing dice, but I'd given them a stern warning about what would be considered appropriate behaviour by Belinus' relatives.) I checked that they'd watered their mules and our two horses, and told them to get on their way home.

As I crossed the yard again, Divico and Lucius approached, walking silently side by side. As they reached me, Esico shuffled slowly out with a tray of mugs. He began handing them round, and when I took mine I realised it contained not wine but native beer, which of course I should have expected. I don't like beer, and this was sharp thin stuff, yet good manners dictated I should drink it as if I enjoyed it. While we drank, Esico and his son talked resolutely about the weather and the sheep, until Illiana came out of the house to join us, and then they talked resolutely about the baby.

We finished our drinks and refused refills, and Lucius returned to the subject of our visit. "Let me say again how sorry we are about Belinus' death. And I mustn't forget to give you the money I owe him, for the work he did for me." He held out a purse to Illiana which, judging from its weight, contained a more than generous amount. She took it and began to thank him, but her brother stepped forward, red-faced with rage.

"We don't need your money!" he burst out, snatching the purse and throwing it at Lucius' feet. "We don't need it, and we won't take it. If he hadn't been so greedy for Roman silver, Belinus wouldn't have got himself killed."

Lucius looked at the young man calmly. "I'm sorry you didn't approve of the work he was doing for me. But he earned this money fairly. It belongs to his family now."

"It's tainted silver," Divico growled. "We refuse it."

"That's enough!" Illiana roused herself and looked animated for the first time since we'd met her. "Belinus was happy to pass on information about the sea-raiders, and the gods know we needed the money. *You'd* have just gone on paying them every time they came round threatening us, I suppose."

Divico was silent, and I seized my chance.

"Esico, what did you mean just now about Magnus being responsible for your misfortunes?"

"It's what I think," Esico answered.

"Father!" Divico was even angrier. "Why do you have to go blabbing our business to all and sundry?"

"If somebody's harassing you," Lucius was stern, "then that makes it my business too. I represent the Governor here, and I can get something done to stop it. But only if you tell me what's been going on, and why you suspect Magnus. First of all, though, please take this." He bent and retrieved the purse, and held it out to Illiana. "It's yours by right, and your baby son's too."

She nodded. "I will, and thank you. We need it for the baby, and like you say, my man earned it." She tucked it into her belt-pouch, ignoring her brother's furious glare.

The old man said, "We've had all sorts of things go wrong. One day a fence was broken down and our cows got out and trampled one of the wheat-fields. Another time our best ram disappeared, and Belinus found his body in the road. And sometimes we see horsemen near the farm, watching us. Or we hear them galloping by at night. All meant to scare us, and take up our time when we should be working the land."

"But aren't they just the sort of things the raiders would do?" Lucius asked.

"They would be," Divico snarled. "But they promised to let us alone, after I paid them last time."

"We'd no choice but to pay them," Esico said sadly. "And up to now they've kept their side of the bargain. These latest troubles are different. They're Ostorius Magnus' work. He wants more land, and he's been round several of the local farmers, offering to buy us out. He's got three nephews, and he says he wants to set them up as farmers on their own."

"He's just greedy, like all Romans," Divico growled.

"Not all," Lucius answered. "But some are, and that's why we have laws to stop people from intimidating their neighbours."

"Was Magnus angry when you refused to sell him the farm?" I asked. "Did he threaten you?"

Esico nodded. "He ended up saying he hoped we'd change our minds, because he'd hate to see any harm coming to us if we stayed on. Belinus said we could take care of ourselves."

"And so we can," Divico said. Brave words, I thought. I only wish they were true.

Illiana's face crumpled and she began to cry. She sat down heavily on the log-pile, and her father went to stand near her and put an arm round her.

Divico looked at them both, no longer angry but sad and concerned. He motioned for us to follow him across the yard out of earshot. "I don't like to see her upset like that," he muttered.

"Nor do we," Lucius answered. "As we've said already, Divico, we'll do our best to help you. Aurelia promised Belinus, and that promise binds me too."

Divico shrugged. "You can't help us. If it's the raiders that are plaguing us, you'll never catch them, nobody will. If it's Magnus, well, we all know how it is. Romans side with Romans. In a quarrel between a rich Roman and a poor tribesman, who do you think the authorities are going to side with?"

"Listen, Divico." Lucius looked the young man squarely in the face. "I accept that you don't like Romans, but that doesn't affect Roman justice. We'll find out who killed Belinus, and who's been harassing you here, and they'll be stopped. It may be the Gauls Belinus spoke about. That seems to me the most likely. But it may not, and it doesn't matter, because we'll catch them and punish them. You have my word on that. Now in return, will you give me all the help you can? We'll have a much better chance if we work together on this."

Divico took a step back, like a scared colt. "I'll not become one of your paid spies."

Lucius laughed. "I'm not asking you to. I only want men who work for me willingly. What I mean is this: will you tell us all you can about what's been going on here? Will you tell us if you have more trouble in the future?"

He hesitated a long time, but finally said, "Aye, all right."

"Will you shake hands on it? We may not be friends, but can we at least be allies, until this trouble is over?" Lucius held out his hand.

There was another long hesitation before Divico answered. "I agree."

Chapter VII

We walked back to where Esico still leaned on the log-pile. Illiana had gone, into the house presumably.

"Esico," Lucius said, "Divico has agreed to let us try and help. Will you agree too?"

"I will. We've tried to manage, but we can't do it no more."

"Then first of all, let's get the facts clear. The attack on Belinus, where and when exactly did it happen? Were either of you with him?"

They both shook their heads, and Divico said, "Day before yesterday it was, in the afternoon. I was cutting wood near the house. Belinus went to check on the sheep. They're about a mile east of here, that's our best pasture. The ewes are lambing now, or have just got new lambs. You need to keep a close eye."

"Have you a shepherd with them?" I asked.

"Oh aye, Cattos is our shepherd—that's Belinus' adopted son. But he's a lazy little tyke, inclined to have a nap in the sun or go off bird's-nesting when he should be watching the flock. Anyhow just before sunset Cattos comes running to the farm saying they've been attacked, and Belinus is hurt bad, mebbe dead. I ride straight over, and we find him on the ground, knocked senseless, blood all over him. And the sheep scattered to the four winds. So I fetched a cart and brought him home. Cattos and the dogs rounded the flock up."

Lucius' expression was grim. "Did he wake up enough to talk? Did he tell you about the attack?"

"Yes, after a bit. Between him and Cattos we got the full story."

"How many men?"

"Three. Strangers, long hair and beards, and weather-beaten looking. Spoke like foreigners. Gauls, they thought."

"Belinus told me that the men intended to kill him, but some travellers on the highway scared them off."

Divico scowled. "That's right. We thought he'd had a lucky escape. Only now…well, anyhow, he was in a bad way, his ribs bashed in and his leg cut, but he said he'd be all right if he just rested up a while. Illiana tried to watch over him through the night, but what with the baby and everything, well, it was too much for her. By morning he was worse, much worse, hot and feverish, talking nonsense, and his leg was still bleeding. So I asked one of the neighbours to take him down to your Greek doctor at Oak Bridges. I couldn't go myself, in case of more trouble here."

"Where's the shepherd boy now?" Lucius asked Divico. "Could we talk to him?"

"With the sheep still. About a mile along the road, like I said."

"He's on his own?"

Divico returned Lucius' sharp look. "Of course he's on his own. I can't spare an extra hand for shepherding, especially now."

"That's not what he means, Divico." Esico looked at Lucius. "You think Cattos may be in danger, don't you?"

"I'm afraid it's possible. If the attackers realise that Belinus is dead, so the lad is the only person who could recognise them again, they may come back for him."

Divico's expression was close to panic. "By the Dagda, I never thought of that. I ought to go after him, make sure he's come to no harm. But how can I? I can't leave my sister, with things as they are."

"Would you like us to check up on the boy?" I asked. "It's on our way. We can make sure he's all right, and let you know if he needs help." I felt pleased that here at last was something practical we could do. "And when we find him, we can ask him about the attack. He might remember something more, something that would help us."

Divico smiled for the first time. "I'd appreciate it, yes. Thank you. I'll give you a dagger to take for him, for a bit of extra protection like. When you find him, tell him I say he's to give you whatever help he can. And tell him be careful. I'll send someone out to keep him company later, one of the neighbours' lads. The gods know who, but I'll find someone. You're right, he shouldn't be out there alone."

"Leave it to us," Lucius said. "We'll be off and look for him straight away."

So we left, and it was a relief to be away from them, even though we were both anxious about what we might find.

The sheep pasture wasn't far away. It lay a mile or so east of the farm, across a shallow valley and beyond a copse of beech trees. My heart sank as I saw it.

The sheep and lambs weren't peacefully grazing, but running in terror, scattering in all directions. In and out among them rode three horsemen, wheeling their mounts and yelling. Of the shepherd boy there was no sign.

We paused and looked at each other. It was one of those times when we each knew what the other was thinking.

"Shall we?" he said.

"Yes."

We screamed "Charge!" at the tops of our voices, and kicked our horses into a flat-out gallop. The three men heard and saw us, and turned to race off towards the sea. We tore after them, yelling like soldiers in a battle. We sped across the open ground and I felt a sudden fire in my blood, as we pelted after our fleeing enemies.

All too soon they disappeared over a rise in the ground, and again, we both had the same thought. We slowed our horses and turned back.

The sheep were already calming down, but where was the boy? I cupped my hands around my mouth and yelled "Cattos! Cattos, are you here?"

Nothing happened.

"Cattos, come out, it's safe now. They've gone."

Still nothing. I felt cold inside. Had we come too late?

"I want to find Cattos the shepherd," I yelled. "We're friends, and we've got a message from Divico!"

Nobody answered or appeared, and I began to be really afraid. "Gods, don't say they've killed the boy. Let's both try."

We filled our lungs and bellowed *"CATTOS!"* fit to wake the dead.

A small figure crawled slowly out from a clump of thorn bushes fifty paces ahead and to our left. He was about ten, still and white-faced, and he stood watching us cautiously, as if about to make a run for it.

We walked our horses towards him and dismounted some distance away. I said softly, "Let me do the talking to start with." I threw my reins to Lucius and moved slowly forward, holding out my hands so he could see I was unarmed.

"Cattos, we're friends of Belinus, and Divico and Illiana sent us to find out if you're all right. I'm Aurelia, and that's my brother Lucius." I stopped, not wanting to crowd him, but I was close enough to see he'd been crying. "You're safe now. Are you hurt? We know someone attacked Belinus here. It looks as if they've come back."

He lowered his eyes." Aye, they've been back. They chased the sheep, and they killed Lightning." He looked across the field towards another clump of bushes. Beneath it I could just make out the body of a dog, mostly white except where red blood soaked the hair on its left side. A second dog, with long brown hair, lay by its mate, but when it saw Cattos, it crossed the pasture to stand protectively beside the boy. It stayed close to him as he set off to where the white dog lay. We followed behind, but stopped when the lad reached his dog and started to shake with sobs as he crouched down beside its body.

"What happened?" I asked quietly.

He wiped his eyes with his sleeve. "I saw them riding up from the sea. Same three as before. I hid in the bush, and called the dogs in, and Thunder came, but Lightning ran out and barked at them. One of them, the biggest one, yelled out, 'We know you're here, Cattos boy, so come out, we want to talk to you.' And Lightning jumped at him and bit his arm, but he grabbed her and—and—he pointed at the livid stab-wound in the dog's side. "I couldn't stop them. They all laughed, and he shouted, 'I don't like dogs with big heads, boy. This one will look much better if it has fewer ears.' The others cheered, and then…" He stopped, on the verge of crying again.

"A brave dog." I took a pace closer, and he pointed at the dog's head. I realised that one of the pointed ears had been hacked right off. I heard Lucius swear and Cattos start to sob. I concentrated on not being sick.

"After that they rode around to scatter the sheep, and he kept shouting, 'Next time it's your turn, Cattos boy. Or maybe we'll go and say hello to little Illiana.' They said horrible things about her…and that's when you came along." He looked up at us. "I feel so useless. I wanted to help Lightning, but I couldn't, so I just had to stay hid. We both did." He patted the brown dog's head. "I wish I could have done *something*. Divico will be furious when he finds out."

"No he won't, at least not with you," I said quickly. "He'll say you did right to hide, you couldn't tackle three of them. He and Illiana need you alive and strong, making the right decision like a man, and that's what you've done."

"Divico asked us to give you this dagger." Lucius slowly drew it out and handed it to the boy. "He says he'll send someone out to help you guard the sheep. You shouldn't be on your own just now."

The boy brightened. "Perhaps Belinus can come when his leg's better."

That was the hardest part of all, telling Cattos that Belinus was dead. We tried to be gentle, but there's no easy way to convey news like that, and the boy hunched himself into a ball and cried. I wanted to shed a few tears myself, for the harsh fate that had taken Belinus' life and left his family so vulnerable. The work

Lucius does is necessary and right, I know that, but sometimes the cruelty of it breaks your heart.

I sat down beside Cattos and put my arm round him, and after a while he raised his head. "Belinus was like my father. He took me in when I was found. My mother left me in a barn. He and Illiana. Poor Illiana, this'll just about kill her, I reckon. She's been so sad and sickly lately, and Belinus was the only one could make her smile. I'll try my best, though." He shook me off and stood up, squaring his thin shoulders. "I'm all right now. I must see to the sheep."

"It's going to be hard for all of you, Cattos. But Lucius and I will do our level best to help you, and punish the men who killed Belinus. That's a promise. We'll have to be on our way soon, but first I think we could do with a drink of wine, How about it?"

The boy's eyes lighted up like torches. "Thank you. I'm starved. I've had nothing to eat since last night."

"Then you must have some honey cakes too." I rummaged in my saddlebag and found the cakes. He fell on them greedily and ate four, by which time I'd poured him a beaker of wine. Lucius and I shared the other beaker.

He drank the wine and coughed. "I've never had wine before." He took another two cakes, and smiled. "Thanks. I wish our Illiana could make cakes like that." His smile faded. "She hardly cooks at all now. She used to be so lively, you know, always busy, always smiling, but since the baby came she's been real miserable. Does it always make women sad, having babies? You'd think they'd be happy, wouldn't you?"

"The gods alone know," I said. "Lots of women are very happy. My sister Albia was as merry as a box of birds when she had her twins."

"Albia's your sister? She and Candidus have been real good to us. They lent us a couple of men last harvest-time, and they said they'd help us when the bastards started threatening us. But Divico's so set on being independent, not letting anyone else know our business. Especially Romans…Oh, sorry, I didn't mean to be rude."

We smiled at him and he went on, "I wish I could get a message to Candidus and Albia about what's happened now. They might be able to do something. But I'm afraid with Belinus gone, the raiders'll get what they want anyway, which is to push us out. I don't see how we can stay."

"We're on our way to see Albia now," I said. "Of course we'll tell her and Candidus what's happened. They'll want to help."

Lucius said, "You think it's the raiders from the sea who attacked Belinus, and are trying to take your farm away?"

Cattos nodded. "Who else? Well, Divico thinks it's that Ostorius Magnus, but it can't be. The men who came after Belinus weren't Romans. Gauls, I reckon. We get fishermen coming ashore here sometimes. They all have long hair."

"What did these three look like?" Lucius asked. "Can you describe them for us?"

"I didn't see much. And the Long-hairs all look the same, don't they?"

"Not really," I prompted. "They've got different coloured hair and beards, for one thing. I didn't get much of a look at the three we chased off today, but one was taller than the others with brown hair, very long, it was blowing about as he rode. The two shorter ones were darker, and one of them had a very skimpy beard. Now you've seen them twice, and you were closer to them than we were. Even if they scared you, your eyes will have seen a lot, and left a picture in your mind. Close your eyes now, and try to look at that picture again with your mind's eye. Start with the one who did most of the talking. Was he the tall one?"

He closed his eyes and screwed up his face, concentrating hard. "That's right, and he was their leader. A head taller than the others, with thick long brown hair, and a white scar on his left cheek running up to where his ear would be, but that was hid by the long hair. It showed up because his face was so brown. They were all brown, like sailors are. The one with the skimpy beard, he had black curly hair, not as long as the others but still a foreign-looking style, and he was small and thin, and not a very good rider. I think he was only a lad. The other one had black hair too but hanging down straight."

"Good! That was an excellent picture. Now their voices. They'll be in your mind too, if you listen inside yourself. You said you've met fishermen. Did these three speak in the same way?"

"Let me think…yes, the leader did. The others just laughed and cheered, I couldn't tell. Yes, the tall one was a Gaul, I'm sure." He looked at me. "That's a good trick you've showed me, finding the pictures and sounds in my mind. I'll remember it."

"We always see and hear more than we think we have. My brother taught me that." I grinned at Lucius. "We used to play games when we were little, looking at a street full of people and seeing how many we could remember. Mind you, Albia's got a much better memory for faces than either of us. Once she sees someone, she never forgets."

We stayed with Cattos a little while longer, reluctant to leave him there entirely alone. We were relieved when a slightly-built dark lad appeared on a pony, followed by a big brindled dog. As they got nearer, we realised that it was in fact a slightly-built dark lass, looking very boyish in trousers and a short cloak, and carrying herself with a swagger.

"Oh, gods," Cattos muttered under his breath. "It's Balca. She's a kind of distant cousin of ours. She's all right, but she bosses me about something awful."

"I know the feeling," Lucius winked at him. "My sister orders me about all the time."

"Only when you need it," I pointed out.

"But remember, the bossy ones are always the best in a fight," my brother added magnanimously. "The nice meek little girls who never argue just turn tail and run if trouble starts."

The boy smiled. "That's true. Balca's not afraid of anything or anyone. She'd be brilliant in a fight." He waved as the girl rode up to us and dismounted.

"Hello, Tom-cat," she greeted him. "I hear you've been having some trouble?"

"Hello, Bossy-boots," he answered cheerfully. "Yes, I have. I was just saying to my friends here, I could do with someone who's not afraid of a fight."

"Well now you've got someone. My father heard the Long-hairs had been here, and he sent me to visit Belinus and Illiana this morning. That's when I found out what's happened. I'm so sorry. "

"Thank you. He was like a father to me."

The boy was nearly in tears again, but she pretended not to notice, and went on briskly, "Who are your friends? I presume they aren't anything to do with the Long-hairs?" She addressed us in Latin. "Good day. I'm Balca. My father is Coriu, the Captain of Chief Bodvocos' Guard. May I ask who you are?"

"Lucius Aurelius Marcellus at your service, and this is my sister Aurelia, who runs the Oak Tree Mansio at Oak Bridges. The doctor who treated Belinus' wounds lives there."

"I'm pleased to meet you." It was Lucius who had her attention. "You came to see Chief Bodvocos a few days ago, didn't you?"

"I did, yes."

"You're the government investigator Belinus was working for, aren't you?"

"You're well-informed, Balca. He was one of my informers, but his work was supposed to be a secret. How did you hear about it?"

"Everybody knows. Even the Long-hairs must have found it out, mustn't they? And are those your men camped on the Headland? Half-a-dozen cavalry?"

He nodded. "I'm on my way back to them now."

"Then I don't suppose you've heard about the shipwreck there? In the storm last night…"

"Oh yes, I've heard about the *Sea Horse*. A Roman ship carrying government papers and stores, wrecked at the northern bay of the Headland. We'll salvage the cargo tonight or tomorrow."

She looked slightly disappointed that he'd already received the news, but she said gravely, "You're well-informed also."

"I try to be." Lucius smiled. "Look, Balca, I'm going to catch these accursed pirates or raiders or whoever they are. I need all the help and information I can get. So I'll ask you, as someone who obviously has the ear of the Chief: will he and your father agree to help me, or do they prefer to keep out of it and leave it to us Romans?"

"They'll help, of course they will. But presumably he told you that when you visited him?"

Lucius shrugged. "We only had a short conversation, and I got the impression he was unsure of me, and hadn't made his mind up about me."

She laughed. "He likes to take his time, sizing up new people. But he wants the raids stopped, and he wants Ostorius Magnus put in his place, and if that's why you're here, then he'll help."

"Good. The Headland is his land, isn't it?"

"Partly his, partly Ostorius Magnus'."

Cattos said, "Can the Chief send anyone to the farm to help us? I don't know how we're going to manage now."

"He will soon, I think. It's difficult just now, because the raiders are still about, and that swine Magnus is up to his tricks again. But *we'll* stay with you, till either you can move the sheep, or Father can send some men." She patted her hound, and Cattos' brown sheepdog went to her for a share of her attention. She looked round and asked, "Where's Lightning?...Oh no, what's happened? Have they been back today?"

"Just now, yes. These two helped me chase them off." I avoided Lucius' eye. If a little boasting made him feel braver, it wouldn't hurt.

She looked at us seriously. "Thank you for helping Tom—I mean Cattos. We are very grateful." Her Latin was good, and though she can't have been more than sixteen, she was calm and self-assured. I was surprised and pleased that a native guard captain's daughter had been so well educated.

"Esico is a kinsman of the Chief," she went on, "so of course we'll avenge Belinus. And we'll look after you all. You can depend on it."

Cattos smiled. "I'm glad you've come, Balca. I know you're only a girl, but I'll feel safer with you here."

"I'm as good a fighter as you, Cattos, and don't you forget it." She turned to me, surveying my cavalry breeches and boots. "We girls are as good as men any day, aren't we?"

"We certainly are. Ask my brother here."

"At least as good," Lucius laughed. "And anyway I daren't say anything else."

"I've brought my dagger, and I'm learning to use a sling," she announced. "There are plenty of the right sized pebbles in this pasture. I've brought a sling for you too, Cattos. We'll practise while I'm here, and if those men come back any more, we'll have a surprise for them. You can kill a man with a sling-shot before ever he can get near you."

"Good. But until you've had a bit of practice, aim for the horse, not the rider," Lucius advised. "Moving targets aren't easy, but a horse makes a bigger one than a man."

"Thank you, I'll remember. Are you a soldier?"

"I used to be. We were all expected to be able to use a sling, though I was never very good at it. But if you're on foot, it gives you a fighting chance against enemies at a distance."

"I'd like to learn to use a bow," she said eagerly, "but Father says it isn't a suitable weapon for a girl. I'll have to get one of the lads in the Guard to teach me when nobody's looking. That's how I learned the sling." She grinned, and I saw that beneath the well-educated grown-up exterior was a lively and very bright young girl.

"Has Chief Bodvocos had trouble from Voltacos' raiders on his own estate?" I asked. "Or perhaps with a well-trained guard, they're leaving him alone."

"We've had no trouble yet. The Long-hairs are going for the smaller places, where the farms aren't fortified. Most of these farms haven't even got a ditch round them, never mind a decent stockade."

"Magnus' place is fortified," Cattos said. "And the raiders haven't gone near him at all. Divico says that's because he's made a deal with the Long-hairs. He tells them where the easiest pickings are, and they leave him alone."

"I shouldn't be surprised. But he leaves the Chief alone, he knows when he's met his match. The most he does is move our boundary markers now and then to try and encroach on our fields."

"I hear he wants to extend his estate," I put in.

She tossed her head scornfully. "So he keeps telling everyone. His land adjoins ours, and he's a pest. But the Chief and Father won't stand for any of his nonsense." She glanced round the field. "Come on, Tom-cat, let's look for pebbles for my sling."

We left them some honey cakes and went on our way, feeling happier. The girl was young, but she was strong and intelligent, and above all, she had close connections with Bodvocos. That surely meant more help would be forthcoming for Esico and Illiana. These tribal chieftains always look after their own. As we rode away, Balca was giving Cattos his first lesson on using a sling. I suspected it would be the first of many.

Chapter VIII

I always enjoy visiting my sister and her husband. You know the way some married couples are so wrapped up in one another that they scarcely have any attention to give to visitors, making you feel like an outsider even though they don't mean to? Albia and Candidus are the exact opposite. From the first, they were happy together and they wanted everyone to share in their happiness, so they have always been open and hospitable, and going to see them is a real treat.

Their farm stood in a sheltered fold of the hills, and was unmistakably Roman with its sturdy brick farmhouse, solid stables and barns, and general air of prosperity. Around the cluster of buildings stretched fields dotted with trees and divided by well-maintained fencing, or thick thorn hedges. Some had wheat or barley growing in them, but most had sheep and lambs, and one patch of rough ground which led into a small piece of woodland was where the pigs and piglets rooted about.

In front of the house was the farm's most important asset, its reason for having been built on just this spot: a small spring, which gave pure water for people and livestock all year round whatever the weather. One of the first improvements Candidus had made when he bought the place two years ago was to divert some of the water to feed a pretty little fish-pond, while the main flow was piped into a big granite basin that would have done credit to a temple precinct. To the left, also near the house, was Albia's garden, her pride and joy. She grew vegetables, fruit, and herbs for the table and the medicine chest. She seemed to have some crop or other ready to harvest whatever season it was, and now there were cabbages, small lettuces, and various sorts of herbs, the kinds that survive through the winter even here in the far north.

A thin lad was digging over a bare stretch of earth. He stopped and smiled at us, and I recognised him as the house-boy.

"Hello, Nasua. Albia's got you helping with her garden, I see."

"Hello, M-Mistress Aurelia. And Master L-lucius too! That's right, I'm learning to be a g-gardener." He stuck his spade in the earth and strolled over, wiping his hands on his tunic. "I l-like working outside. The Mistress is in the house with the twins. Shall I t-tell her you're here?"

"Yes please. We'll unsaddle and give our horses a drink. We've had quite a long ride."

"I'll s-see to them for you. Just leave them there by the trough."

"Everything looks in good order," Lucius said as we dismounted.

"It does. I'm glad."

"And surprised?" my brother grinned.

"Well…Candidus would be the first to admit he wasn't exactly born and bred to farming." His parents had intended him for a political career, but they owned large estates in the south of Britannia, so naturally he'd learned the skills needed to be a gentleman farmer: keep a sharp eye on the finances, and leave most of the hard work to the slaves. The arrangement was clearly a success. Albia loved the farm, and was never tired of saying that this quiet countryside was a perfect place to bring up children. She seemed to be set on proving herself right, with two toddlers already, and a third on the way.

As we walked towards the house Albia and Candidus emerged from it, preceded by the children, who ran round us in circles like excited puppies. My sister had followed the Aurelius family tradition by producing twins, Decimus and Marcella. I like being a twin, and felt sure they would too, when they were old enough to appreciate how lucky they were.

After the first joyful flurry of greetings and hugs, the twins were handed over to their nursemaid, a fair-haired little native girl called Lia, so we could talk without interruption. Albia produced wine, and I unpacked the food I'd brought from the mansio. In no time we were eating a pleasant midday meal by the pond.

Between us, Lucius and I told them about Belinus' death, and Lucius mentioned the shipwreck. But it was the fate of Belinus' family that concerned them.

"Poor Illiana," Albia sighed. "The fates have been cruel to her this past year. Her father's a cripple, and she's grown so melancholy that she can hardly manage to look after her baby. And yet she used to be such a happy girl."

"Belinus and Divico and young Cattos have only just been holding the farm together," Candidus said. "I've lent them a couple of my lads now and then to help, but I can't spare anyone full-time, much as I'd like to. Without Belinus, I don't see how they can go on."

"Chief Bodvocos may be able to help them." I explained about the young lass we'd seen with Cattos. "I hope so. Because Belinus warned me his family are in danger now, and Esico and Divico seem to think so too."

Albia looked worried. "From the Gauls? We keep hearing stories about them, but so far it's just been the usual sort of thieving and threats. Not murder. That's much more serious."

"It's even more than that. They believe someone has a personal grudge against them, and is trying to drive them off their land. Lucius and I wondered if Belinus has fallen out with one of his neighbours, and the harassment is coming from them. But the boy Cattos said the men who killed Belinus were not local, and he would have known them if they'd been from this area."

Candidus refilled Lucius' wine-mug. "I'm glad you're doing something about the raiders. They're a pest. We haven't had any bother ourselves yet, but I've a nasty feeling it's only a matter of time."

"You think they'll attack us here?" Albia exclaimed. "That's dreadful, Candidus. Surely we're too far inland?"

"You're nearer to the sea than Belinus," I pointed out.

"You're right," Candidus agreed. "We've plenty of men, but we've no solid defences. I wonder whether we should think about building a stockade to protect the main house and buildings, and the spring and garden perhaps."

"Good idea," Lucius put in. "The sooner the better."

"No it isn't, it's a horrible idea," Albia objected. "One of the things I love about living here is the feeling of peace and freedom. We can leave our stock in the fields at night without a herdsman, and our doors unlocked day and night, knowing we're safe from harm."

"Perhaps not this summer," Candidus said gently.

"Belinus didn't think the raiders are the main cause of their trouble anyway," I went on. "He thought someone powerful was trying to drive him and his family off their farm. He wouldn't say who, but there are very few men who consider themselves so strong and invulnerable that they'd risk doing a thing like that."

"I can only think of two," Candidus said. "Bodvocos and Magnus. And I can't see it being either of them. We know them both."

"I met Magnus the other day, when he bought some horses from us. I liked him."

"We liked him too," Albia agreed. "He came to introduce himself soon after he arrived." She sliced up more cheese and passed it to me. "And his nephew too, Vividus, *very* dashing. In the old days I'd have called him decidedly fanciable."

"That's not saying much. You used to fall in love about three times a month. What did you think of him, Candidus?"

He smiled. "I didn't find either of them in the least fanciable. But they were pleasant, and full of compliments about our farm. Some of our fields adjoin theirs. I can't imagine Magnus using bully-boy tactics against anyone. He seemed—well, too correct, too much the ex-soldier turned country gentleman, if you know what I mean. Though I suspect he'd be a bad enemy if he didn't get his own way."

"I agree with that." Albia nodded thoughtfully. "But then you don't get to be a centurion unless you can be tough. Father would have made a bad enemy too."

"He's greedy," I said. "Talking to me, he made no secret of wanting more land."

Candidus nodded. "He asked if we knew of any farmers who were selling up. He even joked that if we ever found we had too much on our plates, with the babies and everything, we could sell to him. Well, I assume it was a joke. I asked him whether he meant sell the farm, or sell the babies."

I sipped my wine. "So if he'd made Esico and Belinus an offer for their farm, and they'd refused, you don't think he'd follow it up by trying to force them to leave?"

They shook their heads, and Candidus said, "Divico makes no bones about being anti-Roman. He'd naturally blame a settler for almost anything." He sighed and looked at my sister. "I wish there was something we could do to help them."

She was doubtful. "If Divico's in charge now, he's not likely to accept any help from us."

"Bodvocos will help them, won't he?" I suggested. "I gather Esico is some sort of distant relative of the Chief. Unless it's Bodvocos who's trying to drive them out."

"No, not Bodvocos," Albia said firmly. "He'd never turn on one of his own people. And Esico's family have lived on that farm for years."

We finished our meal in thoughtful silence, and then my brother said, "I can't stay for long, much as I'd like to. But while we're all together, I want to tell you some family news...no, Albia, don't look like that! Aurelia's already asked me if I'm getting married, and the answer is definitely not. This is something much more interesting."

We ignored this sally, and Albia said, "Good news, I hope. We could do with something to cheer us up."

"It'll do that all right. I've met a man in Londinium named Aurelius Rollus."

"Aurelius?" I exclaimed. "You mean he's a relative of ours?"

"Yes. He's our brother."

Our *brother!*

It was pointless to object that we hadn't any more brothers, only Lucius. We knew that. Or we thought we did.

After a stunned silence, I finally managed to say, "Well, if you're waiting till our jaws have stopped dropping, we'll be here all day."

He grinned. "I know how you feel. It shocked me too, when he first approached me in Londinium."

"'Shocked' doesn't quite describe it," I said. "I simply can't believe it. Still, go on. He approached you in Londinium. Just by chance, or had he been looking for you?"

"Oh, he was looking for me. It was about two months ago, and he said he'd spent nearly a year finding me." He took a sip of wine. "He said his mother was a native called Huctia, and she first met father years ago in Glevum, when he was still quite a young soldier."

"He was posted over here just before the Emperor Nero died." Albia rubbed her cheek thoughtfully. "And he was based in Glevum for a few months, I remember him talking about it. It must be…let's see, more than thirty years ago."

"Thirty-one, as far as I can work it out."

"So this Aurelius Rollus must be a little older than we are."

"That's right. Father's cohort was quartered in Glevum, and Huctia was a tavern girl in a bar the soldiers used."

Suddenly it all made sense. I sat back, relieved. "Oh well, if she was a camp-girl, presumably any Roman in Glevum could have been Rollus' father, or any native, come to that, because they use those places too. My guess is this lad doesn't know who his father was, he's just trying his luck, wanting to attach himself to a Roman family by claiming to be a long-lost bastard son. I can't believe you fell for a trick like that…"

"Hear me out, Aurelia, before you judge. I've checked Rollus' story as far as I can. I'm an investigator after all."

He gave me a sharp look, and I held my peace. I had to admit if anyone was capable of checking such a tale, it was my brother.

"Rollus was born in Glevum, and Father had his birth registered in the legionary records there. That much is true. Father couldn't marry Huctia of course because he was still a very lowly legionary. But Rollus thinks, and I agree with him, that it showed Father was looking to the future, and would have been prepared to acknowledge him. But immediately afterwards Father's cohort went on campaign further north, and she lost track of him. Another soldier took her on, and the boy too, and they left Glevum and moved north to Lindum. So when Father tried to get in touch with her later, he couldn't find her, or his son."

"What happened to the second soldier? Did he marry her?"

"He was killed."

"That's sad," Albia said.

"And convenient," I added.

Lucius nodded. "Both, I agree. But eventually there was a happy ending. Father and Huctia and the boy, now about ten years old I suppose, all met up again, by pure chance, when Father came back to Britannia after leaving the army. When he brought us all here, and we spent three months in Lindum, remember?"

I did remember, but not all that clearly after so long. "We stayed with a retired army friend of father's in Lindum, didn't we? And it was bitterly cold, it did nothing but snow all winter long."

Albia nodded. "It was horrible, especially after Pompeii. It makes me shiver just thinking about it."

Pompeii…I don't often let myself dwell on those far-off days nearly twenty years ago when we lost our home in Pompeii. It makes me sad even now, to remember the good life we had known beside the Bay of Neapolis, but in truth we were lucky. Our house was wiped out with the others when Vesuvius erupted, but the Fates had decreed that none of our family were in residence on that frightful day, and the servants, unsupervised, had the good sense to flee before it was too late.

"Fortune was kind to you in a way," Candidus said. "At least your lives were spared. But having your house and land destroyed must have been a nasty blow to your family. And your father was recently retired, you say?"

"About two years before," Lucius answered. "He'd already decided he wanted us to settle in Britannia, and he had a good nest-egg, like all centurions So although losing our house was a setback, it didn't make him a pauper. It just meant we left Italia more quickly than he'd anticipated."

"I often wondered," Albia said, "why he was always so set on Britannia. It was still a very new province then, and pretty unsettled in the north. And after the eruption, come to think about it, he managed to move us all here very fast, in a matter of months, so his plans must have been well advanced. But if he knew he had a son here and wanted to find him, it would account for it."

"Yes, it would." I picked up my beaker and swirled the wine round in it, letting my mind run back across the years. The Aurelius family, like so many, has had its share of sadness. When Father set up house with my mother in Pompeii he hadn't yet reached his exalted centurion's rank, so there was no question of a legal marriage, but they thought of themselves as man and wife and were happy, till she died giving birth to Lucius and me. Our grandmother moved in to look after us, because Father was on campaign in Gaul. Quite soon he met Flavia—Albia's mother—and Albia was born in Gaul. Flavia and Albia lived in various military towns there, following wherever Father was posted. So he didn't see Lucius and me growing up. Flavia died of a fever in Gaul, and Albia came down to join us in Pompeii. Eventually Father managed to pull a few strings and got himself transferred back to Italia to finish his service. When he came out, we had a couple of years of happy family life in Pompeii.

Could it really be true that during all those years, we'd had a brother in a faraway province, and father had been dreaming of going back to see him? I still couldn't take it in.

"Do you know for sure," I asked Lucius, "that father met this so-called son of his while we were all in Lindum? He never breathed a word about it."

"I know for sure. For two reasons. First, he has an Aurelius ring which he said Father gave him." He glanced down at his own left hand, and Albia and I involuntarily did the same. We all had identical rings of twisted gold. "He lent it me, so I could show it to you." He fished in his belt-pouch and produced a thin twisted-gold ring identical to our own.

That, I must say, impressed me: not only that this Rollus had a ring like ours, but that he was prepared to trust Lucius with it.

"But what really convinced me," my brother said, "was a letter he has, from our father to his mother Huctia. And I have a copy of that with me too. Rollus wanted me to show it to you."

He brought out a small roll of papyrus. "The original was on a wooden letter-tablet, and the ink was quite faded, but easy enough to read. This is an exact copy, except it's in my writing, not father's. It's quite short, listen." He flattened out the papyrus and read:

"Aurelius Marcellus to his Huctia, greetings.

My dearest, all is going well here in Brigantia. We've started building work on the mansio, and the twins and Albia are taking to the life like ducks to water. So I'm almost ready to fetch you and Rollus up here to join us. Soon I shall tell them all about you, and I know they will make you welcome. First though I must complete the other business I told you of. Money is shorter than I should like, but Caratacus' gold is waiting. You laughed when I said I would bring you and your son a fortune. You'll see. But I'm not going to reveal its whereabouts even to you. It lies buried in a pit in the noontide shadow of a tall tree, and if you climb the tree you can see the sea. That's all I'll say for now, except that once I have it, all my worries will be over. So be patient for just a little longer, and tell Rollus he will see his papa again very soon.

Lucius passed the papyrus round, and we all took turns to read it.

"It's hard to say from a copy who wrote it," I said, "but you say you recognised father's handwriting, Lucius?"

He nodded emphatically. "I'd swear to it. I'd know his writing anywhere. The odd way he always made the letter R, remember? And how he wrote his own name, with the extra flourish on the A and the M."

Albia said, "Isn't it sad, to think of that poor woman waiting and waiting in Lindum with her son, expecting that every day she'd have another letter from her man, arranging for her to be with him. But Father died, and so the letter never came."

"I wonder what he meant by this reference to Caratacus' gold?" I handed the papyrus back to Lucius. "He writes as if he knew where it was, but he never said anything to us. Now that would be truly sad, to have a father who knew where to lay his hands on a fortune, but died before he could dig it up."

Albia and Lucius laughed, and Albia said, "Remember how the customers in the bar were always talking about it when we first came here? If I had a denarius for every man who told me that he knew where it was hidden, I'd be richer by now than ever Caratacus was."

Candidus was puzzled. "Is this some ancient legend? Caratacus lived in the south of Britannia, surely. He was king of the native tribes there when old Claudius invaded. How could he have left gold in Brigantia?"

"He ran away," I said. "He came up here looking for protection from Queen Cartimandua, only she had the good sense to hand him straight over to Caesar. That much is fact. As for his gold, that part of the story is what our grandmother would have called round objects. Balls, in plain Latin."

"Not necessarily," Lucius put in. "It's possible he buried his treasure to keep it out of Cartimandua's hands."

Albia passed round the wine-jug. "I've never understood why Caratacus came north at all. Why didn't he just jump in a boat and sail over to Gaul? He'd have been much safer there."

"Ah, but Queen Cartimandua had promised to protect him," Lucius said. "Only she'd made a secret deal with Caesar, so when Caratacus came to her, she captured him and handed him over."

"Not very honourable," Candidus commented.

"But necessary." My brother sipped his wine. "It made a stink in Brigantia, of course. The royal household and the warriors were split down the middle. The old men still go on about it even now."

"And just before he was captured," I said, "he was suspicious of Queen Cartimandua, so he sneaked out one night and buried his royal treasure in a basket, hoping to come back for it later. He was carted off to Rome as a prisoner instead, and never told anyone where it was."

Candidus looked thoughtful. "So it could still be in its original hiding-place."

"No it couldn't," I objected. "The whole thing's just a silly dream. There's no treasure, there never was any. If Caratacus had so much warning about being betrayed, why didn't he escape, and take his treasure with him?"

"That's easy, Sis. If he was escaping on horseback, he probably couldn't carry it. He'd have needed a wagon. Only he didn't have a helpful sister who could lend him one in his hour of need." He grinned at me. "His only hope would have been to bury his gold and run."

I saw his point, but I still wasn't convinced. "People have been hunting for Caratacus' treasure for the last fifty years, and never found as much as a handful of copper coins."

"Father thought he had," Lucius said seriously. "And Rollus believes it."

"I daresay he does, but I don't."

"You'll be able to judge better when you've met him," Lucius agreed. "He plans to come north and search for the gold, but first he wants me to bring him to meet you. He wants all of us to have a share in the treasure if he finds it."

"Will he put that in writing?"

"Don't be so sceptical, Sis. He wants to share his good fortune—doesn't that tell you he's genuinely our brother? Otherwise why wouldn't he just come north by himself and hunt for Caratacus' gold on his own?"

"Because he'll have a much better chance if we help him," I said. "If it's a matter of searching for people who knew our father, we'll be more likely to find the facts than a complete stranger with a very tenuous claim to be an Aurelius."

"So here's the question I want you two to answer." Lucius looked first at me and then at Albia. "Will you agree to meet Rollus and make him welcome? Will you treat him as our brother, and help him look for this treasure? It may or may not exist, I accept that. But I for one think that we should acknowledge him and help him. Aurelia?"

"There are several questions there, brother. Will I meet him? Yes. Will I make him welcome? Yes. Will I acknowledge him as our brother? I can't say till I've got to know him a little. Will I help him look for this ridiculous treasure? I suppose if I'm convinced he's our brother, then it's a family duty."

"And you, Albia?"

"I'll answer yes to the first two, and reserve judgment on whether I acknowledge him, and whether I join in his treasure hunting. But even if he turns out not to be our brother, I'll be tempted to help him look for the gold. As long as he promises me a share, of course."

"Thank you." Lucius smiled. "I hoped you'd agree. I very much want you to meet him, and I can get him assigned up here to help me search for the Gauls, so he should be in the area quite soon." He got to his feet. "But now I really must push on to the coast. There's a real box of gold waiting for me there, and a handsome reward when I've taken it safely back to Eburacum."

So he left us, and we chatted on for a while about our mysterious possible brother. Then we played with the children, and strolled round the farm to see the various new projects Candidus and Albia were embarking on. I remember Candidus showing me his new bull, a huge red-and-white animal with enormous horns, which let him walk up and feed it like a well-behaved horse. Albia took me to what she called her "miniature forest", a row of tiny oak saplings, less than a foot tall, growing in a sheltered spot near the woods, and lovingly protected by their own special square of fencing.

"I grew these from acorns I brought here from the mansio. I miss the oaks round the mansio, and there aren't many big trees here on the farm. There used to be some huge ashes, and you can still see some of their stumps, but they've all been cut down. I shall replace them with these." She smiled. "It may take a year or two, but we're not moving anywhere."

In no time at all the sun was sinking low, and I helped Albia prepare supper. April is a hungry time of year in Britannia, when the winter stocks of vegetables are running low, and the spring crops haven't started to come through in any quantity. But Albia's store-room held leeks and onions, and even a few of last year's carrots, and she picked a young cabbage from her garden. Soon we had a huge pot of chicken stew simmering.

By dusk there was still no sign of Lucius or his men, so we ate a hearty meal and went to bed early. I dreamed pleasantly of gardens, and trees, and baskets of gold.

Chapter IX

A thin morning mist hid the sun as I rode Merula east from Albia's farm. She'd insisted I took two of her farm boys to escort me to Lucius, and I was glad of their company, because they knew the coast well, even shrouded in mist. I don't like the feeling of steering blind through unfamiliar country, especially in an area where there are outlaws about.

Fortunately the mist thinned as the sun rose, and by the time we left the Roman highway and followed the small native roads, mere tracks mostly, that crossed the Headland itself, we could see around us clearly enough. With the sun to guide us, we easily found the north side of the promontory and rode along the edge of it. We kept the sea to our left, and before long we saw the small bay where the ship had been wrecked, and two soldiers on guard, facing to landward, not out to sea. I hailed the nearest one and explained who I was.

He saluted smartly. "Your brother said to expect you, Mistress Aurelia. He's probably down on the beach by now, but we've had to wait for the tide to go out. You can get a good view from the cliff top—there look, beyond the fire."

I thanked him and dismissed Albia's slaves, who looked disappointed despite my giving them a few coppers for their trouble. I gathered they'd been hoping to stay awhile, and suggested that I'd need escorting back to their farm later in the day, but I assured them that Lucius and his men would take care of me. I thought my brother wouldn't want strangers hanging round watching. After they'd trotted away I walked my mare over towards a cluster of horses, mules, and oxen which were hobbled in the shelter of some scrubby trees near our covered wagon. A big camp-fire burned not far away, and gathered round it were Taurus and Otho, and a couple of fishermen.

"Taurus!" I called, and he turned and came towards me.

"'Morning, Mistress Aurelia. You found us all right then."

No, I'm still looking for you, I wanted to answer, but of course I didn't. Taurus has always had a tendency for stating the obvious. "I did, yes. How are things here? Did you enjoy camping by the sea?"

"Not much. It was cold when the mist came in, and the sea's a scary place. But it's better now. And the fishermen are making us breakfast."

"Good. Where's Lucius?"

"Just gone down to the beach. The tide's nearly out at last, so he can get the treasure up from the boat." He grinned. "He says it's a big box of gold, and he's promised Otho and me a gold piece each when we get it back to the Oak Tree."

"Let's see what they're up to." I walked to the very edge of the cliff and gingerly peered over. The sea looked a long way down, but what I saw in the bay was interesting enough to make me forget my anxiety.

The wreck lay at the base of the cliff. Even from this distance the damage looked bad. The ship was almost broken in half, the middle section submerged and resting on rocks, the whole framework tipped askew. The sand was still under a couple of inches of water, but the sea was going out, and a group of men clustered round the wreck, Lucius among them. Nearby a small sturdy rowing-boat was pulled up on a high bank of shingle, with more men near it. They were military in appearance but weren't wearing standard army cloaks. They must be sailors from the Britannia fleet, because beyond the beach, the comforting, graceful shape of a Liburnian warship lay anchored about five hundred paces out. The mist had vanished and the sea was blue now, reflecting the sky, and the early sun made a golden path across the water. For once I didn't find the seascape frightening, but beautiful.

"Are you going down to join Master Lucius?" From his smile it was clear Taurus knew the answer. He doesn't like the German Ocean either.

"I will if you will, Taurus."

He laughed. "I'm sure they can manage fine without me. Ah, now they've seen you."

The men on the beach were looking up at us, and Lucius waved and pointed to something on the sand beside the boat, an oblong box about the length and the width of a man lying on his back, but deeper. He beckoned me to go down, calling out "This is it, Aurelia, come and look!"

I called back, "You must be joking!" Even if I didn't find the ocean scary, the path down the cliff was. It appeared pretty well vertical, and I was more than happy to wait for Lucius to bring the box up to me.

An old fisherman with a bushy white beard and whiskers left the fire and came to stand beside me. He looked from me down to Lucius." Good day to you, Mistress. You're that officer's sister, ain't you?"

He spoke in British, and I answered in kind. "Yes, I'm Aurelia Marcella. I see they've found the cargo safe and sound."

"That's thanks to me and my son," he answered. "We were the ones sent the message to the soldiers about the boat being wrecked, and carrying this big wooden box. We saw how it smashed onto the rocks just at sunset the night before last. There was a bad storm, fierce wind. The ship came up from the south, got round the Headland all right, and then the skipper must have decided to pull into the north bay here for shelter. Daft, of course, shows they were strangers. No local crew would have tried that, not in a storm. In the morning we found one of the soldiers, and he said he'd fetch his officer, and there'd be a reward for us if we kept other folks away till he brought his mates. Which we did."

"You did well. My brother says it's an important cargo."

"Must be, to have a warship hanging round out there." He jerked a thumb towards the Liburian. "Well, we've done as we was bid, not touched it, and kept it safe for you. So we thought we'd just stop by to collect the reward money we was promised, and see what was in the chest. We're curious to know what all the fuss is about. So we're making breakfast for everyone while we wait. Nothing like a good fish stew to start the day."

I said casually, "That box looks an awkward shape. I wonder if it's heavy?"

"Aye, it's heavy, and not easy to lift. Flat sides, no handholds."

So they hadn't completely followed instructions about not touching it. Not surprising really. We should thank the gods they hadn't stolen it.

He pointed down at the group on the beach. "Look now, they're doing it the way I suggested."

Two soldiers unrolled a fishing net and spread it on the sand. They lifted the box onto it and tied the net's edges together. One of the sailors came forward and ostentatiously pulled at the soldiers' knots to test them, then added a couple of short rope loops for handles at either end of the long box.

"That's a good idea for a heavy load. I'm sure they appreciate it." I was also sure they'd have managed to come up with it all by themselves, but as our grandmother used to say, it costs nothing to be civil, and makes you feel good.

He sucked his teeth. "We're used to bringing things up cliffs. It's amazing, what the sea brings ashore round here. Gifts from the gods, we call 'em, and we're glad to have 'em mostly, even the sad ones, like the drownded bodies. But this is the first time I've ever known any gods to send a chest of money."

I felt a growing excitement as the two soldiers picked up their burden and made for the cliff path. But I had time to wonder whether Lucius had told the fishermen what the box contained. "Money? What makes you think its money?"

"Stands to reason, surely. You think there's money in there, don't you, else why would you have come? And so does your brother, otherwise why would there be all these soldiers? Not to mention them sailor-boys out there."

Why indeed? I glanced across at the Liburian, and realised the sailors in the bay had already launched their small boat and were rowing out towards their ship. Lucius waved them off, took a last look around the bay, then turned and began to climb up the cliff path. Not very far ahead of him, his two soldiers were hauling the unwieldy chest up the narrow, zig-zag track. Lucius caught up with them and followed close behind. He paused for a heartbeat, glanced up to where I stood, and gave me an exuberant wave.

"Be careful!" I called. "Don't drop it!" Even as I shouted, I thought, don't be silly, Aurelia, of course they won't. And yelling like that will just distract them.

But it didn't seem to. They continued toiling steadily upwards, giving no sign that they'd heard me. The old fisherman laughed. "They'll not drop it, Mistress. Save your breath, I should."

"But that path is steep, and it's all bare chalk underfoot. It must be as slippery as ice."

"It is. But they've got good hobnails on their boots."

"Well I wish they'd hurry up. The sea makes me nervous." I shivered as I watched them, not with cold but with anxiety. They were going as fast as they could, I supposed, but they looked as slow as tortoises.

"Why?" the old man seemed genuinely surprised.

"It's so unpredictable, yet the waves and winds have such power. And I can't stand the way the tide comes in and goes out again every day."

"Twice a day," he corrected. "But what's wrong with that? It's natural."

"Not to me. The way it changes the whole look of the coast, it's scary. It's completely different from our sea in Italia. When I was a child I used to love the beach at Pompeii."

He looked blank. "Where's that? Down south somewhere, is it?"

"It's in Italia. I mean, it was. The sea was always blue there, and calm. And warm enough to swim in, which it certainly isn't here."

"'Course it is. *We* swim in the sea here, and it don't do us no harm. It's just a question of being used to it. But I didn't think you was born here. You've got a Roman accent. Mind, you speak our language quite well, for a Roman."

"Thanks. I've lived in Britannia a long time. Since I was a girl."

"Some Romans who come here never bother to learn our language, however long they stay. They talk to us in Latin, and if we don't understand, they just speak slower and louder."

I laughed. "More fool them." Barbarians know more than enough tricks to play on us settlers, without the added advantage of being able to chat among themselves in a Roman's presence, knowing they can't be understood.

"If that big box has got money in," the old man mused, "how much will there be?"

"I don't know." Lucius had said there was a large amount of gold coin. I tried to work out how many aureii would fit into a chest that size, but I gave it up. It looked reassuringly heavy, and the two soldiers had all they could do to lug it up the treacherous track. Their boots slithered and slipped on the chalky surface, and I sent a silent prayer to Diana that they wouldn't let the chest tumble back into the bay. I'm as religious as the next woman, but I wasn't in the mood to make an offering to Neptune.

Perhaps the sea god heard this impious thought, because even as I prayed, one of the men stumbled and fell to his knees, leaving the other perilously supporting the whole weight for what felt like an hour. Lucius moved forward quickly to help, till the fallen man scrambled up, rubbing his ankle, and took his place again. I heard the fisherman mutter something under his breath, but I couldn't catch the words. I sent another prayer to Neptune, promising him an offering of gold if he'd let us bring the box ashore.

I turned away from the sea to look at the blazing fire where Taurus and Otho still stood, with a younger fisherman, presumably the son of the greybeard beside me. They all seemed uninterested in what was happening far below, and were tucking into bowls of stew which the fisherman ladled out. I caught the faint aroma of fish, and the tangy smell made me hungry. But I couldn't bear to leave the cliff edge till the chest was safely at the top. I watched as Taurus lifted another pot onto the fire, probably warming up some wine.

Beyond the fire stood our wagon, and the various animals, their coats all golden in the low sun. Further back still, the soldiers we'd seen as we came down stood ready, eyes alert and swords drawn, to warn us if anyone approached from inland.

When I turned back to peer over the cliff again, the men and the chest seemed hardly to have moved. "I wish they'd hurry up," I said for the second time.

The old man shook his head. "You need a bit of patience when you've dealings with the sea. That's something you learn, if you're a fisherman."

"Very likely. I'm an innkeeper, and I've never been good at being patient."

"An innkeeper? That sounds like a nice comfortable job. All the beer and wine you can drink, and folk paying you money just to stay under your roof."

"It has its good points. Next time you travel the road to Eburacum, you'll have to drop in at the Oak Tree. The drinks will be on the house, after the help you and your son have given us."

"Eburacum? I've never been there. Not likely to, neither. We don't see the need to gallop all over the countryside like you Romans do. You're forever rushing here, rushing there, never stopping. We take life a bit slower."

"Yes, we can move fast when we have to." Which is why Romans rule the world and barbarians don't, I could have added.

"Except when you're climbing up cliffs." I had to admit he had a point.

At long last Lucius' men reached the top of the cliff, and with a final heave, manhandled the heavy box onto the short grass, and dragged it back till it was several paces from the edge. Lucius was close behind them, looking extremely pleased with himself, as well he might.

I walked over to the chest, and tried to lift one end by the thick rope handle, but I could barely raise it off the ground. If that dead weight were really all gold coin...

"Well done, lads," Lucius said to the soldiers, who were standing panting, letting us know what a tremendous effort they'd made. "Get yourselves a drink while we see what we've got here." He took a knife from his belt, and began to cut the ropes and the fishing net. "Taurus, come and get the lid off this thing, will you?"

"Right you are, Master Lucius." Taurus left the fire and came to stand over the box, then he too tested its weight by lifting one end. "Heavy, that is. Is it really full of money?"

Lucius grinned. "I'd say it's full to bursting, from the weight of it. But there's only one way to find out."

"Saturn's balls!" Taurus gazed at the box in reverent silence. "I've never seen so much money all in one place."

Nor have I, I added silently, as he went to rummage about in the wagon and came back with a large crowbar. "This ought to do it."

The top of the box was of solid-looking planks, and was tightly nailed down all round the edges. With some difficulty he got the point of the crowbar under the lid at one corner, and began to lever it up, grunting with the effort. Gradually, with a high rending noise, some of the nails wrenched free, but most of them held firm. Taurus is as strong as two ordinary men, but he was struggling, and as he continued to force the box open, the planks began to split. With one final Herculean heave he prised a good section of the lid off. As it fell to the ground, we all craned forward to see inside.

In the middle of the box was a round wicker basket containing a man's head. Packed all around the basket, filling the chest to the brim, were thousands of small blue-grey pebbles.

But no gold. Not even any small change in copper.

Chapter X

We all stood like lumps of rock, unable to move or speak. The shock of finding the gold had been stolen was bad enough, but the sight of that head, its eyes open and staring up at us, was like the worst nightmare. Violent death always makes me queasy, and I feared I was going to be sick. It wasn't that the head appeared bloated or decayed. It was remarkably normal, if you can say that about a bodiless head in a basket, which made it much worse.

It had belonged to a man in his late twenties or early thirties, pale skinned and clean-shaven, but with a day's growth of stubble. His eyes were blue, his eyebrows were pale, and his fair hair was unusually long. He'd have been easily recognisable, except I didn't recognise him at all.

Taurus broke the shocked silence. "The poor man. Who was he, I wonder?"

Nobody answered. I glanced at Lucius, and got another shock. He was white and trembling, looking as if he'd seen a dead man's shade. Was he scared? My brother? No, he couldn't be, not of the head itself, appalling as it was. He's used to dealing with violence and death in his job, and it would distress and horrify him, but not scare him. So presumably he must recognise the dead man, and it must be someone important. "Do you know him?" I asked softly.

"No."

He was lying, and we both knew it, but I let it go for now.

He addressed the fishermen. "He must have been one of the crew. Were any other crew members seen when the boat hit the rocks? Or have you found any bodies since?"

The old man replied, "No, sir, nobody at all."

"Voltacos' men must have killed them then, and left us just one. Just this one…but that means they had this chest ready to put into the boat in place of the real cargo. How did they know? Gods, I don't understand this."

I didn't either, but the old fisherman grasped the drift of Lucius' thought. "You're thinking maybe the cargo was stolen before ever the boat got here?" He scratched his beard. "And then the *Sea Horse* was set adrift without a crew, and that's how it finished up as a wreck? Could be so, and that's a fact. There are pirates further south, they say, but they don't come here, they leave Voltacos alone."

"The warship would have prevented anything like that," Lucius growled. "No, Voltacos and his Gauls have done this. They must have."

"Let's see what we can see." The grey-haired fisherman walked to the chest and extended his hand palm downwards over the head, intoning a short prayer for forgiveness from the gods of the bay. I soon saw why. He bent over the basket and gently moved the long hair back from the head.

"No, I doubt this is Voltacos' doing." He gently re-arranged the hair and straightened up again. "He always cuts one ear off anyone he kills. It's his mark, his sign. He lacks an ear himself, see, from an old battle wound. This poor fellow has both ears on him."

I felt my stomach start to heave, and walked quickly away, turning my back on them all and gazing resolutely out beyond the bay. The quiet blue sea sparkling gold in the sun calmed me a little, and I managed not to be sick.

By the time I felt strong enough to go back to the others, my brother was moving to confront the two fishermen, and anger radiated out of him like the heat from the camp-fire.

"You're just making excuses to cover up the fact that you didn't guard the boat properly. You told me you watched it carefully from the evening it landed here, to the next morning when my men came. You're lying."

"We did watch," the old man answered stoutly. "From the time it was driven on the rocks almost at dark, the day before yesterday. Like I told you."

"And you stayed on guard here all night? All night long, in the storm?"

"Yes. We was on top of the cliff, sheltering in them trees, but we never left."

"Then you couldn't have seen if anybody was below in the bay tampering with the cargo, could you?"

"No, but we'd have seen anyone going down the cliff path," the son protested. "They'd have been fools, mind, but we'd have seen 'em, and we didn't. And nobody came in by water, neither, they'd have been smashed to splinters for sure. The waves were crashing into the cliffs like a hammer on an anvil."

"And in the morning?"

"We were here all the time," the young man insisted. "The storm'd blown itself out by dawn, and we sent my brother off to your camp to tell you about the wreck, so's Father and I could stay on watch here."

The old man added, "And all that time there was nobody else here, and no sign anyone ever had been."

"I still say you're lying," Lucius snapped.

"We are not," the old fisherman replied. "Look, sir, see it from our point of view. We were hoping for a reward when you got the box ashore. Your young officer promised us a finder's fee for telling him where the boat was, and a share of the cargo if it turned out to be valuable. Which we thought it was, so we kept a good eye on it."

"Well you're not getting a copper coin out of me today."

"But that's not fair! Me and my son reported the wreck as soon as we could, and we've spent ages here looking after it."

"Looking after it? *Merda,* you've got a nerve, expecting to be paid for letting Voltacos' Gauls steal the cargo, kill a man, and put him…" He stopped, too furious to continue. "Just think yourselves lucky I don't have you thrown in prison for helping them."

"But we didn't help them!" The old man was angry now. "We brought your men news of the boat, and we guided them to it. Why would we have done that if we'd pinched whatever was inside it?"

"He's got a point, Lucius." I spoke in Greek, which I was pretty sure the fishermen wouldn't understand. "I'm not saying they aren't capable of looting a wreck, but they wouldn't have told your boys about it afterwards. Besides, if you go back on your decurion's promise of a finder's fee, you'll never get any useful informers on this stretch of coast ever again."

"But if I reward them for not keeping a proper lookout…"

"You still owe them the usual finder's reward, whatever that is. Pay it and let's get out of here."

Lucius considered, then nodded. "You're right, Sis." He turned to the two natives and spoke in British. "I'm sorry. Of course you're entitled to the finder's reward, and you'll have it. It's just…well… it's all been a shock." He took six denarii from his belt-pouch and handed them to the old man.

"Thank you. A shock for us all, it is." He tucked the coins away in his own pouch. "I'm sorry you haven't found what you wanted. And think on what I've said. Voltacos may be an evil bastard, but he didn't do this. Now we'll be on our way."

"And if you need us again, you only have to ask." The young fisherman winked at me. He understood Greek after all.

They left us, and Lucius walked to the cliff edge and gazed out to sea just as I'd done. I went to stand with him, and touched his arm gently. "You recognise that head, don't you? Who was he?"

"His name was Rollus."

"Rollus? Not the same…"

"Yes. The man I told you about, our half-brother."

"That's dreadful. I'm so sorry."

"I thought you didn't believe in his existence."

"But you do, and you're upset. What was he doing on the *Sea Horse?*"

"The gods alone know. I suppose he must have volunteered to join the crew. To impress me, perhaps…I don't know, Relia. But to find a brother, and then to lose him again so soon, it's a sorry business." There were tears in his eyes.

"At least we can give him a proper burial. Shall I tell Taurus and Otho to start making a pyre?"

"Here? No, certainly not. We'll take him home to the Oak Tree." He lifted his head, and recovered some of his usual decisiveness as he started planning the next few hours. "You and I will ride on ahead, and call in on Albia as we planned. We'll take a couple of my lads with us as escort, the rest can stay here and get back to searching for Voltacos. The wagon can follow at its own speed."

He turned to Taurus and Otho. "You boys load the basket into the wagon and bring it home as quick as you can. Bring the chest too. You can leave the pebbles." If that was meant as a joke, it didn't raise the faintest smile.

Taurus glanced unhappily at the head. "You're not leaving us with….with…*him?*" Taurus is Italian born, but he's as superstitious as any barbarian when it comes to encountering unexpected death. "What if his shade is here now, looking for revenge? Suppose it thinks we killed him? What'll it do to us?"

"It won't do anything," I said. "It'll know that we weren't to blame for this, and you're taking him home to give him an honourable funeral. The important thing is, we must treat him kindly and with respect. Cover him up now, and guard him carefully on the way back to the mansio."

"You ought to say a prayer, though, just to be sure," Taurus insisted, looking at my brother.

"Yes, perhaps we ought." Lucius stepped close to the box and invoked the gods of the Underworld, asking them to protect the dead man. Taurus fetched a blanket from the wagon, and Lucius laid it carefully over the basket, which he carried to the wagon. Taurus followed with the empty chest.

We all felt relieved, and as the tension ebbed away, we realised how cold and hungry we were. Everyone walked to the fire, and I began handing out beakers of warm wine.

Lucius took his mug in both hands and drank its contents down in one go. "Now, boys, get that fire out and the wagon packed, and let's be on our way."

Otho went to fetch the oxen, while Taurus stowed away his tools and the cooking gear. As he was dousing the fire, one of the soldiers on guard called out, "Men coming from the south, sir. Three mounted, with cudgels. I don't think it's a welcome party."

A tall black-haired Roman followed by two natives came riding quickly towards us on quite decent horses. The lookout was right, they were not pleased to see us, and while they were still some distance away the leader yelled, "What's going on here?"

The soldiers quietly formed themselves into a defensive ring surrounding us and our wagon and animals. Lucius took up a position facing the newcomers just outside the ring, and without thinking I went and stood beside him. We waited quietly till the riders came up.

They didn't dismount, but the Roman barked, "I said, what's going on? Who are you, and what are you doing on my uncle's land?"

Lucius smiled amiably. "I'm Lucius Aurelius Marcellus, on the staff of the provincial Governor, and I'm here on His Excellency's business. Who wants to know?"

"Ferox, estate manager for my uncle Ostorius Magnus. And he doesn't care for trespassers on his property."

Lucius ignored his surly tone and continued to smile. "I don't blame him, but this isn't his property. This section of the Headland belongs to Chief Bodvocos of the Parisi tribe. Your uncle's lands start beyond that boundary-marker there." He gestured towards a big white boulder standing some way from us. "And I have Bodvocos' leave to be here, so there's no question of trespass."

Ferox snorted. "Bodvocos claims this bit of land, but legally it's ours. The boundary stone is *there.*" He pointed inland to where an even larger white rock stood. "Bodvocos is a typical native peasant, always trying to scrounge a few more yards of settlers' property. That's why, when I saw you and your men, I thought I'd better come and take a look. And I still want to know what you're doing here."

Lucius and I glanced at each other. We both knew Bodvocos, and he was no peasant, but a powerful chieftain, and friendly to Rome. Still, quarrels over boundaries are common enough among farmers, and the last thing we wanted was to get involved in one. Lucius said, "We came to salvage some government property from that wrecked boat down there." He nodded towards the bay. "We've finished our work now, so we're leaving."

"What property?" Ferox demanded.

"I can't talk about that, I'm afraid. It's confidential. As I said, I'm here officially, on the Governor's behalf. That's all you need to know."

"Officially? Really?" Ferox sneered down at us. "Looks to me as if you've just come for a nice day out by the sea. Brought the girl-friend along, I see. She's here officially too, I suppose?"

"Yes, she is. May I present Aurelia Marcella. She runs the Oak Tree Mansio, west of here on the road to Eburacum. I requisitioned a wagon and some men from her, and she wanted to come along to see the salvage. As she's my sister, I saw no objection. Do you?"

"Whether I object," Ferox snarled, "depends on whether you're telling the truth. But if you're leaving now, I haven't time to waste finding out. So get on your way, and don't let me see you snooping round here again, all right?"

Lucius took a step forward, at the same time pulling something small and shiny from his belt-pouch, and holding it out towards Ferox. "I suggest you look at this."

It was his Government pass, a bronze medallion, the symbol of his authority to act in the name of the Governor of Britannia. He rarely produced it, since mostly he was involved in undercover work. But its effect, when he did show it, was always powerful, and Ferox's expression of consternation was very satisfying.

"I see. Well of course my uncle would want me to do anything I can to co-operate with the Governor's officers."

"I'm sure he would," Lucius answered. "I expect to be meeting him quite soon in the course of my investigations. I'll be sure to tell him how zealously you look after his interests, even on other people's land."

Ferox dismounted and stopped scowling, though he didn't go as far as a smile. "I'm sorry," he said sourly. "As you know, we're new arrivals, and we're still learning our way around." He held out his hand to Lucius. "I meant no offence, and you've taken none, I hope."

"None at all," Lucius said, and they shook hands.

"And no offence to your sister." He turned to me, but didn't deign to shake my hand.

"Certainly not. You were just doing your job." But I didn't like this man's rudeness, nor the way he was laying claim to his neighbour's land.

"You see I have to be on watch the whole time," Ferox said, "and not just because of Bodvocos' tricks. We've been having trouble with raiders on the coast this year."

"So your uncle mentioned," I said, "when I met him the other day. He told me they're becoming quite a problem."

"They are. Well, for the Romans in the area, anyway. They seem to leave the men of the Parisi alone. If you've really got any influence with the Governor, Lucius Aurelius, I wish you'd persuade him to get this coast protected properly. We need more naval patrols along here. Gods, we all pay our taxes to support the so-called British Fleet, but what do we ever see of it?"

"Surely you saw it this morning," Lucius said. "They sent a Liburian to keep an eye on the wreck down there."

"Well yes," he admitted grudgingly. "I did spot the warship. It was there yesterday too. And you arranged that?"

"I arranged for it to escort the *Sea Horse*. I didn't foresee the wreck."

"Let's hope it scares the Gauls off for a bit. But somehow I doubt it."

Lucius said, "I'm here to investigate them. So perhaps you can give me some first-hand information about them. How many are there? And how many boats?"

"About twenty, with two small boats. Opportunists, if you like, and they've got plenty of scope. The farms are all scattered about, and the fishermen's houses too. Easy meat for any kind of outlaws, and if they've got sea transport, there are small bays and caves where they can hide."

"And they've been picking on farmers inland too, I hear."

"They have, but only now and then. Usually they operate near the shore, and it's settlers they prefer to go for, not natives."

"Do they ever interfere with ships at sea?"

"Like that *Sea Horse* boat?" He shook his head. "I've never heard of them boarding ships on the water. But they've been known to set up false guiding-lights on land, especially in bad weather. Unwary captains see the lights and think they've reached harbour, until they find they're on the rocks, with a band of cut-throats waiting to finish them off and take their cargo. I suppose that could be what happened to the boat down there in the bay. Except they didn't take the cargo, seemingly." He looked enquiringly at the wagon, then at Lucius.

But my brother didn't rise to the bait. Instead he said, "Thank you, that's useful. Now, if you'll excuse us, we must be on our way. No doubt we'll meet again. I expect to be in this area for a while, until I've dealt with Voltacos."

Ferox wished us a more or less civil good-bye and rode away. Lucius gave final instructions to his men, while I had a word with Taurus and Otho, and then we set off ourselves. I for one was glad to be leaving the place where our high hopes of the morning had vanished as completely as the sand beneath the tide.

Chapter XI

It was a gloomy ride back to Albia's, despite the blue sky and the sunny, open landscape. I suggested that Lucius send his two soldiers ahead to warn Albia we were on our way, thinking it would be easier to talk if we were private. I suppose it was, but all we did was try vainly to answer a series of questions that we knew couldn't be answered.

Who had stolen the gold from the *Sea Horse?* Could the fishermen just possibly be correct in their suggestion that the theft took place earlier in the voyage? If that was the case, was the theft part of the tortuous negotiations with the Caledonians? Suppose the boat hadn't been wrecked, but had reached the northern chieftain who was expecting a lavish gift from Caesar, and he'd discovered only stones and a head? Why was Rollus sailing aboard the *Sea Horse?* Where was the gold now? Was there any chance of recovering it?

That final question was the only one we could safely answer. There was no chance.

"I'll go through the motions," Lucius said. "I'll have to. But it's lost for good. And I suppose I'll get the blame," he added glumly, "even though it wasn't my idea to send the gold by water, and it certainly wasn't my fault the boat was wrecked."

"You'll be able to explain it all to the Governor. You've had worse setbacks than this before, and come through them. To me, the saddest thing is that now we'll never know for certain who Rollus was, or whether there was an ounce of truth in the story of Caratacus' gold. I suppose some secrets are buried too deep ever to be uncovered."

"I wish it hadn't been kept such a secret. Why couldn't Father have told the rest of us about Rollus and his mother? No, no, don't say it, Relia: because Rollus' whole story was just a web of lies."

"I wasn't going to say that. I don't know whether it was or wasn't. One thing did strike me, though, when I saw the—when I saw him in the basket. He didn't look in the least like Father, did he?"

"No. But then neither do you or I or Albia."

We rode on in silence for a while. I wondered if, like me, Lucius was picturing our father in his mind, tall and handsome in his fine chain armour and centurion's crest. He had a thin face, thick brown curly hair, grey eyes that missed nothing, a high forehead, and a prominent nose and jaw. He had a ready smile, or sometimes a sudden frown that threatened trouble like a clap of thunder. I still thought of him often, and always with pride. I was only a girl when he left the army, but not too young to be aware that he finished his career in a blaze of glory. And the years afterwards, when we lived all together as a family, had been happy ones.

"Father always loved Britannia, didn't he, Lucius? Even when we were in Pompeii, he used to reminisce about the time he spent out here."

Lucius nodded. "And we've inherited his love of the place. Well, I have. I wouldn't want to live anywhere else now. I wouldn't go back to Italia even if I could. Would you?"

"Not to live, no, my home's here. But I'd love the chance to visit Italia again. I've never even been to Rome, and I'd like to."

"Some day we'll go together."

We looked up sharply as hoof-beats sounded ahead of us, and a mounted man came flying along the highway from the west. Lucius' hand dropped to his sword, but we soon recognised the rider as one of his own troopers.

"Ollius, what in the gods' name are you doing here?"

"Trouble, sir," the soldier panted as he pulled up beside us, "bad trouble. At your sister's place. It's been raided, looks like the Gauls. We got there in time to stop them, but…"

"Tell me as we go," Lucius answered. We set off at a gallop.

"Is my sister safe? And the children?" Lucius called to the trooper over the pounding of hooves.

"Yes, sir, they're safe. Scared though."

"Did you catch the raiders?"

"We killed two. Three got away. It might have been nasty if we hadn't shown up. The men drove a flock of sheep and lambs out of their field and all over the garden. Your sister and her children heard the din, seemingly, and went outside to see what was going on. When we got there, the Gauls had all three of them cornered in the garden, but they hadn't touched them."

"And Candidus—her husband?" I asked.

"Don't know, ma'am. He wasn't there, she said he's working in some outlying bit of the farm today. All the slaves too."

"So they're on their own again?" Lucius asked.

"Severus is with them, sir. He'll guard them till we get there."

They picked a good time for a raid, I thought. It was almost as if they'd been watching the place. I spent the rest of the ride planning what I'd do if I caught any of Voltacos' men alive.

As we came in sight of the farmhouse, my stomach tied itself in knots. Trooper Severus stood on the track leading from the highway, his sword drawn. Behind him the garden, Albia's pride and joy, looked like a battlefield, except it wasn't soldiers but terrified sheep that were milling about, churning the ground into a quagmire. My sister sat on the bench by the pond, clutching her children tightly as they cowered on her lap. They were both howling piteously, alternatively burying their faces in her tunic, and staring around in wide-eyed terror. Albia herself sat still, blank-faced and outwardly calm, but I knew that look. She was thoroughly terrified too, only managing to keep control of herself for the sake of the children.

"Albia!" Lucius and I jumped from our horses before they'd stopped, and ran to her, embracing her and the twins. They all looked up at us, and the children's wailing lessened a little.

"Lucius! Aurelia! Oh, thank the gods!" She smiled for a heartbeat, and then began talking softly to the children, trying

to soothe them. Gradually their tears subsided, and she wiped
their eyes and turned to Lucius and me. "It's so good to see you.
Can somebody fetch Candidus and the boys? They're mending
a fence over in the far pasture, the other side of the valley. That's
why we're on our own."

"I'll send one of the troopers," Lucius said, "just as soon as
I've got all the facts."

"Your troopers were wonderful, Lucius. I don't know what
would have happened if they hadn't arrived. Those horrible
men...There, don't cry now, little ones. We're safe, all safe." She
hugged the twins more tightly than ever.

Lucius put his arm round her shoulders. "Yes, you're safe now,
and we'll make sure you have no more trouble. Severus! Ollius!"
The trooper loped over to us. "Aurelia, while I'm hearing Severus'
report, why not take them inside and find some wine, and maybe
a bite to eat? We could all do with something. Ollius will come
with you as bodyguard. I'll join you very soon."

But Albia shook her head. "Not inside, no, I'd feel trapped.
Anyhow I want to hear the report too. Hush now," she put the
children gently down to stand on the ground in front of her,
but kept her arms round them. "It's all over, and Uncle Lucius
and Aunt Relia are here to look after us."

"At least let me fetch Lia. Their nursemaid," I explained to the
soldiers. "Have either of you seen her? Is she inside, Albia?"

She shook her head. "She ran away when the men came. I
suppose she thought if they caught her, they'd...well, you know."
She stopped, remembering the children. "I can't blame her really.
She's only a child herself."

Child or not, she deserves a good whipping, I thought, for
leaving her mistress like that. But I didn't argue. It was typical
of Albia not to blame the slave, and when the girl came back, if
she ever did, there'd be time enough for punishment.

Trooper Severus made a brief, workmanlike report. The men
had arrived just as the raid was beginning. At first when they
saw three horsemen driving a flock of sheep and lambs out of
a paddock, they took it for some normal farm activity, even

though the animals were running amok. But then they realised that two of the band was standing over Albia and the twins in the garden, daggers in hand, and they charged straight in to the rescue. When they saw the soldiers, the raiders all fled, but only the three mounted ones escaped.

"They're not locals," he finished. "Gauls, I'd say. They were all well armed, swords and daggers, and decently mounted." He nodded to where two horses stood tied to the nearest fence. "Once we were sure we'd got them all, Ollius came to fetch you. Now you're here, shall I go and find the lady's husband?"

"Look out! Behind the house!" Ollius yelled, and we all spun round. I couldn't see anyone but I heard horses coming closer fast. I knew they were far too near for safety, because the racket the sheep were making had masked their approach. Surely the Gauls hadn't dared come back?

Albia clutched the children close. Lucius and his two men drew their swords and ran forward towards the sound. I pulled out the knife I always carry when I'm travelling, and stood alongside Albia. A big sheep-dog came and crouched protectively in front of us. We felt very vulnerable and alone as our three men disappeared behind the farmhouse.

Then the dog began barking excitedly, and round the corner of the house came Candidus and four slaves.

"Look, here's Daddy!" Albia jumped up from the bench, still clutching the children, and ran into Candidus' arms.

For the next couple of hours we were busy. With Candidus home, Albia calmed down quickly and was able to persuade the twins that we were all truly safe. Lucius sent Severus to the coast to bring the rest of his small detachment to the farm for the night. Candidus and his farm boys set about restoring the place to some sort of order, while Lucius, Albia, Nasua, and I took the twins into the kitchen and warmed a pan of wine for everyone. Nasua found some bread and honey, because Lucius declared he was starving, and I was fairly hungry myself. Little Decimus, seeing the food, decided he was hungry too, but Albia couldn't persuade Marcella to eat anything, and she herself only managed half a mug of wine.

Lucius suggested Albia should try and rest a little, while Nasua saw to the children, and he went out to help Candidus. But she refused absolutely to remain in the house unless either Lucius or Candidus stayed with her. This was quite unlike my brave, independent-minded sister, and brought home to me how badly the attack had shaken her. I went out to fetch Candidus, and he came straight inside to be with her, leaving Lucius and me to oversee the farm slaves outside.

Fortunately they seemed to know what they were doing. They'd got the sheep safely into a paddock, and counted them. Only one lamb was missing, and not for long.

Trooper Ollius came hurrying up to us. "Sir, we've found the missing lamb, and it's dead. I think you should see it, so I told the farm boys to leave it out the back till you have."

"I'll go," Lucius said. "You stay here, Aurelia."

"I'll come too. It sounds important, and I think I'm hardened to horrors after the day we've had."

The lamb's head had been hacked from its body, and its left ear had been cut off. I realised I wasn't hardened at all. I turned hastily away, sat down against a barn wall, and threw up.

Lucius came and put a hand on my shoulder. "Sorry, Sis, but he was right to show us, wasn't he?"

"Not your fault. I agreed to come. I wish I hadn't."

"But don't you see? It means the raiders here were from the same band that killed Belinus, Voltacos' men. That old fisherman was right, cutting off an ear seems to be their equivalent of a signature. So maybe they weren't the same ones who took the gold from the *Sea Horse*."

"Yes, all right." I felt too lousy to discuss it. "Now for the gods' sake tell them to bury it somewhere."

They took it away, though whether they buried it or cooked it for their evening meal, I neither knew nor cared. I just wanted to sit still until I felt better, and ignore the rest of the world.

Eventually the nausea left me, and I started to feel uneasy for another reason. Three of the Gauls had escaped. Suppose they came back to try to rescue their comrades? I went to find Lucius and asked how long it would be before the rest of his men arrived.

"They'll be as quick as they can. Meanwhile I've posted three farm boys as sentries, now they've got things more or less under control out here. And I've sent Ollius to scout around a bit, to make sure the bastards have really gone."

"The dead Gauls," I said. "Do you want me to look at them, to see if I recognise either of them? I've seen three of them before, remember, including Voltacos."

He shook his head, and I must say I was relieved. "You've given me a description of Voltacos, and so have several other people in the last couple of days. I'm afraid neither of our dead bodies matches him at all."

"So he's still on the loose somewhere. I don't like the idea of that, with darkness coming on soon."

"There's plenty of light yet. Why don't you go in and see how Albia is? I'll stay outside till my men get here."

"All right. I suppose we should do something about supper." I was on my way back into the house when Ollius galloped into view and pulled up beside Lucius. The look on his face was enough to make me turn round and go back to my brother's side.

"Sir, I've found a body, a young girl. The children's nursemaid, would it be? Someone said she'd run away."

"Lia?" I felt sick again. "Don't say she's dead too?"

"Let's not jump to conclusions," Lucius interrupted. "What does Lia look like, Aurelia?"

"Slim, about fifteen, very pretty, with light-brown wavy hair and big hazel eyes."

Ollius nodded. "Afraid so."

"Where is she?" Lucius asked.

"I left her round the back, sir, in a barn. I didn't want Mistress Albia or the children to see her."

"That's sensible. I'll go and have a look. Aurelia, are you up to coming with me? This girl's quite new. I hardly saw her yesterday, I'm not sure I can identify her."

"Well...the thing is..." The trooper hesitated, looking sideways at me. "She's not pretty, if you take my meaning. She's been raped, and then stabbed, and her head damaged..."

"Her head?" I fought down the nausea in my throat. "Her ear, you mean?"

He nodded grimly. "Her left ear's been cut away."

Lucius swore. "In that case you're not coming, Aurelia, and that's an order."

For once in my life I wasn't going to argue. "Thanks. I'll go inside and break it to them all."

"That'll be hard enough," he said sadly. "And be careful what you say in front of the twins. Those little tykes understand most of what they hear these days."

Albia and Candidus were in the large, sunny living-room that formed the centre of the farmhouse. Candidus was on the floor playing a rough-and-tumble game of bears with Decimus, who seemed to be recovering his spirits, shrieking and laughing. Albia sat on the reading-couch with Marcella sound asleep beside her.

I needed to get my sister away from the children. That, at least, was easy. We'd worked together for many years at the Oak Tree, and we had our own special way of alerting one another to trouble without giving anything away to our customers. I said, "Albia, if you like I'll start getting a meal ready for later. I've a new recipe from Arpinum I'd like to try out."

She hadn't forgotten. "Arpinum? All right. Let's go through into the kitchen." She got up quietly so as not to disturb the sleeping child.

Candidus looked up briefly, nodded, and resumed his game. We walked into the kitchen, which was bright and well laid out, though small by the standards of the one at the mansio. She shut the door firmly behind us, and we sat down on stools at the big scrubbed table. "What's happened? More trouble?"

I told her as gently as I could.

"Poor Lia." She wiped her eyes. "She'd have been safer staying here with us, as it turned out."

"That's what she should have done. So it serves her right, really."

"No, Relia!" Albia snapped. "I don't blame her for running. It was terrifying when those men came. I'd have run myself, except that I couldn't leave the children. And so would you."

"I suppose so. But..."

"She didn't deserve to be abused and killed. Nobody does. If we start even thinking like that, those foul men will have defeated us."

Once again, as so often, I felt amazed and touched by the way my sister always looks for the best in people, even in a crisis. I said soberly, "You're right, she didn't deserve it. I'm sorry."

"I'm sorry too, I shouldn't snap like that. It's just..." We hugged, and then she sighed. "I'll miss her. She was good with the children, and they adored her. I'll tell them she's had to go home to her family for a while. Then in a few days I can break it to them that she's not coming back. We'll just have to manage without a nurse for the time being. I'll need a replacement before the next baby comes though."

"I'll lend you a girl from the mansio for as long as you like, till you've had a chance to buy a proper nursemaid. It won't be the same, but she'll be better than nothing."

She leaned forward and put her head in her hands. I could see she was fighting back tears. "This has always been such a wonderful place to live, safe and peaceful. Now, what with these raiders and...Juno protect us, I don't know if I'll ever feel safe again."

With a shock I sensed she was worrying about something else, something even more serious than the physical danger she'd faced. "What is it, Albia? There's something you haven't told me about all this."

"I keep going over and over it in my head, seeing them all riding around, hearing everything, the din of the sheep, the men shouting and bawling. Especially hearing them. That's the worst. That's why I'm so frightened..."

"What did they say? Vile insults, I suppose, and threats?"

"Oh, those were nothing. But they called my name. They knew my *name,* Relia, and they knew about Candidus. And that really scares me."

"You mean this was some kind of personal attack?"

"It must be. I thought when I saw them first that they were just a gang of criminals looking for easy plunder. I'd heard rumours about them, now here they were. Then when I heard them call me and realised they knew who we were…They came here looking for Candidus and me."

"But why?"

"I don't know."

Candidus came through to the kitchen just then, looking tired but more cheerful. "I've told Nasua to stay with the twins for now. Lucius' men are here, they'll camp in the big barn and take turns to stand sentry round the farm.…Why, whatever is it, love? Is it about Lia? Lucius has just given me the news. It's dreadful."

"That's only part of it." When she told him how the Gauls had addressed her by name, he looked shaken, and I could see what an effort it cost him to stay calm. He sat down next to her and put his arms round her, and they clung together, not saying much. I sat there feeling helpless, and sharing Albia's anxiety. I'd assumed that the raiders had picked on this farm more or less by chance because they'd found it practically deserted, and intended just to steal a lamb or two and then go on to harass some other poor victim. But if they'd come here deliberately seeking Candidus and Albia, that put a whole new complexion on the matter. It lent strength to the theory that the Gauls were working for someone else, but who? Candidus and Albia were on good terms with everyone, neighbours, servants, settlers and natives. It was difficult to think of any reason why someone would want to hurt them. No, not difficult—impossible. Yet it had happened.

I didn't say any of this aloud. My sister was worried enough, I didn't want to make matters worse. But I resolved to talk to Lucius about it as soon as I could.

Eventually Albia gently shook herself free and sat up straight. "Candidus, what are we going to do?"

"First, I think we must put up some sort of permanent defences here—a stockade round the farmhouse and the main out-buildings, with a heavy gate that we can close when we need to. We must make it easier to protect ourselves. I know you hate the idea, Albia, but after today I don't think we have any choice."

She nodded. "I do hate it, but I hate even more being open to raids any time of the day or night. All right. Have we enough men for the work?"

"That's going to be a problem, with our busiest time of year coming up. But we'll do it somehow. I'll see if I can hire extra hands locally for the next month or two. If not, I'll have to go down to the slave market in Eburacum and buy some body-guards. We need a new nursemaid for the children too."

"I'll manage," Albia answered. "Lots of women do."

"But that's not what I want for my girl," Candidus said firmly. "Our two are enough of a handful, and you've got the third one to think about as well." He smiled at her. "Only three months to go now. You're bound to get tired more as your time comes nearer."

"I've already told Albia I'll lend her one of our maids for the time being," I offered. "But I've just had a much better idea, something that would solve both problems at once."

"Let's hear it," Candidus said. "We need all the good ideas there are."

"Albia, why don't you and the children come and stay with us at the Oak Tree for a few days, till things get sorted out?"

"Oh no, Relia, I couldn't. Thanks for thinking of it, but it's impossible. Candidus needs me here."

"That's a brilliant suggestion." Candidus smiled at me grate-fully. "Thank you, Aurelia. I'll feel much happier if they're safe with you."

"But Candidus, I can't just drop everything and go away. Who'll look after you? And there's my garden, I must try and put right the mess if we're to have any crops this year. And Relia will be busy at the mansio from now on. You know how everyone gets the urge to travel in the spring. We'll be a nuisance."

"You could never be that. We'd love to have you."

"You know your sister," Candidus added. "If she hadn't meant it, she wouldn't have made the offer. Am I right, Aurelia?"

"Absolutely right. Albia, do say you'll come, just for a short while. You know we've got plenty of room, and however busy we are, our maids will be fighting one another for the privilege of looking after the twins."

Candidus took her hand and said gently, "Love, you know it makes me unhappy to be parted from you and the children, even for a few days. But just now I'll be unhappier if you're here, and I'm worrying all the time about what may be happening to you when I'm not with you. And I can't stay with you every hour, with the farm work to do. So please accept Aurelia's invitation and go to the Oak Tree. You know you'll enjoy it there, and we can keep in touch by letter, every day if you like."

"Every day? You'll really write to me every day?"

"I promise." He kissed her. "So you agree?"

"I agree."

"Then that's settled," I said. "When we've had our food, I'll help you get a few things together, and we'll set off first thing in the morning."

Chapter XII

Getting two young children ready for a journey and a visit always seems to take forever. I remarked to Lucius that Albia would find it only slightly less of a challenge to plan the invasion of a new province.

He laughed. "It's easy for us to say, we haven't had to do it. And they are without their nursemaid, remember."

"I wanted to be away soon after dawn. It'll be noon at this rate before we leave."

"I know. And I've got to get back to the coast now. But I'm leaving Ollius and Severus here, and they'll escort you all to the mansio."

"Thanks. That'll be appreciated."

"This is no time for riding around unarmed, especially with children to slow the journey down. And you can do something for me in return, if you will."

"Of course, anything."

"I want you to make use of the rumour mill at the mansio. Put the word around that there's a large reward on offer for any information leading to the recovery of the gold from the ship-wreck. It's a very long shot, but you never know. And at least it'll help convince the Governor that I've done all I can to find it."

"I will. And if I hear anything interesting, I'll send word to you at the Headland. How long do you suppose you'll have to be there?"

"I wish I knew. When I was sent up here, it was just to gather information, and I thought ten or twenty days would be enough, or a month at the very most. Now, with Belinus murdered and the attack here, I won't just be on reconnaissance, I'll be actively trying to catch them. It could take all summer." He smiled. "Though there are worse places to spend summer, I suppose."

"I hope you won't need that long. Especially now we suspect the Gauls aren't just working for themselves, but taking orders from someone."

"My guess is they're doing both. Quite a lot of the crimes they're accused of are just what you'd expect from a band of pirates turned thieves. Stealing the odd sheep or goat, small-time burglary, robbing unwary citizens as they travel around, especially on the native roads. It's only the raids here and at Esico's farm that are very much more serious, because they include murder."

"Good hunting, and take care, won't you?"

He touched my shoulder lightly. "And you. Look after yourself, and everyone."

"I promise." I waved him off, and after what seemed like an interminable delay, Albia and the twins were ready to leave too.

They travelled in Candidus' raeda, which was a new one, pulled by a couple of steady mules. The house-boy Nasua drove it, a sensible choice, because he was a reasonable driver and good with the children. I rode Merula, and the two troopers brought up the rear. Candidus came with us too, as far as Belinus' farm—we still found ourselves calling it that—to see what help he could offer Esico.

On the way we stopped at the sheep pasture to see Cattos. The sheep and lambs were grazing quietly, and Cattos and Balca sat beside a smoky fire with a steaming iron pot cooking over it. They ran to the road and greeted us all, with a specially warm welcome for Candidus and Albia and the twins.

"You've had no more visits from the Long-hairs, I hope?" I asked them.

Cattos shook his head. "It's been peaceful. Or it *would* have been, only Balca made me tidy up my hut, and then practice sling-shots all afternoon."

"Good for you, Balca," I smiled. "Give him plenty to do, that's the way to keep lads in order."

"Yes, that's what my father says." She grinned suddenly. "And Tom-cat's coming on with his sling. He's good at snaring birds as well, so we haven't starved. There's a stew on the fire now. Would you like to share it?"

I thanked her, but declined. "We've only just had breakfast. And we can't stay long. We've quite a journey ahead of us, back to the Oak Tree. We just wanted to make sure everything is safe here. By the way, how is your father now? Is his arm mending all right?"

"I haven't seen much of him since he got home, but he says he's fine, and your doctor did a good job."

"We're calling in on Esico and Divico and Illiana next," my sister said. "Have either of you any messages for them?"

"Just tell them not to worry about us," the girl answered, and Cattos nodded. "Now come on, Tom-cat, breakfast should be ready."

Esico's farm was a dispiriting sight. A ramshackle cart stood in front of the house with two scrawny mules hitched to it. Esico and Divico were loading a pathetic collection of clothes and household effects onto it, while Illiana sat nearby, rocking the baby in her lap.

The two men walked over from the cart. Esico's limp was more pronounced than ever, but he held out his hand to each of us. "Good day to you. You only just found us here. We're leaving the farm."

"So whatever you want, can you make it quick," Divico added with his usual scowl.

"Leaving the farm?" Candidus repeated. "Have you had more trouble here?"

"They've poisoned our well." Esico said sadly. "Our only water. They've thrown something down it, something dead, a sheep probably. It stinks, and it's tainted the water. It's too deep to reach and get it out. We can manage without most things, but not water."

"That's terrible," I said. "And it's the Long-hairs who've done this?"

"It must be, though we haven't seen them. Anyhow we've talked it over, and we're going to the coast to ask the Chief for help. We'll take what we can with us, and go and see him today. He'll look after us and find us somewhere safe to stay till all this trouble's over."

"We hope," Divico muttered.

"I'm sure he will. He takes care of his own, does Bodvocos. And anyway what else can we do? It's too dangerous here now."

"But is there really no other way?" Candidus asked. "I came to see if I can be of help to you, lend you a couple of men perhaps. If they could get the well cleaned out..."

"It's good of you, Candidus," the old man answered. "But we've had enough. We're finished, we're leaving, and that's all there is to it."

"Then you must come and stay with us," Albia said. "We've plenty of room, and you'll be safe at our farm, but still near enough to your own to come over and check on things here every day."

"Stay with you? Oh no, we couldn't." But we all knew that Esico wanted to accept the invitation, and only his pride prevented him.

"Of course you could," Candidus said. "It's the perfect solution. You need somewhere safe to live, we need extra help on our farm. So come to us, just until these Gauls are caught."

Divico shook his head firmly. "We thank you, but we'll manage with Bodvocos' help. We don't want to be beholden to anyone."

"But you wouldn't be, Divico," Candidus answered. "I'll expect you to help me with my farm work, as well as whatever you need to do here. You'll be doing two men's jobs, but I have the feeling you're used to that already."

"I don't mind hard work," Divico conceded. "But…why should you do a thing like this for us? We're not your kin. You're Romans."

"Because we've got to stand together against these raiders. They'll be caught sooner or later, but till they are, there's safety in numbers, isn't there? I'm suggesting this for our benefit as much as for yours. It'll be as if you paid me rent, but instead you'll be paying me in the work you do."

"Well, if you put it like that…" the young man's grim expression softened.

Esico cut in. "You're agreeable, then, son?"

He nodded. "I'd rather be living near here, as long as the family's safe. So thank you, Candidus."

"And Illiana, you can help me with the children," Albia added. "I haven't got a nursemaid just now. Will you do that?"

"I'll do what I can," she said softly. "I'm with Divico. We'd be much better living near the farm, if you're really sure you have room for us."

"I'll help too," her father added. "I won't be able to do much heavy work, but I can mind children, yours and ours. And I can help a bit in the garden, with the jobs that don't need too much bending. And I can act as a lookout, if you're needing an extra pair of eyes to watch for trouble."

"But Albia," I cut in, "you're supposed to be coming down to the Oak Tree with us."

She smiled. "I shan't need to now, shall I? If we have more people at our farm, we can manage the work and keep ourselves safe. You know I've never been keen on the idea of leaving Candidus."

"But…"

"No, my mind's made up. It was a lovely invitation, Relia, and we all appreciate it, and we will come, but not yet. We'll wait till the times are peaceful again."

"So are you agreed?" Candidus asked. He looked round at them all in turn, and in turn they nodded.

"Thank you," Esico said. "We'll try not to be more of a burden than we can help."

"And it'll only be for a short time." Divico turned away to stare at the cart, but not before I saw he was trying to hold back tears.

"That's right, son," Esico said gently. "Our troubles can't last for ever. Thank you kindly, Candidus and Albia. We'll get the cart packed, and drive up later today."

"At least living with you, we'll be able to keep an eye on Cattos," Illiana spoke up. "He's a good lad, but very young."

"We don't want to lose him. Or the sheep," Divico said.

"He's in good spirits this morning, at least. He said to tell you not to worry about him and Balca." I told them about our visit. "Balca's a tough young lass, isn't she? And her father too, I believe. He's nursing a broken arm just now, and he visited our doctor at the mansio the other day."

Esico nodded. "She's a rare one. Coriu's brought her up as if she was a boy, and there's been nobody to show her how a woman should behave, on account of her mother dying when she was small."

Illiana smiled, and suddenly looked pretty, despite her pallor and rather gaunt features. "The gods know what'll happen when Coriu marries Elli. That's Bodvocos' daughter, you know, and she's not much older than Balca. Her father promised her to Coriu when she was young."

"When's the wedding?" Albia asked. "I did hear it's going to be this summer."

"It's supposed to be. But with all the troubles we're having now, they may put it off perhaps. And I've heard tell Elli isn't all that keen on marrying him."

"Enough gossip, Illiana," Divico cut in, but quite gently, for him. "Let's get this packing finished. And we'll see you later," he said to Candidus.

Esico looked at Candidus earnestly. "You and Albia are good friends to us. We appreciate it, don't ever doubt it."

We said our good-byes and went our separate ways. Candidus took his family back to their farm, and I and my two-man escort headed for home.

I had plenty of time to think on the journey home, but for all the good it did, I might as well have let my mind go blank and just enjoyed the ride. All I could achieve was to collect together the few certain facts in this confused situation.

Voltacos and his sea-raiders had attacked both Belinus' farm and Albia's. They had done damage and shown they weren't afraid to kill. They'd wanted Belinus dead because he was Lucius' informer, and that must explain the other incidents of harassment that Belinus' family had mentioned.

That was where facts ended and questions began. Why had the Gauls raided Albia and Candidus? If all they wanted was to extort a few denarii or steal a few lambs to eat, there were plenty of other farmers nearer the coast they could pick on. But then if Esico and Divico were right, the Gauls were simply carrying out orders issued them by someone else who was paying them to carry out carefully thought-out plans. Who was playing at general, using these criminals like foot soldiers to fight the battles in the field? It wasn't a large choice: either Ostorius Magnus or Chief Bodvocos.

I'm not one of those Romans who believe that everything we do is right, while the troubles of the world are invariably caused by barbarians within or outside our frontiers. All the same, if there's a conflict between Roman settlers and native tribes, my upbringing and instinct make me side with Romans like the Ostorii, however unprepossessing some of them might be. But I didn't know enough about the Ostorii really. Were they ruthless enough to kill for land? And I certainly hadn't sufficient information to make a sensible judgment about Bodvocos. Was he playing a very subtle kind of game, using his local power and influence to harass settlers in secret while professing loyalty to Rome?

As we rode the final mile down the Long Hill, I was sorry not to be bringing my sister and the children home, but at least travelling without the wagon had meant a fast journey. We reached the Oak Tree shortly after noon.

Chapter XIII

"So thanks to Voltacos, you've had an eventful time," Margarita smiled, and poured me a second beaker of red. "Rescuing a shepherd boy, losing a box of gold, finding an unpleasant surprise on the wrecked boat, and worst of all, a band of Gauls raiding Albia's farm. And you've only been away two days!"

"It's good to be home again." I was sitting at a table near the bar, engaged in one of my favourite occupations: sipping my wine while looking round at a satisfyingly busy bar-room. "I tried to persuade Albia to bring the children here for a few days, but you know my sister. She didn't want to leave Candidus and home."

"It must have been a horrible experience for them. But Lucius is doing something about the raiders?"

"Yes, he is. And he's offering a reward for the missing cargo. He wants us to spread the word here. I was wondering about putting up a notice."

"Why not? Tell me what you'd like it to say, and I'll write it."

We grinned at each other. There was no need to add that her handwriting was very much neater and smarter than mine.

"Now tell me your news. Is all well here?"

She nodded. "Very well. Two guests stayed last night, and a very sober and quiet evening we all had—no more birthday parties."

"How's Timaeus? Have there been more wounded for him to treat?"

She delayed answering long enough to take a big jug of beer to a nearby table, where three farmers pleaded that they were dying of thirst. "Two more came yesterday, both from the wold country. One was from the Parisi, the other a young Roman lad. Both said they'd been attacked by the Gauls. The only thing was, the native said the raiders are in the pay of Roman settlers, but the Roman boy said they are working for a local chief called Bodvocos."

"There's certainly some kind of feud going on between those two, but whether it involves Voltacos, we don't know yet. We saw a small example of the quarrel yesterday. Landowners moving one another's boundary stones, trying to steal their neighbours' fields."

"Well, if anyone can sort them out, it's your brother. Oh, I nearly forgot something important: there's a note for you from Chief Councillor Silvanius. It came yesterday." She went over to the bar and reached up to the high shelf where we always keep important messages. This one was in the form of a scroll, neatly tied and adorned with Silvanius Clarus' seal.

"Maybe its an invitation to a banquet. One can always hope." I broke the seal.

"I suppose the messenger didn't let slip any hint about what he wants?"

"Not a word. I explained that you'd be away till at least this evening, perhaps longer, and asked him to tell Silvanius I was sure you'd answer the letter as soon as you could when you got back."

"Good, thank you. Well, I'd better see what he wants."

The message was longer than it need have been, because its meaning was wrapped up in the flowery formal language that Clarus loved. He wanted me to visit him and his sister at his "humble abode"—his enormous villa the other side of Oak Bridges—in order to "partake of a little refreshment, and to discuss a matter of some delicacy with which I believe you can help me."

Margarita made no attempt to hide her curiosity. "Are you any the wiser?"

"Not much. He wants me to visit him, but he doesn't say why. I expect he wants me to suggest some special wines for his next banquet."

"Will you go this afternoon?"

"No, I've done enough travelling for one day. Tomorrow will be soon enough. I'd better send a reply today though. It isn't every day I'm summoned to His Pomposity's humble abode."

I went into my study and wrote a brief note for Clarus saying I'd be delighted to visit him tomorrow. While I was at it, I jotted down what I hoped was enticing wording for a notice offering a hundred aurei for information leading to recovery of Lucius' missing gold. I gave this to Margarita, then took my message for the Chief Councillor round to the stables so that one of the horse-boys could deliver it. As I crossed the forecourt, Taurus fell into step beside me, and I remembered guiltily that I hadn't given a thought to the wagon's slow progress home from the coast, or to its gruesome contents.

"Hello, Taurus. You had a safe journey home, I hope?"

"We did, Mistress. Got back last night. I was wondering...what shall we do with the remains of the poor man from the boat? We've put him in one of the old farm buildings out of the way for now, but he can't stay there, can he? Shall we build a pyre for him?"

"Yes please, in the usual field. Get one of the farm boys to help you. We'll give him a ceremony at sunset."

"Did Master Lucius know him?" Taurus asked. "He seemed to behave very strange when he saw him in the box. Not like himself at all. Made me wonder."

"You're right, Taurus, he did." I reflected that this big, simple slave wasn't anywhere near as stupid as most people thought. "The man was a—an acquaintance of Lucius', from down south. It gave him a shock, coming on him like that."

"It gave us all a shock, Mistress. Right then, I'll organise the pyre, leave it to me."

In the stable yard I found Secundus, who said he'd see that my message went to Oak Bridges within the hour. I asked how things were going.

"Everything's fine with the stables." There was an odd emphasis in the way he said those last few words.

"That's good. Anything else I should know about?"

"Just one thing. Our Victor will be home sometime today. A courier from Eburacum, one of his mates, called in to tell me he's on his way."

"Really?" I paused, not sure what to say to him. He'd be pleased to see his son, we all would. And yet the circumstances were so sad. "You'll let me know when he gets here, won't you? And tell him I'm sorry for what happened, but I'm proud of him too. It's not every day I meet someone who's saved his company's standard."

He smiled. "Aye, I will. By the gods, look at this beauty!"

I followed his gaze, and wasn't too surprised to see that the "beauty" was a horse, not a woman. One of the boys was leading an extremely handsome white gelding into the yard. It was a very fine animal, big and well-muscled, with a brilliant white coat and thick mane, and it stood out among the usual travel-worn mounts like a rose in a thistle patch. Its saddle and bridle were smart and new, with fancy bronze trimmings.

"Beauty is right, Secundus! Where's he from, I wonder? I've never seen him before, I'd remember a gorgeous horse like that." I've a good memory for horseflesh—my family say it's better than my memory for people—and I envied the man who owned such a lovely creature. Presumably he was in the bar now. I must make a point of congratulating him.

"Superb, isn't he?" A voice behind us made me spin round, and my heart gave a great leap as I saw the tall fair-haired man walking towards me, smiling and holding out his hand. It was Quintus Antonius Delfinus.

"Why, *Quintus!* Welcome to the Oak Tree!" Of course that wasn't what I really wanted to say. I felt like running into his arms, and, between kisses, telling him how happy I was to see him again. But that wasn't our way. We were lovers, but we kept the fact discreet, so a proper greeting would have to wait till we were by ourselves. I simply took his hand and smiled into his eyes, and then nodded towards the horse. "I'm just wondering if I can get away with stealing that gorgeous beast before the owner finishes his drink."

"You've left it too late. He's mine." He was standing beside me now, and I had to make a considerable effort to stay so near him without touching.

"Yours? You'd never ride a flashy animal like that." Quintus is an investigator like Lucius, but a more senior one, working directly for the Emperor. "You always try to be inconspicuous when you travel. If he's really your horse, I'm the Queen of Brigantia!"

He made me a deep bow. "Well, Your Majesty, he's truly mine. I won him two nights ago in a dice-game in Eburacum, from a staff officer with more money than sense." His purple-blue eyes flashed, and I knew that the win itself would have given him as much pleasure as the prize. "So I thought, where can I try out such a wonderful animal? Of course, I'll visit Oak Bridges for a few days, and show him off to Aurelia."

"I'm very pleased you did." That was putting it mildly. I hadn't seen him for six months, but we could make up a lot of lost time if he was planning to be at the Oak Tree for a few days.

"Mind you," he added, "that's if I haven't died of thirst in the meantime. I thought you innkeepers were supposed to be generous and hospitable, and here you are, keeping me chatting in the yard, and you haven't offered me so much as a beaker of water!"

I laughed. "You should have said that's what you wanted. I thought you'd come here just to gloat about your horse."

We didn't linger in the bar-room, pausing only long enough for me to ask Margarita to send wine and food through to us. Then we headed for my private sitting-room, where we threw away discretion and I gave him a real welcome. Soon a knock at the door announced Margarita with a tray of wine and food. She greeted Quintus cordially, though not quite as enthusiastically as I'd done, and smiled at me as she put down the meal on the table.

"Everything's under control in the bar, Aurelia. And you and Quintus Antonius will have business to discuss, so I'll see that you're not disturbed for the rest of the afternoon."

"Thanks, Margarita. We appreciate it."

"She's a sensible girl," Quintus said when we were alone again and could resume our greeting.

"She is. And if she's prepared to cover for me this afternoon, let's make the most of it."

I poured the wine and we drank to each other, sitting side by side on a couch. He moved closer and murmured, "I've missed you."

"And I you. Tell me, have we business to discuss, as Margarita put it, or is this just a social call?"

"Business and pleasure together." He leaned back and stretched out his long legs.

"I think I can guess the pleasure. And the business might be connected with a band of pirates?"

"Not directly, though I'm afraid I shan't be able to avoid dealing with them. But the Emperor's had a report from a Roman landowner, a fairly new settler, that the Parisi tribesmen near the coast are making trouble, and may be hatching some kind of conspiracy against Rome."

"That would be Ostorius Magnus complaining about Chief Bodvocos, I expect."

He spread his hands and gave me a rueful smile. "I might have guessed you'd know all about it. I swear you get news of events before they've even happened! I don't know why I don't just set up my headquarters in your bar-room, and gather intelligence from there."

"Isn't that what I'm always telling you? But how does Caesar come into this? Does Magnus have connections at court?"

"One of his old army friends is highly placed in the Praetorian Guard." He bent close and kissed me. "But don't let's talk about it now. We'll have to face work soon enough, but I want this afternoon to be for us two. Can you really leave Margarita to run the bar?"

"Just watch me! There's only one thing I must do, and that's at sunset. But we've plenty of time before then."

We had more than enough time for love. We flew like birds soaring over the green hills, absorbed in each other to the exclusion of everything else. But even birds must leave the sky sometime, and glide gently back to earth.

"I'm hungry," Quintus announced.

"So am I." I fetched the tray of food Margarita had brought, and served each of us a plate with bread, olives, and slices of sausage, while he poured more wine.

"This is a feast!" he exclaimed with his mouth full. "And while we eat, you can tell me what you know about Ostorius Magnus and Bodvocos, and these accursed Gauls."

He listened without interrupting while I went through the events of the last few days in order, and stopped me when I came to the shipwreck with its unpleasant cargo.

"What was the head like?"

"He had long fair hair, a pale complexion, no beard, blue eyes, no scars. A youngish man I'd say, not more than thirty-five. You can see him for yourself if you like. He's in one of our out-buildings. The funeral's at sunset."

"No, there's no need. I just wanted to be sure."

"Was it one of the boat's crew?"

"No. *Merda,* it's a pity I missed Lucius. I hoped to catch him before he left Eburacum, but I was too late. I have to see him, it's one of the reasons I'm here. I'll ride over to the coast tomorrow. I hope he's not feeling too downcast about the missing gold? It wasn't his fault."

"I told him that, but he was depressed about it, and annoyed, because he thought the *Sea Horse* had been under observation the whole time after it came ashore. And…" But something stopped me telling Quintus that Lucius knew the identity of the man in the chest.

"And?" Quintus prompted.

"And," I improvised, "he reckons that if Voltacos stole the cargo, he must have had help from someone ashore. Perhaps even the fishermen who appeared to be so helpful."

"He probably did, but that isn't the point. Can I tell you something in confidence?"

"Of course not. I'll spread it all over Brigantia. Really, Quintus, don't you know by now that I can keep secrets?"

He took my hand. "Sorry. It's just that this is sensitive. The gold was never in the *Sea Horse* at all."

"*What?*"

"It was removed before it sailed from Londinium, and a substitute chest put in to replace it."

"But Lucius said he helped prepare that cargo himself. He said—and here's another secret I've managed to keep!—that it was a chest full of gold coin to bribe some Caledonian chieftain."

"So it was. But just before it was due to go north, our agents in Caledonia sent word that the chieftain Caesar was about to honour with such a marvellous gift was playing fast and loose with us. He was going to take the gold and then lead a collection of natives tribes across our frontier and down into Brigantia. Using, if you please, Caesar's gold to finance it."

"Devious, but pretty much in character for those northern tribes. Why didn't you just stop the boat sailing?"

"The Governor's advisers never do anything simply if they can introduce a complication or two. They decided to let the *Sea Horse* go as intended but minus cargo, and act as bait to attract any pirates along its route north. The plan was that if raiders tried to capture it, our men on board, plus the warship that was escorting it, would be able to capture *them*."

"Some plan!"

He shrugged. "I never said it was a good plan. One of the Governor's new young men dreamed it up. He's fresh over here from Rome, and as green as a lettuce leaf."

"So the shipment of gold wasn't so much a secret as a lie."

"Exactly so. Our agents further up the coast spread a few choice rumours about the value of it. The gods know if they did any good."

"But why add such a horrible touch, including that head in the box? That was done in Londinium too, presumably?"

He nodded. "It was meant to be horrible. If the boat eventually made it to Caledonia, we wanted to teach the chieftain a lesson. The head belonged to someone he knew, one of our men in Londinium who'd turned traitor."

"A *traitor?* Are you sure?"

"No doubt about it. His name was Rollus, and he'd been involved in the negotiations with the Caledonians, and switched sides. We found out he'd been encouraging his new master to take our money and run. What's the matter, Aurelia? You've gone as white as marble."

"Nothing. Just the thought of that head, the way we found it in the basket." But my mind was in turmoil. So the long-lost brother Rollus was a traitor! It wasn't a family connection to be desired, even though it was Rollus who had sought out Lucius and made all the running, not the other way round. But how many people knew that Lucius and Rollus had become friends? If Lucius had only told the immediate family, we could keep it secret. But then if we did, and it was discovered later, that would make us look like traitors too.

"Something's wrong," Quintus said gently. "Why not tell me? Whatever it is, I'll help if I can, you know that." He slid his arm round me. I wanted desperately to confide in him, and perhaps indeed he could help us. But should I reveal our secret to him without asking Lucius first?

"It's difficult, Quintus. I don't know."

"It's about the head that was in the boat, isn't it? You know who he was. Otherwise why would it matter if he was a traitor?"

"Yes. The trouble is it's a secret. I don't just mean officially, I mean it's private Aurelius family business. So if I tell you, you'll be discreet?"

"I'll spread it all over Brigantia, of course."

So I told him. I expected he might be shocked, or at least surprised, but he was excited, and made me report everything Lucius had told us about Rollus. I left nothing out, and as I saw his growing interest, I became more and more worried about how the situation might be misunderstood.

"Quintus, you've got to understand Lucius was only interested in a possible family connection with the man, not in his work. He'd no idea about any treachery…"

"Of course he hadn't. Lucius is in no danger, his loyalty's well enough established. But he may have met some of Rollus' contacts and be able to lead us to other men who are working against Rome. This could be a real breakthrough. As for his not knowing about the treachery, I think we'll find he did know."

"No, Quintus, he didn't. I can swear to that."

"But he did, Aurelia! He knew, or suspected, right from the start." His purple-blue eyes were full of mischief. "He was investigating Rollus, playing along with him in order to find out exactly what he was up to. And the sooner he realises that's what he was doing, the better."

Relief flooded into me. Of course, the obvious solution, the answer to any accusations, should they happen. I hugged Quintus, but he pulled gently away from me and stood up.

"This makes it more urgent than ever that I talk to him." He glanced through the open window, assessing the height of the sun. "If I leave now on a fast horse, I can get a good part of the way to the coast by dark, say as far as Albia's. Then tomorrow morning early I can see Lucius."

My heart sank. We'd had such a short time together, I couldn't bear the thought of it ending so soon. "I haven't any fast horses available. And even if I had, the wold country's not a safe area to be riding through towards the end of the day when the roads are deserted."

"I can take care of myself."

"So you say. But if you're wrong, I can't afford to lose a fast horse."

I saw the beginnings of a smile. "You don't think I should go then?"

"Quintus Antonius Delfinus, if you go away again today, it'll be over my dead body."

He sat down again, smiling as he picked up his wine-mug. "On second thoughts, I ought not to miss Rollus' funeral."

"Gods, the funeral! Shouldn't I cancel it, now I know who—I mean *what*—Rollus really was?"

"Cancelling it at such short notice would cause too much comment. Let it go ahead as you've planned it. After all, traitor or not, the man was still your half-brother."

So Rollus got a more dignified send-off than he deserved, and for the rest of the evening Quintus and I forgot about him altogether.

Chapter XIV

Next morning we breakfasted in my private sitting-room, but after that we both knew play-time was over. I looked into the kitchen to check that everything was running smoothly. It was, except that Cook was moaning because too many of the spring cabbages were being eaten by caterpillars. I suggested he should invent a way of cooking the caterpillars themselves, but he didn't see the joke.

Margarita smiled at me. "Don't expect any sensible culinary suggestions from Aurelia this morning, Cook. She's got other things on her mind."

"Of course I have, very important things. I'm visiting our esteemed Chief Councillor later on, aren't I?"

I found Quintus near the big paddock in earnest conversation with Secundus. "I've just been hearing about young Victor. I didn't know he'd been discharged. And I didn't know he'd come home."

"Come home? I didn't know either." I turned to Secundus. "When did he arrive? Why didn't you tell me?"

"He arrived yesterday very late, while you were holding that funeral ceremony. Margarita said you weren't to be disturbed."

I felt a pang of guilt, but only a small one. "How is he?"

"They've patched him up pretty well. He can ride all right without using the fingers of his left hand, although he says it's more tiring that way. But he's up and about now, and I reckon he'll be glad you're here, Quintus Antonius. He always had a lot of time for you. Mebbe you can help cheer the poor lad up. Try and make him see that having to leave the cavalry isn't the end of everything, which he thinks it is."

"Maybe I can, at that." Quintus looked thoughtful. "Yes, maybe I can."

"Where is he?" I asked.

Secundus nodded towards the next paddock. "He's in there, looking over the horses and mules. There's quite a lot of new stock since he was last home. He was quite taken with yon flashy white one of yours," he said to Quintus.

"So I should hope! It'll need regular exercise, of course. If Victor has time to spare, I'd appreciate it if he'd take him out for me later."

Secundus smiled. "I'll tell him."

" I'd like a chance to talk to him, but without making a big thing of it. Aurelia and I have to go into Oak Bridges this morning to see Silvanius Clarus. Could Victor drive us in a raeda?"

I wondered what Quintus was up to. Last night he'd been talking about leaving to see Lucius urgently. Now he'd just invited himself to my meeting with Clarus.

But Secundus' smile broadened. "I don't know. Let's ask him." He put two fingers into his mouth and gave a shrill whistle, and then called, "Victor! Someone to see you here!"

Titch came walking across the paddock, and I hardly recognised him. His body was much the same, compact and lithe, and his left hand was out of sight, tucked away under his tunic. But his face was quite changed. He still had bright red hair and ears that stuck out, but instead of the alert eyes and the cheeky grin that we were all used to, there was a sullen stillness about him. He strolled over to us slowly, looking down, and when he did raise his eyes, they had no sparkle in them.

"Hello, Victor," I said. "Your dad's told me they've discharged you. I'm so sorry."

"Thank you," he said dully.

Quintus held out his hand. "Victor, it's good to see you. You're something of a hero, I gather. We're all proud of you."

They shook hands, and Titch grunted, "Some hero, falling off me horse and getting me arm broke! And I'm finished as a soldier now. Finished altogether, if you want the truth."

"No you're not." It was my instinctive reply, meant to comfort him, but I should have known such facile words would only upset him more.

"No? Then what do you reckon I'm good for? You going to give me a job here, are you?"

"Yes, I am. There'll always be a job here for you, Victor, if you want it."

That at least made him look me directly in the face. "That's good of you, Mistress Aurelia. Thank you. But..."

Quintus finished the sentence for him. "Being a stable-hand at a mansio isn't what you want, is it?"

He shook his head. "I want to be a soldier. It's what I've always dreamed of, ever since I was a bairn. When I was accepted for the cavalry, it was like me dreams had all come true. And when we went into battle, I felt it was where I should be. I could make a difference somehow, fight for the Empire, show the barbarians what it means to be a Roman." He was animated now, and we saw the familiar, lively, determined character we'd all liked so much. But the animation died as he added, "Now I've got nothing left to live for. I wish the barbarians had killed me, along with me mates."

Quintus said gently. "I know it doesn't seem like it now, but you're lucky to be alive, lad."

"Oh aye? And what would you know about it? You've got a job you like, a good job that's worth summat." Suddenly he was tense, furious, as if he needed anger to give him strength. "And don't call me 'lad'! Don't you ever call me that again! I'm a man, and I'll not have anyone treating me like a boy."

"He didn't mean..." I began, but Quintus waved me quiet.

"Calm down, Victor, and don't take offence where there's none intended. You're not a boy, I know that. You're one of the brightest young men I've come across lately. And you can still fight for the Empire, if it's what you want to do, only in a different way."

"I don't see how."

"I'll tell you, but this isn't the time. Look, Aurelia and I have to go into Oak Bridges this morning to see Councillor Silvanius, and we need a driver. Your dad says the horse-boys here have their hands full. Are you too grand to drive a carriage these days?"

"Me? Why, no, I suppose not. But I don't know if I can."

"You can. The question is, will you? As a favour to us?"

"Well…" He hesitated, then shook his head and dropped his gaze. "No, I reckon I need a day or two before I'm ready to face folk. You'd best find someone else."

"Why? You've come home a hero. A man who saved his squadron's standard from capture. That's what people round here think. The sooner they see you in person, the better. Face them now, that's my advice."

"I don't need your advice, thanks all the same. I wish you and everyone else would stop telling me what to do. Nobody knows what it's like for me."

"I do," Quintus answered steadily. "I know very well."

Victor looked up in surprise. "How's that?"

"Why do you think I left the army? I was an officer when your father was serving in Germania, you know that. I was an engineer, I specialised in designing and building bridges. I loved the work, and thought it was what I wanted to do for my whole life. But I was injured one day, not in battle, but falling from some scaffolding. I hurt my back so badly I could hardly stand for a while. It got a little better after a few months, but it was still painful, and the doctors said I'd never be able to ride any distance again. So eventually I was discharged." He paused and flexed his shoulders. "They were wrong, as it happened, but it took me a year to find a doctor who could really help me. He put me on a regime of exercises and diet to get my full strength back. By that time I'd—well, I'd joined a different kind of service, which I preferred. And still do."

"I never knew," Titch said. "Is your back all right now?"

"It is, except for the occasional twinge in wet weather. But most old soldiers have a few aches and pains, don't they?"

"Well then, you know the way their minds work in the army, when you're hurt but they still want to keep you on."

"Did they offer you some sort of desk job?"

"They offered, but they could see I'm not interested in pushing a stylus around. Horses are what I like."

"So then—let me guess—they suggested you could move into the transport section. Supplies, was it?"

Victor smiled without humour. "Transport Officer, they called it, which sounds grand enough, but in plain Latin it's just playing nursemaid to a load of brainless mules and even more brainless drivers. Bringing supplies up from base to the battle area, riding up and down, up and down, safe behind the lines while other men do the fighting, and getting shouted at by the quartermasters because you've brought everything except what they want! I couldn't have stood that, and to be fair, they didn't push it."

"Good, because I think you're worth something more. But we've really got to get moving. If you don't want to drive us today, that's all right. Secundus, could you spare one of the other lads please? We mustn't be late for our meeting with the Chief Councillor. You know what he's like."

The meeting wasn't at a fixed hour, and I opened my mouth to say so, but fortunately realised in time what Quintus was doing, and held my peace.

Secundus nodded. "Of course. I'll get Malchus to harness up for you."

"There's no need," Titch said. "I'll do it, if you're stuck. Only if I make a mess of it, don't complain."

"If you can't handle a couple of mules, then I'm the Queen of Brigantia."

He brightened a little. "There was a tavern girl in Eburacum used to use that expression. It reminded me of you whenever I heard it. I mean...no offence, like."

"None taken. As long as she was pretty, of course."

"She was that all right."

"We haven't got time for the story of your love life, Titch—er—Victor," Quintus grinned. "We'll be ready as soon as you've harnessed up."

The lad actually smiled. "You know, in the squadron I couldn't get me mates to call me Victor, any more than folk here. It was always Titch. So I don't mind if you want to call me Titch as well."

We didn't wait to watch how easily Titch managed to prepare the carriage and mules, but his driving was as good as ever, and the journey to Silvanius' villa was uneventful. As we trotted through the centre of Oak Bridges we passed various acquaintances and gave them a wave or a few words, and Titch received as many greetings as we did. He answered them barely politely at first, but then it must have begun to dawn on him how many friends he had who were pleased to see him, and he visibly relaxed.

We trotted up the long drive that led to Silvanius' huge villa. The gardens on either side were bright with spring flowers and new leaves, and as we came near the house we could hear noises of hammering and sawing. Quintus exclaimed, "By the gods, this place gets bigger every time I come. Is that another wing of rooms he's adding at the back?"

"He's re-designing his bath house," I said. "He says it isn't big enough. He must be expecting to entertain several cohorts of visitors at once."

"Mebbe his guests are just very dirty," Titch suggested, and I didn't have the heart to rebuke his impudence. It was so good to see his cheeky smile, and the way he held his head high as he led the raeda off to the stables.

Chief Councillor Publius Silvanius Clarus was waiting for us in his library. It was a big room, like all the public rooms in his villa, and pleasant in the mornings, when a large open window let in the sunshine. Most of the other three walls were covered in book-pockets, each containing several scrolls neatly rolled and labelled. Clarus prided himself on owning all the books a

Roman gentleman should possess. I'd never seen him reading any of them, but then many Roman gentlemen take the view that actually perusing a library's contents isn't essential.

Being Roman had always been very important to Clarus. He was unswervingly loyal to the Empire, and he was a citizen, as Roman in his ways as any patrician with ancestors who were present at the foundation of the Republic. Yet he was born in Britannia of one of the old native aristocratic families, and he was a typical Briton in appearance, tall, square, and fair. He was about fifty, with traces of white showing in his hair, but he was as vigorous as ever, a man of power in Oak Bridges, physically and politically. Of course he was wearing his toga, even for this informal meeting. He delighted in proclaiming his Roman-ness in every way he could.

As we came in he was dictating to a secretary, but he broke off and welcomed us with his usual mixture of warmth and pomposity. "Aurelia, my dear, thank you so much for coming. It's always such a delight to entertain you in my humble abode. And Quintus Antonius, what a pleasant surprise. You are indeed welcome. I think you may very well be able to help with the matter that concerns us today." He turned to his slave. "Ask my sister to join us, and then get on with making fair copies of those letters. I want them sent out today."

"I hope you don't mind my coming with Aurelia," Quintus said. "I only arrived in Oak Bridges yesterday, and when she said that she was visiting you, I couldn't resist the chance to come too. I'm afraid it's not quite the done thing, but we're old friends."

"I should have been mortified if you hadn't come," Silvanius smiled. They began exchanging small-talk, while I gazed out of the window at the garden. I knew Clarus would be pleased to see Quintus, not only because he'd helped the Chief Councillor in the past, but because of Quintus' important government connections, which made him exactly the kind of friend Silvanius liked to receive.

His sister Clarilla came in, smart and well-groomed as always. She was wearing a fashionable pale blue tunic secured with fine silver brooches, and her fair hair was piled up on her head in a style I hadn't seen before, under a silvery net studded with small blue stones. She greeted me and Quintus affectionately.

"I wish I'd known you were coming, Quintus Antonius. I'd have organised a dinner party for you. Are you staying long at the Oak Tree?"

"No, unfortunately, just a day or two. I have to go over to the coast to see Aurelia's brother."

"Ah, the coast." Clarus said. "I heard that Lucius is pursuing these wretched pirates. More power to him. I'm told the situation in those parts is deteriorating rapidly."

Clarus' stately major-domo brought in refreshments. Clarilla kept the best table in the district, as well as the most lavish. We drank our white wine from silver goblets, and the food arrived on silver platters: a selection of mouth-watering pastries, and some pears in spiced syrup served in individual silver bowls.

While we ate, we exchanged news. When our hosts heard about the attack on Albia's farm they were both horrified, and I had to reassure them several times that my sister and the children hadn't been harmed, just very frightened.

"That is an appalling thing to happen," Clarus exclaimed, "though I cannot say I'm surprised. We've been hearing disturbing reports of trouble in the wold country. To be frank, that's why I asked you to visit me, Aurelia. I thought you might have up-to-date news of the state of things there from your sister. But I never expected such grim happenings. Has Candidus enough men to protect his farm? Is it safe for Albia to remain there?"

"Not really, and I tried to persuade her to stay with me at the Oak Tree for a while, but she won't budge. I've been wondering about going over to Eburacum to buy some bodyguards for them all."

"There's no need for that. If Candidus will allow me to help, I should be glad to lend him half-a-dozen strong lads to guard him and Albia."

"Clarus, that would be wonderful, thank you. Are you sure you can spare them?"

"Indeed yes, I've more guards than I need here, and my man Brutus will be pleased to lead them. You know he'll do anything to help you and your family."

"Brutus will be in charge of them? He's worth three legionaries all by himself! That would be such a weight off my mind."

"Brutus?" Quintus asked. "The ex-soldier who helped you out at the Oak Tree a few years ago? He's an excellent man."

"He is, and if Candidus and Albia have him to guard them, I'll know that they are safe whatever happens."

Clarus smiled. "Good. It shall be arranged then. I'll send them over to the Oak Tree this afternoon."

I thanked him again from my heart. For all his pomp and pride, he'd repeatedly shown himself a good friend to our family.

"Might you be visiting your sister again soon?" Clarus put the question diffidently, but I sensed it was important to him. Could I have stumbled on the reason for his generous gesture of help for my sister?

"I expect so, yes. I'm worried about them all, and if Albia refuses to come to Oak Bridges, I'll have to go to her. Why? Is there some errand I can do for you while I'm there?"

"I confess there is, yes. Nothing onerous, just collecting information and impressions. Oh dear, this is a somewhat delicate matter. I should hate what I'm about to ask you to become widely known."

"Then it won't, Clarus. You can rely on us."

"Of course, of course. Well, let me explain a little. My late wife was a cousin of Chief Bodvocos, and we still keep in touch with him and his family, even after all this time. The roots of kinship run very deep, you know. And Bodvocos has considerable local power among the Parisi."

"As you do among the Brigantes."

Clarus acknowledged Quintus' compliment with a smile. "Exactly so. I've always felt that we who have been chosen to hold positions of responsibility in the Empire must work together, especially when it comes to preserving the Roman peace. And until this year there has been peace in the coastal areas, more so than here in Brigantia. I'm sure Bodvocos must take credit for that. But now I fear things have changed."

"Because of a couple of boatloads of Gauls?" Quintus raised an eyebrow. "Are they really such a menace?"

Clarus took a long drink of his wine. "Not on their own, no. But a serious dispute has arisen between two powerful estates, and the pirates, bandits, whatever one should call them, are taking the chance to cause trouble at the same time. Bodvocos is one party to the dispute. The other is a settler called Ostorius Magnus, who's bought a big parcel of land near the Headland. Do you know him, Antonius?"

"I've heard of him, but we haven't met yet. What's the dispute about?"

"Oh, not one particular thing, a score of minor issues. Boundaries, and livestock straying or disappearing, and farm boys getting into fights when they have drunk too much beer. All the usual rural problems, and individually each cause of contention is very small. Taken together they mean that the two men and their households are at daggers drawn most of the time. And I'm worried for Bodvocos' safety. Not so much his physical well-being, I'm sure he can protect himself. But if he were to allow himself to be drawn into some long-running feud, and the Roman authorities got to hear of it…"

He has, and they have, I thought, but I left the talking to Quintus.

"Who started it, do you know?"

Clarus smiled. "That depends upon whose account you believe. Bodvocos says the Ostorii are behaving badly, throwing their weight about among their less powerful neighbours, who are merely retaliating when they go too far. Ostorius is apparently claiming the exact opposite. he says Bodvocos' people are harassing his, because the Parisi are hostile to Roman settlement."

"They never have been before," I pointed out. "I can imagine a dispute between two rich farmers, that happens everywhere, but I simply don't believe the Parisi have suddenly decided they don't like Romans. Do you, Clarus?"

"I don't know what to believe, Aurelia. I certainly hope you're right. Bodvocos has written to me asking for my help, but I don't in all honesty know what I can do. Intervening from this distance would be a major step to take. Before I decide, I'd like more information about the Ostorii, and indeed whether the situation is as serious as Bodvocos represents it."

I could see where he was driving. He found it hard to believe that Roman settlers would disturb the peace, yet the people whose peace was being disturbed were his own kin.

"So you'd like me to go and stay with Albia, and while I'm there, ask around a little? Try to decide whether Magnus or Bodvocos is to blame for the trouble, or whether the whole affair is just an argument between powerful men that has got out of hand, and allowed a band of raiders to operate undisturbed?"

"My dear, as always you hit the mark exactly."

"I'll be glad to find out what I can, Clarus. If you're helping keep my sister safe, that's the very least I can do for you. And Quintus will be able to form his own opinion too, while he's in the area. Won't you?"

"Certainly. And you're right not to rush into action without more information, Clarus. You show good judgment. Mind you, your judgment is always sound in matters like this."

Clarus beamed. "Oh, thank you both, that's excellent. I find it painful even to contemplate taking sides with either of them against the other. But if I must, I want my actions to be rooted in fact, not rumour. Magnus is a well-respected Roman, just the sort of man we need to make his home in this province. But Bodvocos is my kinsman. We visited him this time last year, you know, for the feast of Beltane. A splendid occasion, wasn't it, Clarilla?"

Clarilla had remained silent throughout all this. At mention of her name she stirred in her chair and said "Oh yes indeed," reminding me of the way I'd answered the talkative trader Curtius when my mind was fully occupied elsewhere. I hadn't long to wait to find where her thoughts had been taking her.

"Aurelia, I believe you had a visit from Ostorius Magnus recently, didn't you?"

"I did. He and his nephew Vividus came over to buy horses. And Vividus had a bad tooth, poor man, which Timaeus pulled out for him. They were talking about their ambitions to make their farm bigger and better, and they mentioned that they'd met with some local hostility, but didn't go into much detail."

"What did you think of them?"

"They seemed very pleasant, especially Vividus, who's a real charmer. Magnus was civil enough, inclined to be a shade grumpy, but I don't think it was anything personal. Vividus was very good company. I'd say they'll be an asset to the area, although I'd guess they would make bad enemies if one got on the wrong side of them. But I don't know them well, they were only at the mansio a few hours. They visited you here, didn't they?"

"Indeed they did," Clarus answered, "but as you say, it is impossible to form a true impression in just a few short hours."

"Do you think they'll really take to life in this part of the Empire?" Clarilla asked. "They're both ex-army, and they've only recently moved north into Britannia."

"I don't see why not. They seem efficient and determined to make a go of their land. A bit raw, perhaps, like so many Romans when they first arrive to live in a new province. What did you both make of them?"

"I liked them both," Clarus said.

"But I did *not* like them," Clarilla said firmly. "I didn't take to either of them, though I agree they tried their best to be likeable. I thought that Magnus was an overbearing bully, and Vividus was too much in love with himself to have time for anyone else."

This unfavourable assessment surprised me. Clarilla was usually easy-going and tolerant, and enjoyed making friends with everyone. But I couldn't deny she'd unerringly picked out the two men's major faults. "I do agree that Vividus fancies himself as the gods' gift to women. He tried out his charms on me, but it was all very gentlemanly, just harmless flirting."

"I've no objection to a little flirting," she smiled. "*That* wasn't what worried me."

"Then what?"

"They both struck me as too greedy, with all their talk of enlarging their property by buying out the smaller farmers. There was a ruthlessness there that made me wonder how far they would go to get what they want."

Quintus said, "Surely there's nothing wrong in wanting to expand one's farm? One man's greed is another man's healthy ambition."

"Indeed, that was my thought. And ambition is what has made our Empire great," Clarus declared.

Clarilla frowned. "That's as may be. But they don't care what they do to other people, they'll just roll over any opposition and crush it. They're powerful, and rich, and they can use the law to get their own way."

This was so like what Divico had said that it made me sit up and look at Clarilla closely. There was more to this than met the eye.

"Clarilla, they've obviously upset you in some way. I agree they're a bit rough-and-ready, but they'll calm down when they've lived here a while."

"I'm not so sure. They made some very disparaging remarks about people here. For instance Magnus told us he'd encountered hostility from the tribesmen near the coast, but it didn't worry him, he said, because 'the natives in northern Britannia are all barbarians, even if they don't wear blue paint nowadays.'"

"Ouch! That was wrong of him, as well as stupid," I said, and Quintus nodded in agreement. I picked up my goblet and took a drink of wine, to give myself time to think. Privately I couldn't help agreeing with Magnus to some extent: many of our natives *are* still barbarians under the skin, but by no means all, and certainly not Clarus and his sister. They were examples of how people born in Britannia can become completely Roman. And the Ostorii had taken them for Romans from Italia, or at least from one of the older provinces, Spain maybe or Gaul. In one sense that should be a source of pride to them, because they strove to be Roman in everything. But their family in Britannia was an old and aristocratic one, relatively civilised even before our legions came, and they'd made it clear already that they weren't in the least ashamed of their origins.

"I suspect they're not used to civilian life in a frontier province," Quintus said. "That's the most likely explanation for such rudeness. As Aurelia says, they'll settle down and learn to behave themselves. Forgive me for asking, Clarus, but I get the feeling that your interest in the Ostorii goes a bit beyond what they may or may not be doing to your kinfolk on the coast. Have they offered you some kind of business proposition?"

Clarus smiled. "They have, Antonius. Magnus has proposed a marriage between his nephew Vividus and Clarilla."

Clarilla wasn't smiling. Her grim expression told its own tale.

"I'd offer congratulations, Clarilla," I said, "but you don't look exactly happy about this."

"I'm not." She pushed back a strand of fair hair that had escaped from the elaborate silver net. "I know that marriages in a family such as ours are, as my brother says, business alliances. If I marry again I'm not expecting to fall in love like a silly slip of a girl. But if I take another husband, I want someone I can at least like and respect."

"These—ah—intuitive feelings are important, of course, my dear," Clarus said, patting his sister's hand. "And for that reason I have not given Ostorius a definite answer, but told him I must consider it, and talk to you about it. But it would be an extremely suitable match for you, you know. They're a good Roman family, and wealthy in both money and land, as I understand it. Once they've established themselves here, they're going to be important people in this part of Britannia."

"Not as important to me as you are, Publius. You need somebody here to run your house and act as hostess when you entertain. I enjoy doing that, and I'd much rather go on doing it than be tied to Ostorius Vividus."

"My dear, you know I don't want you to be unhappy. But I think you're being a little over-hasty, since we hardly know the Ostorii as yet. Once Aurelia and Quintus have had time to do a little investigating for us…"

"Yes, of course. I know you'll both do your best, won't you?"

We both assured her again that we would, and I sensed that our meeting was over, and it was time to be on our way. "If you'll excuse us, I think we should be heading back to the mansio now. You know what it's like when you've been away from home for two days, you come back and find at least three days' work has piled up in your office."

Clarilla smiled. "Just before you go, Aurelia, I've made a copy of that recipe you wanted for preserving grapes through the winter. If you come along with me to the kitchen, I'll give it you now."

"Recipe?" My mind was as blank as an unwritten note-tablet.

"Yes. You said you'd give it to your cook to try." She gazed at me intently, while I racked my brains and completely failed to remember asking for a recipe. And why would I want to think about grapes at this time of year?

"It really won't take long," she said, and her voice, usually so warm and easy, held an underlying note of—what? Anxiety? Warning? Desperation?

Sometimes I'm so slow I'd have trouble keeping pace with a tortoise. Clarilla must be wanting to talk to me on my own, and this was her way of getting me away from her brother. I stood up. "Of course! I'm amazed you've persuaded your chef to part with one of his famous recipes…"

"There's nothing more important than good food." Clarilla chattered brightly as we went out into the corridor, and headed not for the kitchen, but for her own small study. She closed the door firmly once we were inside, and we sat down.

"Aurelia, I'm sorry to drag you away in that cloak-and-dagger fashion, but I need a private word. Private from Publius, I mean, not from Quintus. You and he are my only hope."

"Gods, Clarilla, what is it? You know we'll help if you need us. Is it about this proposed marriage with Vividus? I could see you're not keen on it, but surely Clarus won't force you into it against your will?"

"That's part of it. I know my brother wants the match, but he would never compel me to marry someone I really hate, and anyway he couldn't. I have money of my own, left by my late husband's will, so I can do as I please. But I'm hoping—I'm wishing, if that doesn't sound too horrible—that you find something about those Ostorii that would make Publius consider them an unsuitable connection."

"I can promise you Quintus and I will find out everything we can about the whole Ostorius family. If they have any skeletons in their clothes-chests, you'll be the first to hear."

"Thank you. But I want to ask you to help over something else, something concerning a favourite young relative of ours. It's Bodvocos' daughter Elli. She's in some sort of trouble and has written to me begging me to visit her. I can't go immediately, because Publius is giving a big banquet here in a few days and I am to be his hostess as usual. And anyway, Publius has forbidden me to interfere in Elli's problems, for fear of offending Bodvocos." She smiled. "So any action I do take will have to be discreet."

"Point taken. Has Elli told you what sort of trouble she's in?"

"She's in love with one man, and betrothed to another."

I sighed. "Ah. She's promised to Coriu, isn't she?"

"She is."

"I heard it was more a marriage of convenience than a love match. Who's the lad she's in love with?"

She replied with another question. "Did you know that Magnus has a nephew called Aquilo? A younger boy, and not in the least military like Vividus."

"Magnus did mention him. But—you're saying Elli is in love with the youngest Ostorius boy?"

"I think so. She hasn't mentioned any names in her latest letter, but earlier this year when she wrote, she was singing his praises very loudly."

"And you want me to find out if it really is Aquilo she's fallen for, and discourage her?"

"I don't know about discouraging her. I haven't met Aquilo, but I've heard a little about him. By all accounts he's a thoroughly likeable young man, quite different from his brothers and his uncle. He's never been in the army, so he hasn't an ounce of military ambition. He says he just wants to live peacefully with everyone. *Everyone,* settlers and Parisi."

"All Magnus said about him, rather disparagingly, was that he likes music and writes poetry, and wants to go and study in Greece. That made me like the lad already."

She nodded. "It appears that he's the most civilised member of the family. Could you find a way to meet him while you're staying with Albia? And then give me your honest opinion about the boy?"

"I'm sure I can manage that. Candidus and Albia are on good terms with all their neighbours."

"Oh, I'd be so grateful. I trust your judgment, you're not easily taken in. Then I'll know whether I should be encouraging Elli or dissuading her."

"Do you want me to visit Elli too, and hear her side of the story?"

"Oh, would you? *Could* you?"

"I don't see why not. If you give me a letter for her, or perhaps a small present, that'll give me an excuse for a visit to Bodvocos' place without making him suspicious."

"I will. I'll write a note with a small gift, and have one of our boys bring it to you at the Oak Tree. And I'll get Publius to write a short letter to Bodvocos, then you'll have a chance to meet him too. I won't mention Elli, but I can persuade Publius that you ought to meet our relatives, to help with your investigations, and he'll write you a letter of introduction."

"Excellent. What's Bodvocos like?"

"Pleasant enough, in a rather lofty way. His family is very old and very high-born, so he looks down his nose at most of the world."

"Not you and Clarus, though, surely."

"Oh no, we're family. If it wasn't for that, I don't suppose we'd feel we have much in common with him. He's quite old-fashioned, prefers the traditional ways of doing things. Even to the spelling of his name—ending it in -os, as his forefathers did, not in the Roman style, ending in –us." She smiled. "He gets very annoyed if Romans call him Bodvocos. Which many of them do."

"Including the Ostorii, I expect."

"Coriu's not a bad young man at all," Clarilla mused, "and I think Elli would have been happy enough with him if she hadn't met Aquilo. You know, the poets go on ad nauseam about the joys of true love, but in real life it can be rather an inconvenient emotion, don't you think?"

There was more, but that was the gist, and I was longing to talk to Quintus about it. But Clarilla had made me promise to tell nobody but Quintus, so I couldn't discuss it in front of Titch. However, we could discuss our latest travel plans.

"So I'm off to see Albia, and you're off to visit Ostorius Magnus," I said to Quintus. "You'll be setting off tomorrow, presumably?"

"I could go today."

"If you wait till tomorrow, I'll come with you. I need a few hours here before I disappear again. Margarita's very good, but I can't just leave her to do everything."

"All right. Getting to know the Ostorius family can wait another day."

"Excuse me," Titch spoke up, "but is this the same Ostorius family that came to buy horses from you the other day? Me dad was telling me about Uncle Magnus."

"Yes, the same. Why, do you know them?"

"Only by reputation. I hope you got paid for the horses."

"I did, yes. Why? Tight with their money, are they?"

"Magnus is what you might call a legend in the legions." He stopped. "I don't want to speak out of turn if they're friends of yours. I was just interested, that's all."

"They're not special friends," Quintus said. "So come on, why is Magnus a legend?"

"He's the greediest man you'd ever want to meet. He's got the name Magnus Midas, because he wishes everything he touches could turn to gold. What actually happens is, everything gold he touches turns into thin air and vanishes."

"He steals, in plain Latin."

"So they say. It was never proved, otherwise he wouldn't have made centurion. You didn't mind me mentioning it, did you?"

"Not at all, no. It's interesting."

Nothing more was said till we were through Oak Bridges and almost at the main highway, where we'd turn left towards the mansio. Then Titch stopped the mules and turned to look full at Quintus. "Could I talk to you before we get back? It's a bit private."

"Yes. What's on your mind?"

"I've been thinking on what you said this morning, about how I could serve the Empire even if I'm not in the army. Like you do, did you mean, investigating for the Governor?"

"Something like that, yes. But I investigate for Caesar, not for any particular provincial governor."

Titch said slowly, "But the Governor here thinks a lot of you, doesn't he?"

Quintus didn't answer, so I did. "Yes, that's right."

"And they do in the army too, them as has heard your name. They say you help keep the Empire safe."

"You've seen me at work a time or two. Do you think that's what I do?"

"I reckon it is. You stop conspiracies, and catch rebels. You fight enemies inside the Empire, while the army goes out to fight 'em on the frontier."

"That's about the size of it."

"But you don't always work in Brigantia, do you? Or even in Britannia?"

He shook his head. "I'm not attached to any particular province, so I have to work anywhere I'm sent, like you did in the army.

I think the chance to see the world is one of the good things about the job. The pay's not bad either." He paused. "Could you see yourself doing the sort of work I do?"

"I…I'm not sure."

"I'll spell it out in plan Latin. I'd like to offer you a job as an imperial investigator. You'd work for me to start with, while you were learning, but eventually you'd be given assignments on your own. You said you want work where you feel you can make a difference. I can offer you that. What do you say?"

"I say thank you for the offer." He glanced down at his left hand. "But do you really think I can do it, now I've been wounded?"

"Why not? You can still use a sword, can't you?"

"Yes."

"And ride a horse?"

"Aye. Not both at once, though, and I can't carry a shield properly."

"How many investigators have you seen charging about on horseback brandishing swords and shields?"

Titch laughed. "So what would the work be? From day to day, like?"

"No two days are the same, that's another good thing about it. I look for enemies of the Empire, and destroy them when I can."

"Domitian Caesar…" Titch stopped. "I don't want to speak treason."

"Domitian's dead, so nothing you say about him can be treason now. If you were going to remark that he was paranoid, and made arbitrary decisions, and took out his personal spite on individuals, I'd say yes, he did."

"But did he make you investigators do that for him? Get rid of people because Caesar didn't like them, not because they'd done wrong?"

"I think the men based at court probably had to sometimes. I never did. I made sure I stayed out of Rome, and out of court politics. I only went after people I believed were trying to subvert the Empire."

"Quintus," I put in, "if you two want to finish this discussion privately, I can easily walk back to the mansio from here."

"Don't go on our account, Aurelia. If Titch doesn't know by now that you're good at keeping other people's secrets, he's not the man I take him for. All right, Titch?"

"Of course. Can I ask another question? Would I get some real investigating work to do even when I'm just starting, or would I be like a servant, looking after the horses and that?"

Quintus said, "You wouldn't be my servant, but you'd probably have to see to the horses now and then. You'd get real investigating, as you call it, but remember that much of the work would be boring and not very glamorous. I'll tell you what I look for when I'm recruiting junior investigators, shall I? First, I need men who are quick with their wits as well as with their blades. That's the most important thing. Second, I need men who believe that defending the Empire is a worthwhile occupation. I know you well enough to be sure you could pass muster on both of those."

"Yes, I reckon I could."

"The next point is harder. I need men who'll usually do what they're told without arguing, and yet have enough sense to recognise the rare occasion when they must disregard orders and use their own initiative. In the past, you've probably erred too much on the side of going your own way, but I imagine the army's knocked some discipline into you. Am I right?"

Titch half-smiled. "The army isn't keen on lads using their own initiative, even if they turn out to be right."

"And last but not least, I need men who are brave. I don't mean fools who aren't afraid of anything, because a man without any fear at all is a danger to himself and his comrades, and probably won't live long. But men who, in spite of being scared, get on with their assignment and see it through. Now, you've been through a terrible ordeal, which would have broken many soldiers, so there's no shame in owning up if your army experience has made you, shall we say, a bit more cautious about combat." He looked the lad squarely in the eyes. "If after everything you've suffered, the idea of working with danger, putting yourself at risk, doesn't appeal…"

Titch flared up like a volcano. "I'm no coward, and you've no right even suggesting I am! Cautious about combat? Well naturally I'm cautious, like any sensible soldier, but I've not lost me nerve. By Mars, if anyone else but you had suggested I had, they wouldn't live to brag about it after. So you get this straight. I can take on any job and not let anything frighten me out of it, if I've a mind to. I can be the best investigator in the Empire, if I reckon it's worthwhile. Just because I've had to leave the army, that does *not* make me into a coward. Have you got that?"

Quintus answered softly, "I never said it did."

They stared at one another in silence. Then Titch began to smile, a real smile that showed in his eyes. "Why, you cunning, devious old…by the gods, I walked into that one, didn't I?"

"I'd say you rode into it." Quintus was smiling too.

"I've never in me life met such a…no, perhaps I'd better not call you what you deserve."

"Feel free. I've been called most things in my time."

"It wouldn't be right. If you're going to be me boss."

Chapter XV

The forecourt was filling up nicely. Hitched to the railings were several native ponies, a couple of farm carts, and one official gig, and the main door stood wide open, showing the bar-room more than half full.

Quintus helped me down, and turned to Titch, saying softly, "Get something to eat, and we'll do the same. Then come and find me. We've got plans to make for tomorrow."

Titch saluted. "Yes, sir."

"No salutes. We're both civilians now, working with the army but not part of it. If anybody asks, we're engineers from the Governor's highways and bridges secretariat, and I'm giving you training in surveying and designing bridges. We can't disguise from your friends that you've left the cavalry, but we can stop them finding out what you've decided to do instead."

Titch grinned. "I'm sure anyone can design a bridge. Just hammer a few stakes into a river bed and lay some planks flat on top to walk on. It can't be that hard, can it?"

Quintus laughed. "There you are, you're a natural. I'll show you some of the basic skills as we go along. For what we're doing now, it's a very useful cover, because it lets a man go almost anywhere."

"Is it all right if I tell me dad?"

"Yes, Secundus knows the work I do. But remind him if he breathes a word to anyone else, I'll have his guts for catapult springs."

"I will. And, Quintus Antonius, one more thing…"

"Yes?"

"Thank you. I'll not let you down."

As soon as I could, I took Quintus somewhere private to tell him about Clarilla's revelations. It was a perfect spring day, so we walked out behind the mansio and into the woods that slope down to the bank of our little river. The trees all had their spring leaves, and I marvelled at just how many different shades of green there are in a wood, from the pale new grass to the golden-green of the oak leaves. The path threaded its way more or less parallel with the river below, and we could see a couple of maids doing the day's washing, and a short distance upstream one of the farm boys fishing. But there was nobody within earshot, so we sat down on a fallen log in the sunshine.

I told Quintus how Clarilla had asked for our help in pre-venting the proposed marriage with Vividus.

He wasn't surprised. "Clarus is keen on the marriage, she's right there. *He* wants our help to convince Clarilla it would be a good match for her. So he's hoping we'll find that the conflict near the coast isn't any of Magnus' doing, but is being stirred up by Bodvocos and his people. Clarus did say he wouldn't force Clarilla into an alliance she really objected to."

"How very considerate of him."

"No, I'm sure he means it. He's very fond of her, and I did point out how much he'd miss her if she no longer lived at the villa."

"Well done. But she's given me another assignment. She wants me to visit Bodvocos' daughter Elli." I told her the gist of it, including the part about Clarus forbidding her to interfere.

Quintus was delighted. "It couldn't be better. It fits in beauti-fully with my plans."

"Really? How? I thought you were concentrating on Magnus and his family."

"I am. I must check them out, I hope by staying with them for at least a day or two. I'll give the impression I'm on their side, of course, and hope to win their confidence and find out their secrets, if any. But I also need to discover what Bodvocos is up to, and I was wondering how to manage that, if I'm apparently in cahoots with Magnus. I couldn't think of any convincing reason for visiting Bodvocos without making him suspicious. Lucius can visit him, in fact he probably has already, as part of his search for information about the Gauls, but even he can't make social calls. But you can, you have the perfect pretext. You'll call on Bodvocos socially, and then visit his daughter, bringing her a letter from her beloved aunt Clarilla. With any luck you'll be able to go there more than once, because Elli will want to write a reply. You'll be staying with Albia, who hasn't taken sides in the dispute, even though she's been a victim. They'll never suspect."

"Yes, it should work nicely. While you get to know Magnus and his family, I'll be rubbing shoulders with Chief Bodvocos and Coriu, as well as Elli. And we can meet at Albia's from time to time to compare notes."

"Or even if we can't meet, we'll be close enough to keep in touch easily. Titch can act as messenger, if we need one."

I smiled at him. "You did well there, Quintus. Thank you."

"No thanks needed. I've always thought that boy would make a fine investigator, and so he will, as long as I can get him to obey orders once in a while. He's too intelligent for the army."

"Most men are," came a voice close by, and we spun round as a slightly-built dark man emerged from the trees behind us. "Greetings, Quintus Antonius, and greetings, Aurelia."

"Hawk!" I exclaimed, "you made me jump out of my skin. You might whistle a tune or snap a few twigs, to let us know when you're about."

"That would spoil the surprise." Hawk is my favourite native huntsman, a good friend and the most accomplished tracker I've ever seen. His clothes always blend into the colours of the forest, whatever the season, so today he was wearing a homespun cloak of leafy green. He had his hunting-bow over his shoulder, and his big wolflike hound at his heels. "I came to look for you, Aurelia. I'm glad Antonius is here too."

"I haven't seen you for a few days," I answered. "Mind you, you've probably been here all the time, just keeping out of sight."

"That would be telling." He sat down beside us on the log. "As a matter of fact I've been away visiting a very old friend. And I heard some odd news that I thought would interest you." As usual he spoke in British, while I spoke in Latin. We always conversed like that, even though we understood each other's languages well enough. I daresay it sounded odd to some people, but not to Quintus, who was used to it.

"Your news is always interesting," he said. "Tell us more."

"Aurelia, was your father called Lucius Aurelius Marcellus, like your brother?"

"He was. Why?"

"One more question first. Is it true Lucius is hunting high and low for Caratacus' gold?"

"No, he's looking for a missing Government cargo which the Gauls have stolen. But it isn't Caratacus' treasure hoard."

Quintus laughed. "It's gold though, Hawk. And he's offering a generous reward, so if you've found it yourself…?"

"Ah, now I begin to see. There are two missing hoards of gold, one stolen from a boat, and the other the hoard Caratacus is supposed to have buried."

"So it seems," Quintus answered guardedly. "What have you heard?"

"There's a very old man, a friend of mine called Nertacos, who lives over towards the coast. He's very lame and almost blind, so he hardly leaves his house these days. I'm fond of him, and I look in now and then for a beaker of beer and a chat about old times. He was a famous hunter and tracker when he was young, one of the best. I was with him the other day when Lucius' name came up in conversation, something about his men camping on the Headland. Nertacos said he used to know another Lucius Aurelius Marcellus who was in the army here thirty years ago. Could that be your father, Aurelia?"

I felt my heartbeat quicken. "It could, in fact it almost certainly was. Father served in Britannia in Nero Caesar's time."

Hawk nodded. "Nertacos knew him then. And he says Aurelius senior found Caratacus' gold, and Nertacos helped him hide it."

"Gods, Hawk, I thought that story was just a pleasant family myth. Now I'm starting to believe it."

"It's true then?"

"I don't know. I wish I did. We've heard that it may be possible our father found some gold coin and buried it, meaning to come back for it, but he never did. He didn't tell any of us about it, except one—er—distant relative."

"But he came back to Brigantia to set up the mansio. Didn't he go and look for it then?"

"We don't know if he did or didn't. We assume if he'd found it, we'd have heard. Tell us more about this Nertacos."

"He was employed by the Roman army as a local guide and tracker, and your father enjoyed hunting, so the two of them became friends. Good friends, when Aurelius saved Nertacos from being killed by a wild boar. Then Aurelius found a basket of gold in a wood while he was hunting on his own, and told Nertacos about it. He gave him half, and asked him to bury the other half for him at a certain spot they both knew, where they were sure it would be safe. They both swore an oath to keep it secret till Aurelius came back for it."

"Where?" Quintus and I asked together.

"Ah, that's the question! He wouldn't tell the exact place, he claimed he couldn't remember, but I don't believe that. His body is failing him, but not his mind. All he'd say was that the gold is in a basket, and the basket is in a pit in the noontide shade of a tall tree. From the top of the tree you can see the sea."

"In the noontide shade presumably means north," I said. "He didn't say what kind of tree?"

"No. Just that it was a big one."

"If Nertacos had a share of the gold when he was young, what did he do with it?" Quintus asked. "If a fairly humble hunter suddenly came into money, surely it would be noticed?"

"I asked him that. He said he went off travelling round the Empire for a couple of years, seeing the world and spending money on wine and women and adventures. Then he came back to his home near the coast here, met a girl, and settled down again as a hunter. Of course that could just be another of his tales, but knowing him, I can believe he'd do that when he was young and free."

"Then tell me honestly, Hawk," I asked, "can we believe Nertacos' story? Do you believe it?"

"I think so. Though of course his family don't. They've always regarded him as a muddled old man who rambles on about days gone by."

"When Aurelius never came back," Quintus wondered, "why wasn't Nertacos tempted to dig up the rest of the treasure for himself?"

"Perhaps he was tempted. But he wouldn't break a promise to a friend who'd saved his life."

"What I don't understand," I said, "is why in the gods' name didn't Father simply take his share of the gold with him? Why bury it, especially if that meant entrusting the job to someone else?"

"It was quite a large amount, apparently, and your father thought it would be impossible to keep it secret, or safe. His cohort was on the march most of the time, living in temporary camps, moving on every day or two. There was nowhere he could safely hide such a quantity of coin, and he was afraid it would be stolen. He said there was a known thief in his unit, or I suppose a strongly suspected one, who would have made off with it."

"Sounds like Magnus Midas," I joked, remembering Titch's story.

"That's extraordinary!" Hawk exclaimed. "That was the name Nertacos remembered. So you know this story after all?"

"Not all of it, but it ties in with something else I've heard about those old days. Hawk, could we meet Nertacos ourselves? If he does know the hiding-place, he might be prepared to reveal it to Aurelius' children. Perhaps if we bring Lucius too…"

"Why, yes, he'd love to see you. You're his friend's children, and what's more, you're a fresh audience for his tales. He lives with his daughter, their hut's not hard to find." Hawk gave us directions, but added, "The gods know whether he'll tell you where the gold is. But mention my name, and good luck." He smiled. "I'll expect at least a gold piece as a reward, you know, if he tells you."

"Of course," I agreed. "We won't forget."

He became serious again. "I'm only teasing. I'm not sure I'd want it, if I'm honest. Gold is deadly stuff, it brings out the worst in people."

"You're telling us to watch our backs?" Quintus asked, serious also.

"I am. I wish you good hunting, but take care, both of you. And bring me news of Nertacos when you come back." He stepped into the trees, and vanished from view.

Quintus and I sat for a while, trying to digest this astonishing information, and decide what we should do about it. I don't know how long we sat there, but eventually we heard a voice calling our names, and walked back through the trees towards the paddocks. Titch was standing by the fence, beckoning us to hurry.

"Brutus and his men are here, sir. They're on the forecourt now."

"What do you want them to do—go to Albia's today?" Quintus asked me.

"I think so, yes. Albia may as well have some extra protection straight away. We three can leave in the morning, can't we?"

We hurried to the forecourt to greet them. Brutus was as solidly reassuring as ever. I told him how glad I was that he'd be helping us, and introduced him to Quintus and Titch. "Can you leave for Albia's farm today, Brutus? You might not get all the way, but..."

"Maybe not immediately, but certainly in about an hour, when I've made sure these lads are reasonably well armed and prepared. Could we borrow a couple of pack mules, please, for equipment?"

"By all means. Take a carriage if you'd rather, or a wagon."

"No, I want to travel light. Mules will be fine. Are you coming up to your sister's place too?"

"For a few days, yes, just to make sure everything's in order. But Quintus and I will stay here tonight, and leave tomorrow. I only got back from there yesterday, and I need a little time here to make arrangements before I go away again. You know Albia, of course, but I don't think you've met her husband Candidus. Or the children, come to that."

"I didn't realise you knew Albia," Quintus put in. "That's good."

"I've known both the ladies for many years," Brutus smiled. "Well they were girls when I first met them. I served under their father, you see, and we left the army at more or less the same time. He invited me to stay once at their house at Pompeii. 'Course, we were all a lot younger then. We had good times though, didn't we?"

"We did. Quintus' home was in Pompeii too. Until...you know."

We were all silent a few heartbeats. The others were perhaps thinking of Pompeii. I was reflecting that Brutus had known father, and that might mean he knew...well, there was only one way to find out.

"Brutus, when you knew Father..."I stopped, suddenly realising as I formed the next few words how odd they were going to sound. "That is...we've had a bit of a surprise in the family lately. We've heard that Father had a son born here in Britannia, a half-brother to me and Albia and Lucius, that none of us knew anything about. It's hard to believe a thing like that after all this time, and we can't help doubting the truth of it. I don't suppose Father ever mentioned..."

I paused, because Brutus had lost his smile and was staring at me as if I'd just thrown a pail of cold water over him. "Well...that is...yes, he did, as it happens. But it's difficult, because I took an oath not to say anything to a living person until your father had told all of you about it."

"But he never did, Brutus. And he never will now."

"What have you heard about this brother?" Brutus asked.

"Father knew a native girl called Huctia in Glevum when his legion was based down there. They saw a lot of each other, but then Father's cohort was moved to Lindum, and he lost touch with the girl. She had his baby but he never knew about it, until he found out by pure chance years later. By that time the son was a grown lad called Rollus, and father wrote to Huctia saying he planned to bring them both up to Brigantia, because he was just setting up the mansio at Oak Bridges. He died soon after. So he never brought them up north, and he never mentioned anything about Huctia and Rollus to us."

Brutus scratched his chin thoughtfully. "It can't hurt to tell you now what I know, as you've found out so much already. When we were together in Pompeii, Aurelius told me about Huctia, and that he had a son born to her over here. He said more than once that he planned to settle in this province to be near the boy. 'Course, I've never met him. Have you?"

"Lucius has. Albia and I have only seen his dead face."

"He's dead? That's sad. Your dad was proud of you three children of his marriages, and of the boy Rollus too. He'd have liked you all to meet. I remember he joked about Rollus being the only one of his children who looked like him."

"But that's not right," I said. "He didn't..."

"He resembled Aurelia's father?" Quintus interrupted sharply, startling me because I'd forgotten he was there. "What did Aurelius senior look like? I never met him, you see."

"No, you wouldn't have. Well, he had brown hair and grey eyes, a high forehead, and of course a great big nose, and a heavy jaw. And Rollus took after him. A chip off the old marble."

"That sounds like Father," I agreed.

"But not the man in the box," Quintus said.

I felt excitement rising inside me. "Brutus, you're sure about the description? After all it's a long time ago."

"'Course I'm sure. Why?"

"Never mind, it doesn't matter." But it did matter, because Brutus' description in no way matched the man who'd claimed to be our brother, with his fair hair and eyebrows, thin nose, and blue eyes. So he wasn't our brother after all! He was a traitor, but not an Aurelius traitor.

Suddenly I realised what a burden I'd felt our half-brother's treachery to be, even though Quintus had reassured me that Lucius was safe from suspicion. And the burden had just fallen off my back. My heart was lighter than it had been for days.

Chapter XVI

We left at the first cock-crow, before it was fully light. There were four of us: Quintus, Titch and I, and Taurus, who insisted on coming too. And if you think a slave can't insist on anything, you've never owned a servant like Taurus, who's not only completely loyal, but has been with us so long he's more or less family. I tried to dissuade him, but he was adamant. "I can look after the children while everyone is busy. They know me, they won't be so frightened with me there. You and Master Quintus and Master Candidus probably can't be at the farm all the time. I can. Please don't say no."

So I said yes, and was glad of his presence as we rode up the Long Hill and along the highway.

Nothing of note happened till we got to Belinus' farm turning. Here Quintus called a short halt, and said he'd like to see the farm for himself, so he and I rode slowly down the rutted track towards the farmhouse. Taurus and Titch followed along out of curiosity, or perhaps to show that if *we* didn't need a rest, then neither did they.

The place looked more forlorn than ever now it was empty, with not even a few poor fowls scratching about among the weeds. Taurus dismounted and went towards the well, but I stopped him, remembering that Esico said it had been poisoned. When we looked over its side an indescribably unpleasant smell drifted up to us.

"Listen! I can hear someone round the back." Titch whispered suddenly. He jumped from his horse and began to run towards the rear of the house, pulling out his knife. Quintus and I did the same, moving fast but quietly, and when we reached the open ground behind the building a very odd sight confronted us.

In a field some distance away four men were digging a deep trench in the ground, about five paces long, under a group of tall trees. They were singing as they dug, and facing away from us, so we couldn't identify them, but at least we had time to watch them before they noticed us. They were dressed in the usual serviceable scruffy clothes that any peasant, or for that matter any sailor, might wear.

One of them must have heard us or sensed our presence, because he looked round, dropped his spade, and called out, "Visitors, boys! Let's go!" The others dropped their spades too, and they bolted away across the field. We couldn't catch them, they had too big a start.

We all stood gazing at the trench, until Taurus said, "Quite good spades, these. I'll take these along to Mistress Albia's."

We made a quick search of the house and barns, but found nothing amiss. It seemed the men hadn't gone inside at all. We re-mounted and resumed our journey, speculating about what the men had been doing.

"They must have been burying something," Titch said. "A dead sheep, or a cow?"

"The trench is the wrong shape for that," I objected. "It'd be about right for a body or two."

"Aye, that's it! They're Voltacos' men, and they're disposing of someone they've killed."

"They hadn't a corpse with them," Quintus pointed out. "Perhaps they were sinking a new water-channel, or a pond? But if they were doing something as useful as that, why run away?"

"They might be digging an underground hiding-place for weapons," I suggested. "Maybe Bodvocos has been collecting arms and wants to store them well off the beaten track."

Taurus said, "You know what I think? You're looking at this from the wrong side of the gate. I don't think they were burying anything. I think they were looking for something that was buried already."

I laughed. "You mean like Caratacus' gold?"

"Yes, why not?"

"Well then, they haven't found it."

"Not yet," he agreed, "but we interrupted them. It could still be there. Perhaps it's buried too deep."

"Perhaps it isn't there to find."

We were still arguing when we reached the sheep pasture, We couldn't see either Cattos or Balca, but everything was reassuringly calm, the sheep grazing quietly and the lambs eating or playing. When Titch gave a piercing whistle, the two youngsters came out from behind the wooden hut.

"Good morning, Aurelia." Balca smiled at me, and cast an appraising glance over the rest of the group. "Have you brought us more reinforcements? We saw the men come up here yesterday."

"Yes, we're here to help too, and we're going to be staying with Albia and Candidus for a while, till the trouble here blows over. Brutus and his men, who came yesterday, will give everyone more protection, including the sheep pasture here, and they'll patrol down as far as Esico's farm."

"Thank you," Balca said. "That's excellent."

I made the introductions. I described Quintus as a government official who'd come to investigate the raiders, and she greeted him with formal courtesy. I said Taurus was one of our most useful guards, and she nodded politely. But when I presented Titch as Quintus' assistant, she responded with a warm smile and a flash of eye that he didn't miss, though he pretended to.

"Have you seen any more of the Long-hairs since we were here last?" I asked them.

They both shook their heads. "I expect they've heard we've got sling-shots now," Cattos suggested.

"Slings are fine for emergencies," Titch said. "But you could do with some bows and arrows here."

"Just what I've been thinking," Balca agreed. "I'd love to learn to use a bow, and I'm sure I could, I'm as strong as any lad my age. But Father says it isn't a proper weapon for a woman. I've asked a couple of the boys in the guard to teach me, but they're all too scared of Father to risk it."

"I can teach you, if you like," Titch offered.

"Would you? Would you really?"

"If Quintus Antonius can spare me for an hour or two. It's not the teaching that'll take the time, it's practising hard."

"I'd practise all right. Are you a soldier then?"

Titch nodded. "I enlisted in the cavalry, and I learnt to shoot a bow there, because we were quartered next door to a squadron of Syrian archers. I've transferred to a more important unit now," he added loftily. "But I still keep up my weapons practice, naturally."

The girl's obvious admiration must have pleased him. I managed not to smile, and avoided looking at Quintus, who had developed a sudden coughing fit and turned away.

"That'd be all right, sir, wouldn't it?" Titch asked Quintus. "I can spend some time here, giving Miss Balca archery training? I'll be well placed to keep an eye out for any trouble, and I can ride back to the empty farm every now and then and let you know if anyone unauthorised goes there."

"You can stay till noon," Quintus answered. "Then ride up to Albia's farm. I'll want you with me this afternoon when I go to visit Ostorius Magnus."

Balca exclaimed, "You're going up to the Fort? Whatever for?"

"Part of my enquiries about the sea-raiders. I'll be visiting several people with land near the coast in due course. But I'm intending to go to Ostorius' house, not to any fort."

Balca laughed. "That's what we all call his house, because it's built like a fort. Well on the outside, anyway. I've never actually been in it."

"Like a fort? How extraordinary," Quintus said. "You'd think after years and years in the army, the last place he'd want to live would be a building that reminded him of army life."

"He and his nephews are all ex-army," she said. "Except the poet. I wish you joy of the lot of them."

Quintus smiled his most dazzling smile. "That sounds as if you don't like them much."

She said nothing.

"I've never met any of the Ostorius family, so you can give me some advance briefing, if you will. What's Magnus like?"

She shrugged. "I don't know him well."

"But what you do know, you dislike?"

"Oh, if he was just a typical greedy settler, I could put up with him. But I think he's somehow conspiring with the Gauls. I'm sure he was behind the attack on Belinus, though it was some of Voltacos' men who actually did the dirty work. And my father had his arm broken when he was caught out on his own at night by a couple of them. He's pretty sure that was on the orders of Magnus, or maybe Vividus or Ferox. One's just as bad as the other."

"That's a serious allegation," Quintus said, as if considering it for the first time. "Have you any definite evidence that the Ostorii are making trouble?"

"I've never actually seen them," she admitted. "But for one thing, they've never been troubled by any raids themselves. They have pastures on the Headland, you'd think the bastards would help themselves to a sheep or a goat now and then. And second, the folk that are getting attacked are all our men from the Parisi tribe, never Romans. Like poor Belinus. And now they've killed Nertacos, one of the oldest men of the tribe, even older than the Chief..."

"Nertacos?" I stared at her. "Nertacos the huntsman?"

"That's right. He used to be, years and years ago. He's been too old and blind lately, except in his dreams, poor old man. But now he's in the Otherworld, so he'll be hunting again. Did you know him?"

"An old friend of his at Oak Bridges was telling me about him just the other day, and I promised to visit him and bring him greetings. But you say the raiders have killed him? What happened?"

"His daughter found him, quite close to their house. He was lying at the bottom of a steep bank, where the ground drops down almost sheer. His neck was broken. He'd been pushed over the edge, everybody says so."

"He couldn't just have fallen?" Quintus asked. "You said he couldn't see."

She shook her head. "He knew every inch of that land, with his eyes or without them. And his body was covered in bruises, and a couple of his fingers were broken. His daughter didn't know what to make of it, she's a simple girl. But Father says he must have been beaten and tortured."

I felt cold inside. "Tortured? But why?"

"Perhaps," she said slowly, "they thought he knew something important that they wanted him to tell them. But I bet he didn't. He could be a stubborn old mule."

"I'll miss him," Cattos put in. "I used to love the wonderful stories he told us when we went round there."

Balca smiled. "We never knew if they were true, but while he was telling them, we believed every word."

"Did he have a story about buried treasure?" I asked.

Cattos looked at me in surprise. "Why yes, how did you know that? It was about Caratacus' gold, he said he knew where it was hid. Mind you, he didn't ever tell the exact spot, just that one day he'd go and dig it up, so he could be very very rich."

"I never believed that one," Balca said scornfully. "Everybody between here and the Humber has searched for Caratacus' gold for years, and never found any..." She stopped suddenly. She had seen the same connection I'd made. "You think that's what the Gauls are looking for?"

"There's a rumour that they are," Quintus said cautiously. "If you don't mind a bit of advice, I wouldn't go around repeating Nertacos' old story about it, except to people you know you can trust."

She said gravely, "No. No, we won't."

"And now we should be moving," Quintus said. "You've been very helpful. I expect we'll meet again." He darted a quick sideways glance at Titch.

"Are you coming to our Beltane feast?" she asked. "The Chief keeps open house for everyone in this whole area."

"Beltane?" I never can remember when these native festivals are. "Isn't that quite soon?"

"Yes, the first day of May—the Kalends, you'd call it. Only two days away. It's always a wonderful party. Do come if you can. If you're staying with Albia and Candidus, you can come with them, they're bound to be there. Or if you stay with Ostorius Magnus, come with him," she added with an air of disgust. "Chief Bodvocos has invited the Ostorii too, though the gods know why. He says it's traditional to include everyone, especially the neighbours, and Ostorius' land adjoins ours on the Headland, so he has to. But I bet he's hoping they won't turn up."

"I've never been to a Beltane feast. What's it like?" Titch asked. "Would I be able to come as well?"

"Oh, you must!" Her eyes lit up. "It's one of the best days of the year. It starts at dawn with the fire-lighting, and then we all watch the Mother-gift ceremony in the big bay south of the Headland. The priests dedicate a gift to the sea, the Mother-gift. It's a special boat with offerings in it to bring good fortune for the year—corn and a honeycomb and a lamb, and two rag dolls made like a mother and child. When the tide is halfway out, they launch the boat into the water and let the sea gods take it away on the ebb. They say in the old days they used to put real people in the boat, but of course they don't now." She sounded almost regretful. "And after that we all eat and drink as much as we like. There are roast oxen, and deer, and piglets, lambs, fowls, and beer and wine and mead, more than we can possibly get through, and it's there all day long. By the afternoon some of the lads are always drunk, and Father's men have to drag them into the sea to sober them up and stop them fighting. It's terrific fun. And then in the evening we go up on the cliff and there's a huge fire, and the bards take turns to tell stories and sing songs. Do say you'll come."

"It sounds grand. I will if I can." His look said he'd make certain he could.

"And so will I," I said, "if you're sure the Chief won't mind strangers being there."

"No, it really is open house. Candidus and Albia will tell you. And they'll be bringing the twins this year, I expect. Grand little tykes, considering. Not that I'm all that keen on children as a rule myself."

"We'll give them your best wishes," Quintus said. "Now we must push on to their farm, they'll be expecting us. Thank you for your help."

"A pleasure to meet you, Quintus Antonius." But we could all see it was Titch she was pleased to have met. As we made our way back onto the road, the two of them were talking and smiling, too absorbed to wave us good-bye.

"Well!" I said when we were out of earshot. "So Titch fancies the guard captain's daughter. She's certainly a lively youngster. Isn't love a wonderful thing?"

"Wonderful. But if he's not ready to leave for Magnus' with me, I'll have his guts for catapult-springs."

"This Beltane feast," I mused. "If Magnus and his nephews can be persuaded to go to it, what would be the chances of getting them and Bodvocos to make some sort of public declaration of peace?"

"Pretty slim, from what we've heard so far."

"But surely neither side wants this feud to go on indefinitely. They just need a way of ending it without anyone having to back down. Perhaps their leaders would agree to drink a formal toast together, and declare publicly that they'll stop squabbling and combine against the Gauls. We could at least suggest it."

"But if either Magnus or Bodvocos is really in some sort of secret alliance with the Gauls, the last thing he'll want to do is promise peace, and even if he did, he wouldn't keep the promise."

"But it would mean he'd have to stop his part of the trouble-making for a while at least, probably while you were in the area, and that would buy us some time to find out what's really happening. Whatever he thought privately, he couldn't refuse to make peace publicly without giving himself away."

"That's true. But how could we manage it? They're both powerful men with reputations to keep up. Neither would want to be seen as the first to suggest a compromise, in case it's seen as a sign of weakness."

"Then we must suggest it to each of them separately, giving the impression that the other has already agreed. You're going to see Magnus today. I'll make a visit to Bodvocos today too, on pretext of delivering the letters from Oak Bridges. He's already invited the Ostorii to the feast, so perhaps he's halfway there. Beltane is the day after tomorrow, so we can't delay."

He nodded slowly. "It's worth a try. What have we got to lose?"

Chapter XVII

Albia's farm was as busy as a hive of bees. Brutus and his men were hard at work building a defensive stockade, an earth rampart with a wooden fence on its top and a ditch in front of it. It would be tall enough to give basic protection against intruders, and it would eventually surround the house and the part of the garden that contained the spring. It was a big project, but Brutus in his legionary days had helped build scores of similar defences, and the work was going well, with encouragement from Candidus and plentiful supplies of food and beer from Albia.

We got a warm welcome from Albia and Candidus, and the twins were delighted to see Taurus. He offered to help with the digging, but the children refused to allow this at first, and he went off happily to play with them.

"Where's Illiana?" I asked. "And her father? Divico's out in the fields, I presume?"

"He's helping with the stockade," Candidus said. "Esico and Illiana are inside. Poor Illiana's little boy died yesterday, so she doesn't want to see anyone but her father just now."

"It's terrible for her," Albia said. "The poor little mite was all she had left of Belinus. But he was never really strong or healthy from the day he was born."

She fetched wine, and we all sat down by the pond to discuss our plans.

"These men Clarus has sent us are a gift from the gods," Albia said as she handed round beakers. "I must say I don't like the idea of having a fence around our house, but Candidus says we have to have one for now, and if that's so, I want it built as well as possible. And it's very comforting to have so many strong lads about the farm just at present."

"Clarus has given Quintus an assignment while he's in this area," I said, "and Clarilla has given me one." We told them the details, and they were amused by our dual functions. They both offered any help they could give.

"Thanks, I think we'll be more than glad of it," I said. "To start with, could I borrow a raeda please, to visit Bodvocos? I don't think he's likely to be impressed if I ride up on horseback in my cavalry trousers."

"Of course," Albia said. "When will you go?"

"This afternoon."

"You've already had a long journey, Relia. Can't it wait till tomorrow?"

"I'd like to see Bodvocos' daughter as soon as I can. Clarilla's quite worried about her. And Quintus and I want to persuade Bodvocos and Ostorius Magnus that they should stop their silly feuding and think about making peace."

Albia smiled. "I wish you could. Relia. We feel as if we're caught between Scylla and Charybdis here, in the middle of somebody else's quarrel." She turned to Quintus. "Will you be going to see Bodvocos with Relia?"

"No, I'm off in the other direction. I plan to visit the Ostorii family, and if I leave it till fairly late to arrive, I should be able to get myself and Titch invited to stay with them overnight. That'll give us a better chance of seeing what the Ostorii are up to, if anything."

"Titch?" Albia exclaimed. "Titch is coming here too?"

While we were explaining about Titch, his new job and his latest romantic interest, the house-boy Nasua brought out the midday meal of bread, cold mutton, and tiny sweet onions. We set to hungrily, but eating didn't stop us talking.

"Young Balca mentioned," I said, "that Bodvocos is giving a big Beltane feast, and everyone for miles around is invited. Will you be going?"

"Oh yes, all being well. It's always a good day out, and the twins are just about old enough to enjoy it. Will you come too?"

"I'd like to, certainly. And we thought that, if we can get Magnus and the Chief to agree to some sort of public declaration of peace, the Beltane celebration might be the ideal place for it—somewhere public, a festive occasion, no threats of any kind."

Albia nodded. "It would be perfect, if you could bring it off."

"There's one practical problem that I can see," Candidus spoke up. "It's not a good idea for you to go alone to Bodvocos' place."

"I'll be safe enough, Candidus. I'll have whoever drives the carriage, and I can take Taurus along as a guard."

"I wasn't thinking about safety. But Bodvocos is extremely old-fashioned in his ways, and he simply wouldn't receive a woman he'd never met who called on him unannounced, except in a man's company. He'd be perfectly polite, but he'd have one of his people show you straight into his daughter's presence, so that you could have a nice womanly chat together. If you want to talk to him seriously about making peace with the Ostorii, you'll need a man with you to break the ice. I'd offer to escort you myself, but I really need to be here while Brutus and his men are at work."

"That's a blow, but I take your point. Quintus, could you escort me there before you go off to Magnus' estate?"

He shook his head. "I'd rather not visit Bodvocos so soon. I'm anxious to get Magnus and his nephews to trust me, which means giving them the impression I'm on their side in whatever quarrel they've got with the local people. If they found out I'd been to Bodvocos first, they might be harder to convince."

"Then Lucius will have to come along, I suppose. As soon as Titch gets here, can we send him to Lucius' camp with a message?"

"Well, I suppose so…"

"I've had a better idea," Albia said, and I noticed a thoughtful gleam in her eyes that I recognised from long experience.

Candidus had spotted it too. "Do we stand up and cheer, or run for cover?"

"Relia, if none of the men are available to escort you to see the Chief, why don't I go with you? He knows me, a respectable Roman matron, and I'm sure he'll agree to receive us together. Two Roman ladies, calling on the local chief and also on his daughter, will be respectable enough even for him. What do you say?"

"I say yes, let's do it."

"But will it work?" Candidus looked at us doubtfully. "He's so conventional."

"We'll make it work," my sister declared, and that settled the matter.

Quintus grinned. "Poor old Bodvocos. He won't have an inkling that you two sisters are a far more dangerous combination than if either of you were accompanied by a mere man."

"Of course he won't," I replied. "That's what makes it such a good idea."

As we were finishing our meal, Titch arrived, late but not disastrously so, with a broad smile and an excuse about not having realised what the hour was. We all teased him, even Quintus, though not before he'd said something quietly in Titch's ear which wiped the smile off his face for a few heartbeats.

"I want you to escort Aurelia and Albia on a visit to Chief Bodvocos," Quintus told him. "You'll drive them in a raeda, and Taurus will go along as guard. Not that they need one, if you're there, but to make the right impression. Bring them back here when they're ready, and then join me at the Ostorius estate, the Fort as they call it."

"Right. And when we get there, while the ladies are drinking their wine, I'll try and get to know a few of the native lads, like Coriu and his guard."

"You have an acquaintance in common, so that shouldn't be too hard. Unless Balca already has a young man among the guard, of course."

"She says not." He stopped, blushing, then hurried on. "Well, I'll harness up."

Albia's raeda was new, and her mules were a good pair from our own stables, steady and strong. Titch drove them at as good a pace as was sensible, given the rough country tracks we had to follow through the hills, and we enjoyed the chance to talk. I passed on all our news, including the information that thanks to Brutus, we now knew that Rollus wasn't, in fact, our brother.

"Poor Lucius," she said sadly. "He'll take it very hard. Still, if the man was a traitor, it's for the best."

We discussed how we'd try to persuade Bodvocos to make peace with the Ostorii. Albia was optimistic, and she had firm ideas about the best approach. What it boiled down to was that I was to let her do the talking, especially at first.

"He's a funny old stick, but I know him, and more important, he knows me. He'll give our suggestion more consideration if it comes from me rather than from a stranger. So just leave it to me. All right?"

"Willingly. From what I keep hearing about him, he's a scary old man."

She nodded. "Scary and powerful, used to his own way. But I think I can handle him."

The Chief's grand residence stood on a slight rise of ground, about two hundred paces from the sea. It looked imposing in the mid-afternoon sun, even though it was an odd construction to Roman eyes. It wasn't a roundhouse, as you'd expect a native dwelling to be, even on a grand scale. It was oblong, with a short two-storeyed corridor of rooms jutting out to one side towards the back. Yet its walls were of timber, not brick or stone, and the roof was thatched with straw and had no chimney.

Clustered quite close around it were several other smaller houses, and assorted barns, workshops, store-rooms, and stables. They were all contained within a vast enclosure, surrounded by two tall earthen walls, one inside the other, each with a deep ditch in front of it. We drove through the outer wall by way of wide wooden gates, hospitably open now, only to find that the entrance through the inner rampart was offset some distance to the left, forcing us to turn and drive slowly along between the two banks for some way. The gates of this second entrance were open too, and there were no obvious guards about, but in the blink of an eye both gates could be slammed shut, to turn the whole area into a fortress.

Titch headed for the main door, and before we'd covered half the distance, a young man stepped out in front of us, and we pulled up. "Good day to you," he greeted us in reasonable Latin. "What can I do for you?"

He was a typical fair blue-eyed native, but the weave of his fawn tunic was a shade finer than the other men's, and his boots and belt were of good leather. Then I gave up speculating, because Albia greeted him by name.

"Good day, Vulso. I've brought my sister Aurelia to see the Chief and deliver messages from some of his kinfolk at Oak Bridges. Aurelia, let me present Vulso, one of the Chief's senior guard."

The man smiled and gave a small bow. "Forgive me, Mistress Albia, I didn't know you at first. Welcome to our house, and welcome to you, Mistress Aurelia."

"Thank you," we both said. Not for the first time I was grateful for Albia's wonderful memory for faces. If she recognised the Chief's household with such ease, our visit would go more smoothly than I'd dared to hope.

She returned Vulso's smile, with a convincing and quite un-Albia-like air of diffidence. "I hope the Chief will forgive our coming unannounced. My sister only arrived to stay with us today, and we didn't want to lose any time delivering her messages."

"I'm sure he'll be delighted to see you," Vulso answered. "I'll escort you to him. Your men can take your carriage round to the stables and give your mules and themselves some refreshment."

He came towards the carriage door. I nearly forgot we were supposed to be behaving like refined ladies and began to reach out a hand to open it for myself, but remembered just in time, and changed the movement to a more feminine gesture, patting my hair to tidy it. Vulso opened the door and helped us alight, and as we followed him across to the house, I saw a servant directing Titch and Taurus towards the stable block.

We climbed the few steps into a big hall, which took up most of the building. There was a dais at one end of it with some doors leading off it, a vast fireplace in the centre, and a few more doors leading to rooms down the side opposite the entrance. Vulso sat us down at a small table near the door. "I'll go and tell the Chief you're here. I'm sure he'll be able to receive you very soon."

"*Be able to receive us very soon?*" I repeated the words to Albia, speaking softly although they roused my indignation. "He gives himself airs, doesn't he? As if he's some great nobleman or a high official."

She nodded. "He is, Relia, at least in these parts. His family come of the old native aristocracy, and they've always been friends to Rome. So when the administration was sorted out here, Bodvocos was left with a lot of his old power. After all it makes no odds to the authorities really, provided his people keep the peace, and pay their taxes on time."

"And it means he has quite a lot to lose, if he or some of his men are caught out harassing Roman farmers. Has he any sons to follow in his footsteps?"

"No, only Elli. That's why everyone sets such store by a marriage between Elli and Coriu. Bodvocos needs an heir." But there was no time for more, because Coriu himself appeared from a doorway at the far end of the hall and strode briskly towards us. He was informally dressed, in a leather kilt and boots and a sleeveless jerkin, and he made a very handsome figure even though his arm was still pinioned to his side.

He greeted us warmly. "Welcome to you both. Albia, how good of you to call. Are you well?"

"Very well, thank you, Coriu. Candidus sends his regards, and his apologies for not coming with me. He's anxious to stay on the farm at present, at least until our new stockade is finished."

"I understand. And you're welcome at any time. This is your sister Aurelia?"

Albia nodded. "You've met her already, I think? She's the innkeeper at the Oak Tree mansio, where you went to have your broken arm set."

He smiled at me. "Of course, just briefly. Please tell that Greek doctor my arm is feeling much better, and I'm being good and not trying to use it yet, even though it's very frustrating."

"I'm glad it's healing well."

" Vulso tells me you've brought some messages for Lord Bodvocos?"

"For the Chief and for his daughter, from Chief Councillor Silvanius and his sister Clarilla. They're friends of ours at Oak Bridges, and when they heard I was coming to visit Albia, they asked me to bring letters for you." I decided to follow Albia's example and behave as he'd expect a Roman lady to do. "I hope it won't inconvenience them, my coming to see them without sending word first. I've just arrived at Albia's, and I didn't want to delay delivering the letters. In these uncertain times..."

"Uncertain is right," Coriu agreed. "The Chief will be pleased if you'll join him now. As for Elli, I'm sure she'll be delighted with some female company. She's been unwell for the last few days, and has had to keep to her room, which I know she finds very boring."

"I'm sorry to hear she's unwell," Albia said. "She was in radiantly good health when I saw her last month. It's nothing serious, I hope?"

"I hope not too. One of these mysterious women's complaints, which is making her very tired. Seeing new faces will cheer her up."

We followed him into a large, light room, overlooking the front portion of the enclosure, with the two earth banks in the foreground, and beyond them a slope of ground and a distant glimpse of the sea. The room was set out as a kind of audience chamber, and the furniture was well-made, with rich inlays and good carvings. Bodvocos sat in a huge throne-like chair with elaborate back and arms, and a cushioned foot-rest. It was impressive, though it didn't look particularly comfortable. There were several more chairs, a couple of small tables with inlaid tops, and a polished desk in one corner where a thin elderly secretary sat writing. Bodvocos was keeping him busy, to judge from the pile of papers and note-tablets in front of him.

Bodvocos didn't get up as we entered. Coriu introduced us both, and he said, "Welcome, ladies," and gave us a rather con-descending smile. "It's good of you to visit us. You'll take some wine?" His Latin was fluent, with a native lilt to it.

We all sat down, and a manservant came in and placed a tray on one of the small tables. He poured out wine, and handed round plates with nuts and small slivers of cheese, and some odd-looking brown cakes. The wine was a good Italian white, and the jug, beakers, and plates were of pewter.

There was a longish pause while we all sipped and chewed and wondered what to say. I took the chance to study the Chief. I meet plenty of natives, but apart from Clarus, I'd never met one with this much clout. He was older than I'd expected, perhaps fifty-five, with a lined face and a small neat grey beard. His hair and eyebrows were grey too, but the blue eyes beneath them were sharp. He wore a finely-woven wool tunic, and he had a thick gold collar round his neck and a couple of gold bracelets on his right arm. So if he was a Roman citizen—and I assumed he must be, if he was acting for the government—he preferred not to flaunt the fact by wearing a toga.

The silence lengthened. The Chief must be waiting for one of us to explain why we were calling on him. Quintus had said it was against the custom for a woman to pay him a visit by herself. Even with Albia there, and armed with my messages from his relatives, the Chief's welcome was only what basic politeness demanded. I could make a conversational opening, but Albia had warned me to leave the talking to her.

"It's good of you to receive us, Lord Bodvocos," Albia said. "My sister has been so looking forward to meeting you, having heard about you from your relatives in Oak Bridges."

"Indeed?" He relaxed a little.

I said. "I hope you won't think it's impertinent when I say I know you already by reputation. Chief Councillor Silvanius has talked about you often."

A small smile twitched his mouth. "What has he said?"

That was a tricky one. I could hardly tell him Silvanius wanted to know whether he was allowing his men to harass Romans. "He mentioned visiting you at Beltane last year," I improvised. "He and Clarilla enjoyed that enormously. And he's always saying what a peaceful district this is, and how he admires the way you govern your people." I picked up one of the scrolls I'd brought with me, and crossed the room to hand it to the Chief, who accepted it with a nod. "Here's the letter he asked me to bring, and he said I was to convey his and Clarilla's greetings and good wishes."

"Thank you." He opened the scroll carefully and read through it. His expression softened a little more, and he looked at me with growing interest. "My kinsman writes a pretty letter."

"He's always had a way with words," I answered.

"He says that you are among his most valued friends, and he sometimes even seeks your advice in his dealings with the authorities, because your brother is on the Governor's staff. You take an interest in public affairs, do you?" It was half question and half accusation.

"I'm afraid I do, though people tell me it's not really a woman's sphere. But I'm my father's daughter, and he was a retired centurion, always fascinated by politics and government. He taught us that every citizen, man or woman, must be aware how the Empire is ruled. Didn't he, Albia?"

She nodded. "I believe you knew father, Lord Bodvocos, when he first established the Oak Tree mansio."

That broke the ice, and the Chief smiled at her. "I did. A fine man, and a brave soldier in his youth, they say. How long is it, since he set up the mansio? It must be almost twenty years ago."

They continued to exchange compliments and memories for a while, until Albia steered the conversation back to the present.

"And now our brother Lucius is on an assignment here. He came to see you the other day, I believe."

"He asks for my help against these accursed Gauls. Of course I've told him I'll do what I can. But if they were easy to apprehend, we'd already have caught them, wouldn't we, Coriu?"

"We certainly would. Aurelius has a squad of soldiers camped on the Headland, but I don't think they're having any luck tracking the raiders down."

"Our father used to say that local criminals can always outmanoeuvre soldiers," I put in. "They know the terrain so much better."

The two men nodded their approval at this statement of the obvious.

"I hope the raiders are caught soon," Albia continued. "Perhaps you heard our farm was attacked, and one of our servants killed. It was horribly frightening. We're building a stockade now."

"You're wise," the old man said. "But have you enough men to guard it?"

"Chief Councillor Silvanius has sent us half-a-dozen guards to help give us some protection. This has always been such a peaceful, safe part of the world, and I hate the feeling of being under siege. I shan't be truly at ease until the raiders are caught."

"I heard about the attack," the Chief said. "I'm sorry it happened. You and your husband have always been good friends and neighbours to everyone. I wish I could say that all those who've come to settle in this area show as much consideration."

Albia neatly took her chance to move to the topic we wanted. "You're thinking of the Ostorii, perhaps?"

Bodvocos looked at her keenly. "You've heard what they're doing? I appreciate that you'll feel sympathy for fellow Romans, but surely you can't approve of the way they're behaving?"

"So far," Albia said carefully, "I've heard only vague rumours of trouble between them and some of your people. They say they want to live peacefully with all their neighbours."

Coriu gave a scornful snort. "They've a funny idea of living peacefully. Plaguing our farmers, moving boundary markers, breaking down our hedges and fences so that animals wander, or sometimes disappear altogether. And if you ask me, they're working hand in hand with Voltacos' men."

"Of course I wouldn't approve of any such thing," Albia answered. "Romans or not, that's no way to behave. Have you evidence of what they're up to?"

The men shook their heads. "Not evidence that would stand up in one of your Roman courts," Bodvocos admitted.

"I think the old uncle, Magnus, is greedy," she went on, "and I can well believe he's antagonising people by his efforts to get more land. He says he wants to build up a huge estate for his three nephews. But joining forces with a band of rogues…with respect, that doesn't seem very likely to me."

"Why not?" the Chief retorted. "What better way for him to get more land than to frighten a few farmers into selling him their homes?"

"And you've got to admit it's our own Parisi people who are being harassed," Coriu put in.

"Not exclusively," Albia said softly.

"I'm sorry, Albia," Bodvocos said. "Coriu was mistaken. You have suffered along with our people. Perhaps that's because you and Candidus have always been on good terms with the Parisi people. What you're doing now for Esico and his family…we know about it, and we appreciate it."

"Thank you," Albia said. She paused. "May I ask your help with something, Lord Bodvocos?"

"Certainly, if it's in my power."

"This—this trouble between you and the Ostorii. It's disturbing, and it's also taking time and resources away from fighting the Gauls. It seems such a waste to me."

He nodded. "To me too."

"Then is there no way you could make this quarrel stop?"

"We're not the ones…" Coriu began, but Bodvocos waved him quiet.

"What have you in mind, Albia?"

"Couldn't you get them to declare publicly that they'll settle any outstanding disputes with you and your household, and then live at peace with you?"

Coriu said, "We're not the ones disturbing the peace. They must surrender to us."

"But I'm not asking you to surrender anything to anyone," Albia said quickly. "Not at all. I'm just suggesting that you take the lead in bringing about peace. That you and the Ostorii should set aside any differences you may have, and work together to destroy Voltacos and his men. *They're* the men who are disrupting the peace, and I believe they're encouraging rivalry between your people and the settlers, so they can carry on their criminal activities with less risk."

"You've met Ostorius Magnus, presumably?" Bodvocos asked her.

"I have, yes, and so has my sister."

She glanced at me, like an actor giving a cue, and I took it. "I met him at our mansio when he came to buy some horses from us. We had quite a long chat, and he expressed himself as extremely worried about the Gauls, and the way this peaceful district has been suffering at their hands. From what he said, I think he'd jump at the chance to make it clear to everyone that he'll co-operate with you in destroying the pirates."

"He's bluffing, surely," Coriu put in. "Trying to disguise the fact that he's prepared to use the raiders for his own ends."

"But do we know that for sure?" I looked at him, and then at the Chief, and neither of them answered. "And even supposing he is in some sort of alliance with them, he's hardly in a position to admit it. He'll accept a proposal for peace, and if it's made before all the people—say at your Beltane feast—you'll be able to ask for his help against the raiders, and he'll have to promise to give it whether he likes it or not."

"But he won't keep the promise," Coriu growled.

"If he's innocent of conspiring with the raiders," I said, "he'll keep it. If he isn't, he may not keep it for ever, but he'll have to do so for a while or be publicly dishonoured. And consider this: if it's true he has been making use of the Gauls now and then, surely your best hope of putting him in his place is to destroy the Gauls as soon as possible. Then he can't."

Bodvocos smiled at me. "I think my kinsman Silvanius may be right when he says you offer good advice."

"I wouldn't presume to advise, Lord Bodvocos. But I'm worried for my sister and her family. I'd do anything I could, in however small a way, to help reduce the risk to them, and to other farmers."

"And you really think that if I ask him, Ostorius Magnus will agree to come to our feast at Beltane and publicly promise peace between his people and mine?"

"I'm sure of it."

Bodvocos sat still for a long time, considering. "Very well. Like you, I want peace, and I'm prepared to try to negotiate with him. I've already issued a general invitation to all our neighbours to come and celebrate with us. I'll send Ostorius a personal invitation today, and we'll know by his answer whether your assessment of him is correct."

Coriu gave me a look that would have curdled milk. "My lord, I want peace too, we all do. But not at the price of…"

"Yes, Coriu, I've made up my mind. I'll write a note straight away, and you'll send one of your men to deliver it, please. And now," he turned back to me, "I believe you have a letter for my daughter from Clarus' sister?"

"Yes indeed. Would it be possible for me to see your daughter while I'm here? I bring her greetings and messages as well as the letter."

Bodvocos inclined his head. "I'm sure she'd be glad to see you. She's a little indisposed this afternoon, but I'll send someone to enquire." He rang a small bronze hand-bell, and instructed the young page boy who appeared to find out whether Elli was receiving visitors. "Tell her that Albia and her sister Aurelia Marcella are here, with a message from her aunt Clarilla."

I said, "I hope Elli's indisposition is nothing serious?"

"Just some woman's complaint, I gather. Her mother's been nursing her, but she continues to stay in her room. Our wise woman here, who deals with our sick and wounded people, seems to be at a loss. Ah, here's the boy. Well?"

"Lady Elli will be delighted to receive Aurelia Marcella and Albia," the boy said. "Please to come this way with me."

Elli's room didn't lead directly out of the main hall, but was one of those off the side corridor, and it looked south, so the first thing that struck us as we entered was a flood of bright sunlight. A middle-aged woman with a careworn expression rose to greet us. "Albia, how good to see you. And this is Aurelia Marcella? Please come in. I'm Elli's mother."

We stepped in, and saw Elli lying full-length on a highly ornamented couch with wooden carvings on its back and arms. Her head was propped on a couple of cushions, her knees were drawn up, and one hand rested on her stomach, which was quite distended. A young maid sat beside the couch, gently bathing Elli's face with a cloth, but she stopped and left the room as we entered.

I could see at once that Elli would be strikingly beautiful when she was well. But now her skin was greyish and there were lines of pain across her forehead, and her blue-grey eyes had no sparkle, only a tired, blank expression. Her pale gold hair was long by Roman standards, but it hung limp and unkempt.

Her mother said, "I'm sure you girls will have plenty to talk about, so I'll leave you to chat for a while. Call out if you need me." She left the room and closed the door firmly behind her.

Chapter XVIII

"Forgive me for not getting up to greet you." Elli spoke good Latin with hardly a trace of an accent. "I'm not feeling my best at present. But I didn't want to miss the chance of seeing you, Albia, and meeting your sister. Any friend of Aunt Clarilla is very welcome."

I took the seat by the couch. "We're sorry to find you unwell. Clarilla will be too. She was worried about you, and I promised to let her know how things are with you. I hope whatever ails you is nothing too serious?"

"Not serious in itself, no. But for me, it couldn't be more serious." She hesitated, and there was an odd look in her eyes, of fear, almost panic. I thought, here's someone exercising an iron control over herself. Was she in severe pain, or was there some other unhappiness that she was trying to suppress?

I took her hand. "What's the trouble? Is there anything Albia or I can do to help?"

"I doubt that, thank you. I…well, I don't think anyone can help me."

"Tell us what's wrong," Albia said, pulling up a chair at the other end of the couch. "I've quite a store of herbs that help the aches and pains we women have to suffer. Is it your time of the month?"

"No, Albia, it's not that. I'm grateful that you should try to help, but…Aurelia, Mother said you've brought a letter for me from Aunt Clarilla. May I see it? She's such a sweet person, her letters always cheer me up."

I produced Clarilla's scroll. She untied it and read it slowly. Suddenly her face crumpled and she began to cry. I sat quietly holding her hand till she had herself more or less under control.

"Clarilla says you'll be a friend," she murmured, so softly we had to lean close to hear her. "And I know Albia is my friend too. Gods, I need friends now. Can I trust you both to keep a secret?"

"Yes. I promise." We both answered together.

"I'm not really ill, that's just an excuse to let me stay out of Father's way. I'm with child."

I stared. "*With child!* Are you sure?"

"I'm sure. And I expect it to be born any time."

It was hard to believe. Her stomach was a little swollen, but not exceptionally so, and her breasts weren't very big. She must be one of those girls who can carry a baby inside them for nine months without a change in shape that a generously-cut tunic wouldn't disguise.

Albia voiced my thoughts. "You don't look as if you're about to give birth. I was as big as a house when I was carrying the twins. And you've managed to keep it a secret from everyone?"

"Mother knows, and my maid. Otherwise nobody."

"Your father?" I asked.

"My father would kill me if he found out."

"Even though you're betrothed? Surely if you married Coriu now..."

"It isn't Coriu's child."

So the punishment would be brutal indeed. Bodvocos would consider she'd disgraced him, and Coriu would feel the same. Brides of the Parisi tribe have their marriages arranged for them by their families, and they're expected to be virgins.

"I haven't even told Aquilo. I wanted to, but I couldn't find the right words at the right time. I've enough trouble just seeing him now and then."

"Aquilo? *Ostorius* Aquilo?" Albia exclaimed.

"Yes. We're in love, and we want to be married."

So Clarilla had been right. "Your aunt realised you were in trouble. She suspected you were involved with someone…" I searched for a better word than "unsuitable," Clarilla's description, "…someone your father would disapprove of."

"Involved?" She laughed. "That's such a horrible word. In love, that's what we are. And neither Father nor Magnus can stop us loving one another. They can stop us marrying, especially Aquilo's uncle, because of the Roman laws about having to have consent from the head of the family, which Magnus would never give us. But once the baby's born, we hope both of them will realise they've got to make the best of it. And if they don't, we'll run away together."

Albia said, "And it's really due any time now?"

"Today, tomorrow, I'm not sure precisely, but it won't be long."

Albia got up and stood over her, and very gently put her hands on Elli's stomach. She nodded slowly as she took her hands away again. "I can feel it moving. I'd say it's wanting to be born."

"And neither your father nor Coriu have any idea you are carrying a child?" I asked.

Elli spread her hands. "Why should they? They don't expect me to…and they're men, it's not hard to put them off the scent. Tell them you have a 'woman's complaint', hint about bleeding and attacks of nausea…they'd rather not know the details. As for Coriu, I haven't seen much of him these past few months in any case. In fact he's been very aloof lately, not just to me but to everyone. I shouldn't be surprised if he doesn't want to marry me any more than I want to marry him. Perhaps he'll accept it when I tell him I can't go through with it."

I refrained from saying this was as clear a case of wishful thinking as one would care to meet. Coriu would never willingly accept such a thing. Whatever his feelings for Elli, he must want the marriage very much, because it singled him out as Bodvocos' heir, second in power and prestige to the Chief. But there was no point saying any of that. "Ideally, we need to get you away from here, Elli, to have the baby in peace and not be worrying all the time about being discovered. Would you be prepared to move out to somewhere else, if we can arrange it?"

"Prepared? Oh, it's what I've been hoping and praying for. But where? I wondered about going to Aunt Clarilla, but it's a long way to travel, and anyway she says her brother Clarus has told her not to interfere in my family's business, so I might not be welcome." She smiled suddenly. "But she's brought you to me, Aurelia. It's lucky for me that she doesn't always do what she's told."

"Neither does your mother, it seems. She's been protecting you and your secret."

She sighed. "Mother's been wonderful. But she's frightened of Father, he can be a bad-tempered bully at times. If he finds out—I suppose I mean *when* he finds out—I don't think she'll be very good at standing up to him. Aquilo and I will be on our own. That's why we may have to go away from here."

"If we could get you over to our farm," Albia suggested, "you can have your baby there. I know you'd miss your mother's help, but I'd look after you."

"Oh, Albia, if I only could. But I couldn't impose on you. You've got your own children, and you're expecting another, aren't you? It's a wonderful idea, but I can't."

"Of course you can. Take it as definite that I'd like you to come to me. Is it what you'd like too?"

Her face lighted up with sudden hope. "More than anything."

"Then no more argument," my sister said. "We'll take you home with us now."

"But Father will never allow me to leave here without a good reason. And what reason could I give?"

"Would he let you come to Albia's," I wondered, "if our Greek doctor Timaeus was there? He's a first-class man, and we could tell Bodvocos that he might be able to find the cause of your mysterious illness."

"A Greek doctor? The man who set Coriu's broken arm? Is he staying with you, Albia?"

My sister smiled. "No. But we can say he is. We can even send for him if you look like needing medical help. I don't think you will. You're young and strong, so all you need is somewhere peaceful where you and your new baby will feel safe."

Elli sat up on the couch and swung her feet onto the floor. "I've been praying to the gods, and my prayers have been answered. Thank you. Thank you both! I'll pack a few things to bring. Can my maid come with me?"

"Hold your horses," Albia said. "Don't do anything till we've persuaded your father. That may take a little time."

First we told Elli's mother what we planned, and she promised to help persuade Bodvocos. So she and Albia and I went back to his room, and found him deep in consultation with Coriu and Vulso. They politely broke off their discussion as we came in, but the Chief, despite courteous words of enquiry about Elli, gave the unmistakable impression that we were an annoying interruption to much more serious matters.

When we suggested that Elli needed to see Timaeus, who was at present staying at Albia's house, Coriu nodded approvingly. "He's a good man. Can he really help Elli, do you think?"

"Yes, we believe he can," Albia answered. "He's knowledge-able about women's complaints. He's visiting me because I've been having...but no, you gentlemen don't want to know the details, I'm sure." Her coy smile was a masterpiece, and the men all shook their heads.

"But why can't this Timaeus be summoned here?" Bodvocos demanded. "My daughter shouldn't have to go traipsing across country to see him if she's unwell."

I answered "Timaeus can't leave my sister's house just now, I'm afraid. Besides helping with Albia's problems, he's looking after Illiana, Esico's daughter. She's lost her baby, you know, and is quite gravely ill. So the doctor has his hands full, but if Elli's in the same house, he can care for her too, and find out what's wrong with her."

Bodvocos turned to his wife. "What do you think? Would Elli do better going to this Greek fellow than staying here with you?"

She nodded, and said quietly, "She ought to see this Greek doctor. The sooner the better."

Bodvocos shrugged. "I suppose she could visit Albia for a day or two. But she must be back here for the Beltane celebrations. She has to help prepare the Mother-gift." He glanced at Coriu. "And I'm planning to announce her betrothal to you during the festivities. I can hardly do that if she's not here, can I?"

"It will depend on what the doctor says," his wife answered. "Of course she'll be here if she's well enough, but you won't be able to announce it if she's ill, will you? You haven't seen her for a day or two, but as she is now, she can hardly stand on her legs. What with the dizziness, and being sick, and the bleeding…"

"Very well, very well. I'll take your word for it. Are you telling me she may not be in a fit state for her part in the Mother-gift ceremony either?"

"Not unless she improves dramatically in the next two days. I think we should prepare Balca to take her place."

"Balca?" Coriu smiled. "She'd be honoured, and she would do it well, I'm sure. If Elli really can't manage it, I mean, of course. But we want the ritual to go smoothly, my lord, don't we, or people may say it's a sign of the gods' disapproval."

"That's true," Bodvocos agreed thoughtfully. "I hadn't thought of that. Well then, send word to Balca that she may be needed. She'll know what she has to do, she's watched the ceremony every year. And, Coriu, if Elli is really ill, perhaps we should postpone the public announcement of your betrothal until she recovers. What do you think?"

"Perhaps we should. I'm not exactly fighting fit myself." He glanced down at his right arm, still held rigid at his side.

"I think it would be better to delay the announcement for a while," Elli's mother suggested. "Say until midsummer?"

The Chief looked at Coriu. "Well?"

"If you wish, of course. As long as the marriage itself still takes place this year."

"Then that's decided." The Chief turned to Albia. "Thank you for your kind offer, Albia. We accept, and hope your Greek fellow can find the cause of my daughter's trouble and make her well again, by Beltane if possible. I'd like her to be with us here for the feast day, even if she's not able to take much part in the celebration. It's a day for families to be together, after all. But you can tell her from me that if she really is too weak and ill to prepare the Mother-gift, Balca will be on hand to do it instead."

"Let's hope that won't be necessary," Albia said. "We'll do everything we can to get her well again, you can be sure of that."

"Thank you. Now I must ask your pardon, but I have work to attend to. I wish you all a safe journey, and my daughter a speedy recovery."

The Chief provided his largest raeda for Elli, who lay propped up on cushions, with her maid sitting beside her. I kept looking back at her from our carriage, wondering what I'd do if she went into labour on the journey, and we were all relieved when we reached Albia's house.

As it happened the first person we saw was Quintus, who was standing in front of the house chatting to Candidus. I jumped down from our carriage and hurried over to him. "I'm glad you're still here. We've had quite an eventful time."

"I've seen Lucius already," he explained. "I met him on the road, which saved me going all the way to the coast. He's had a small piece of luck. His men caught one of the Gauls and made him talk. He admitted that the raiders sometimes take orders from a local landowner who pays them well for what he called 'occasional services.' He didn't seem to know the name, he said their leader keeps that bit of information to himself. But he said one or two of the raiders aren't very happy working inland, they'd rather stay near the sea and their boats. I thought I might as well wait here for you and tell you that, and also hear how you got on with Bodvocos. Who have you brought back with you?"

"The Chief's daughter Elli." I followed his glance to where Albia and the maid were helping her down from the raeda. "Clarilla was right about her being in trouble. She's due to have Aquilo's baby any day now. If her father finds out, he'll kill her."

"*Merda,*" was all he said, but that summed up the situation pretty well.

Candidus greeted Elli warmly, as I'd known he would. Esico and Illiana gave her a respectful but friendly welcome, and Illiana stirred herself into activity to help as Albia put Elli to bed in the biggest guest room.

"You mustn't worry," Albia said. "We'll take care of you here, and the baby, when it comes."

"Thank you. Thank you all," Elli said. "When Aurelia came to me with my aunt's letter, it felt as if—I don't know, as if I'd been sentenced to death, and then reprieved. My mother and I could never have managed to keep my baby secret for long, living under the same roof. And then…" She shivered. "According to our custom, my father could put the baby to death, and me too."

"But would he really be so harsh?" Albia asked. "His only child…surely he wouldn't actually go through with it?"

"I don't know," she answered miserably. " I've been hoping against hope that Aquilo could think of a way out of this, but it's all such a mess." She covered her face with her hands, and then raised her head again, as if the thought of her lover had given her new courage. "I mustn't give in. There'll be something we can do, there must be. Could we get a message to Aquilo today, without the rest of his family finding out?"

"Quintus is going over to see Magnus today," I said. "Write a note for Aquilo and he'll deliver it. Or dictate it to me, if you're not up to writing."

But she summoned enough strength to sit up in bed and write a short message on a wooden tablet. I took it outside to the stables, where Quintus and Titch were saddling fresh horses, and Titch was reporting a conversation he'd had while he was at Bodvocos'. He repeated it for my benefit.

"Two of Coriu's lads, Mistress Aurelia. They were in one of the guard-rooms, and I heard them mention Caratacus' gold, so of course I pricked me ears up. One said, 'They'll never discover it, they're only a load of ignorant Long-hairs.' And the other agreed, and said, 'The captain should send us out to look, we'd soon find the right spot.' Then they realised I was just outside, and stopped. I made a point of talking to them in Latin, so they'd think I hadn't understood anyway."

"Well done. What do you conclude from that snippet of conversation?"

"Why, that the raiders have been told to find the gold, by Bodvocos or Coriu."

"That's how it looks, certainly. Aurelia, you actually met the great chief himself. How did it go?"

"I was surprised how amenable he was to the idea of a public declaration of peace. He's promised to invite the Ostorii to his Beltane feast, he's sending them a personal message today. He agreed quite easily, provided the Ostorii would agree too, and I told him they had already, in principle. So you'll have to make sure they do."

"I will. Though whichever of them is working with the raiders—Bodvocos, it seems—will no doubt break any agreement they make."

"Bodvocos himself said that, about Magnus of course. But whoever it is, they'll hope to keep things nice and peaceful for a while, long enough so you'll go away happy that the problem's resolved, and Lucius will take his men to some other trouble spot in the province. That gives us time to find out more, and also to track down the gold, if it really exists."

"Gods, Aurelia, don't say you're finally accepting the story of Caratacus' gold as fact?"

"Only as a remote possibility."

"And then you saw Elli and her mother, and decided to bring Elli here. Didn't Bodvocos object?"

I told him how we'd managed it. Quintus nodded, and said, "Titch, remember, not a word of any of this at the Fort. I'll be with Magnus and the nephews, you'll be with the servants, picking up what you can. We're presenting ourselves to them as imperial investigators, looking into Magnus' complaint about rebel elements among the natives, and we're letting them believe we're on their side."

"I understand. No mention of me giving weapons training to the guard captain's daughter."

"If that's what you were doing. Now, are we ready?"

"Speaking of Balca…?"

"Well?"

"Will you need me to stay at Magnus' tonight?"

Quintus looked at him warily. "Why wouldn't I?"

"I wondered if I ought to stand guard over at the sheep pasture with Cattos and Balca. With that old huntsman getting killed, they shouldn't be on their own in the dark. The raiders might come back for Cattos."

"We'll see." Quintus was smiling. "If I don't need you, you can go and play shepherds and nymphs. But I want you with me now, to meet Magnus and his family and their servants. I expect you'll be carrying messages to and fro in the next few days, and it's important they recognise you and trust you."

"It's just—I don't like to think of them out there on their own…"

"I said, we'll see. Now let's go. Take care of yourself, Aurelia." He gave me a swift kiss, then they mounted and rode away.

Chapter XIX

The days are long here in the north, and this one seemed longer than usual, with events crowding on one another's heels. But finally in the late afternoon Albia and I found a little space to sit and sip wine by the pond. We were just congratulating ourselves on having survived the busiest part of the day when Titch returned.

From the state of his horse he'd ridden like the wind. But not for the delight of our company or even Balca's, I soon realised. The pace had been set by another man, a slight, slim figure with dark hair and eyes and unmistakeably Ostorius features.

"Here's Aquilo," Albia said, as the two horses skidded to a halt.

"Albia, I came as soon as I heard about Elli," the young man said as he dismounted. "What wonderful news. Where is she? Is she all right? May I see her straight away?"

Albia got up, smiling. "She's fine, Aquilo, and of course you may see her. Bu you haven't asked the most important question of all."

"What question? I don't understand. Please, Albia, I've no time for games."

"The question you should ask is, how's the baby?"

"The baby's born already? *Already?*"

"Your son is here waiting for you. And he and his mother are very well. Come in and see for yourself."

They went indoors, talking and laughing. I stayed by the pond, determined at least to finish my wine in peace. It had been quite an afternoon. No sooner had Quintus and Titch left us than Elli had gone into labour. And contrary to the usual experience that first babies are never in a hurry to be born, this one had popped out in about an hour. Albia knew what to do, and Elli's maid helped with the fetching and carrying, so my contribution was mostly keeping the twins amused and out of the way. It's odd, but I felt quite squeamish about the birth and was glad nobody wanted me to help with it, yet I've seen foals born, and pups, and calves, and piglets, and never turned a hair. Still, I've always known that when the gods doled out to each of us our personal gifts, Albia got an extra portion of mothering skills, and I got none.

Titch was watching me. "The bairn's come since we left? Gods, that didn't take long. Just as well we got Lady Elli away from her father's place."

"You're not joking. Are you staying for a quick drink to celebrate the arrival of the new Ostorius?"

"I'd better not linger. I'll just see to the horses and get myself a fresh one, then I'm off again. My orders are to get back to the Fort as soon I'd escorted Aquilo here."

"You were escorting him? It looked to me as if you were racing him, and he was winning hands down."

"Aye, well, he was in a bit of a hurry. And he showed me a short cut across country that's really useful."

"See to the horses then, but before you go, I'm sure Quintus Antonius told you to report to me or Albia about the Ostorii. I'd like to hear what you both thought of them."

Titch grinned. "Actually he didn't tell me that, but I'm sure he meant to. All right then, thank you, I'll take a quick drink."

He walked the horses about to let them cool off, gave them a quick rub-down and a drink, and turned them loose into the paddock. He managed it all extremely well despite his injured hand, and was soon sitting by the pond holding a mug of wine.

I let him quench his thirst before I asked, "Well? Why is Quintus so anxious for you to ride back to the Fort? Some sort of trouble?"

"Could be. I was hoping to go to the sheep pasture tonight to look after Balca," he said regretfully. "But there's a poisonous atmosphere there, like a tavern when a fight's about to start, except nobody's actually drunk. Quintus Antonius wants me there in case there's any violence."

"Who's fighting who, then? It's in the family, presumably?"

"Aye, they've been rowing like cats and dogs ever since we got there, and before we arrived too, I shouldn't wonder. About whether to go to Chief Bodvocos' Beltane ceremony, the one Balca was telling us about. The three nephews all have different ideas about what they should do. Ferox, the middle one, doesn't want them to go at all, any of them, because he says they're enemies and it would be dishonourable to accept their hospitality. Vividus wants Magnus to go because he says it'll look odd if he doesn't show up, but he doesn't want him to promise anything about peace with the Chief because he doesn't trust him." He paused to take a long drink. "Aquilo wants them all to go and make a public peace declaration."

"And Magnus himself?"

"That was the most surprising thing. He was siding with Aquilo and favouring peace, at least that's how it was when I left."

"I agree, that is a surprise. Was he putting on a performance for Quintus' benefit?"

"We couldn't be sure. He said he was real glad Quintus Antonius was here, and Master Lucius with his soldiers, because it meant the Governor was taking him seriously when he complained about the natives making mischief. He said he'd only ever wanted peace with everyone, and he's prepared to say so publicly at the feast. Now that Aquilo's over here instead of at the Fort joining in the argument, the old boy may change his mind I suppose."

"Probably not, if he wants to make a good impression on Quintus."

"I don't think Quintus Antonius is that easily impressed," Titch said.

Just then Aquilo came hurrying out of the house, and almost ran to where we sat.

"Aurelia, have you seen my son? He's wonderful, absolutely beautiful. Oh, you *must* come in and meet him. And you, Victor, you must come and say hello to him too. Gods, I'm so happy, I feel as if I'm flying!"

"He's lovely," I agreed. "I've seen him already, and he's a beautiful little fellow. So I won't go in disturbing Elli again just now, and I don't think Victor should either, not when the baby's so very new. There'll be time enough later."

Titch gave me a quick grateful smile, which Aquilo failed to notice.

"Perhaps you're right. I'm glad you're still here, Victor," he added in a slightly calmer tone, "because I'd like you to take a message back to the Fort for me. I'm going to stay here tonight, and probably most of tomorrow too. Will you tell my uncle and my brothers this is where I shall be?"

"I will, sir, of course. What reason shall I give?"

"Reason? Why, the obvious one…oh no, I see what you mean. Uncle Magnus and the others don't know about Elli and me. I'll have to tell them soon, but I can't do it in a message." He looked perplexed. "I don't know what's best. I've got to say something, they're bound to be wondering…oh, my mind's whirling so much I can't think straight."

"Your uncle mentioned," I said, "that you're interested in music and poetry."

He looked even more perplexed. "I am. I don't see how that helps."

"Suppose you'd discovered from Quintus Antonius that Albia was entertaining friends from Eburacum—no, better still, Londinium—and one of them was a musician, an acquaintance of yours whom you haven't seen for years. You've rushed over to see him, and Albia has offered to put you up for the night so you can spend some time together."

"That's perfect! Thank you, Aurelia."

"Titch, can you make Aquilo's message about his reason for staying here sound convincing?"

He nodded. "I can. Just one detail to make the picture complete. What's the name of this old musician friend?"

"The name?" Aquilo smiled. "How about Trimalchio?"

We all laughed, but I was doubtful. "A character from a famous book? Won't they smell a rat?"

"Not they! None of the rest of my family read anything but treatises on warfare."

Titch rode off into the gathering dusk, and Aquilo went back to sit with Elli and their son. Albia, Candidus and I ate supper, and I found I was so tired I was falling asleep over my bowl. I went to bed early, and whether the new baby cried in the night I don't know, because I slept like the dead.

At home I'm always up with the dawn, and I couldn't break the habit of waking early, but I enjoyed the luxury of lying in bed awhile instead of rising to look after guests and prepare for a day at the mansio.

When I finally made my way to the kitchen, a good hour after sunrise, Nasua offered me warmed wine and bread and honey for breakfast, so I took a plate and beaker and strolled outside. Brutus and his men were hard at work on the defences, which were now beginning to look quite formidable. Candidus was talking to a couple of his farm boys, and Albia was looking over what remained of her garden after the recent raid. She waved a greeting and came over to me. "Relia, good afternoon! It is Relia, isn't it—my energetic sister, who used to boast she never could stay in bed once the sun appeared?"

I laughed. "You fed me too well last night, Albia, and I had a really good peaceful sleep. But how about you, and Elli and the baby? How is everyone?"

"All fine. We all managed to get a bit of sleep eventually, including Elli. The baby's feeding well, but it was a slow start, because Elli doesn't seem to have enough milk for him."

"So you'll have to look for a wet-nurse. What a nuisance."

"We've got one already. Illiana still has milk, and she's feeding him for now."

"Really? She doesn't mind doing that, after losing her own child?"

"No, in fact she offered to help, and it seems to be comforting her. She knows Elli of course, which makes it easier. I'll bring my breakfast out here and join you, then we can look in and see them again."

We were just finishing a leisurely breakfast when Candidus walked over to the pond. "Brutus says the stockade will be finished today, and they may even get the gate fitted. That's good, isn't it? Oh, 'morning, Aurelia. No need to ask if you slept well. I'm glad our comings and goings didn't disturb you."

"I was too comfortable for anything to disturb me, Candidus. Your boys have done really well, to get your stockade ready so soon."

"Yes, they have. Brutus' army experience made all the difference. I'm afraid my one year as a military tribune didn't equip me for fortifying farms. And I'll be glad when we can shut ourselves inside it if we need to."

"Presumably the other farmers round here are all putting up the same sort of defences?"

"One or two, but mostly not. They haven't the manpower, of course, but all the same it's odd. They don't seem to think extra protection is necessary." He sat down beside us and helped himself to Albia's half-finished mug of watered wine.

"I agree," I said, "that's odd."

"I've spent quite a bit of time lately visiting our neighbours, the other farmers between here and the coast. Most of them are natives, but there are one or two settlers, and I went round all of them. I wanted to encourage them to band together, so we can defend ourselves and one another. But most of them aren't interested."

"They don't take it seriously, you mean, or are they paying the Gauls protection money to be left alone?"

"A few may be paying, perhaps, but not the majority. They mostly agree Voltacos' men are a menace, and they've heard alarming rumours of their crimes. But they haven't suffered themselves. I asked all of them whether they'd had any trouble on their own farms, and they said no, not personally, but they knew the situation must be getting worse because of all the rumours. I couldn't find a single farm inland that's been raided by the Gauls except ours and Belinus'."

"Do you think the Gauls are deliberately spreading rumours to frighten people, so when they do attack anyone, their victims will be readier to give them whatever they want?"

"I suppose that must be it. But I was hoping I could persuade all the threatened farmers to combine against the Gauls, help each other, share information, that sort of thing. They all said they're willing in principle, but don't feel it's very important at this stage."

"Disappointing for you. But at least you're well protected now, thanks to Brutus and his boys."

"But I'm wondering if there's more to it. Suppose, just suppose, that in fact the only farms the sea-raiders have seriously attacked are Esico's and mine. Suppose we're not dealing with random raids by a gang of opportunists, but someone has deliberately chosen to harass Esico and his family, and us?"

"But why would they pick on you? You're on such good terms with everyone, you and Albia. From what I've heard, you haven't an enemy in the world."

He shrugged. "I can't imagine. Anyhow, let's forget about raids and pirates and all that gloomy stuff, and go and see Elli and the baby."

Elli was sitting up in her bed with Aquilo beside her. She wore that tired-yet-happy expression that new mothers tend to have, and Aquilo looked as happy and proud as if he'd just found Caratacus' gold. I made the usual enthusiastic remarks about the little one, his size, his beautiful blue eyes, his resemblance to Aquilo, his appetite. All babies look much the same to me really, but I know one isn't expected to say that, and I did my best. I tried not to think about Elli's remark of yesterday: "My father would kill me if he found out."

I said, "Elli, do you want us to send a message to your mother? Secretly, of course, but just to let her know she's now a grandma?"

"I've been wondering about that. Do you think Candidus could spare a servant to take her a note from me?"

"I'll ask him if you like." I strolled outside again and spotted Candidus some distance away in earnest conversation with Brutus. Before I could reach them, the twins came charging out of the house to see me, with Nasua following in their wake, ready to prevent them jumping all over me. In fact I wasn't the centre of their attention for long, because a rider came cantering down from the direction of the main road, and they shouted and waved as he pulled up by the pond.

"Titch!" I called. "Are you on your way to see Balca?"

"Not this morning. Later if I'm lucky." He swung down, and let his horse have a drink while he bent to greet the children. "All right, you young terrors, you go along into the house while I talk to Mistress Aurelia. You've got your hands full there," he grinned at Nasua. "Being a nursemaid is hard work, eh?"

Nasua flushed, feeling he'd been insulted, though I don't think that was Titch's intention. But I didn't want any ill feeling between these two. "He's their bodyguard. He keeps them safe for us, don't you, Nasua?"

"Yes." He smiled proudly. "N-nobody will hurt them while I'm here." He rounded up the twins and marched them off inside.

Titch said, "I've some news I didn't want them to hear. Magnus has been murdered."

My heart sank. "Murdered? Oh, *no!* This is what we've been dreading, the quarrel with Bodvocos getting completely out of hand. We'll have a job to stop a civil war breaking out now."

He shook his head. "It's true some of the Ostorius lads are blaming Bodvocos, but it doesn't look like the murderer was one of the Parisi, nor the Gauls neither."

"Who then?"

"He was stabbed while he was taking a bath. That means it must have been one of the family. No outsider could have got into the Fort, let alone into that bath-house, without being noticed and stopped. When you see the layout of the place you'll understand. It's as secure as a real military camp. More so than some I've been in."

"Who found the body?"

"One of his slaves, and he wasn't quite dead, but near enough. She said he muttered summat about being betrayed by the family, and mentioned Aquilo. He wasn't making much sense mind, and he died soon after."

"When was this? Last night?"

"Dawn today."

"Then at least the murderer can't be Aquilo. He's been here all night."

"Ah." Titch nodded. "That's what Quintus Antonius asked me to check, because we thought he hadn't been anywhere near the place."

"If this slave is speaking the truth, and the murderer was one of Magnus' family, it can only have been either Vividus or Ferox."

"Vividus was with Quintus Antonius most of the time, and Ferox has disappeared."

"Has he now? Interesting…Does Quintus want Aquilo to return to the Fort?"

"He does, as soon as possible. And he says could you please go too?"

"Try and stop me! I've been wanting an excuse to visit the Ostorii."

"He thought you'd say that. And he said he'll spill the rest of the beans when you arrive."

I laughed, because "beans" was Quintus' favourite password, and it meant he needed my help. "Are you riding back there now, Titch?"

"No, I'm to go and fetch Master Lucius and his men. They can look for Ferox, and if we end up having to arrest either him or Vividus, we'll need extra muscle. They've got half a cohort of guards in the place. Seems like everyone who ever served in the army with either the uncle or the nephews got a job from them afterwards."

"Right, I'll ride over with Aquilo. You'd best be on your way."

"I expect I'll see you later." He vaulted onto his horse cavalry fashion, to show he'd no need of a mounting-block. "That is if I haven't been sent off on another errand. I swear I'm covering more miles these days than I did in the army!" And he rode off, waving cheerfully.

The news of Magnus' death was received with horror, and everyone jumped to the conclusion that he'd been killed either by one of Bodvocos' men or by the Gauls.

"I don't think so," I said. "It sounds more like someone from inside the household." Aquilo wanted to ask questions, but I cut him short. "Let's talk as we go, Aquilo. Quintus Antonius wants us to ride to the Fort as fast as we can."

"Us? You're coming too?"

"Yes. Quintus has asked me to. You need someone who can vouch for the fact that you were here all of last night."

He looked shocked. "You mean they might accuse me of killing him? In that case I suppose I've no choice. But I hate to leave Elli and my son."

"I'm sure you can be back here again tonight, if you want to."

"And you know we'll take good care of them for you," Albia reassured him. "Now I suggest you go and tell Elli what's happened. The sooner you start, the sooner you can come back. Candidus, could you organise horses for them please? Relia, I wonder if you ought to pack a spare tunic and a comb and strigil in your saddlebag? You might end up staying overnight at the Fort."

"And people say *I'm* the bossy one in the family!" But I did as she advised, because I'd a feeling she might be right.

Chapter XX

Aquilo and I took the short cut Titch had mentioned. Apart from the first mile or so it was all across country, following rough native tracks that meandered between farms, and sometimes using no tracks at all. From the higher points we could catch occasional glimpses of the sea, blue and sparkling in the morning sun. It was more interesting riding than the roads would have been, and quicker.

To start with we set only a moderate pace so that we could talk. Aquilo wanted to know exactly what Titch had told me, and when I relayed the account of Magnus' dying words, he let fly some curses that I wouldn't have thought came naturally to a poet.

"Gods. I suppose it was Niobe who found my uncle."

"Who's Niobe? One of your family slaves?"

"My uncle's concubine. None of us brothers are married, so she rules the roost as mistress of the house. A scheming little piece. She's never liked me. I don't like her either."

"It's as well for you that you were with Albia and Candidus last night. Your friend Trimalchio can't be brought to give evidence, but they'll stand witness for you, and they'll be believed. Now according to Titch—well, according to Quintus, I suppose—the murderer must have been one of your household, someone your uncle trusted, because an outsider couldn't have found a way into the bath-house unobserved."

"No, especially not now. We keep a guard on the gate all the time, and sentries on patrol at night." He smiled. "All our neighbours used to laugh at my uncle's military ways, I know they did. But just lately, with these pirates about, I don't think they're laughing so loudly."

"Had your uncle..." I stopped to choose my words carefully. I wanted to ask Aquilo about the likelihood that either of his brothers was a killer. "Had your uncle quarrelled with anyone in the house over the last day or two?"

"He'd had rows with nearly everyone yesterday, especially Vividus and Ferox. I heard them quarrelling myself. Well I could hardly avoid it, I expect ships passing the Headland could hear them, the din they were making. But that wasn't so very unusual. We're the kind of men who have furious arguments in the morning, and make our peace by lunch-time. I never dreamed...Surely Vividus or Ferox wouldn't have...I mean we owe Magnus a great deal, the three of us. "

"We haven't got all the facts yet, Aquilo. It sounds grim, I know, but we can't be certain of what happened till we get there."

"You ask a lot of questions." His tone was accusing. "And you said that investigator Antonius asked you to come with me. Are you some kind of assistant of his?"

"I sometimes help a little in his investigations." Time for a change of subject, I thought. "Aquilo, I think we ought to get moving. The quicker we get there..."

"Yes, I know, the quicker I'll be home. By the way, please remember none of my family know about Elli yet. You won't tell them, will you?

"I won't tell them. I promise."

So we urged our horses on and rode flat out, or as nearly so as the country would allow. He was a good rider, as Titch had discovered, and the fast pace was exhilarating. I forgot the grim circumstances that made it necessary, at least until we came in sight of the Fort.

Then sheer astonishment caused me to bring Merula to a stop so I could sit and stare. "What an amazing place!" With a name like the Fort, I expected it would be some sort of foursquare, mili-tary-looking structure. But this was built along standard military lines. The outside wall was a stone rampart with a walkway on its top and a deep ditch in front of it. The main entrance was through a huge heavy gate that needed only a couple of sentries outside it to make it look like any porta praetoria belonging to any legion in the Empire.

"My uncle's pride and joy," Aquilo remarked dryly. "What do you think of it?"

"Impressive. Very impressive." That was the only positive description I could come up with, and indeed it *was* impressive. But it was also sinister, and simultaneously almost comic, because in this green, gentle landscape it was utterly out of place.

Aquilo laughed. "Tactful. Very tactful. And I suppose you're right, it is impressive in its own weird way. Uncle and the others love it, it reminds them of their glory days. I hate it." The last few words were said softly but bitterly.

We rode through the gate, and inside the rampart I was relieved to find the resemblance to a fort was less complete, but still too overwhelming for my comfort. There was a road leading straight ahead to a central range of buildings, where presumably the family lived. In front of these buildings was a large open space, and other buildings were spread out in a rather higgledy-piggledy fashion, at any rate not in the serried ranks and rows that characterised military bases. They were more typical of a farm too: store-rooms, stables, carriage and cart sheds, and barns. "The main house is built round a courtyard," Aquilo said. "And you'll be glad to hear there's a bath-house just behind it." Indeed I was relieved. In a real fort the baths would have been outside the walls, or at best in an annex.

We paused just inside the gateway, and I realised there was a sentry of sorts on duty after all, he just wasn't visible from outside. He came forward to intercept us, and I recognised him as one of the big Gaulish bodyguards who'd accompanied Magnus and Vividus to the Oak Tree when they came to buy my horses. He gave a military salute, which Aquilo didn't return. "Master Aquilo, thank the gods you've come. We've had a disaster here. Your uncle, our old master…I'm afraid he's dead."

"I've heard, Rinacus. A disaster indeed. I came straight back here as soon as I got the news. I was staying with friends last night…never mind that now. Where are my brothers?"

"Master Ferox is out, sir. We think he's on the farm somewhere, he usually is at this time of day. Master Vividus is with that investigator Antonius. Shall I tell him you're here, you and…er…your friend?" He glanced at me uneasily. I thought, why do the Fates keep directing my steps to places where an independent-looking lady is such a novelty?

"This is Aurelia Marcella," Aquilo said. "Aurelia, Rinacus is our chief guard."

"We've met before, Rinacus, I believe, when you came with Magnus and Vividus to the Oak Tree Mansio."

"Ah yes, of course." But it was clear he didn't remember me.

I said, "I'm a colleague of the investigator Antonius, and I've brought urgent information for him."

"Equally important," Aquilo said, "she's here as my guest, so make sure she has everything she requires to make her visit comfortable."

"Of course, sir. Will she be staying the night here?"

"I don't know, but I'll tell them to prepare a guest room just in case. Now we'll go straight to Vividus, don't bother announcing us. Where is he?"

He nodded towards the house. "At Headquarters, sir, in the big sitting-room. If you'd like to leave your horses here, I'll have one of the lads take care of them." He gave a shrill whistle, and a thin stable-lad came and took the bridles.

"Headquarters?" I asked as we walked across the wide space towards the big main building.

Aquilo grunted. "Another of Magnus' whims. It's positioned where the garrison headquarters would stand in a real fort."

But the house itself, to my great relief, wasn't military at all. It was considerably bigger than it appeared from the gate, because it had two wings of rooms jutting out at right angles behind it, forming in effect three sides of a courtyard. The fourth side was open, and there was a wide space with a few troughs and tubs of plants, meant to make the place look homely I suppose, but to me they just accentuated the grey drabness of it all.

The main part of the house was two-storeyed, which surprised me because there was plenty of space for building at ground level. When we mounted the stairs to Vividus' sitting-room on the upper floor I realised the reason for the design. It was pleasant to have some rooms high enough up to look over the ramparts and out into the countryside beyond.

Aquilo knocked, paused for a heartbeat and then walked in without waiting for a reply. I followed, and as we entered I heard Quintus' voice, half irritated and half amused. "But none of this is real proof, is it?"

Quintus and Vividus were seated on chairs on opposite sides of an ornately carved round table. Before them stood a young slave, a house-boy from his dress, white and scared. A beautiful woman was sitting on a stool near the window, but something about her pose told me she wasn't part of whatever discussion was going on. A jug of wine and several beakers stood untouched on a side table.

Quintus and Vividus turned towards the door as we entered, and Vividus jumped to his feet.

"Aquilo, where have you been? I've had men looking all over for you." I thought he was going to embrace his brother, but instead he went to the door, took a pace out onto the landing, and yelled, "Guard!"

Two burly men appeared. Vividus pointed at Aquilo.

"Secure Master Aquilo. Tie him up."

"Now wait, Vividus," Aquilo protested. "You can't do this! Don't touch me, any of you."

The guards hesitated, as well they might, but Vividus barked, "Do it!" and they obeyed. I expected Quintus to intervene, but he sat looking on impassively while the guards tied Aquilo's hands behind his back. The woman by the window watched closely too, but said nothing. The young slave boy glanced quickly round him and scuttled for the door, and nobody stopped him.

"Now," Vividus said, "we'll get to the bottom of this. Where were you last night, Aquilo?"

"I sent you a message by Antonius' lad Victor," Aquilo said, trying his best to keep his dignity. "I stayed with Candidus and Albia last night, because I got word that an old friend of mine from Londinium was visiting there."

"Can you prove it? Have you witnesses to confirm you were there all the time?"

"Of course I have. Why?"

"Why do you think? Because our uncle has been murdered, and with his dying breath he accused…"

"Vividus, let's do this in a seemly manner," Quintus cut in. "This is private family business." He glanced at the woman by the window. "Would you leave us, please, Niobe? We'll need to talk to you later, so please stay in your quarters."

She glanced at Vividus. "Do you want me to leave?"

"I suppose it's best, just for now. Off you go, girl."

As she glided across the room I saw how exceptionally lovely she was, tall and long-legged with shining brown hair and delicate fair skin. She was dressed in a fine linen tunic, and was entirely self-assured, walking confidently with her head held up, not at all the down-trodden slave. I remembered Aquilo saying that she ruled the roost here at the Fort, and that was certainly the impression she gave.

Aquilo began shouting at Vividus: "You're accusing me of killing Uncle Magnus? Gods, it'd be a laughing matter if it wasn't so serious. Of course I didn't kill him. I can prove I was at Candidus' place. And why are you being so high-and-mighty? Where were *you* last night and at dawn this morning?"

"How dare you…"

"Gentlemen," Quintus interrupted, "this is getting us nowhere. Vividus, I don't want to issue orders in another man's house, so I'll make this a request. Please would you tell your men to release your brother Aquilo." The brothers gazed at him almost in surprise, as if they'd forgotten he was there.

Vividus shook his head. "No, Antonius. I'm sorry, but until I have proof of where Aquilo was last night…"

"*I* have proof," Quintus answered. "Or at least my assistant has. Aurelia?"

Vividus noticed me for the first time, and looked at me in surprise. "Aurelia Marcella the innkeeper. This is an unexpected pleasure. You're welcome of course, but…"

"Thank you. I'm very sorry for your less, and I'm not here to intrude into your grief. I've come to deliver some information requested by Quintus Antonius."

"Oh? What information is that?"

Quintus stepped in. "Aurelia acts as my assistant sometimes. Her wealth of local knowledge and contacts can be extremely helpful." That was how we would play it in public, because we both knew the idea of a woman investigator was too far-fetched for most people to take seriously. In private he'd treat me as his equal though, and that was all that mattered. "Well, Aurelia, have you the information I need?"

"I have, yes." Vividus and Aquilo were both watching me with close attention.

"Where was Aquilo last night?"

"At Candidus and Albia's house. All night, and this morning, until Victor came and asked us to ride here as quickly as we could."

"You'll swear to that?" Vividus snapped.

"By any gods you care to name. So will Candidus and Albia, and everyone else at their house last night."

"Thank you. Does that satisfy you, Ostorius Vividus? Or shall we ride over to Candidus' farm now and interview them all?"

He sighed. "I suppose I'm satisfied, yes."

"Then I'll make my request again. Will you now tell you men to untie your brother? For one thing, I expect he wants to go and pay his respects to your uncle's body, don't you, Aquilo?"

"Yes, I do. Where is he?"

"Untie him," Vividus snapped at the guards, "then leave us." The guards obeyed. "Uncle's body is in the shrine room. He'll stay there until the funeral, which will be tonight."

"I'll go and see him straight away. But first, you haven't answered my question, Vividus. Where were you last night and at dawn today?"

"Last night I was in my bed. At dawn, which we assume is when the attack took place, I was with Quintus Antonius."

Aquilo looked enquiringly at Quintus, who nodded. "I can't speak for last night, but we met at sunrise, and were together when Niobe came to us and said she'd found that Magnus had been stabbed."

Then the murderer must be Ferox or Niobe. The words hung in the air, unspoken, as Aquilo left the room.

Quintus looked at me. "You've brought the rest of the information I asked for?"

"Yes, Antonius." I hadn't a clue what this meant, but I'm good at sounding confident when I don't know what's going on.

"Is it in writing, or have you memorised it?"

"It's in my memory. I prefer not to carry written messages at present, in case they fall into the wrong hands."

Quintus nodded and turned to Vividus. "Then will you excuse me while I find out what she has to tell me? I'll take the opportunity to show her the place where your uncle met his death. Unless you'd rather...? No, I thought not. I'm sure you don't want the distress of visiting it again."

"No, I leave that to you. The priests will be here soon for the ritual cleansing, so if you want to see the place as it is now, you'd best not waste any time. Meanwhile, what do you want me to do?"

"We need to find your brother Ferox as a matter of urgency. If you could send men out to look for him, that would aid our enquiries. You'll have a good idea of where he's likely to be found, if he's just carrying out his usual duties as estate manager."

"All right, I'll send out a search party."

"Thank you. And please tell your gatekeepers that nobody else is to leave your compound until further notice. In particular, Niobe is under instructions not to leave. Now, come with me, please, Aurelia." He got up quickly, and I followed. We were

out of the door and down the stairs before Vividus could say
another word.

At the bottom of the staircase, just inside the wide house-
door, Quintus pointed to a smaller door on our right. "That's
the room they've assigned me as an office. It's just big enough
for a desk and two chairs, but it's in a good position for watching who comes and goes into the house. We'll go straight to the
baths now, though. We can talk privately there."

We left the house and turned right, and then right again
alongside the corridor of rooms that jutted out behind. I noticed
a door leading into the corridor from the courtyard, and counted
six windows. The baths were towards the back of the Fort,
near the outer wall. Not far really, but distant enough that you
couldn't see their entrance from the front of the house at all. It
was a smaller bath-house than ours at the Oak Tree, having only
one set of rooms, not separate suites for ladies and gentlemen as
we have. But it was extremely luxurious, with high-quality tiling
and mosaics, and good-sized pools for the bathers.

Needless to say nobody was using the facilities now, and the
outer door was locked. Quintus produced a key, and when we
were safely inside, locked the door again, muttering, "We can't
be too careful."

We entered a wide lobby with several doors leading from it.
I could see a changing area, and a cold plunge pool. Quintus
took me into a kind of sitting-room next to it, meant presumably
for bathers who wished to relax for a while over a cup of wine
or a philosophical discussion. I felt sure that in the Ostorius
household the room saw more drinking than debating.

At last he turned to face me and gave me a proper smile. He
put his arms round me and kissed me hard, then stepped back
and said softly, "Gods, I'm glad to see you. Thank you for coming
so quickly. This is a horrible situation. Having you here makes
me feel we might just possibly get through it without the whole
district being engulfed in a bloodbath."

"Of course I came. But you really think there's likely to be
open war now between Magnus' family and Bodvocos?"

"Unless we identify the murderer by Beltane, I'd say it's odds on. Most of the men here are clamouring to take revenge on Bodvocos and his people."

"You mean at the feast tomorrow? But there's no evidence…"

"None, but they're angry, and they're determined. They're a wild assortment of ex-army toughs, with more energy than discipline, especially now Magnus is gone. So far I've kept them under control by showing them my imperial pass, which carries quite a lot of weight in such a military setting. When Lucius gets here I'll be able to put men on the gates. But if their resentment reaches boiling point before I find Magnus' killer, they may just ride out of here whether I like it or not, and start massacring every native in sight. With Vividus' full consent, I suspect. It's probably he who's been putting ideas of vengeance into their heads."

"That would be a nightmare. At least Aquilo has an alibi for last night and this morning." I smiled at him. "Elli's well, by the way, and so's the baby. Thanks for asking."

He ran a hand through his hair. "Gods, yes, with all that's happened here I'm forgetting you've had your share of drama too. You know, in a way it would have been simpler if Aquilo had done it. We could have announced the fact, shipped him off to Eburacum, and that would have been that. As it is, there are three obvious suspects in the family, and I haven't even started interviewing the servants yet."

I looked round the elaborately tiled room, with its cushioned benches and marble-topped table. "This is pretty much a standard bath suite, is it? Changing room, sitting area, cold plunge, warm room, hot room, furnace down below underneath the building?"

He nodded. "And only one entrance for bathers to go in and out."

"How do the furnace slaves get in? They have their own door, presumably?"

"It's at the very far end. They get to it from an alley near the wood store and the latrines. It lets them into a small room where they can leave their clothes, and they go from there through another door to the stokehole itself. Vividus told me they're here stoking well before dawn, so Magnus can have a really good hot bath."

"Is there a door between the slaves' area and the baths? You know we have one at the mansio, to make a second exit for bathers in case of a fire."

"Yes, there's a small door from the slaves' changing-area that leads through into the bath suite, at least into a spare lobby right at the far end that's not used. The door's never used either, and it's kept bolted from this side, so nobody can ever get in that way. At a push someone from this side could unbar it and get out."

"Was it bolted this morning?"

"It was, by the time I came to examine it. Whether anyone unbarred it earlier, I've no way of knowing."

"All the same," I said, "a private bath-house is a fairly intimate place, isn't it? Surely only the family and their personal slaves could have come and gone in here as they liked."

"I agree. I don't think we're dealing with a mystery killer who sneaked in from outside through the back entrance. Magnus would have heard an intruder coming in that way, he'd have turned to face him at least. I'd say the attacker must have been Vividus or Ferox, or the girl Niobe, who I think counts as family in this situation. But you see the problem. Whoever did kill Magnus will try to place the blame elsewhere, and who could be a more convenient guilty party than Bodvocos?"

"Well then, let's get to work." I kissed him. "Don't worry, we've faced worse than this before. And Lucius will soon be here, and that scamp Titch, if he hasn't run off to his shepherdess. So now," I pulled away from him, "kindly give your humble assistant a briefing. Let's take the three family suspects first. You said that you were with Vividus when the attack happened?"

He smiled. "Actually that's what *he* said. I'm not making assumptions about when the attack happened at this stage. But it's true that I met him, by arrangement, just after they blew reveille."

"They blow reveille here? Gods, how appalling! Do they have other bugle-calls to regulate the day?"

"No, just a sunrise one. I suppose you get used to it. Vividus had suggested I meet him then, so he could show me the night-time security arrangements here. They're pretty formidable. All gates locked at sunset, and the chief guard brings the keys to Vividus every night, except for the main gate key. There's a sentry on duty all night there, to unlock that big gate for anyone who wants to go in or out. They never do, unless it's a real emergency."

"So in effect there's a night-time curfew. *Merda*! Remind me never to marry a military man!" For a heartbeat I wondered what Clarilla would make of a household like this, but put the thought aside. "Tell me about how the body was found. By this concubine Niobe, I gather?"

"That's right. She found him in the hot room here, just after dawn. She said he wasn't quite dead. She asked who had killed him, and he answered, 'He's finished me, Niobe. After all I've done for those boys, they betray me. Even Aquilo…too late now.'"

"No wonder Vividus was all for locking Aquilo in chains when he came back. But is Niobe's account reliable?"

"I wish I knew. She's not an easy character to read."

"She's quite a beauty, isn't she?"

He nodded. "She was Magnus' concubine, not his wife, but they've lived together for some years, and the nephews seem to accept her as part of the family."

"Does any intelligence lurk inside that pretty head?"

"I think so. I'd have said definitely so, except that if she's not telling the truth about Magnus' last words, her efforts to implicate Aquilo in the murder were rather stupid. Granted she didn't know where he'd gone last night, but she couldn't be sure he hadn't got witnesses to vouch for him."

"So you think she invented Magnus' last words, and threw suspicion on Aquilo to protect herself, or somebody else?"

"I honestly don't know. She must have realised that, as the person who found him, she'd be the one everyone suspected of having killed him. Yet to invent a story that could be so easily checked…As you saw for yourself, she's quiet but confident, as if she's got herself and everything else well in hand. She was the master's favoured slave, yet she doesn't push herself forward, at least she hasn't since I arrived."

"She can't afford to now, can she, with her protector dead?"

"Only one of her protectors."

"Only one! You mean more than one person in the house is taking her to bed? Who told you that?"

"Vividus makes no secret of it. He says both he and Ferox fancy the girl, and to avoid petty jealousy, they, as he put it, each use her in turn. Vividus and Ferox can have her company in the evenings when they want, they just agree it between themselves. Night-time and early morning she spent with Magnus, if he wanted her to, and everyone knew he liked her to bathe with him."

"Poor Niobe. I don't suppose anyone knows or cares what she thought of the arrangement?"

"That's one of the things I'm hoping we'll find out, or I should say, I'm hoping *you'll* find out. She'll almost certainly respond better to a woman than a man. We'll arrange matters so you and she have a private, woman-to-woman chat about everything, especially the insensitivity of men, who simply don't understand the difficulties of her position."

"I daresay I can manage that. I've every sympathy with her, if she's being treated like that."

"Niobe says that this morning she came in here to join Magnus in his bath. They used to take their morning bath together regularly. Wine too, from the look of it." He gestured towards a small table near the door, where a silver tray held a jug and a couple of glasses.

I went over and looked at the wine in the jug. It was a rich red, looking almost black against the white marble. I sniffed it. Campanian probably, and quite good. There was nothing unusual about its bouquet. I looked at the glasses too. You don't often encounter wine-glasses, and these were fine examples. Any family that owned these and casually drank out of them in a bath-house was not just rich, but flaunting the fact.

"These two are still clean," I said.

"Yes. They could have been swilled out afterwards, or replaced with fresh ones. You're wondering about poison?"

"It crossed my mind. It would be easier to stab a man if he'd drunk something that paralysed him, or made him very sleepy. But then if the murderer had a supply of poison, he or she would surely have killed Magnus with that, not half-used it and finished the killing off with a dagger."

He nodded. "That's the conclusion I came to. There was no indication on Magnus' body that he'd eaten or drunk anything unusual. No foam near his mouth, and his face wasn't discoloured."

I shivered. "Anything else about the body? I'd just as soon not have to look at it unless it's absolutely necessary. Where is he?"

"They've put him in a small room with a shrine in it, where the household gods are kept, and all the decorations and awards the family have won over the years. They regard it as sacred, and that's where he will stay until the funeral, which will be today at sunset. No, you don't need to see him. But I'd like you to look at the spot where he was found."

He led the way through to the hottest room, where steam was rising from the round marble-lined pool, and the air was heavy with moisture and the sickly smell of blood. The water in the pool was tinged reddish, but most of the blood was on a low marble bench near its edge. "He lay here," Quintus indicated the scarlet stain that spread over the bench and dripped down onto the pretty blue mosaic. "Quite relaxed, apparently, there doesn't seem to have been a fight of any kind. He was stabbed in the neck, about *there*." He touched the right side of my neck just above the spot where my collar-bone joins my shoulder. "The blow came from in front, and needed just one stroke of a narrow blade. It was quite clumsily done because it missed the important veins, so he didn't die immediately."

"He just had time to accuse his family of killing him. Very convenient."

"You don't sound as if you believe Niobe's account of his last words. The wound wasn't deep enough to be fatal straight away. He'd have had time to say something."

Suddenly I felt queasy. "Quintus, can we get out of this room now? I've had enough of the scent of blood."

Back in the sitting-room I felt better. Quintus put his arm round me. "Go on about Niobe. You doubt her word?"

"I haven't heard the story from her own lips, so I suppose I shouldn't judge. But if we only have her unsupported word for what happened, he could have been dead when she came in here. Or maybe she killed him."

Quintus looked at me steadily. "Maybe. What's your reason for suggesting that?"

"For a start, it sounds as if the attacker wasn't experienced at killing with a dagger. That would rule out army men like Vividus and Ferox, wouldn't it?"

"Not necessarily. Don't forget an experienced professional killer might want to disguise the fact, and botch the job to give the impression the attacker was an amateur. So for instance, a right-handed man could strike with his left hand."

"You always like making matters more complicated than they need be, Quintus. Let's take the evidence as it appears for now, and assume it wasn't a professional killer. Niobe had the perfect opportunity to do it. After all if everyone knew she would be visiting the bath-house, nobody would think twice when they saw her come here, and there'd be no interruptions while she stabbed him. But afterwards she couldn't just walk out and pretend she knew nothing about it."

"Why not? If she'd had the nerve that's exactly what she could have done. She'd have gone about her day's work and waited till someone else found Magnus, a cleaning-slave perhaps, or till another member of the family noticed he was missing and went searching for him. She'd tell everyone she hadn't gone bathing with Magnus this morning, she had no idea anything was wrong. They'd all say, as you just have, that if she had killed him, she couldn't simply walk out, therefore she must be innocent."

"The way people watch each other here, she may have thought that someone had seen her come into the baths at her usual time—or been afraid they had. So she couldn't pretend she hadn't been here. She had to say she'd found Magnus close to death, and she made up the tale of Magnus' final words, to deflect suspicion from herself."

He rubbed his cheek thoughtfully. "Yes, I'll admit it's a possibility. But why would she kill Magnus? If he was her main protector, what would she gain from his death? And if she wanted to divert blame from herself, why not throw it on Bodvocos and his men? Everyone would believe that. As I said, most of them do anyway."

"I don't know. But let's put her at the top of our list of suspects."

"She's on the list, but not at the head of it. That position belongs to Ferox. He's disappeared. He could be out and about on the estate, but isn't it more likely he's run away? He killed Magnus in a quarrel, panicked, and bolted."

"Titch told me you were worried because both Ferox and Vividus had serious rows with Magnus yesterday. Aquilo mentioned them too."

"Quite right. They were arguing when I arrived, and went on quarrelling all last evening. Not just squabbling, out-and-out blazing rows."

"About whether to make peace with Bodvocos and the natives?"

"Yes. Specifically, how to respond to the Chief's invitation to the Beltane feast."

"Bodvocos was as good as his word then, trying to persuade them to attend his party. And Magnus agreed to go?"

"Yes, I believe he'd decided to."

"In spite of their protests?"

"He kept a pretty tight rein on his nephews, and if he'd made his mind up about something, he'd have ignored their objections and gone ahead."

I thought about it. "This makes less and less sense, you know. Vividus and Ferox disapproved of the idea of peace, but

Aquilo was keen on it. So why would Magnus say that Aquilo had betrayed him? It seems to me Aquilo was the one nephew who gave him wholehearted support."

"We've come back to the question we asked before. Is Niobe telling the truth about Magnus' dying words, or is she making them up?"

"And if she is making them up, we're faced with another question: why would she want to kill Magnus?"

He nodded. "We'll know more when you've talked to her."

"Thanks for your confidence. I'll do my best. Suppose…yes, suppose Magnus was acting the heavy-handed master, and doing something she didn't want him to do, or maybe forbidding something…Yes, of course. Magnus had proposed that Vividus should marry Clarilla, and Niobe didn't want that to happen, because she'd lose her position as the most important woman in the household."

Quintus laughed. "That sounds like the plot of a Greek love story. If she was really so angry about the idea of Vividus marrying a Roman lady, why not kill Vividus himself? That would put a permanent end to the scheme."

"Ah, but perhaps Vividus wasn't really keen on the marriage, and won't go ahead with it now that his uncle isn't there to crack the whip. Perhaps Niobe even wants Vividus for herself alone, only she had to get his uncle out of the way first."

"Gods, that's enough!" He stood up. "Let's stop guessing and start asking some questions. I'll start interviewing the servants. You go and pay a call on Niobe."

Chapter XXI

Niobe's sitting-room was as soft and elegant as she was, and its luxurious feminine atmosphere made a welcome contrast to the military air that pervaded the rest of the Fort.

"This is beautiful, Niobe. Fit for a princess!" My remark pleased her, which was what I wanted, but my admiration was genuine. She couldn't have asked for more, I thought, if she'd been the mistress of the house in law as well as in fact.

"I'm glad you like it. I wanted a good view of the countryside." She indicated the big glazed window which stood open to show pastures and trees, and the sea in the distance beyond. "When they were building this place, I said to Magnus, you may enjoy living in a fort, but I'm not a soldier, and I'm not spending half my life gazing out on nothing but a rampart. You can give me one of the upstairs rooms. So he did. Take a seat, won't you?"

The seats were comfortable couches, each of which had a lavishly carved low table beside it. I chose one near the window, and she sat opposite.

"Would you like some wine?"

"No, thank you." Something in my tone or my face must have caught her attention, because she smiled.

"Afraid of being poisoned, dear? Don't worry, you'll be safe enough with me." She got up and fetched a flask of red and two glasses from a table in the corner. She poured us each a glass and held both out to me. "Choose one. Go on, I'm sure you could do with it."

I took one, but still hesitated. "Thank you."

She raised hers to her lips, and drank heartily.

I couldn't help smiling. "You've talked me into it." The wine was Gaulish, very pleasant, and I savoured it as I took time to look around and appreciate the room. Good taste and money had combined to make its decor something special. The wall-paintings were excellent, and one wall was mostly covered by a large coloured hanging that, incredibly, seemed to be made of silk.

She nodded, once again guessing what was in my mind. "Pure silk, that is. Aren't the colours lovely?"

"They are. I've never seen such gorgeous turquoise shades. And what an enormous piece!" The only silk I own is a small square blue scarf my brother bought me once, and it cost him a small fortune. "Magnus obviously thought a great deal of you."

"Oh this wasn't from the old man. He did buy me things occasionally, but he'd a mean streak when it came to what he called 'feminine foibles.' Vividus bought it for me when he was in Egypt, although it doesn't come from there, it's made somewhere on the eastern edge of the world."

"You're lucky." I sipped my wine. "Not just having such a wonderful present, but a man who's prepared to give you anything you want."

"Men are easy," she answered lightly. "And I'd say your man would give you pretty well anything, if you'd only ask him."

"My man?"

"Your Antonius What's-his-name, the investigator. There's something between you two, isn't there? Else why would he bring you along here? You're not telling me you actually help in his work."

"If only. " Suddenly I saw how I might get under her guard by gaining her sympathy. "I do help him, yes. I've got plenty of local contacts, and my brother's on the Governor's staff. That's all there is to it, unfortunately. I'd like it to go further. Perhaps one day…"

She laughed. "You're obviously not handling him right. Men are like fish, you know. All you have to do is throw the bait into the river, they'll come for it. He's a handsome enough fellow, pleasant, a bit more civilised than my soldier-boys, but not weak. You'd better watch out, I might go after him myself."

My answer to this would have been too unladylike for such a beautiful room, so I said nothing. My silence made my thoughts clear enough to someone as perceptive as Niobe.

"Don't worry, dear, he's safe from me. I've got a good setup here, I shan't endanger it. The Ostorius men believe in keeping love within the family, if you take my meaning."

"Except Aquilo?" I suggested.

She tossed her head. "True, the stuck-up little fool. Not my type at all."

"But I'm curious…no, I mustn't ask."

"Ask what?"

"Aquilo. Why did you try to make out he'd murdered Magnus? Putting words into the old man's mouth like that…was it because he wouldn't take your bait?"

She looked surprised. "I didn't put any words into his mouth. I quoted exactly what he said to me. Poor old boy, he was nearly dead, but even then he hadn't lost his wits."

"But he must have been confused, to say that Aquilo attacked him?"

"Ah, that wasn't what he said." Her expression was pure mischief, like a little girl who's played a particularly good trick on a room full of adults. "They misunderstood his meaning, Vividus and your Antonius."

"Exactly what did he say?"

"He said: 'He's finished me, Niobe. After all I've done for those boys, they betray me. Even Aquilo…too late now.'" She repeated the words exactly as she'd told them to Quintus, I noticed. The sign of an accurate memory, or of careful rehearsal?

"And you don't think he meant Aquilo stabbed him?"

"No, if he'd meant that, he'd have said so. 'He's finished me' could mean any of the brothers. He mentioned Aquilo because of something quite different."

"What was that?"

"This stupid affair of Aquilo's with the native chieftain's daughter. The old man was quite taken aback when he heard about it, especially the baby. He said he thought Aquilo's only chance of getting a woman with child would be to sing her a love-song while a real man did the business." She smiled with more than a touch of malice. "But he was angry as well. He threatened to cut Aquilo out of his will, but he hadn't time. That's what he meant about it being too late."

"How in the gods' name did he know about Aquilo and Elli?"

"From me, of course. And I got it from Antonius. Last night I overheard him telling Aquilo that Elli was at Albia's farm having his baby."

"Ah." I gave a conspiratorial smile. "A bit of eavesdropping's useful now and then."

"And dead easy too. My bedroom is nearly above the main house-door, with a good view of the main gate too. In the warm weather I need to keep my window open wide, and voices carry very easily from down there to up here. If your Antonius ever whispers sweet love-words into your ear on the threshold of the headquarters building, believe me, I'll be the first to know."

"I'll bear it in mind." I grinned at her. "But let's stick to yesterday. After Quintus Antonius told Aquilo about the baby, what happened?"

"Aquilo rode off in a great hurry, presumably to see his sweetheart. Then later on that red-headed lad, the investigator's assistant, came riding in, and had the cheek to interrupt us while we were at dinner, with some ridiculous message from Aquilo, that he was staying the night with your sister because he'd met his old friend Trimalchio. *Trimalchio,* I ask you! Mind you, it would probably have got past Magnus and the boys, they're not great readers. But I smelt a rat."

"So you told them all what Aquilo had been up to?"

"Just Magnus, nobody else. I thought he had the right to know first, and I told him last night before he went to bed."

She'd said, "before *he* went to bed," which made me ask, "Did you spend the night with him?"

"No. He didn't often want a bed-companion these days, but he always liked me to be there when he bathed. Early mornings were our time together." She picked up her wine-glass and twisted it in her hands, gazing down at the swirling liquid. Then she shrugged. "Funny to think I shan't ever see that ugly old body again."

Being stoical is one thing, I thought, but that's downright callous. It was as well she didn't seem to expect any words of condolence, because I couldn't have managed any. Again, uncannily, she knew what was in my mind.

"You think I'm heartless, talking like that. In my position, love's something you dream about, but you don't expect to find it in real life. If the masters are kind to you and don't beat you, or humiliate you in public, that's enough. I haven't chosen the life I live here, but I have learned how to make the best of it."

"I'm sorry. I didn't mean to offend you. You have a knack of knowing what's going on in my mind."

"That's because I think you're a lot like me. You know where you stand, and you know what you want. Only you were born free and I wasn't."

"You're more beautiful than I'll ever be."

She nodded, accepting the fact. "But not more intelligent."

We found we were smiling at one another, and some kind of understanding passed between us, making us allies in spite of our differences. I can't really explain this, it was something instinctive, and my instincts about other people are usually safe to trust. Now I knew for certain Niobe hadn't killed Magnus. She was too clever to have murdered her master in such a crude, obvious fashion. She could have killed him, certainly, but she'd have disguised the death as an accident.

"Niobe, let me ask you this and then it's done. Did you murder Magnus?"

"No, I did not."

"Do you know who did?"

"No."

"I believe you."

"Thank you. But most people won't."

"Then you must help me convince them, by finding out who did. Will you?"

She sat silent a long time, staring out of the window. Finally she said, "Yes. But I don't want to give evidence for a trial. I won't let them torture me. I'll take my own life first."

I didn't blame her. Whichever of our forefathers decreed that the courts would only recognise evidence from slaves if it was obtained by torturing them, he was both cruel and ineffective. Quintus felt the same. "Then I'll promise you that if you help me, you won't be tortured to provide evidence. I can speak for Antonius on that."

She smiled. "Can you now?"

"Yes. You have my word."

"All right, I'll give you all the information I can. Where shall I begin? This morning, I suppose. I went to Magnus in the bath-house, and I was late."

"That's as good a starting-point as any. Why were you late joining him? I mean any special reason, or did you usually make him wait for you?"

"I actually woke up early, so I should have been ready when he was. But I couldn't find my rose-scented oil. It was his favourite, he liked to rub it on my body after we'd bathed, and I didn't want to go without it. I wasted time hunting around for the flask in here and in my bedroom. I found it eventually in quite the wrong place. My maid must have moved it when she cleaned the rooms yesterday. Anyhow when I got to the bath-house…"

"Was this before or after the sunrise bugle-call?"

She frowned. "A little before, I think. Yes, I'm sure. I went into the changing-area and realised that Magnus had somebody with him."

"You heard voices?"

"I knew even before that. There were two cloaks hanging up there. They were similar, both scruffy leather things. I expect you've noticed, or you soon will, how most of the men here seem to like wearing their old army clothes, and they seem to think the sagum is the height of fashion for the outdoor man." She gave a scornful sniff. "I recognised which was Magnus' because his night-tunic was beside it. The other cloak was on its own."

"Someone had gone into the bathing area with a tunic on? Wasn't that unusual?"

"It happened sometimes, if one of the boys wanted a quick word with Magnus first thing in the morning. I knew if he had someone else with him he might want me to wait till they went. Frankly I was relieved. I thought, if he's got company, he may not realise I was late arriving. He hated to be kept waiting. I went through the cold and warm rooms, and by then I could hear voices coming from the caldarium. Magnus was shouting at someone, it sounded like an argument."

"Could you hear what they were arguing about?"

"Not really. Magnus was yelling, 'By the gods, I've had enough of this, do you hear? It's time I taught you a lesson.' I was on the point of turning back to wait outside, but something made me sneeze, so they heard me. Magnus shouted, 'Niobe! Are you there, girl?' And I called, 'Yes, it's me, my lord.' 'Well go away and come back later. I'm busy. Gods, can't a man have a private conversation in peace even in his bath?' Then there was more yelling, something about not being pushed around, and I didn't stay any longer. I went back to my room."

Without thinking I poured myself more wine. "Sorry, Niobe. Once an innkeeper, always an innkeeper. Do you want a refill?"

"Yes please." She held out her glass.

"Did you recognise the voice of whoever was arguing with Magnus?"

"No. They all of them sound alike, Magnus, Vividus, and Ferox. And I didn't wait around trying to listen."

I smiled and raised an eyebrow. "You didn't?"

"No fear! I expected someone else would be coming out when the argument ended, and I didn't want to be seen. But thankfully, no one did come..." She stopped, realising what she'd said. "I mean..."

"It's all right, I know. You were relieved he hadn't caught sight of you."

"I was. I knew that if one of the boys had got a tongue-lashing from Magnus, he wouldn't want to think anyone else had heard it, especially not me."

I thought how difficult life must be for someone on intimate terms with more than one man from the same family. Niobe was right, she and I had a good deal in common, but that was a situation I could never have endured. "And then you went back for your bath later as if nothing had happened?"

She nodded. "There were only Magnus' things in the changing-room, so I knew he was on his own. I hung up my cloak and tunic, and went through to the hot room. I saw him lying on the bench, blood everywhere. I think I screamed. I ran to him, and I thought he was dead at first, but when I knelt down beside him and called his name, he opened his eyes. I got a towel and tried to staunch the bleeding, and I said, 'Who's done this dreadful thing, my lord?' And he answered, 'He's finished me, Niobe. After all I've done for those boys, they betray me. Even Aquilo…too late now.' I said, 'I'll fetch help, my lord.'" But he said, 'Don't leave me, Niobe.' His eyes closed again. I sat down on the bench and took his head on my lap, and just held him still until he died." There was a catch in her voice, and I realised Magnus' death had affected her more than she was prepared to admit.

"It must have been a dreadful shock for you."

She shrugged, and took a long drink of wine.

"But I don't understand why Magnus felt Aquilo had betrayed him by his liaison with Elli. He'd just decided to make peace with Bodvocos, and of all the three brothers, Aquilo was the one who supported him in that, because he wanted an alliance with Elli's family. How could that be a betrayal?"

She looked at me pityingly. "Gods alive, I'd have thought it was obvious. Elli's father will be angrier than an exploding volcano when he hears what's happened. Their code of honour is strict, he'll want to put Elli to death. So will Coriu. Aquilo will try to stop them, and they may make him fight Coriu for her. He'd probably do it too, the stupid young idiot, he's so much in love. Coriu could kill him with one hand tied behind his back."

She smiled suddenly. "Even with his broken arm, he could wipe the floor with Aquilo. Vividus and Ferox couldn't accept that. Don't you see? At the very moment when we might have got everyone to agree to peace, Aquilo and Elli have provided a whole new set of reasons for Bodvocos and the Ostorii to hate each other for ever."

"Let's hope you're wrong. Most of the guards here are already spoiling for a fight with the Parisi, blaming them for Magnus' death. So the quicker we can find the real murderer, the better."

She nodded.

"As I see, it, if you didn't kill him, and I accept that you didn't, there are three possibilities. Tell me which you think is the most likely. Either it was one of his nephews—Vividus or Ferox, as Aquilo was miles away."

She nodded. "That's possible."

"Or it was someone else in the household, a servant with a grudge perhaps."

"That's possible too, but not very likely. The old man could be harsh, I'm not saying he couldn't, and some of the slaves resented it. But none of them ever went into the bath-house first thing. It was cleaned and tidied each night at bed-time, to be ready for the master and me at dawn. Everybody knew that, and if one of the others had sneaked in, he'd have been noticed."

"Unless he went in there last night and hid until morning?"

"That'd be quite hard. The servants aren't allowed to be away from the Fort at night, and they all sleep in the slave block near the back wall. Each section of the block has a senior trusted slave in charge, who'd report if anyone was missing. I'm not saying it's completely out of the question, but it wouldn't be easy. And it seems a bit far-fetched to suggest that one man had a blazing row with Magnus, then left him, and a different man came out of hiding and stabbed him."

"It does, I admit. And the same goes for my third possibility, which I think is the least credible, but we can't ignore it, as it's the most popular theory in the household…"

She nodded. "Bodvocos, or Coriu, or the Long-hairs, or all three of them together. No, I don't believe that. It's an Ostorius pastime, blaming the natives or the pirates for everything that goes wrong. And because they're all so obsessed with security and protecting themselves, the Fort gets more and more like a real military base every day. No outsider could have got into the main area unobserved, even through the Achilles gate, never mind finding a way into a private place like the baths."

"The Achilles gate? Which one's that?"

She smiled slyly. "Can you keep a secret?"

"I'll have to pass it on to Quintus Antonius, but nobody else, I promise."

"The Achilles gate is the smallest one in the back wall, nearly in the corner, tucked away behind the slave block. It's kept locked all the time. But it isn't hard to get hold of the key."

I felt a twinge of excitement. "So if one of the lads fancies a night away from the Fort, he could ask, for instance, that big Gaul Rinacus for a favour, and borrow a key for a few hours?"

I'd mentioned Rinacus because his was the only name I knew so far, but her look of surprise told me it was a lucky guess.

"You don't miss much, do you? Yes, Rinacus is the man for fixing most things here at the Fort. He'd never put his masters in danger, but he's not above making a silver piece or two for himself. I suppose he learnt that in the army. He's stashed away enough to set himself up in business, if he wants to, but Magnus would never hear of him leaving. And he enjoys the power he has here, so maybe he'll stay a while longer even with Magnus gone."

Something in her tone made me ask, "A special friend of yours, is he?"

"Let's just say he sometimes asks favours as well as granting them."

"Favours?"

"I told you. Men are easy."

"Well then, we come to the most important question." I paused, knowing it was also the most difficult for her to answer.

"You said you thought you heard either Vividus or Ferox arguing with their uncle. If you had to say which one it was…?"

"I don't know. It could have been either. They both have hot tempers, and both are strong enough to kill a big man like Magnus with a dagger. He was used to both of them coming into the baths sometimes, even if it was for an argument. He was like their father. Fathers and sons always row, don't they, especially when the boys get older and want to assert themselves. Both of them had been officers in the army, and Magnus respected that in a way, but then he thought that he, as the senior officer, should be able to boss them about as if they were still in the legion. Naturally they didn't like it. I've wondered sometimes if it was such a good idea, Magnus bringing all his nephews here to run a family farm. They might have been better with a bit of distance between them."

"They could have refused to join him," I pointed out.

"It wouldn't have occurred to them. The Ostorii have always been a close family, they see their lives and their futures together. Except Aquilo. He's a fool in most things, but he wants to get away from the others, live his own kind of life, with his poetry and his music. I've a sneaking admiration for that. I doubt if he'll ever do it though."

"Aquilo is out of the running here. Vividus and Ferox are in the lead, neck and neck. You won't even guess which of them would be more likely to get so enraged with Magnus that it ended in murder?"

"No, I won't." She returned my gaze calmly. I knew I couldn't get any more out of her for now.

"Fair enough." I stood up. "You've been a real help to me. Thanks for being so honest about everything."

"And thank you," she answered gravely, "for accepting that I'm telling the truth."

I turned at the door. "Niobe, if you think of anything else that might help us catch the killer, you will tell me, won't you? Because you realise that while he's still free, you may be in danger yourself."

"Me? I don't think so."

"How sure are you that you weren't seen leaving the bath-house this morning? Or even if you weren't seen, the man who killed Magnus would know that you usually went there at dawn and might have noticed something. If he thought you'd identi-fied him…"

For the first time since we'd met, her confidence wavered, and she looked alarmed. "But I've told you, I've told everyone, I don't know who it was!"

"And I believe you, but the killer may not, or he may not want to take chances. So watch your back, Niobe, and if anything else comes to your memory that would be useful to me, then don't hesitate to come and find me. All right?"

"All right." She forced a smile. "Gods, you certainly know how to cheer a girl up, don't you? And," she added, "you watch yourself too. The Ostorius family aren't keen on outsiders enquir-ing about their private affairs."

"We'll look out for each other, then, shall we?"

"It's a deal." We shook hands, and I left her, feeling that I'd made a friend.

Chapter XXII

"So you like Niobe?" Quintus asked. "Yet before you met her, you had her singled out as the killer."

"I know. I was surprised myself, but I do like her, and I think I also trust her. But as you said yourself, she's not an easy person to get to know. She's intelligent, and she's aware her position here is vulnerable, which makes her potentially dangerous. Like an unbroken horse, calm and in control most of the time, but if something threatens her, she'll do what she must to protect herself."

"I've rarely seen anyone who looked less like a horse, but I see what you mean."

We were crowded into Quintus' cramped little office—me, Quintus, and Titch, who'd just arrived with Lucius and his men. My brother had led his patrol straight out onto the farm to look for Ferox, while I told Quintus and Titch about my talk with Niobe.

"And she really couldn't be the killer?" Titch asked. "Being the one who found the body, it makes her look the most likely."

"I didn't say she couldn't be a murderer under any circumstances. I say she didn't murder Magnus. If she decided to kill her master she'd make a much better job of it."

Quintus said, "Interesting that she mentioned a secret way in and out after dark. I'd assumed there'd be an escape route, because you can't keep a bunch of active young men cooped up in a small place like this unless you're really in the army, and sometimes not even then. Titch, did you pick up anything about this Achilles gate? You talked to some of their lads after supper last night, didn't you?"

He grinned. "I did. We had a nice friendly game of dice in the stables."

"Did you win?" I asked.

"'Course not. I want them to play again tonight. It was only a few coppers, and I reckon it can come out of our expenses, can't it?"

"That depends on whether you learnt anything useful."

"I heard one or two mentions of the Achilles gate, quite casual like in conversation. But I didn't get why they call it that."

I laughed. "Really, Titch, didn't they teach you any military history while you were in the army?"

"Not much. They wanted us to learn about battles we'd be fighting now, not stuff from the olden days."

"But you *have* heard of the Trojan War?"

He performed a comic show of thinking deeply. "I believe I have. A long siege job, which would have been shorter if Achilles hadn't spent a lot of it sulking instead of fighting."

"And what was special about Achilles?"

"He couldn't be killed except by a wound in his heel...Now I see. Achilles' heel. So yon little gate is the weak point of the Fort. I'll find out more about it, now I know."

Quintus nodded. "Anything else?"

"They all really hate the chief guard. They're loyal to the Ostorii as a family, because most of them owe their jobs to Magnus or Vividus. But there's no loyalty to Rinacus, except out of fear, because he uses his fists a lot. When we'd all had a few beakers of beer I was sympathising with them about serving under bad-tempered officers, and one lad says, 'Rinacus saved one of the masters from being convicted of murder when they were serving together. He wouldn't be captain here now if the master didn't owe him.' And another one says, 'But he doesn't want to stay. He keeps saying he's going to leave, only he's signed a contract so he can't go right away. I say the sooner he goes the better.' And the first one says, 'He may be kicked out regardless, if anyone finds out he's sniffing around after Niobe.' I asks, 'Does she fancy him then?' But he says to me, 'Keep your nose out, boy, the Ostorii don't like outsiders asking questions.'"

"Niobe told me the same. She mentioned Rinacus too, so I suspect she may not be turning him down out of hand."

"So the chief guard has some sort of hold over one or more of the family," Quintus mused, "and he's allowed to break a few rules. He's unhappy here, and he could be making somebody jealous over the girl. But I can't see him letting outsiders in here, can you?"

Titch shook his head. "That'd be going too far. He may let the lads go off for a few hours' drinking or whoring, but nobody's letting strangers inside the defences, they're too scared. They're all very jumpy about the Gauls and Bodvocos' men, they feel like they're kind of under siege here. They'd not tell tales on one another, but they'd report a stranger."

"I agree. Good information, Titch. Off you go now, but remember please, I need you back here by dark. I want you to pick up more gossip tonight. I realise it isn't as interesting as your little chats with Balca. It's a hard life, isn't it?"

Titch grinned. "Oh, I don't know. And I'll tell you something else interesting, shall I?"

"If you feel you must."

"You know I've been teaching her to use a bow? Well I had a job to demonstrate it at first, with this bad hand and all. But I do believe me hand is getting better. I can move the fingers just a bit."

"That's very good news, Titch," I said.

"I suppose it is," Quintus conceded. "But if you have the use of both hands again, you'll be wanting to go back to the cavalry. I've almost got used to having you around."

"I've almost got used to it too," the lad grinned. "Well, it's early days to be making decisions. I'll see you both later. Or…" he turned to me. "Are you riding back to Mistress Albia's? If so I'll ride along with you, make sure you get safe there."

"Thanks, but I'm staying here for a while longer. I'll go back to Albia's tonight, so we can all leave for Bodvocos' feast together tomorrow. You're going, presumably?"

Quintus said, "He's going, because Balca is, and I don't think there's a threat in my power to make that would keep him away."

He grinned. "She's performing the Mother-gift ceremony instead of Elli. I'm taking her over to Bodvocos' place later. So I'd best make the most of the afternoon."

People who know that I help Quintus sometimes—that's only my family and close friends—tend to assume that investigating is an exciting business, full of dramatic events, lightning-flashes of intuition, brilliant deductions leading to logical solutions. Those things happen sometimes, but mostly the work is tedious in the extreme. We had a taste of tedium now, for what seemed like a whole day, but was probably only a couple of hours.

We interviewed the men of the guard, from Rinacus down, and the trusted servants who were in charge of night-time security in the slave quarters. There were over forty of them, and we didn't get one single useful piece of information. Quintus asked the questions, while I went through the motions of making notes. They all denied knowing anything about a secret way out of the Fort; they all assured us they'd seen nothing unusual in the place last night or early this morning. They all hated Bodvocos and his people, who, they were sure, had murdered their master. They all loved working for the Ostorii, and thought Rinacus was a first-class commander. They were all tense and wooden-faced, giving terse answers in more or less the same words.

The only exception was Rinacus. He was a big, solid man, who seemed even larger than life in our small room, and he was relaxed and confident. He offered no useful information either, but he gave the impression he was anxious to help. He spent some time boasting about the high level of protection he and his men provided from the natives, and the impossibility of anyone from outside the Fort ever getting into it. He had a great respect for his masters, and was devastated by Magnus' death. He loved his job, and if Vividus would keep him on as commander, he would never want to leave.

"The only thing we can safely conclude from all that," Quintus grumbled after the last one left us, "is that Rinacus feels sure of himself, and has a strong enough grip on the others to make them say exactly what he wants them to."

"I always thought drill was something soldiers practised on the parade-ground," I said. "He's got their minds drilled as well."

We were sitting there staring gloomily at one another, when there was a brisk knock at the door, and we were both delighted when Lucius came striding in.

"Lucius, you're a welcome sight!" I gave him a hug. "Have you come to tell us you've caught Ferox?"

"Yes, we've caught him—well found him, really. He didn't seem to be hiding or trying to escape. He was inland on the very edge of the Ostorius property, where it borders Albia's. I tried in that direction because everyone else was searching around the Headland. When he saw us he came riding up, just as he did the other day when we went to the shipwreck, demanding to know what we were doing there. When I told him we were arresting him and taking him home, and my lads drew their swords, he wasn't best pleased, but he came along with us quietly enough."

"Excellent," Quintus said. "Good work. How does he seem now? And where has he been all this time?"

Lucius grinned. "He's his usual charming self. He says he's been riding round the farm since first light. He's obsessed with the idea that the Gauls are going to raid here soon, he kept on about it all the way back. And he started telling off the chief guard as soon as he got in through the gate, saying there should have been more men out on patrol during the night. The guard said he was out all night himself, and saw nothing at all to indicate trouble. I broke the argument up, but it was interesting to hear that Rinacus wasn't in the Fort last night."

"Yes, I agree. Where's Ferox now?"

"He's in his office, which is downstairs in one of the outbuildings near the main gate. I left a guard on his door so he'll have to stay put. It seemed better to put him there than keep him standing in the open, and I assume you don't want him to talk to the others till you've questioned him. He's extremely annoyed and keeps demanding to see Magnus or Vividus."

"*Magnus?*" I said. "You mean he doesn't know Magnus is dead?"

"He doesn't seem to, though he could just be play-acting. Are you going to see him now, Quintus?"

"I most certainly am. You two come as well."

So we trooped out of the house and across the big open space in front of it. Ferox's office was a large room with big windows which were open to give a good view of the entrance gate and also the main door to the house. Its interior looked like any estate manager's lair, untidy and littered with note-tablets, scrolls, styluses, and ink-pots, not to mention used wine-beakers, some with wine still in them.

Ferox leapt from his chair as we entered, and confronted Quintus. "Are you responsible for my being treated like this, Antonius?"

"I'm afraid I am."

"Well it's disgraceful. I demand you release me at once and let me talk to my uncle or my brother. You've no business to hold me a prisoner here as if I'm some sort of criminal."

"I'm sorry, Ferox. I'm afraid it's necessary. I need to ask you some questions. What time did you leave the Fort this morning?"

"Before dawn. What about it?"

"Just answer my questions please, if you would. You were up early, it seems. Are you usually such an early riser?"

He looked uneasy. "Sometimes. Why?"

"It helps us to get a picture of life here at the Fort, if we know what a normal routine day is like. Is there a special reason why you sometimes get up early, or is it just as the mood takes you?"

"If you must know, I'm a poor sleeper, and I sometimes suffer from bad dreams. Really unpleasant ones, I mean, and if I've woken up after one of them, I'm not likely to go back to sleep that night. So however early it is, I get myself up and make use of the time to do some work."

"Work? In the middle of the night?" I asked.

He glanced round his cluttered office. "There's always plenty of paperwork to be done, till it gets light enough to ride out onto the farm. I like to patrol our land as often as I can myself. That way I can keep an eye open for trouble, and also supervise what my workers are up to."

Quintus asked, "Did you see your uncle this morning before you left?"

"I didn't. I told you, I left before dawn, which is when he gets up and takes his bath. Believe me, when I do see him and tell him how I've been treated, he'll throw you all off our property. And I intend to see him now. Out of my way." He took a couple of paces across the room.

Lucius went to stand with his back against the door, while Quintus took a step forward and faced Ferox squarely. He said softly, "I'm afraid I've some bad news for you. Your uncle is dead."

"*Dead?*"

I was watching him closely, and I could swear his surprise and horror were completely genuine. If he was acting, he was doing it supremely well.

Quintus went on, and he too was observing Ferox carefully. "He died this morning at dawn. To be precise, he was *murdered* this morning at dawn."

Ferox said nothing for a few heartbeats, then he exclaimed, "Magnus dead? I can't believe it!"

"I'm afraid it's true," Quintus said.

"But…how will we manage without him? He's been like a father to me, to all of us boys after our mother died. Gods, it's my fault. All my fault!"

"Your fault? You're admitting you killed him?" Quintus asked.

"Of course I didn't. But I knew the Gauls would be attacking us about now, I just knew it! And I thought we were well prepared, so my best way of protecting us all was to spend as much time as possible on patrol, out on the estate. I should have stayed at the Fort, but I never thought they'd try to murder anyone inside the walls here." He looked stricken, deathly pale and staring straight ahead at nothing.

"You think the sea-raiders killed him?" Quintus asked.

"Who else? Under orders from Bodvocos, no doubt. They've been harassing all the settlers in this district. We're the only ones they haven't dared touch so far, because we've plenty of men and a good solid rampart around us. But I knew it was only a matter of time, we all did. Personally I thought they'd try something on Beltane, that was why Bodvocos was so keen to lure us away from here to attend his feast."

"What if I told you," Quintus said, "that your uncle couldn't have been killed by an outsider, whether one of the Gauls or one of the Parisi?"

"Couldn't? Why not?"

"Because he was killed in a place where no outsider could have penetrated, in the caldarium of your bath suite. The murderer must have been someone from this household, almost certainly someone close to Magnus, whom he knew and trusted. There was no sign of a struggle in the hot room. Whoever was there with him was able to come up close to him and stab him, without Magnus suspecting his intention."

"One of our own people?" He shook his head. "Not very likely. What's your evidence?"

"Niobe overheard a quarrel in the bath-house only a short while before she found your uncle there. He wasn't dead when she discovered…"

Ferox barked, "Niobe found him?"

"Yes," I said. "She says she went to join Magnus in the bath-house, heard an argument in progress and went away again. When she came back, Magnus was almost dead, and she heard his last words."

"Heard them? Or made them up?"

"You don't like Niobe?" I asked.

"Oh, I like her well enough. She's beautiful, and she knows how to make a man feel like a man. And she's been kind to me sometimes…But if she found my uncle, isn't it likely she killed him, and made up a story to cover herself? What does she claim my uncle said to her?"

"'He's finished me, Niobe. After all I've done for those boys, they betray me. Even Aquilo…too late now.'"

Ferox' expression was of complete astonishment. "Aquilo? Aquilo couldn't hurt a fly. He certainly couldn't kill a man, even in a quarrel. And what would he be quarrelling about anyway?"

"Perhaps you can tell us," Quintus invited. "We've heard already that there were several disagreements among the family yesterday."

"Oh yes, we were arguing all day long. About whether any of us should go to the Beltane feast. Bodvocos sent Uncle Magnus a message suggesting they should meet and publicly declare they wanted to live at peace and join forces against the Gauls. I thought it was a trap, and thought we should refuse to have anything to do with it. Vividus wanted Magnus to go and promise peace, but he said we should be prepared to go on defending ourselves because he was sure Bodvocos' men wouldn't keep to their side of it. Aquilo wanted peace at any cost, and agreed that my uncle should go and make an agreement, one that we'd all have to stick to. So if Aquilo quarrelled with my uncle, it can't have been about that. And as I've already said, Aquilo hasn't got it in him to be a killer…"

"We know it wasn't Aquilo who killed your uncle," I interrupted him. "He stayed at my sister's house last night. I was there, and I can vouch for that."

"Then who…?" He stopped, realising the answer. "You think I killed my uncle?"

We said nothing.

"You must be mad! You're not seriously accusing *me* of murdering my uncle?"

"We haven't got as far as accusing anyone yet," Quintus answered. "What we're doing is checking the movements of anyone who could possibly have killed him. That's anyone who was known to your uncle and familiar with the routine of the household."

"And," I added, "anyone who wouldn't have been afraid to visit Magnus while he was at his bath, even though, as we understand it, he disliked interruptions when he was bathing alone or with Niobe."

"That's what Niobe said, I take it," he exclaimed scornfully. "She's always made the most of her position with Uncle Magnus, pretending he'd prefer to be with her rather than discussing family matters. The truth is, Vividus and I quite often took the chance of a chat with the old boy first thing in the morning, before we all got too busy with our day's work."

"So if you weren't with your uncle in the baths this morning," I said, "Vividus could have been there?"

"He could, I suppose. But—no, it's ridiculous to suggest he'd kill Uncle Magnus. None of us would. As I said to start with, this is an outsider's work. One of the Long-hair raiders, or one of Bodvocos' young men. That's my view, and I suggest you stop wasting your time on fanciful theories based on tales made up by a concubine, and start hunting for the real killer."

And we couldn't get any more out of him. I didn't like the man any more than I had before, but his story seemed convincing, as did his shock at the news of his uncle's murder. We'd no choice but to accept his account of events.

Just as we were leaving I asked him casually, "By the way, Ferox, we've been picking up rumours that there's some kind of secret way in and out of the Fort that the men use at night. One of the gates, which is supposed to be kept locked, but there are spare keys in circulation…"

He grunted. "If you mean the so-called Achilles gate, it's true. The lads use it sometimes when they want to slip out and see girls. They think I don't know, but I'm prepared to let it go as long as they don't start bringing girls in here, or any other strangers, and they aren't such fools as to try that."

"Does anyone else know?"

He scratched his head. "Vividus, probably, he's pretty observant. Magnus didn't know, he'd have been upset by something so undisciplined."

"Thanks, Ferox," Quintus said. "We'll leave you free to get on with your work. Spring's a busy time for farmers."

Ferox growled something we couldn't hear, but its meaning was clear enough: he felt he was busy enough without having to answer our unnecessary and foolish questions.

Chapter XXIII

"The more we learn, the less we know," Quintus remarked irritably, leaning back in his chair. We were in his office again, having sent a servant to bring us some refreshment. The sky had clouded over so we had no sunlight to show us what hour it was, but our stomachs told us it was more than time for our midday meal. Now we were eating stale bread and ancient cheese, washed down with sour wine.

"Better than nothing, though not by much." I cut away a mouldy crust from the bread, and took an unenthusiastic bite. "Jupiter's balls, if this is the usual standard of food at the Fort, I'm surprised there aren't more murders. But there is one good result already. The report we take back to Clarus and Clarilla will convince them both that the Ostorii aren't the sort of family that Clarilla should be marrying into."

"That's true." Quintus nibbled at the cheese. "This takes me back to my army days, except I think our rations were better. Perhaps we should be encouraging Clarilla to take over the housekeeping here and improve the cuisine. She could bring her wonderful chef."

"He's Clarus' chef, and whoever Clarilla marries, her brother won't let her take him." I washed down the bread with a swallow of vinegar pretending to be wine. "Clarilla was right to be worried about Elli, though, wasn't she? We got her away from Bodvocos' just in time."

There was a soft knock at the door and Quintus called "Come in." Aquilo entered the room, looking calm but tired. I remembered he hadn't had much sleep the previous night, and offered him the stool, and a beaker of wine.

"Thanks, I'll have some wine. But…where on earth did you find that revolting-looking food?"

"We asked one of the slaves for refreshments," Quintus said.

"And they gave you yesterday's leavings? That's outrageous! Wait, I'll get you something better."

He went out again despite our protests, which in truth weren't very loud, and soon returned followed by the same slave who'd served us before, carrying a tray with fresh bread, cold mutton, and even some lettuce leaves, and a flask of white wine.

"Get this muck out of here," Aquilo told the man, "and if I catch any of you treating our guests like this again, you'll all be eating mouldy bread and water for a month. Understand?"

The slave nodded, picked up the rejected tray, and left. If he'd had a tail, it would have been between his legs.

"I'm sorry," Aquilo said.

"Don't worry. This is a feast." I cut up the new bread and cheese and we ate it gratefully.

"How are your investigations going?" he asked. "Do you know who killed my uncle?"

"Not yet, but we're close," Quintus answered, and I nodded agreement. A lie like that needed all the support it could get. "At least we're certain it wasn't you. But there's a strong possibility it may be someone within your family."

"So I gather. Ferox has been bending my ear about how you accused him. But I don't see it being old Ferox, or Vividus for that matter. We all had our differences with my uncle from time to time, but we all owed him a great deal, and we've never forgotten it. He took us all into his house and brought us up when our parents died. They both contracted some dreadful fever, and died within days of each other. Our nurse got us away from the house and brought us to Magnus, and he didn't hesitate to make us welcome."

"Do you think he'd have given consent eventually for you to marry Elli?" I'll be honest: this was nothing at all to do with our enquiries, but a girl can't help being curious.

He ran his hands through his untidy mop of hair. "I don't know, and now I never will. Perhaps." He sighed. "My brothers aren't happy about it. I've just had yet another row with Vividus, this time about my future."

"You told them about your baby?" I asked.

"Not yet. That has to stay secret till after Beltane. I daren't risk word getting back to Bodvocos about it. No, I just told them that I'm in love with Elli, and intend to live with her, whether we're legally married or not. So if they feel that would bring disgrace on the name of Ostorius, that's just too bad. But I'm trying to make Vividus see that the best thing is for him to give his formal consent as head of the family, it'll cause much less of a scandal. We'll be married, and I'll have my share of the inheritance, and take Elli to live somewhere I feel more at home. Londinium perhaps, or even another province, Italia or Greece."

"What did Vividus say to that?"

"He blustered and ranted, but he didn't say an outright no. He'll agree in the end, especially after tomorrow when we've made formal peace between ourselves and Bodvocos. Because surely once we've made peace, Bodvocos will give his consent, and Vividus won't want to appear less generous than a native."

Neither of us commented on this hopeful prophecy, but he didn't seem to notice. "I'm going to the feast to represent the family, did you know that? So I'll be the man making the pledge of peace with the Chief. Neither of the others want to go, but they've agreed that I'll attend, and we all hope that once Bodvocos and I have shown everyone publicly that we're no longer enemies, then these destructive quarrels will stop, and we can all put our minds to getting rid of the Gauls. You'll be coming to the feast too, won't you?"

"We plan to, if we're sufficiently far on with our work," Quintus said.

"Then I hope to see you there." He stood up. "I'm off back to Albia's now, to be with Elli and my son. I'll see to it that Elli gets to her father's house in plenty of time for the festivities tomorrow. But she won't be needed to perform the ceremony where the boat is launched on the tide. Coriu's daughter is doing it in her place. You know, I've dreamed of being able to bring peace back to this district. Tomorrow we'll make a start."

Once again I threw in a final irrelevant-seeming enquiry. "Going back to your uncle's death, Aquilo. Did you know there's a secret way in and out of the Fort that some of the men use at night, after the main gates are locked?"

"The small back gate in the corner? Yes, I did, in fact I'm the one that named it after Achilles. It's harmless enough, some of the wilder lads sneak out that way on summer nights and go courting. I went that way myself a few times last year, when I visited Elli."

"You don't think an outsider could have used it to enter the Fort, and attack your uncle?" Quintus asked.

"Gods, no. Getting through the wall is one thing, but moving about among the buildings, especially near the baths...no, that has to be someone familiar, someone in the household or close to it."

"It's the same story from everyone," I remarked to Quintus after Aquilo had gone. "We seem to be going round in circles."

Quintus stood up and stretched. "Gods, I feel like a lion in a cage. Let's go outside for a walk, and breathe some fresh air."

We strolled towards the back of the Fort, and out of the main rear gate, which stood wide open. Beyond the walls was a cleared strip of ground, and then fields stretching away to the sea. In the nearest one I spotted the four black horses Magnus had bought from me, and I walked over to the fence. They came to me for a bit of attention, and I talked to them and rubbed their glossy necks.

"Ah, Aurelia! Saying good-day to your horses?" Vividus asked, as he emerged from the Fort and came to join us.

"Yes. I hope they've settled in all right?"

"They're fine, just what we wanted." He hesitated, then gave me his most charming smile. "I'm glad I've caught you. I wanted to ask you something—oh, not about your investigations, that wouldn't be proper at all." He'd recovered his flirtatious manner, so I decided to play up to him.

"Not proper at all, no. But I'm sure there are plenty of other things you can ask me."

Quintus ambled off along the fence towards another bunch of horses, apparently completely absorbed in looking them over.

"I wondered if you've seen Silvanius Clarus lately."

"Yes, only a few days ago."

"Did he mention…I mean, did my name come up in conversation at all?"

I smiled, both outwardly and inwardly. It was as well he couldn't see the thoughts in my mind. "Yes, indeed it did. You've made a proposal of marriage to his sister, I understand."

"I have, but I'm still waiting for their reply. Silvanius said he wanted time to think about it, which is natural enough, of course. I suppose he didn't give you any idea of whether…that is, what…I mean, d'you think he'll accept?"

"They both talked about it," I answered, "and to be honest, I think they were still undecided. May I speak frankly, Vividus?"

"Please do. But that sounds ominous. Wasn't he in favour of it?"

"He was, but Clarilla was a little less certain. I think she found your uncle a little—er—direct in his speech."

"I was afraid of that. He can, I mean could, be quite insensitive sometimes. Just his way, you know, but he believed in plain speaking, no nonsense, and if it offended anyone, that was too bad. Did he say something to offend her?"

I nodded. "She was a little disturbed by one or two of your uncle's disparaging comments about natives, and his implication that all the native-born Britons are still barbarians at heart. Of course perhaps your uncle didn't realise Clarus comes from the old Brigantian aristocracy, and has never been ashamed of it, though he's proud to be a Roman citizen. His sister feels the same, so your uncle's comments were rather unfortunate."

Vividus sighed. "He was always making crass mistakes like that. I know I shouldn't speak ill of the dead, but sometimes I used to wish he'd think before he spoke."

"He was used to dealing with barbarian enemies, so he tended to treat inhabitants of a new province in the same way?" Gods, why was I making excuses for the old man's rudeness? But my instinct told me this could be important.

Vividus looked relieved. "You understand very well. Do you think now that Uncle's not here, they might look on my proposal more favourably?"

Not if I have anything to do with it, I thought. "It'd certainly be worth approaching them again, if you haven't had an answer in a month or two. You'd need to allow a decent interval to pass after the funeral, I think."

"Of course. I'll do whatever it takes. I want that marriage, Aurelia. It's important to me."

His vehemence surprised me. "May I ask why? You don't know Clarilla, so it isn't a love match. And you're an eligible bachelor, if ever I saw one. You could take your pick among the wealthy families of Britannia. Or anywhere else in the Empire," I added for good measure.

"Thank you. We've good reasons for wanting to be in this part of the province now…"

I gave him my merriest laugh. "Oh, of course. Caratacus' gold?"

Did I detect a flicker of surprise on his face? His loud answering laugh came so quickly that I couldn't be sure. "Ah, so the secret's out! And I thought nobody suspected that all those little holes in the ground, and the newly-turned patches of soil, were my doing." He laughed still louder. "Sad to say I haven't found it yet."

"But there's still hope. Neither has anyone else."

"Luckily my future plans don't depend on it." He became serious. "But they do depend on an alliance with a powerful

Brigantian like Silvanius. I want to make my way into public affairs. In this province, I mean, I'm too old to dream of Rome and senatorial purple. So marrying Clarilla is of great importance to me, and I'll do it, whatever it costs. Nothing is going to stand in my way." He stopped, looking self-conscious. "I'm sorry, I shouldn't rant on like this. Thank you for listening, and for your encouragement."

"I've enjoyed our chat." Well perhaps enjoyed wasn't quite the right word, but I'd certainly found it interesting. It had made me aware that Vividus had a motive for wanting his uncle dead.

Chapter XXIV

As Quintus and I walked slowly back from the horse field, we realised how the weather had changed. A north wind had risen and was pushing big dark clouds across the blue sky. As we reached the wall of the Fort, a scattering of raindrops fell, and we heard the faint roll of thunder in the distance.

"I hope we're not in for a storm," I said. "I don't mind a few splashes of rain, but I don't fancy riding back to Albia's in a downpour. Only I do want to get home tonight."

"Must you go?" He smiled at me. "I had dinner with the Ostorii last night, but I doubt if Vividus will invite me to join him tonight, with the funeral and all. So I've a long solitary evening ahead. But if you stay..."

"Aurelia!" We looked round to see Niobe beckoning us from her sitting-room window upstairs. "This isn't an afternoon for going walking. Come up to my room and have a glass of something to warm you."

The rain was getting heavier with every pace we took, so we accepted her offer and hurried inside to join her. Quintus paused outside the office. "Let's make sure we're not being spied on," he murmured. He plucked a long hair from his head, and positioned it high up on the hinge side of the door. If anyone opened it, the hair would break. Then we climbed the stairs and Niobe welcomed us in, smiling warmly at Quintus.

"Now tell me how your enquiries are going," she said as she handed round glasses. "Or is it all a deadly secret?"

"Most of it is," Quintus returned her smile. "But you never know, after a glass or two of wine we may not be able to stop ourselves telling you everything."

"Oh good, that's what I'm counting on."

Her room was comfortably warm and smelled of rose perfume. We sat down near the window, which was closed now against the rain. We parried her questions about our enquiries, and she flirted outrageously with Quintus, who enjoyed himself being charming and amusing for her benefit. Eventually she turned to me with a mischievous smile.

"Aurelia, I hope you're not thinking of riding back to your sister's in this deluge. Listen to it!" Indeed the rain was now lashing at her window out of a sky as black as ink, and the rolling thunder-claps were almost continuous.

"I was hoping to," I answered, "but it looks and sounds pretty awful out there."

"Then you mustn't even dream of it. We'd be delighted to put you up here, I'll tell the servants to get a bedroom ready for you. It'll be in the guest wing, where Quintus Antonius' room is." I avoided Quintus' eye. "I'll get them to serve you dinner too. I'm afraid it won't be a family meal. The boys and I will be attending Magnus' funeral."

"In this weather?"

"Oh yes. Most sensible people would put it off, I expect, but my two tough ex-centurions have told me in no uncertain terms that Magnus wouldn't have been deterred from his duty by a mere storm, so we mustn't be either." She made a wry face. "Sometimes I think young Aquilo has the right idea, you know, even though he is a silly little idiot. But I'm sure poets and musicians wouldn't insist on braving the elements. Anyway I don't imagine he'll come back now, do you?"

"No." I hadn't imagined he'd come back at all tonight, but I suppose he'd had to tell his brothers he would attend the ceremony.

"Well then, have I persuaded you?" She smiled at me. "Will you stay overnight? You'll have plenty of time to get back to your sister's tomorrow, if you want to change into something special for the Beltane feast. Or you can go direct from here, if you'd rather."

"When tomorrow comes, we'll decide what we're doing. But thank you, I think I should like to stay tonight."

We heard a footstep outside the door, and Vividus came in without waiting to be asked.

"Sorry, Niobe, but I need to see Antonius. I wonder if I could have a word with you please?"

"Of course. We'll go down to my office."

"Oh, there's no need to trouble Aurelia. I need to talk to you alone, if possible."

"I'd prefer Aurelia to be with me. Since she's helping me in this matter, it's best she hears what you tell me direct from you, not at second hand afterwards."

"But I need…I want…I must be able to rely on your complete discretion. Both of you."

"You can rely on it. You have my word."

"And mine," I put in. "Discretion is one of the most important of an innkeeper's qualities. Our customers may gossip, but we can keep quiet when it's necessary."

"Very well." Vividus looked at each of us in turn and heaved a loud sigh. "Then we'll go into my office."

"Thank you for the wine, Niobe," I said, as we left. Though I'd have insisted on being present at Vividus' talk with Quintus, all the same I felt reluctant to leave her warm, pleasant room.

"This isn't easy for me, or pleasant," Vividus said when we were all seated in his room. "But I must do my duty." A flash of lightning made me realise that the sky was growing even darker, though it wasn't yet night-time.

Quintus said, "What's the trouble?"

"I've been talking to my men, especially the guards, because they are trained to observe people's movements around the Fort, and I felt sure one of them must have noticed something unusual this morning. It turns out one of them did."

"Good," Quintus said. "Who, and what was it he noticed?"

"My chief guard, Rinacus. I'd like you to hear his account for yourselves." He rang a small silver bell, and sent the servant who answered it to fetch the chief guard.

I thought, this will be interesting. I wonder if he knows we've interviewed Rinacus already?

"Has he been with you long?" Quintus asked.

"About two years. Since before we came to Britannia, anyway. He's ex-army, and Uncle Magnus took him on as a bodyguard in Gaul shortly after he left the service. He was a good soldier, and he's been extremely useful here, especially since we began having trouble with the natives. As chief guard he's in charge of the day-to-day security here. A top quality man."

The guard captain knocked, came in, and stood to attention. He looked ill at ease, more like a legionary who was expecting a reprimand than an officer with important information to deliver. His relaxed pose of the morning had deserted him.

Even when Vividus told him to sit down he was still as stiff as a spear, and made his report in terse military style. "I was on early duty this morning, and just as it was beginning to get light I noticed Master Ferox going in the direction of the stable yard, and I followed him for a few paces, to make sure he was all right."

"Why shouldn't he be all right?" Quintus asked. "Has he been ill?"

"Well, no, sir, not ill. But sometimes he has had dreams, and even walks in his sleep. If he's seen around in the night or the very early morning, we're under instructions to keep an eye out for him."

He glanced at Vividus, who nodded. "My poor brother does suffer very badly with nightmares, I'm afraid."

Rinacus cleared his throat. "This morning he was fine. He waved to me as he went to the stables, and a short while later I saw him come out with a saddled horse. I expected he'd head off for the main gate, or go and get some breakfast, but he didn't. He left the horse tied up and went to the bath-house."

He paused, and now I saw why he was so uneasy. He was about to accuse one of his masters of murder.

"Did you follow him there?" Quintus asked.

"No, I didn't. The master—the old master, Lord Magnus— liked to take his bath early in the morning, and hated any of us to disturb him while he was at it, except for Niobe of course. I thought Master Ferox must have had pressing business with his uncle, to go in and interrupt him, but that wasn't any affair of mine. So I went on my way."

"You didn't linger just for a short while, to make sure all was well?" I asked. "Nobody could have blamed you for being conscientious."

"No, ma'am."

"So you didn't happen to hear voices raised inside, some sort of quarrel going on?"

"No, sir."

"Did you see Ferox come out of the baths again?"

"No. Like I said, I went on my way."

"Did you see Niobe?" I asked.

"I saw her crossing the courtyard, and assumed she was going to join the master, but I didn't actually watch her enter."

"And that was after you'd seen Ferox go in there?"

"Yes, ma'am, well after."

"You know what your statement implies, Rinacus?" Vividus asked him. "You're quite sure of your facts?"

"I'm quite sure, my lord. I know what I'm saying, and I'm very sorry to have to report something so…something like this."

"Any more questions for him, Antonius?" Vividus asked.

"Just one. Rinacus, we spoke to you this morning and you didn't mention any of this. Why not?"

He looked down at his feet, a picture of embarrassment. "I'm sorry, I know I should have spoken out, and I wanted to. But it seemed sort of disloyal, to inform on Master Ferox. I wanted a chance to talk to Lord Vividus first. He advised me that whatever the consequences I must tell you everything."

"And you've told us everything now? There's nothing else you'd like to add?"

"No, sir."

Vividus dismissed him, ordering him to stay inside the Fort in case he was needed later. "A sound man, that, very loyal and honest. I trust him, and, sad though I am, I believe what he's just told us."

"You'd take his word against that of your brother?" Quintus asked.

"I'm afraid I would. Ferox has been acting strangely these last few months. As Rinacus said, he's not exactly ill, but he has these recurring nightmares, about something that happened to him on his last campaign—a fire at a camp where several of his friends were killed. The bad dreams come most nights, often more than once, so he doesn't have much sleep."

"A man can get used to going without sleep, though," Quintus pointed out. "It happens for days on end in the army. Men on long, difficult campaigns, or on siege work...."

"But this has been going on for months. We've done our best with him, kept him busy, let him know that we sympathise with him. He's a very competent farm manager, and he believed in all the new ideas for this place that our uncle brought with him to Britannia. But he's become too wrapped up in our quarrel with Bodvocos, and with the raiders. He thinks of little else now."

"I still don't see how that could make him responsible for your uncle's death," I said. "When we spoke to him earlier, he was saying how much your uncle did for you three brothers, taking you in as boys after your mother died."

"I know. But I think this whole idea of making peace with the natives was too much for him to accept. He spent most of yesterday arguing with Magnus about it. He wanted no part of any peace-making initiative, he said it was a trap being laid for us by Bodvocos, and that if we went to the Beltane feast we'd all be massacred. They rowed for hours about it." He turned to Quintus. "You heard some of it, Antonius, didn't you, when we were all having dinner last night?"

Quintus nodded. "I did, but I have to say, Vividus, that I heard you rowing with your uncle too."

"I admit it!" he exclaimed. "I was worried about the dangers of accepting, yet I didn't want to refuse Bodvocos' offer outright. I agreed that Magnus should attend the Beltane feast and even go through some kind of formal peace-making ceremony if it was unavoidable. I hoped that would at least quieten them down for a while, so we could deal with the Gauls. The gods know that nobody else is having any success controlling them. Young Aurelius…I know he's your brother, Aurelia, and I'm sure he's done his best, but he's got nowhere so far. How can he? Half-a-dozen men coming in from outside aren't anything like enough."

"I'm inclined to agree with you about that," Quintus said. "But let's keep to the matter in hand. You'll allow me to arrest Ferox then, and send him under guard to Eburacum for the authorities to deal with? If he confesses to the murder, he'll be exiled, but if he protests his innocence still, there'll probably have to be a trial, with Rinacus and yourself as the principal witnesses."

Vividus nodded. "I know all that. Believe me it gives me no pleasure. But I want my uncle avenged."

"If we need to hold him prisoner, have you a suitable room where we can keep him securely under lock and key?"

"We have a small lockup. Rarely used, but if any of the lads are caught brawling, or drinking too much too often, a spell in there brings them to heel."

"Then we'll interview Ferox straight away," Quintus said. "You'll come with us, Vividus, please."

We talked to Ferox for some time, but it can all be summed up in a couple of sentences. Vividus accused him of murdering Magnus, and brought in Rinacus to give his account of seeing Ferox enter the bath-house. Ferox vehemently denied laying a finger on his uncle, called Rinacus a liar, and insisted he'd left the Fort before dawn. It was one man's word against another.

I think Quintus felt as I did. Neither Ferox nor Rinacus were likeable, but Rinacus seemed the more reliable, and Vividus supported the guard's word against his own brother. So eventually Quintus told Ferox formally that he was under arrest for Magnus' murder. Since it was late in the day it wasn't practical to escort him all the way to Eburacum, so he would be kept under guard at the Fort overnight, and taken to the town in the morning.

Ferox roared like a cornered bull, and tried to break out of his office. It took Lucius and two men to hold him and march him off to the lockup, which was a small dingy room at the back of the main house. It had metal bars across the window opening and outside bolts on its shutters, and there was no furniture but a bench and a moth-eaten blanket. With some difficulty they shackled Ferox' feet to a chain that was let into the stone wall, and left him there, still proclaiming his innocence and swearing that he'd been betrayed.

"Well he would claim that, wouldn't he?" I remarked to Quintus as we headed for our office.

Quintus, as usual, was more cautious. "Does it seem to you that this is all a bit too convenient?"

"Not really. I've never liked the man, and I'm not surprised he's a murderer."

"Perhaps you're right. It's just…I don't know. Well, he can appeal to Caesar, that's his right as a citizen. The whole case will drag on for months, and his military record will stand in his favour."

"At least now we've an Emperor whose justice we can trust."

"They say he takes his duties very seriously…Look, that was lightning, wasn't it?"

A clap of thunder echoed round the Fort, and I swore at it, and at Jupiter, who, if you believe the priests, is responsible for such happenings.

"Careful," Quintus joked, "you're insulting the King of the Gods."

"And he deserves it. But for this storm I could be on my way home to my sister's. I expect he's just making some bad weather to spite me, so I'll have to endure the Fort's food instead of Albia's good cooking."

Oh, me and my big mouth! One should never insult a god, even as a joke.

Chapter XXV

In the pitch black middle of the night, something woke me. I lay in bed, less than half awake, feeling lazy and lethargic. I vaguely thought I ought to be curious about what had roused me, because it was something unusual, a noise that shouldn't have been there in the dead of night. But I was warm and comfortable and very sleepy. I'd had a long day rounded off with a good dinner, and perhaps a beaker more wine than I should. And after all, I was in someone else's house, and some of the night-noises were bound to be unfamiliar.

The storm was still battering my window with pelting rain, and filling the air with rolling thunder now and then. Nothing unusual about those noises, and I was glad I'd decided not to travel back to Albia's. Perhaps there'd been an extra loud clap of thunder? I was too fuddled with sleep to care. I yawned and let my eyes close.

A flash of lightning made me open them again, and I froze, now fully awake. I wasn't alone in the room. A man stood at the foot of my bed, looking down at me and smiling. He whispered, "So you're awake at last, Aurelia Marcella?" Then darkness hid him again.

"Who's there? Whoever you are, get out of here." But the words didn't come out as a challenge, just an inaudible mumble. I tried to sit up, but in horror I realised I couldn't. My body felt as heavy as lead, and my arms and legs refused to move. It was like the paralysis you get in the worst kind of nightmare. Was

I drunk? Or sick? Or going mad? Only my mind operated at something like the proper speed, and I understood that I was in serious danger: there was a man in my room, and he could do whatever he liked with me, because I couldn't stop him.

My only hope was to scream for help, which I did, as loudly as I could. My cry didn't last long. He growled "Quiet, bitch!" and threw himself on the bed on top of me, putting a hand over my mouth. With his other hand he reached under my head for the pillow and pressed it over my mouth instead, leaning his weight on it so that I couldn't shift it. At least I could still breathe through my nose, but I felt stifled and trapped, unable to throw him off because my movements were as feeble as a child's.

"Keep quiet! Quiet and still!" he whispered. His words were slurred, and his breath stank of beer, which wasn't comforting. I've had enough experience of drunks to be aware how dangerous they can be. So I lay as quiet and still as a stone.

"I don't want to hurt you." The whisper was almost conversational. "But I will if you act stupid. Here's my knife, see?" I couldn't see, but I could feel the way he moved his right arm, pulling something out of his belt, and then the touch of a sharp point pricking the soft skin of my neck.

"What do you want?" I asked, and this time the words were more or less intelligible.

"To give you a message, that's all. A piece of good advice from a well-wisher." He laughed softly. "Keep your nose out of Ostorius family business, or you'll be sorry. Got that?"

I didn't answer.

"I said got that?" The knife-point dug into my neck, not hard, but I felt blood on my skin.

"I've got it."

"Go away from here tomorrow and don't come back. Got that?"

"Yes." Gladly, I added silently. If I ever see tomorrow…

"Good." He eased his weight a little so that he lay alongside me rather than on top. It was a relief, but then he pressed his body hard against me, and I realised that giving me advice wasn't all he wanted now.

"You're not bad looking, really," he whispered. "Well all women are beautiful in the dark, I suppose." He laughed to himself, and I had to lie there, knowing what he intended but completely helpless to prevent it. I was in a house full of people, with Quintus' room and Lucius' room only a few paces down the corridor. But in the dark, with a thunderstorm going on, nobody would be up and about to see or hear. And I was so tired and weak. Why was that? They must have put something in my food or drink at supper, some poison to prevent my moving. Perhaps they'd poisoned the others too.

Panic engulfed me. Had they used hemlock? Was I experiencing the beginning of the paralysis that hemlock brings before it kills you?

Strangely, the terror of this idea brought me strength, a sudden influx of energy that overcame my body's weakness. I wasn't dead yet, and I wasn't going to die without a fight. And the man on my bed wasn't expecting me to die either, otherwise why would he have come here to threaten me? So I could take control of this situation. I *must*. But how?

The drunk himself gave me the answer. He began to run his hands over my body—both hands, I realised, which meant he'd abandoned his knife, and he wasn't holding down the pillow over my mouth. I shook my head very gently, and the pillow slid away, but he didn't even realise this as he moved to lie on top of me again. If I could muster the strength, I could take him by surprise and get away. But I must do it now.

I took a deep breath and let out another scream for help, and this one was ear-splitting. At the same time I brought my knee up into his groin, and as the pain hit him, I twisted my whole body to the right and managed to wriggle out from under him. With a final push I flung myself off the bed.

He cursed and grabbed at me with both hands, but he missed, and I rolled away from the bed just as he jumped off it, landing with a thud that shook the room. I stood up, feeling shaky still, but my strength was coming back. I seized the wooden stool from beside the bed and held it up high in front of me, its three legs pointing away from me into the dark. He lunged at me and I felt the legs smash into his face. He grunted in pain and grabbed at the stool, trying to wrench it free, but I hung on till the flimsy thing broke. So now we each had a weapon of sorts, and of course he still had his knife. But I was out of his reach, at least for now.

I was still screaming "Help! Help!" as loudly as I could, and he was shouting in drunken fury, telling me what he'd do when he caught me, which I knew he could still do unless I could get out of there. I stopped screaming and for a few heartbeats I had the advantage of knowing where he was while he couldn't hear me, but then he fell silent too. I began to move softly round the edge of the room towards where the door must be, though I couldn't be sure in the blackness. There was no sound now but the rain on the window. We were both holding our breaths, and stepping quietly enough not to be heard.

Lightning filled the room with brightness and we found we were very close together, almost touching. He had his right arm raised, and one of the broken stool-legs in his hand. I dived under his raised arm and bolted towards the door.

I stopped, because I saw the door was opening, and as darkness came again, someone rushed into the room. A peal of thunder split the silence, and Quintus' voice rang out. "Aurelia, get into the corridor while I deal with this scum."

"He's got a knife," I called out, jumping to the right so my voice didn't give my position away.

"So have I."

I felt a flood of relief, but the fight wasn't over yet. I began to move again, continuing my progress towards the door. At least now I knew where it was. Then I felt myself flung out of the way so roughly that I fell over, and the intruder gave a final curse and ran for the door himself. I shouted a warning and heard sounds of a scuffle, and then the rush of heavy footsteps running away along the corridor, followed by the bang of the outside door into the courtyard.

"Aurelia? Are you all right?"

"I think so. " I picked myself up and groped for the bed to steady myself. "Are you?"

"Yes." He came close and put his arms round me. My legs felt as weak as water, I wanted to sink onto the bed and lie down. But I wanted still more to feel him holding me, so I just stood there for a while, resting my head on his shoulder, till I'd stopped shaking and my heartbeat had slowed down from a gallop to a fast trot. Then we both sat on the bed.

"Better now?" he asked.

"Yes." I kissed him. "Thank you, Quintus. If you hadn't been there…"

"Don't think about it. I suppose you didn't recognise him?"

I shook my head. "I didn't even get a good look at him. But I hit him in the face quite hard with a stool. He'll have a few bruises tomorrow, with luck."

"I'm sorry I took so long to come to you." He kissed me gently. "Your screaming woke me up, and I knew you must be in trouble, but I felt dreadful and could hardly move. It was as if I was ill, or very drunk. I'm still half-drugged now, but it seems to be wearing off."

"Me too. I thought I was dying at one point."

"They must have put something in our food or drink tonight, so we'd sleep soundly."

I got up. "Before I do anything else, I'll light my candle. I don't like being in the dark. Thank the gods for sending the lightning!"

"I know. I suggest we spend the rest of the night in my room. I've lighted my candle already, and anyhow there's safety in numbers. We ought to take turns to keep awake."

I laughed. "Tired as I feel, there's no danger of me sleeping another wink under this roof."

The corridor lamps were out, but Quintus' door was only a few paces along from mine, and the reassuring strip of light shining under it made it easy to find. All the same I was nervous as we covered the dark space between, and relieved when we were able to step inside and sit down on his bed.

"Some wine?" he suggested.

"No thanks. I'm not eating or drinking anything till we're safely back at Albia's."

"This is wine from my own flask, the one I brought with me from Albia's. It's safe, and there's enough for a few mouthfuls each."

"In that case, yes please." He poured us each a small measure. It tasted like the nectar of the gods.

"I wonder," he mused, "who it was who wanted us to sleep so soundly tonight, and why?"

"Perhaps they planned to kill us both in our sleep." I shivered. "When I woke up and saw the man standing there by my bed…"

"Just standing there? With a weapon in his hand?"

"No, he drew his knife later to shut me up. Listen, I'll tell it from the beginning."

When I'd finished, Quintus said, "That doesn't sound much like the way a killer would behave. Surely he'd just enter the bedroom, stab his victim a couple of times, and get out as quickly as he could. And there's one good thing about all this."

"There is?"

"If somebody's taken the trouble to drug us, and then to warn you off, it must mean we're getting dangerously close to the truth. Perhaps we've even arrived there…"

He stopped, as a series of loud yells echoed through the night. A man was shouting the single word "Run!" over and over again. It was coming from somewhere outside and fairly close by, and it wasn't especially loud, but the terror in the voice made me jump up and look wildly round the room. "Quintus, that must be what woke me up tonight. I knew it was something scary, but I was so full of sleep…What does it mean?"

"I'll go and take a look." He crossed the room and picked up his travelling-cloak. "Judging from the direction, it's coming from the room where we're holding Ferox. There's a guard on the door there, but I'd better make certain nobody's trying to take their private revenge on him. You'll be all right here while I slip outside?"

"Not on your life. I'm coming too…no, don't argue, Quintus, I'm not staying by myself in this room. Just let me get my cloak."

Quintus knows me well, and he recognises those occasions when it's pointless to argue with me. He lighted me to my room with his candle, and lit mine while I put on my heavy cloak. We left one candle burning on a shelf in the corridor, and tiptoed along till we came to the door that led out into the courtyard.

It opened quietly, and we stood looking out onto the wet paving-stones, letting our eyes adjust to the very dim light coming from a scattering of wall-mounted torches around the courtyard. Quintus leaned close and whispered, "Follow me."

But before we could move, a flash of lightning showed us the whole courtyard as bright as day, and I almost cried out. Two men were standing there quite close to us, against the wall of the main building. Both were wearing thick hooded cloaks, and the taller one had his back to me. But I recognised the other, even though his face was mostly hidden. "Rinacus," I breathed, and Quintus nodded.

"Well?" Rinacus spoke softly, but we could hear easily. "Did you check?"

"I did."

"And are they asleep?"

"Yes."

"Good. Then get over to the gate and let him in and bring him here."

"Alright."

The man left, and Quintus breathed, "At least we know why they wanted us out of the way. Rinacus is expecting company."

Before long we heard footsteps, and the guard brought a third man to stand beside the wall. Rinacus waved the guard away, and another brief glare of lightning showed him exchanging a silent handshake with the newcomer. I saw that the new arrival's leather cloak and hood were soaking wet. He'd been out in the rain for some time. If only we could see his face…

Rinacus said, "I'm glad you've come. I wasn't sure you would, in this weather."

"I didn't exactly have a choice." The man's tone was surly. "He can't come himself, and it's urgent. Anyhow at least there won't be anyone watching on a night like this. We've heard about these investigators you've got staying here, nosing around into everything."

"They're sound asleep, we've seen to that. So let's not waste time. What's so urgent?"

"Tell your boss there's a change of plan. We'll have a much better chance if we do it tomorrow."

Rinacus swore. "Tomorrow? We can't start messing the plans about at this stage! Listen, you're not trying to tell me he's backing out, are you? Because if he is, I…"

"Of course he isn't. Just the opposite. He says it'll be much better tomorrow than in two days' time, because folk will all be at the feast."

"But doesn't he have to be there himself? Oh, I get it, he's asking us to do all the work while he sits around at home drinking his beer…"

"Close your gob and open your lugs, can't you? He doesn't have to be at the feast now. He's supposed to show his face, but he can say he's heard some rumour about a raid by the Gauls, so he can leave any time." He laughed. "It'll be true, in its way. You can use the same excuse on old Magnus."

"We won't have to. Magnus is dead."

"Dead? What from?"

"It wasn't old age," Rinacus sneered, "but more than that I don't know, and I'm not asking. Vividus is master now, and he can do as he likes. He doesn't even plan to be at the feast at all. He's sending Aquilo."

"So much the better. Well then, the new plan is, we meet there as agreed, only change the time to tomorrow at noon."

"Somebody's told the Gauls?"

"Yes, and they're up for it. So we meet, we do the job, we come away laughing. Laughing and rich. We'll all be home well before dark. Probably nobody'll even miss us. All right?"

Rinacus sighed. "I suppose so. All right. It makes sense. I always said Beltane would be the best day. You're quite sure they'll be at the feast?"

"Yes, they're all planning to go, taking some of the guards as escorts. They reckon it'll be a day of peace, so the farm'll be safe."

"But they'll leave a few lads behind, I suppose."

"Bound to, but they'll be easy enough. They won't be expecting us, and they'll probably have a Beltane drink or two themselves when the bosses are gone."

"Then tomorrow it is." Rinacus' voice rose excitedly. "I'll see you there, Vulso."

The man's reply was drowned by another wild burst of shouting, "Fire! Fire!" this time, coming from somewhere to our left.

Rinacus swore. "You'd better go. Ferox is having one of his dreams again, and shouting 'Fire' will bring people running. Quick, let's get you out of the gate." Their footsteps receded as they walked swiftly away.

Quintus grabbed my arm. "Let's get to Ferox."

The guard standing outside the prisoner's locked room was Ollius. He was looking round uneasily, and was extremely glad when Quintus and I appeared.

"Sir, the prisoner's going mad in there, shouting and yelling. I don't know what to do. Now he's calling out that there's a fire, and I don't think there is, but…"

"Give me the key." The guard handed it over. "We'll go in. You stay out here on guard. This could be a diversion, to make us unlock the door so someone from outside can get Ferox out."

"Or a trap to persuade one of us to go in," Ollius suggested.

Quintus drew his knife, then put the key into the lock and turned it softly. He threw the door open and stepped slightly to one side, knife held ready in case the prisoner rushed out.

Nobody emerged, and no running footsteps from the courtyard disturbed the silence.

We stepped into the small room, dimly lit by one torch on the wall, and found a truly pathetic sight. Ferox was sitting on the bench, apparently convulsed with terror. He was hunched up, rocking backwards and forwards and moaning to himself; he was shivering and sweating, and tears streamed down his face. For all his size and his powerful physique, he looked more like a frightened boy than a man. If I hadn't known him for a murderer, I'd have been tempted to put my arms round him to comfort him.

"It's all right, Ferox," Quintus said softly. "There's no fire. You're safe, and nobody's going to hurt you. Was it a bad dream?"

He nodded. "The fire in the woods. At the camp. I was there, it was happening all over again. I couldn't make them hear…"

"You're at the Fort now, and there isn't any fire," I said.

Behind us a woman's voice spoke sharply. I looked round and was surprised to find Niobe berating the guard.

"Don't be a fool, man, I've got to go to him. Aurelia, tell this idiot to let me through to Ferox. He's had one of his nightmares, he needs me with him."

"Let her come in, Ollius," I said.

She stepped into the room, wearing a heavy wool cloak which incongruously carried the smell of her rose perfume. She sat down beside Ferox and put her arm round him, speaking to him very quietly.

"There now, Ferox, it's all right. I'm here, and I'll keep the bad dreams away tonight." She repeated more or less the same comforting words over and over, like a mother reassuring a scared child.

Gradually he became calm and still, then raised his head and looked round at us all. "I didn't kill him. I know you think I did, but you're wrong. I didn't."

"Then who did?" The words came out before I could stop them. "You were seen going into the bath-house, Ferox. You went into the hot room, quarrelled with your uncle, and stabbed him…"

"For the gods' sake!" Niobe snapped at me. "This isn't the time or the place. Ferox has had a bad night. He needs some of his sleeping medicine, it sometimes helps him. May I fetch it for him, and then stay with him through the night? You can leave your guard outside if you must."

"We must, I'm afraid," Quintus said. "But please fetch his medicine and anything else that will help him."

She stood up, careful not to move too fast. "I won't be long now, Ferox, and these others will stay here till I get back." She turned, still moving slowly, and only when she was out of the room did she break into a run.

"I'm sorry I woke you," Ferox said. "It was just an awful dream. I get them quite often and they make me shout out, silly confused messages, but I don't know I'm doing it. I'll be all right now."

I said, "Nevermind, Ferox, we were awake anyway." Neither of us could think of anything else to say. Niobe was right, this wasn't the appropriate setting to discuss Magnus' murder. Anyway what was the point? We had a reliable witness, sure of his facts, who had seen Ferox go to meet his uncle. He couldn't talk his way out of that.

We were glad to leave him when Niobe returned. "Don't let anyone in or out of here, Ollius," Quintus said as he locked the door and handed the key back to the guard. "Are you here all night, or will someone relieve you?"

"I'm due a relief at bugle-call."

"Make sure he understands the situation. Nobody to enter or leave that room without me or Aurelius being present."

"You're still thinking this might be some sort of ruse?" I asked when we got back to Quintus' room.

"I'm just being sensible. We'd look pretty foolish if it was."

We sat down side by side on his bed. "Well, what do you make of Rinacus and the messenger? From Coriu, presumably?"

"Yes. I couldn't see the man's face, but I caught the name Vulso, and he's one of the senior men of the Chief's guard."

"And while everyone is eating and drinking themselves into a stupor, he and Coriu will be mounting some sort of raid. With Vividus, we assume, as he referred to Rinacus' boss."

"He could have meant Magnus."

"No. When he heard Magnus was dead, that didn't alter the plans. And the Gauls are involved too somehow."

"And all of them will be descending on Candidus and Albia's farm."

Quintus nodded. "I take it that was where they meant. They were annoyingly vague about it."

I smiled. "They were, but there's no doubt, to my mind. And the whole family plan to be at the feast—or planned, I should say, because presumably they won't go now. But what's the purpose of it, I wonder?"

"Obviously they're looking for the gold. Even you must accept that now, Aurelia."

"I suppose I must."

"It all fits together. They've been trying to get access to Esico's property, and to Albia's. Nowhere else, not in the same way. They must be certain the gold is buried on one of those two farms."

"They must have thought so for some time. First they tried to get hold of the farms legally. Magnus offered to buy out Esico and also Candidus, but neither would sell."

"Then they used terror tactics, paying the raiders to do some dirty work, and that scared Esico away, so they've looked round his empty farm, but found nothing."

I nodded, remembering the freshly dug trench we'd seen on our way up from Oak Bridges. "And now they think the gold is on Albia's land. The terror tactics didn't work there, though." I felt a surge of pride in my sister and her husband. "They showed they couldn't be bullied or frightened off their farm like poor Esico."

"So the only course left them is to go there in force and search," Quintus said thoughtfully. "If they're right, Albia and Candidus are sitting on a fortune—*if they're right*."

"We've been saying 'they' are doing this and that, but I still find it astonishing that Vividus and Coriu are working *together*. They've been at each other's throats for months."

"Apparently that was all for show. But I got the impression the two of them are working privately, I mean without telling their families. Vulso said that Coriu could use an excuse to get away from the Beltane party. If Bodvocos knew about the raid, he wouldn't have to bother with excuses. And he said that the same excuse would do for Magnus. That must mean neither of the older men know about it."

"Oh come on, of course they do. There isn't anybody north of the Humber who *doesn't* know about it."

"About the gold, yes. But this is different. Vividus and Coriu now know where it is, or they think they do. And they're not telling anybody else."

I felt suddenly chilled, and pulled a blanket round me. "So then. We need to send an urgent message to Albia and Candidus. Did Titch get back all right last evening?"

"No, he didn't. I suppose the storm would have made travelling quite difficult, and he preferred to keep his shepherdess warm."

"Then one of Lucius' men will have to go, storm or no storm."

"We ought to wake Lucius anyway. I'll go to his room now. It's only just along the corridor. Leave the door open, I won't be long. I wonder if anyone tampered with his supper too?"

They had, but Lucius had been woken by Ferox' shouting, and Quintus met him walking a little groggily along the corridor in our direction.

As he heard about the night's adventures he became fully alert. "Gods, what a lot I've missed! It's a good job you two managed to see what was happening." His green eyes were anxious as he looked me up and down. "Are you sure you're all right now, Sis?"

"I'm fine, except that I'm thirsty and cold. In other words, in need of a drink, but I'm not touching any of the wine from here, and we've finished up Quintus' flask. You haven't any of Albia's wine left, I suppose?"

He grinned at me. "That's a relief. At least I know you've suffered no permanent ill effects. You fight off a drunken rapist, you overhear plans for a raid on our sister, and all you can think about is wine! As it happens, I've a flask in my room."

After he'd fetched it and shared out its contents, we began to make our plans.

"First," Quintus said, "are we all agreed that we need to send as many men as possible over to Albia's farm, to deal with the raid that Vividus and Coriu are planning?"

We all were, but Lucius pointed out that he needed to send a couple of his troopers to escort Ferox to Eburacum.

"If you take four men to Albia's, that'll be enough," Quintus said. "We'll have surprise on our side, and Candidus has Brutus and his lads there already."

"You're going there too?" Lucius asked.

"Of course. But I can go direct, on pretext of escorting Aurelia. You'll have to go roundabout. The last thing we want is for Vividus or Rinacus to realise that Albia will be getting reinforcements."

Lucius nodded. "Understood. We'll leave at dawn, and I'll tell the boys we're heading back to our camp on the Headland. We'll ride a mile or so towards the coast and turn west again when we're well away from here."

"Good. Then there's just one more matter to be settled."

Lucius looked grim. "Who tried to rape Aurelia, and how do we find him?"

"Aurelia, you said you couldn't identify him from the brief glimpse you had in your room. Did you get a better view when we saw him later?"

"No, I'm afraid not. I couldn't even tell whether his face was bruised, but I hit him quite hard, so he should have some marks on him by morning."

"Do you want us to organise a full parade of all the men here, so we can pick out the intruder? We'll execute him here, once we're sure we've got the right man."

I thought it over carefully, then reluctantly said no. "I'm afraid we'll have to leave it for today. I want the bastard caught, but it's more important to go to Albia's. Picking the right man out from all the other guards here could be a long process, there are so many of them. And that's assuming he's still here and doesn't make a run for it, which I imagine he will. He must know even Rinacus can't protect him if he's guilty of attempted rape."

The men both nodded, and Lucius said, "That's the right decision, Sis."

"And a brave one," Quintus added.

The rest of the night passed surprisingly quickly as we finalised the details of our plans. Lucius roused his men, and left instructions with Ollius and Tertius about escorting the prisoner to Eburacum. Ferox himself was asleep when we looked in on him, with his head in Niobe's lap. She whispered that she'd stay with him till daylight. I whispered back that we'd leave instructions for her to be released then, but by daylight I'd be on my way to my sister's. She seemed genuinely sorry to say good-bye.

Chapter XXVI

We left the Fort as soon as there was light to see. We were earlier even than the morning bugle, but the gate-guards let us through, probably glad enough to see the back of us. The storm had blown itself out, and a thick white mist covered everything, It seeped clammily through our clothes and deep into our bones, and as I'd refused breakfast, I felt the cold in spite of my heavy cloak. But I was so pleased to be leaving the Ostorii that I hardly noticed.

We were delayed slightly because we couldn't find Vividus. We'd decided it would cause comment if we departed without observing the courtesies, and anyway we wanted to convince him that we suspected nothing about his planned attack on my sister. But nobody knew where he was. Rinacus said he assumed his master had gone out early to ride round the farm, since Ferox wasn't now available to do this. We had to accept his explanation, even though we'd a pretty shrewd idea what Vividus was really up to. For the sake of form we left a message of thanks and farewell with Rinacus, to be passed on to Vividus on his return.

We'd barely ridden through the gates when Titch arrived. We heard hoof-beats first, then saw him looming up out of the mist. He and his horse were sweating despite the fog.

"Good of you to join us," Quintus said as the panting horse skidded to a standstill. "Better late than never, I suppose. Where were you last night?"

"Sorry, sir, I stayed at Bodvocos' place because of the storm. But I've got something urgent for you. I set out as soon as I could. It's very important. It might be life and death."

"Spit it out then. We've no time to waste, I'm taking Aurelia back to Albia's now."

Titch glanced at the gate, then up at the ramparts. Through the mist we could dimly see a sentry pacing the walkway.

Quintus said loudly, "Ride with us a few paces, so you can tell Lucius too. He's off to the coast now, so this is your only chance." We all trooped along the track that led towards the sea, and halted when we were well away from the Fort. "Good luck, Lucius," Quintus said in his normal voice. "I'll see you later.

"Now, let's have your report, Titch. What's so urgent?"

"Have you found who murdered Magnus yet?"

"Yes. Ferox."

"Then that's the start of my report. It wasn't Ferox. It can't have been."

"Oh? We've a witness who saw him go into the bath-house at the right time yesterday."

"He's mistaken. Or lying."

"Why?"

"Ferox was wandering about on Esico's sheep pasture yesterday, just where it joins onto Albia's farm, from dawn till the middle of the morning. Riding up and down, round and round, searching for something seemingly. He was even making notes. Balca saw him."

"Balca did? You're right, this is important. How sure is she?"

"Definite. She'd not make up something like that."

"No, but she could be wrong. Think carefully, Titch. Did she really see Ferox, or just a distant rider in a heavy cloak and a hood, who was snooping around in an odd or secretive way, and she just assumed it was Ferox?"

"She saw Ferox. She spotted him from the hut, but at the start he was quite a way away, and she couldn't identify him. He was on his own so she rode over to have a closer look. She shouldn't have taken a risk like that, but now she thinks she can use a bow...."

"Yes, yes, stick to the point. How near did she get?"

"To within fifty paces, and she knew him without a doubt. She called out his name, and he looked round, she says it was only then that he noticed her, because he was so wrapped up in his own thoughts. He didn't answer, just turned and cantered away, and she didn't follow. She told me all this yesterday. I'm sorry I couldn't get back here last night to report."

"So Ferox couldn't possibly have been seen going into the bath-house at dawn," I said. "And yet he must know Balca would give him an alibi. Why for Mars' sweet sake didn't he tell us where he was and prove his innocence?"

"Because whatever he was up to, he shouldn't have been," Titch answered.

"And perhaps he thought Balca wouldn't speak up for him," I suggested, "given the hostility there's been."

"Balca would always say the truth," Titch said. "It's one of the things I like about her. Most girls just tell you what they think you want to hear, but Balca says what she thinks."

I felt my heart sinking. "Gods, this has opened a whole new box of beetles. We can't leave now till we've sorted it out."

"You can, Aurelia. I know you want to get to Albia's urgently, and Titch can escort you there now, while I..."

"You're joking! I'm staying too. Yes, I do want to get away from here, but not if it means leaving without catching the murderer. If Ferox didn't kill Magnus, then whoever did it is still free, and believing he's got away with it."

"Whoever did it? That's fairly clear now, surely," Quintus said. "Rinacus lied about Ferox."

"But to protect himself? Or Vividus?"

"Either way, we must arrest him now, and release Ferox. Come on, let's do it."

"First things first, Quintus. We still need to get an urgent message to Albia. As we can't take it, could Titch go?"

"Yes, good idea," Quintus said, "but only once we've got Rinacus under lock and key."

But Rinacus had disappeared. None of the other guards knew where he was, or at any rate none were telling. And Vividus hadn't returned.

We sent Titch to get himself a fresh horse, while Quintus and I released Ferox from the lockup. He was clearly relieved, and he strode out of the small room stretching and breathing in great gulps of the misty morning air. He looked surprisingly none the worse for his ordeal, but it hadn't improved his temper. You might have thought he'd be just a little grateful for our efforts, but all he said was, "I've been telling you I'm innocent all night long. Rinacus was lying his head off, the bastard. Where is he? I'm going to break him in pieces with my bare hands."

"We can't find him," Quintus answered. "We think he's run away."

"Run away? Yes, I suppose he would, if he murdered my uncle and realises his lies have been found out. Well, I'll catch him, never fear. He can't have got very far. Nobody accuses *me* of murder and gets away with it."

Quintus said, "Ferox, I'd appreciate a private word with you. Can we go to your office please?"

He settled behind his untidy desk as if he'd never been away, and for the first time in our acquaintance, I found something to admire in him. Strange he might be, bad-tempered, haunted by evil dreams and convinced his home was about to be attacked, but physically he was still as resilient as in his army days.

"Well?" he barked. "I hope you're going to start by apologising."

"We do apologise," Quintus said. "We made a mistake. But we wouldn't have made it if you'd told us where you were yesterday morning, and that you'd seen Balca while you were there. Then we'd have realised you couldn't have been with Magnus, and we wouldn't have believed Rinacus' accusation."

"Vividus believed it too!" he exclaimed angrily. "My own brother! How could he? He just accepted Rinacus' word, he never even came to talk to me himself. And he didn't let me attend Uncle's funeral…yes, maybe I'll have it out with him first of all. A man shouldn't behave like that to his brother. Where is he? Will you send for him, please?"

"He's disappeared too. He's been missing since dawn at least."

"Disappeared?" He stared at Quintus as a possible reason dawned on him. "Then was he the one who killed our uncle?"

"We think that was Rinacus," Quintus said.

"Then why has he gone away just when I need him here?' He made a sound somewhere between a groan and a growl. "Gods, is there nobody who'll help me?"

"We will," Quintus answered. "We'll do all we can, but we're only a handful, five of us in all. Not enough to make a thorough search quickly. If you can use your men to check that neither of them are in the Fort, we've got a couple of other bits of business to attend to. If you don't find them, we'll put our heads together to plan the next move. All right?" He stood up, and so did I.

"All right. First I'll check to see that all the others are here, then I'll organise a search room by room." We left him to get on with it.

Back in our tiny office, Titch was sitting at the desk with a tray of bread and cheese and a wine-skin. "You're here just in time," he told us cheerfully. "I might have scoffed the lot."

"Where did you get this?" I asked warily. "Someone tampered with our supper last night, Rinacus presumably, so we're avoiding the kitchen's offerings."

"It's not from here. Balca made me up a bag of food, enough for a cohort."

While we all ate and drank, we told Titch what had happened in his absence.

"I'm ever so sorry I wasn't here," he said. "I'd have come, storm or no storm, if I'd known you'd be in danger."

"Well, you're here now." Quintus smiled at him. "And you and Balca have prevented a serious injustice. What we have to decide next is why Rinacus tried to put the blame on Ferox like that? Was it his own idea, or was he under orders to protect Vividus?"

"He was protecting himself, surely," Titch said through a mouthful of cheese. "He wasn't happy here, he wanted to leave, but Magnus wouldn't let him. Or maybe Magnus threatened him with all sorts for chasing after Niobe. Either of those would be enough of a motive for a murder in a man like that."

"But we know Vividus had a motive as well," I put in. "He thought he'd stand more of a chance of marrying Clarilla without his old uncle offending Clarus and his ancestors. What if he ordered Rinacus to do the killing, and in return he'll let him leave the Fort, probably with a handsome nest-egg."

"Or Vividus stabbed his uncle, and Rinacus found out after," Titch suggested. "He agreed to say nothing, provided he got well paid and was allowed to disappear without a fuss."

Quintus looked at us, and I recognised the sparkle of rising excitement in his eyes. "So the two of them were working together? They're both guilty? That makes sense. And they'll both be punished, whichever of them actually stabbed Magnus."

"I think," I said, wiping breadcrumbs from my tunic, "that I'm going to have a chat with Niobe. That girl sees and hears most things, and she must have some kindly feeling towards Ferox, the way she looked after him last night."

"Right. Titch, I'll give you the message for Albia, then you ride over there as fast as you can."

I climbed the stairs to the upper storey, but Niobe wasn't in her spacious sitting-room. Through its half-open door I could see a tray with the remains of a sumptuous breakfast on it.

I looked along the corridor, which was wide enough to have rooms on both sides of it, and examined the doors opposite me. One of them was Niobe's bedroom, and she'd mentioned that it was positioned almost above the main house door. I tried to work out where that was, gave up, and decided to try a more direct approach.

"Niobe!" I called softly. "Niobe, it's Aurelia. I need your help. Are you here?"

For a few heartbeats nothing happened, and then a door further along opened, and Niobe's face looked out. She was pale and drawn, and her finger was to her lips. I nodded and tiptoed along to the barely-opened door, and into a large and over-furnished bedroom. There wasn't time to admire the surroundings. Niobe, still signalling silence, motioned for me to move across to her window. It was open, and as I drew closer I could hear voices below.

I ventured a quick peep over the sill, and saw Rinacus. He was looking in through a downstairs window to our left and addressing someone inside, someone I couldn't see, but whose words were clear enough. Not that he spoke much. The chief guard did most of the talking.

"I'm getting out of here. I don't know what's gone wrong, but they've released Ferox, which must mean they know I never saw him. You'll cover for me, as we agreed?"

"Of course. But it's as we agreed. Money up front."

"I know, I've got it." There was the chink of coins, and when I peeped over again, I was in time to see Rinacus handing a small leather bag through the window. "Ten gold pieces."

"You said fifteen."

They started haggling. As I listened, a detached part of my mind was desperately trying to think how to stop Rinacus escaping. Hearing what was in effect a confession was all very well, but I couldn't reach Quintus before Rinacus made his run, and if I yelled from here, that would simply make him run faster. I looked round the room and saw a big water-jug on a table, heavy and solid. I stepped carefully towards it, but Niobe, guessing my intention, pointed under the bed, and I realised there was an even better weapon there.

I bent and picked it up just as more money was handed over down below, and the invisible man said, "That's more like it. You can rely on me. Where will you go?"

"Somewhere safe where I can hide till all this has blown over. I'll get the blame for Magnus, but they won't know about

Vividus. When he's got the gold, he knows where to find me, and he'll see me right."

"Good luck then."

"Thanks, but I don't need luck. I've got it all worked out."

I raised my improvised weapon. Niobe grinned hugely, and leaning out from the window, murmured, "Rinacus, aren't you coming to say goodbye?"

He looked up just as I upended the chamber-pot over him. I let out a wild triumphant yell as its contents hit him first, and then I dropped the pot squarely on his head.

He jumped to one side and flung it from him, and his howl of protest was drowned by a shout from Quintus as he raced out of the house. I didn't see the actual capture, because I'd collapsed onto Niobe's elegant bed, helpless with laughter.

Chapter XXVII

I soon stopped laughing.

Quintus was swearing like a centurion when we got downstairs. He was still outside the door, standing over Rinacus, who lay dead, a knife gripped in his hand and the broken pot near his head. Quintus' own knife was red to the hilt. "I didn't mean to kill the bastard," he growled. "He drew his knife on me, and I hadn't time to think, I just hit back. I wish I could have taken him alive. There are a lot of questions I'd like to have asked him."

"We can answer most of them, I think, thanks to Niobe." I smiled at her. "Thank you for helping. But first hadn't we better dispose of the body?"

Quintus gave orders for Rinacus' corpse to be removed and the blood cleaned up. Then he sent for the deputy guard captain, and informed him he was now in charge of the Fort's security. "Rinacus was involved in murdering Lord Magnus," Quintus told the man. "When we found out and confronted him, he attacked me."

The new guard captain didn't seem either surprised or particularly upset. "Rinacus got up to all sorts, sir. And he always had a foul temper. I hope you weren't hurt?"

"No, thank you. I need to discuss this with Vividus straight away. Is he back yet?" Of course this was merely for show. None of us expected Vividus to come back till much later.

"No, sir," the guard answered stolidly. "I'll make sure he's fully informed about it when he returns."

Once inside the office, Niobe and I told Quintus what we'd overheard, and he nodded in satisfaction. "Thank you, Niobe. You've been an enormous help. If you hadn't let Aurelia hear that conversation..."

"It was lucky she was there, but I'd have reported it anyway."

"You would? Why?"

"Because when you let Ferox go this morning, I realised how Rinacus had lied to make Ferox look guilty. I asked myself why, and of course the reason must be that he killed Magnus himself. I was scared, realising that, but I was angry too. I wanted justice for Magnus. So I went looking for Rinacus, but the lads in the guard were very cagey and secretive when I started asking for him." She smiled slyly. "One or two of them owe me a favour, and eventually I found out he was still in the house, waiting his chance to make a run for it. I was up in my room by then, and I was wondering how to warn you, when I saw Rinacus large as life almost under my window. Another piece of luck, that his brother was in one of the rooms near the main entrance, so when he went to say goodbye..."

"His brother?" I exclaimed. "He has a brother living here?"

"Yes, he's one of the guards. No, don't bother even trying to catch him," she said as Quintus sprang up. "He'll be long gone by now, and good riddance. He was an unpleasant oaf, and drunk as a senator most of the time. And," she added, giving me a sudden smile, "he had a couple of nasty bruises on his face this morning. Now I wonder how he came by those?"

"So you heard someone came calling on me last night?"

"I heard. And you," she smiled at Quintus, "came galloping to her rescue, didn't you?"

"Gods," I grinned at her, feeling a flood of surprise and relief. "I'll never know how you manage to be so well-informed about everything that happens here."

"I was going to tell Ferox to give him a good flogging," she said. "Now he's run off and saved everyone the trouble."

Quintus said, "Well, at least before he went, Rinacus as good as admitted the murder. Presumably his reason was that Magnus wouldn't let him leave here and set up on his own?"

She nodded. "He resented that, certainly. He never stopped moaning about it. I suppose he thought once Vividus was master he'd be free to go as soon as he liked. Those two were always as thick as thieves."

"He must have had some sort of understanding with Vividus," I agreed. "We overheard him saying that Vividus would protect him, and see him right later on. What was it now: 'I'll get the blame for Magnus, but they won't know about Vividus.' The two of them were involved together somehow."

"As you suggested earlier," Quintus said. "Vividus put Rinacus up to the murder, and offered him protection afterwards."

"Well, we know he had his own reasons for wanting Magnus out of the way."

"What reasons?" Niobe asked.

"He was desperate for the marriage with Clarilla to go ahead, and he thought Magnus was spoiling his chances. He was right there, of course, but I don't know…"

"Marriage?" Niobe looked shocked. "Vividus was planning to *marry?*"

"Didn't you know?"

A stupid question, given her reaction. So we told her how Magnus and Vividus had visited Silvanius and made an offer for Clarilla. She was angrier than a fighting tigress, not only because of the proposal, but because she hadn't been told about it.

"*Merda,*" she growled, "so that was his big idea. Kill his uncle, get a new wife…and where would that leave me? Would he have deigned to inform me about the new mistress of the Fort before the wedding day, I wonder, or would she have arrived in her wedding veil, and I'd have been expected to serve wine at the party? Gods, I've always known he was a devious bastard. Now it seems he's a coward too."

We reassured her that neither of the Silvanii would want the marriage now there'd been a murder in the Ostorius family, but her fury hardly lessened. I thought, I wouldn't be in Vividus' sandals when he comes back to the Fort. If he comes back.

"We really ought to be on our way," Quintus said, getting up. "I must just see Ferox to tell him about Rinacus, and then I must take Aurelia to her sister's."

"There isn't time to get to Albia's first, Quintus. I think we'd better go direct to Bodvocos' feast. I'm sure Ferox will lend us a raeda. I'd have liked to change my clothes, but it can't be helped." I glanced down at my tunic. It was a serviceable russet-coloured wool, clean enough, but not what I'd have chosen for a party, even an outdoor one. "In this fog it probably won't be seen, I'll be wearing my thick cloak all day."

Niobe, as so often, knew what I was thinking. "I can lend you an over-tunic for warmth. You're right, it'll be bleak and cold at Bodvocos'."

"Could you? Thanks, that would be wonderful."

"I'll go and talk to Ferox," Quintus said. "But don't spend too many hours going through Niobe's entire collection of clothes. Even if we don't go by way of Albia's farm, we're going to arrive late."

"Spoilsport! Don't worry, I won't be long."

"Thank you, Niobe. This is really good of you," I said as she led the way upstairs and into the room next to her bedroom, which proved to have several racks of beautiful clothes in it.

She laughed. "You may not thank me when I tell you I feel I owe it you. I was the one put the sleeping-stuff in your wine last night."

"*You!*"

"Vividus asked me to, and I didn't see any harm. He said he and several of his boys were having a meeting to make plans for some escapade they've got lined up, a raid on a farm—one of Bodvocos' peasants I assume. He thought you or your Antonius might be tempted to spy." She shrugged. "If I'd known he'd be sending that drunken lout to check up on you…well, I didn't. I hope a party tunic will pay my debt. Now, let's see. With your fair hair, you can wear almost any colour, you lucky thing."

I hadn't time to revel in all her beautiful clothes. I picked a lovely peach-coloured linen over-tunic with white trimming, and two silver brooches to fasten it. When I gazed at my reflection in her bronze mirror, I knew I looked good.

Niobe nodded. "You'll do, Aurelia. And don't worry about returning it. If you like it, keep it as a memento of your stay at the Fort."

"Niobe! Are you there, Niobe?" a strident male voice called from below.

"I ought to go," I said. "You're wanted down there, and so am I. Why, whatever's the matter?"

She was standing rooted to the floor, pale and frightened.

I went to the window and looked out. "It's only Ferox, down by the door."

"It sounded like Magnus," she breathed. "Just for a heartbeat I forgot…you know. They sounded so alike, those three. I used to tease them about it. All of them looked alike and spoke alike. And he used the same words."

"The same words."

"Those were the words Magnus shouted at me when I came into the bath-house yesterday. 'Niobe! Are you there, girl?'"

"But Ferox didn't say that." I felt a stirring of excitement, and tried not to show it. "He didn't call you 'girl', he said 'Niobe'. Did the brothers all call you by different names?"

She sat down heavily on a stool. "Jupiter's balls, Aurelia, I never thought of that. The only one who ever called me 'girl' was Vividus. Magnus and Ferox used my name. So the voice that shouted out to me yesterday…it must have been Vividus. He must have gone in to see Magnus, and didn't want to be disturbed…because he was about to kill him."

"Or because he had already stabbed him," I said, "and thought that he'd killed him."

"But Magnus was still alive then, and I don't mean in the sad state he was in when I got there. I heard his voice."

"Tell me again exactly what you heard."

"I heard Magnus shouting at someone. 'By the gods, I've had enough of this, do you hear? It's time I taught you a lesson.' The I knocked, and he shouted, 'Niobe! Are you there, girl?' And I called, 'Yes, it's me, my lord.' 'Well go away and come back later. Gods, can't a man have a private conversation in peace even in his bath?' So I went away, back to my room."

"And you heard more shouting as you left?"

She paused, remembering. "More or less the same as before. I think the exact words were, 'I'll teach you a lesson once and for all.'"

"And what did the other man answer?"

"I don't know. I hurried away to the outer door. Magnus in one of his rages was like a wild animal. You'd best keep out of his way."

"*Was* there any answer? Think carefully."

"I don't know," she said again. "Perhaps there wasn't. I just assumed…you mean Vividus was the one doing the shouting, but letting me think it was Magnus? He was threatening to teach Magnus a lesson, not the other way round?"

"Does it sound right? You're the one that heard it."

She nodded. "I think so. Except how could Vividus have got into the baths? He keeps telling everyone he never went near them, and he's got witnesses. Your investigator was with him after bugle-call, and Rinacus earlier on. He wasn't by himself at all."

"Rinacus could have been lying. That would be his side of the deal that he spoke of—to protect Vividus by giving him an alibi."

There was a knock at the bedroom door, and it opened softly behind us. Quintus said, "Aurelia, aren't you ready yet? Why, what is it?"

"We think it was Vividus," I said, "who killed Magnus."

We explained it, and he listened quietly, but then shook his head. "Just one thing doesn't fit. If Vividus had stabbed Magnus, especially in the rather clumsy way it was done, he'd have had blood all over him. He couldn't help it. Yet he hadn't. I know, because I met him in the courtyard as we'd arranged, just after the morning bugle-call. He was by the main gate, talking to Rinacus, and there wasn't a spot of blood on him. He wouldn't have had time to get back to his room and change his tunic."

"He'd wash his hands and arms in the pool," I said. "The water was tinged red, wasn't it? As for his tunic…What was he wearing when you met him?"

"A heavy leather sagum. Old and well-used, but perfectly clean…ah, wait, I see where you're driving. If he put that on over his tunic, it would cover everything, bloodstains and all. Yes. It all fits. I hope to be seeing Vividus later. I'll ask him about it."

Niobe looked surprised. "You know where he is?"

"I think I do, and I hope to arrest him sometime today. Meanwhile, I suggest we keep this conversation between the three of us. We don't want Vividus or anyone suspecting that you've helped us, Niobe. And you *have* helped us, more than we can ever repay. So thank you."

"Yes, you have. Thank you for everything." On impulse I gave her a hug. "You're a real friend."

"So are you. Now off you go and enjoy Beltane."

Chapter XXVIII

Bodvocos' Beltane feast was magnificent, I'm told. I missed most of it, but that was hardly my fault.

I arrived about the middle of the morning, though you can't easily judge how the hours pass outdoors when the sun isn't out. The fog grew ever thicker and clammier as we neared the coast, blanketing the entire area of land around Bodvocos' house, and hiding the house itself until we were practically at his gates. But if you live in Britannia, you soon learn that the weather will do as it likes without reference to gods or men. Bemoaning the fact is a waste of breath.

As Quintus pulled up our borrowed carriage in front of the main gate, we could make out only dim shapes in the mist as people clustered together in groups. But though we couldn't see much, we could hear plenty of animated chatter and some singing, and the air carried smoke from several cooking-fires, mixed with the scent of roasting meet.

Quintus helped me down, then climbed back into the raeda again. "This seems like a good party. Enjoy yourself, and take care. I'll see you later."

"Take care yourself. Your party won't be as enjoyable as this one."

"Oh, I don't know. I'm quite looking forward to it." He grinned and drove away.

We'd already agreed that he wouldn't linger, because he was anxious to reach Albia's farm as soon as he could. All the same as he vanished into the mist, I felt very much alone.

The feast was held on the large flat area of short grass between Bodvocos' house and the sea. I turned away from the house and headed into the mist, looking among the people I passed for a familiar face. Before I'd gone many paces a tall figure caught my eye, the bulky shape of Taurus, head and shoulders above almost everyone else. I steered towards him like a ship heading for a harbour light, and was relieved to see Albia, the twins and Nasua with him.

"Relia, how nice!" My sister greeted me, and the twins danced excitedly up and down.

"Good to see you all. You got our message, I hope?"

"Yes, we got it, thank you. Lucius arrived too. All's well. Is Quintus with you?"

"He couldn't stay, unfortunately."

"We're in the same boat then. Candidus couldn't come either. Still, never mind, we're going to enjoy ourselves. Come on, let's go and say good-day to Bodvocos. I'm told there's an enormous table right in the middle where he's receiving visitors, but I don't know if we'll ever find it in all this fog." She chattered on, smiling brightly, but I caught her underlying feeling of uneasiness. I know my sister, and I can tell when she's putting on an act, even when it's a very good one.

"Decimus, Marcella," I said to the twins, "Mummy and I have got to talk about some boring grown-up things. Why don't you go with Nasua and Taurus and find something to eat?"

"Yes, do that, little ones," Albia said. "And stay close to Nasua and Taurus. You two men, don't let the children out of your sight even for the blink of an eye, will you?"

They all strolled off into the crowd, and I gave Albia's hand a squeeze. "Try not to worry. I know you're thinking of the raiders."

"I wanted to stay with Candidus, and if it hadn't been for the twins, I would have done, whatever he said. But he insisted we're safer here. Divico has brought Illiana and the baby too."

"The men will feel happier without any women or babies about," I agreed. "They'll want to concentrate their whole attention on catching the Gauls. Not to mention…" I looked around cautiously. With such a thick fog, it was hard to be sure we weren't overheard. I lowered my voice. "Lucius told you exactly who's expected at your house today, I presume?"

"He did. Quite extraordinary, isn't it? And he told me you had a horrible time last night. Are you all right now?"

"Yes, I'm fine. In fact, if this mist ever lifts, you'll see I'm looking fine too. Niobe, Magnus' mistress, has lent me a lovely over-tunic to wear." I undid my cloak part-way so she could admire it, and kept her chatting about inconsequential topics as we threaded our way through the guests towards where we thought Bodvocos' central table was.

It stood on a raised platform, which on a clear day should have made it easy to see for everyone, but it was surrounded by a thick crowd of guests, so we couldn't get close enough for a proper view of the old Chief. As we drew nearer a horn blew, and a loud-voiced herald called out, "Pray silence, everyone, if you please. The Lord Bodvocos wishes to welcome all his guests today."

We could hear his short speech, but it was frustrating not being able to see him properly. His bade us all welcome, invited us to enjoy his hospitality on this special day, and said that the tide would be right for the Mother-gift ceremony very soon. His words were greeted by an enthusiastic cheer from the crowd, who had clearly been enjoying his hospitality for some time already.

"But what about the peace-making declaration with Aquilo?" Albia whispered anxiously in my ear. "Pray the gods they both go through with it. Otherwise whatever happens at our farm today, it may start a war."

I took her hand. "Aquilo is determined. He'll make it happen."

As if my remark was a cue, the herald blew his horn again and called out, "Chief Bodvocos extends a special welcome to his neighbour Ostorius Aquilo, and they propose to drink a peace-cup together."

We elbowed our way further into the crowd, till we could see Bodvocos in a ceremonial white robe, and next to him Aquilo, resplendent in his best toga. Each held a large silver goblet.

Bodvocos made a masterly speech, worthy of the subtlest politician. I wish I could remember the exact words, the clever way he suggested that it was high time for everyone in the area to live in peace and harmony and put aside petty quarrels, without once allocating or accepting any blame. He didn't even mention the Ostorii by name, but he didn't have to, everyone knew where he was driving. I was closely watching the reactions of the people around us, and was pleased to see that his suggestion was well received. When he ended with a rousing call for everyone to unite against the sea-raiders, the crowd roared their approval.

Aquilo replied with a simpler but obviously heartfelt plea for good neighbourly friendship, and pledged himself and his family to co-operate in catching the Gauls and restoring the peace and prosperity for which Bodvocos' lands had always been so justly famous. That won him an approving cheer too.

The two men raised their goblets and Bodvocos declaimed, "Let us all drink to peace."

"To peace," Aquilo replied.

They drank, while the crowd echoed "Peace," and people who had anything to drink in hand, which was nearly everyone, joined in the toast.

For the third time the horn blew, and the herald announced that Bodvocos would lead the Mother-gift ceremony on the beach, and invited those not involved in the time-honoured ritual to look on from the cliff top.

We weren't onlookers in any literal sense, because the ceremony took place a hundred paces down the beach, and we couldn't see anything of it through the fog. Fortunately Elli came up to join Albia and me. She was full of praise for the peace-making, and then she told us in a whisper that she would have a chance to meet Aquilo privately later, and that Illiana had brought the baby along for the feast too. "We'll all three be together," she murmured. "Then my day will be complete."

Meanwhile, she told us what would be taking place down below. Bodvocos would invoke the sea-gods, aided by two priests, while Balca packed the figures of the mother and child together with the other sacrificial objects into the little wooden boat. Then Balca would speak the special prayer for fertility and fruitfulness, and four specially chosen young warriors would launch the boat into the waves, wading out chest-deep to push it far enough for the tide to carry away. Everyone would wait and watch anxiously till the ebbing tide took the boat in its grip and floated it further out still. When it was lost to view there would be general rejoicing, because they had fulfilled their duty to the gods, who in return would give the people good fortune in the year to come.

Elli described all this so beautifully that we felt we'd been involved in the ceremony. As for watching the boat out of sight, Elli laughed and said those on the beach wouldn't be too downcast that it vanished so rapidly in the mist, because they could return all the quicker to the feast. We soon saw them all troop up the cliff path and head for a warm fire and some festive food and drink.

Elli seemed in no hurry to go back to the feast once the Mother-gift was safely given. I'd have joined the crowds around the cooking-fires, but I didn't want to leave her on her own, and she seemed disposed to dawdle, glancing around now and then as if expecting someone.

I realised that she probably was. "Are we waiting for somebody, Elli? Aquilo, by any chance?"

Her face lit up. "He sent me a note to say he'd meet me here. By those trees over there, where it's a bit more private." We began to stroll over to a dark mass a hundred paces or so away, which resolved itself into a small spinney as we drew near. "I hope he comes soon. I miss him so much, even more since the baby. I can't be properly happy unless we're together. And now that peace has been publicly made…"

"You're taking a risk, though, having a private meeting with Aquilo when you're still officially betrothed to Coriu."

She mistook the cause of my disapproval. "You go and enjoy the feast, Aurelia. Don't worry about me, I'm happy to wait for him here."

"You're not waiting alone, it's not safe. I'll stay with you till Aquilo comes."

She smiled. "Thank you. You're so sensible, and I seem to have lost my wits just now."

"Everyone does when they're in love. Aquilo made a good little speech, I thought."

"He did, and so did Father. And with Magnus in the Other-world…I know this sounds horrible, but I'm glad he's dead if it means there's a real chance of peace now."

As we entered the cover of the trees, two men with knives sprang out at us and seized us. It was so sudden, so completely overwhelming, that we hadn't time to cry out, and I couldn't even get at the dagger I was carrying under my cloak. I must admit it was professionally done, and all without a sound. I silently cursed myself for a careless fool in not having foreseen the possibility that we could so easily fall prey to the Gauls.

Because these were Voltacos' men. I'd seen them before. One had lank black hair, and the other had black curls and hardly any beard. Lucius and I had chased them away from Cattos' sheep. Had they come to get me because I'd seen them there? Or was it Elli they were after? Perhaps they just wanted a couple of hostages, and we happened to be available.

Elli broke the silence, and she did it in style. "Let us go at once," she ordered, in the crisp imperious tone of a chief's daughter. "Chief Bodvocos will have your hides for a prank like this, but if you let us go straight away…"

"This is no prank," the man with the lank black hair growled. "Just keep quiet and do what you're told, or it'll be the worse for you. Which of you is Elli?"

"I am." I said it instantly and without thinking. Beside me, the real Elli echoed, "I am," but I'd said it first.

"Two of 'em!" the younger raider laughed. "Shall we take 'em both?"

"Be quiet, Albia," I said sharply to Elli. "Don't try any silly hero-
ics with these scum. They're Voltacos' Long-hairs, aren't you?"

The younger one nodded.

"Well I'm Elli, daughter of Chief Bodvocos. This is Albia, a
friend of mine. So what do you want with me?"

Elli exclaimed, "But Aurelia…"

"Aurelia will be very annoyed if her sister gets mixed up in
things that don't concern her. So be quiet please, Albia. I'll deal
with this. Well?" I stared at the black-haired raider, and he stared
back. "I haven't got all day, I'm expected at the feast. What do
you want?"

"Oh you've got all day, my lady, make no mistake. Because our
captain's planning a little affair of his own, and he requests the pleasure of your company." He glanced at his companion. "Tie yours
up, we've no quarrel with her. We'll leave her here, somebody'll
find her eventually, but not till she's missed the feast."

"What a shame. Now keep still, or your friend Elli will pay
for it." The curly-headed youth tied Elli's hands, then her feet,
and finally bound a cloth across her mouth. She stood without
struggling, and I was glad of it.

"Now," the lank-haired man ordered me, "pull the hood of
your cloak right up over your head. That's right. I'll do the same
with mine. You and I are going to walk out across the open
ground, arms around each other like a couple of lovers. We'll
take the path down to the beach, where I've left my boat. My
friend here will stay close to this—what's her name, Albia?—and
he'll watch us all the way, and if you don't behave yourself, he'll
stick his knife in her. Won't you?"

"It'll be a pleasure."

"Let's go. See you at the boat," he threw over his shoulder,
and began to walk me out of the trees, his arm round my waist.
"Now come on, let's make this nice and friendly-like. Put your
arm round my shoulders. That's it. Don't be coy, or my friend
will give your friend a bit more than a lovers' kiss…" He kept
on murmuring to me, but his words were threats, not sweet
romantic nothings.

My mind was racing, but I knew I had to do as he said. At least I'd saved Elli from capture. But what would happen to me when they found out, as they'd be bound to, that they'd got the wrong captive? I must try and delay that discovery as long as I could, to give my friends and Elli's time to realise we were missing. So I walked as slowly as I dared with him across the grass and down the zig-zag path to the beach below. We were now, I knew, pretty much invisible from above. All any onlooker would see was a couple of cloaked figures, impossible to identify in the fog.

As we approached a small hide boat, the other Long-hair came quickly down to us, and the two men helped me aboard it at the water's edge. I stumbled and splashed and delayed as long as I could, but eventually we were afloat, and heading out onto the foggy sea. The water was calm, and the white mist flowed round us as we turned north and headed leisurely in the direction where the Headland must be. By then I knew that nobody from the feast could see us, or if their eyes were sharp enough, they might just discern three cloaked figures disappearing from view.

The two raiders—I never did learn their names, so I mentally called them Black-hair and Curly—rowed with quiet efficiency along the coast towards the Headland. It wasn't far, but it remained hidden in the fog until we were almost underneath it. I thought they'd pull into the beach on the south side, but instead they simply stopped rowing and let the boat drift, giving an occasional thrust with an oar to keep the bows facing the swell. Soon another small boat was rowed out to us, manned by two oarsmen, both enveloped in heavy hooded cloaks. Our boatmen started rowing to meet it, and before long I could see who was approaching us. I recognised Voltacos, the raiders' leader, the third of the men who'd been chased from the sheep pasture by Lucius and me. His companion looked vaguely familiar, what I could see of him beneath his hood, but I hadn't time to think about that because before the two boats had fully closed in, Voltacos let fly a string of oaths at Black-hair. He'd seen me, and realised his men had brought him the wrong prisoner.

The argument and abuse that followed were satisfying in a way. It's always pleasant to watch your enemies falling out. If Voltacos had been in our boat, I believe he'd have struck Black-hair, and Black-hair himself must have thought so, because he kept his boat just far enough away from his leader's to make it impossible. But he wasn't intimidated by all the swearing.

"How was I to know?" he snapped back. "I did what you said, sent a note for Elli arranging to meet her lover on the cliff. Two women showed up, and this silly cow here said she was Elli."

"But she hasn't got a baby, you stupid…gods, the Chief's going to be furious about this." Voltacos turned his attention to me, and I got my own string of colourful abuse. "I don't know who you are, but you're not Elli, and the gods know what I'm to do with you. It's Elli I need today."

Black-hair said, "I don't see why you can't make do with this one. One woman's much like another. But if you don't want her, I'll take her. *I* can find a use for her." He laughed, and Voltacos swore.

I should have been afraid, but I felt only anger at the way they were talking about me. As I saw it, I'd nothing to lose, they could do whatever they liked with me. So I gave my anger free rein. "Neither of you are going to do anything with me or to me. I'm a Roman citizen, Aurelia Marcella, and if you lay a finger on me, you'll wind up nailed to a cross or fed to lions and tigers in the arena. If you don't fancy that kind of death, all you've got to do is put me ashore somewhere near here and I'll make my way back to Bodvocos' place. And don't come looking for Elli. By now the Chief's people will have found her, and they'll make sure she and I are well protected."

"Listen to it!" Black-hair jeered. "Who does she think she is, the Queen of the Nile?"

"I'm a citizen of the Empire. And my brother's Lucius Aurelius, an investigator for the Governor, and he's on your trail, you one-eared barbarian."

I knew that would enrage Voltacos. He drew a knife and made as if to throw it at me, but his companion grabbed his arm and restrained him. "Go easy, Voltacos. If she's really a Roman citizen…"

"Shut your mouth, or I'll shut it for you. Now, you Roman whore, I've decided what we'll do. Can you swim?"

"Yes, a bit."

"It'll have to be enough. Toss her over the side, boys, let the fishes have a meal or two."

"Untie her hands first," the man in Voltacos' boat said. "If they find her, and she's drowned because she can't reach the shore, nobody will know we had anything to do with it. If she's drowned because her hands are tied, they'll all know it was us."

Voltacos growled, "All right, get her untied and chuck her in. And then get back to the feast and bring me the right ones this time. Elli and her baby. Got that?"

They cheered as they threw me overboard into the icy cold water. I hit it with a resounding splash, went under, and immediately came up again. For a few heartbeats I stayed on the surface, buoyed up by the air trapped in my heavy cloak. I had time to gulp in a couple of huge breaths and to look round. The boat that had brought me was already just a dim blurred shape in the fog. I began to swim. I must stick close to the coast, because if I went very far out to sea I'd lose my bearings completely. I struck out towards the Headland, but Voltacos' boat was still there, blocking my way towards the shore, the men laughing as they watched me. Then the water soaked into the heavy woollen fabric of my cloak, and I began to sink. My head went below the surface, the heavy wool pulling me down and down. Under the water it was grey and gloomy, and seemed to be getting darker, presumably because I was sinking away from the surface. My chest was beginning to tighten, and I felt panic reaching out to engulf me. Supposing I just went on down and down till I came to the bottom of the sea, and stayed there forever?

No, I thought, that's not going to happen. I began kicking with my feet and using my hands to claw my way up towards the light. Slowly, slowly, I rose through the water, and just at the point when I thought my chest would burst, my head broke the surface. I trod the water as I got my breath back and looked around anxiously for the raiders' boats, but they were gone. I had the sea to myself.

So you're on your own, Aurelia, I told myself sternly. Think what's best to do. First, get rid of this clinging cloak, you'll never swim anywhere with a burden like that. I undid the bronze brooch that fastened it at the neck, and felt a great surge of relief as it fell away from me.

Now look around and get your bearings. There, that dark mass ahead of you is the Headland. Turn left and keep swimming with the Headland on your right. Just keep swimming, swimming, till you reach the landward end of it, and you'll see the big sandy bay.

How far was it? I didn't know. How far was I capable of swimming? I didn't know that either. Father had taught the three of us to swim when we were children in Pompeii, but we'd never ventured far from land. Probably the most I'd ever swum was half a mile. Surely I could keep going for much further than that if I had to. Again I felt the icy touch of panic, so strong it threatened to paralyse me. But thinking about Father comforted me, and I ploughed on.

I'm not a very good swimmer, slow and clumsy even in the warm blue waters of the Bay of Neapolis. Here the cold of the German Ocean was seeping into me, and I didn't know whether there were offshore currents that would sweep me out to sea. I suppose there must be, or the Mother-gift ceremony would tend to produce a bad omen, if the boat and its sacrificial cargo found their way back to shore. The tide was still ebbing, but would soon turn, and that would help me. Or would it?

Anyhow, I reasoned, I won't have to swim the whole way. The beach in the big sandy bay to the south is wide and easy to approach. I can get ashore there and just walk steadily along the sands till I come to the area below Bodvocos' estate. There the Beltane feast will still be in progress, and all I have to do is climb the cliff, and I'll find all my friends waiting for me, with a hot fire and a mug of warm wine, and some dry clothes, and a chance to rest...

Thinking of warmth and rest made me realise how cold and tired I was. My hands had turned white, and I had hardly any sensation in my fingers. A small wave slapped me across the face, then another. Gods, the sea was getting rougher. If the wind got up and disturbed the dead calm of the water, I was finished. But I couldn't feel any wind, and the waves still looked flat and friendly. So it must be that I was swimming lower in the water, failing to keep my head up high enough. And that would be why the Headland seemed further away than it had before. Yes, surely that must be the reason its bulk was less solid in the white gloom. Or perhaps the fog itself was growing thicker, making it harder to discern the outline. Or perhaps I was drifting away from it...no, I wouldn't let myself even think about that.

I tried to make my arms and legs go faster, and with more force in each stroke. I began to pray to Father Neptune. He's not a god I've had much to do with, but I asked him to hear me and spare my life because I'd tried to protect Elli. Then I prayed to Diana, my guardian goddess.

Another wave buffeted me, almost washing over my head. Water splashed into my mouth and in a fright I breathed some in through my nose too. I began to cough and splutter. Was this how it felt when you started to drown? My body tensed, and my chest and throat were tight, but the coughing went on, and I swallowed more water. As I fought to get my breath, I felt a sudden agonising cramp in my left calf, all the way down to my foot. I screamed with the pain of it, and stopped swimming, just managing to flail my arms enough to keep my head above the surface.

I sucked in a desperate breath of air and yelled, "Father Neptune! Holy Diana! Help me! Help me now!"

Out of the fog I heard an answer. "Hold on there. Hold on! We're coming!"

I felt a sudden rush of hope. There was someone else out here. It wasn't Father Neptune, even in my despair I knew that. The voice hadn't the majestic cadence of an immortal god. It had a gruff barbarian accent that came from Britannia, not Olympus. But it was *someone!*

Before I could call out again, yet another wave caught me full in the mouth, and I swallowed more water. I felt myself going under. I made one last effort not to sink. When I surfaced, the voice was there again, much closer. "It's all right, we've got you. Why, it's Aurelia Marcella. Now what in the gods' name are you doing here?"

I remember thinking that was a particularly silly question, as strong hands grasped my tunic and pulled me from the ocean and into the bottom of a fishing-boat.

Chapter XXIX

I don't remember being taken back to Bodvocos' beach. I suppose I must have fainted. In fact I recall nothing at all till I woke up in a bed.

I opened my eyes and wondered where I was. The small room wasn't familiar, but that didn't seem important really. I was warm and dry and very tired, and all I wanted to do was rest.

"Relia," Albia's voice said softly. "You're all right. You're safe, and I'm here."

"Albia?" She was by my bedside on a stool, holding my hand. So we must be at her farm. That was odd, I thought I should be at Bodvocos' house. Well, if Albia was with me I needn't fret. I started to sit up, but it was an enormous effort, so I lay down again.

"Don't try to move, just relax. You're quite safe. We're at Bodvocos' house."

"Why?" And why did she keep saying I was safe?

"Because of the Beltane feast. You've been in the sea, and some fishermen found you and brought you back to land. Do you remember?"

"In the sea? No, I'd never go in the sea. It's too cold. And the tide would take me...oh, gods!" Suddenly I did remember. "Albia, it was awful! The Long-hairs threw me in. I swam, and I prayed to Neptune, and then someone saved me. They wanted Elli." I was wide awake now, and I sat bolt upright. "Elli, they tied her up. Is she all right?"

"She's safe, and being well guarded."

"And the baby. He told them to come back for it. Is it safe too?"

"Elli says you were very brave, letting the raiders take you instead of her. Someone found her quite soon after you disappeared, and she sent all the local fishermen out in their boats to look for you. The ones who picked you up were the same two who told Lucius about the shipwreck."

"But the baby, Albia. Is the baby safe?"

She hesitated. Albia and I don't lie to each other.

"Gods, they've got the baby?"

"We're not sure. But Illiana and the baby have been missing for some time."

"Then Voltacos has them." I told her what I could remember of Voltacos' words. She was horrified, and got to her feet.

"I must find Divico. He's been going nearly frantic, looking for them. Will you be all right here by yourself for a little while?"

"Of course. I'll get dressed and come outside. Maybe I can help. And I'm starving hungry. Will there be any food left at the feast?"

She giggled. "Ah, that's a good sign. There's some bread and cheese over on that table. And I made you some mulsum. It's not very warm now, but it's sweet, and it'll help you get your strength back. Have something to eat and drink while I see Divico. I promise I won't be long."

Normally I think mulsum is much too sickly-sweet for my palate, the flavour of all that honey spoiling the wine. But just then it was delicious. I drank two beakers, ate a couple of slices of bread, and thought, "Now I'm ready for anything." Well almost anything, because my muscles screamed in protest when I got out of bed, and it was an effort to dress myself. But I did it. Only later, when I stopped to think, I realised that the clothes draped ready over a chair weren't mine. Of course they weren't. Mine were either soaking wet or lost in the sea. But at the time all that concerned me was that they were the right size, and would keep me warm.

There was a soft tap at the door.

I called, "Come in, if that's Albia."

"Yes, it's me, and Lucius is here too. He's just arrived from the farm."

They both came in, and Lucius looked at me anxiously. "You do like getting into scrapes, Sis, don't you?"

"I'm all right. I thought it was a nice day for a swim, that's all. What's the news from the farm? Did the raid happen?"

"It never even got started. We ambushed the bastards before they reached us."

"Candidus and the others? Are they all safe?" Albia demanded.

"And Quintus?" I added.

"All safe and sound. It was even better than we planned, because we had a piece of good luck. One of the pirates deserted, and came to warn us of the attack, and which way they'd be coming. We thought at first it was some kind of trick, but he convinced us he wanted to help, and we ambushed them on their way to us. They didn't know what hit them."

I asked, "Did you get them all? Vividus, Coriu…"

"Every last one of them, all killed. Vividus, Coriu, Voltacos, and nine assorted guards and raiders. And none of us have even a scratch."

"Oh, that's wonderful news," Albia exclaimed. "Well done!"

"Yes, congratulations, brother. An excellent day's work." I grinned at him. "I suppose you didn't find Caratacus' gold while you were at it?"

"Not yet. But Candidus has all his boys digging over his land yard by yard. If it's buried there, they'll find it."

"Has Quintus come over with you?" I asked.

"He'll be arriving soon. He had to make arrangements about some of the bodies—Vividus and Coriu. We couldn't just bury them in a pit with the rest. And he's bringing over the raider who deserted. There are a lot more questions we want to ask him." He grinned. "And I think you'll want to meet him too."

"Me? To see if I recognise him, you mean? I'll certainly have a look at him. Did he say why he deserted?"

"Only that he and Voltacos quarrelled over something important, and he didn't want to work with him any more. Perhaps he'll be more forthcoming now Voltacos is dead. Come on outside and wait for them, they won't be long."

So I wrapped up warm, and we all trooped out into the mist, where the feast was still going on at full gallop.

The later stages of a party are always more enjoyable if you've been part of it all the way through, rather than leaving it and then returning. The drunken youths, the courting couples, the over-enthusiastic singing and dancing…well, I suppose I just wasn't in the mood for them. But among the merrymakers a quiet group waited round one of the bonfires. Divico, Elli and Aquilo, and Balca with Titch in close attendance, clustered together, and we three joined them. Neither Bodvocos nor his wife were there, and I wondered who would be given the job of telling them about Coriu.

We joined the group, and Lucius and I gave accounts of our respective adventures. The congratulations (for him) and the sympathy (for me) were interrupted by a shout from the direction of the road, and five figures loomed out of the fog: Quintus, Brutus and two of his men, and a tall man in chains. They brought the prisoner to us, and when I got a proper view of him, I felt a shock that was almost physical. Before I could stop myself, I cried out, "Gods, he's the image of father!"

Beside me, Albia muttered, "Jupiter's balls, you're right. That's just how father looked when we were children."

Lucius said softly, "I thought so too. I wanted you girls to see for yourselves."

The man was tall, thin, and brown-haired, with the familiar high forehead, sharp grey eyes and prominent nose and jaw. Incredibly, he had father's way of holding himself, erect and alert, even now when he was a captive in chains.

I stepped up to him till I could almost touch him. "What's your name?"

"Rollus."

"Who was your father?"

He frowned. "What's that to you?"

"Just answer the questions." Lucius had come up to stand beside me. "Who was your father—if you can name him, that is."

"I can name him, but what's the point? You'll not believe me."

"Listen, scum." Quintus gripped the prisoner's tunic at the neck and shook it hard, making his head jerk like a puppet's. "Don't push your luck with us. You gave us some help today, and we appreciated it, but you're still an outlaw, and I carry the Emperor's authority to rid the world of filth like you. So do as my friend here says. Answer the questions."

He released his grip and stepped back. Rollus said, "My father was a Roman soldier named Lucius Aurelius Marcellus. He was based in Britannia for a while in the Emperor Nero's time, but he was born in Italia."

"And your mother?" I could hardly get the words out.

"My mother was Huctia, originally from Glevum, which is where she met my father."

"Are you in contact with your father?" Lucius asked. "Or any of his family?"

The prisoner laughed. "Of course not. I hardly remember him. I was only a baby when he left us, and then much later we met once in Lindum, when I was almost a man. He wasn't exactly a resident *paterfamilias*. But he cared for my mother, or so she always said. He was prepared to acknowledge me as his son. He wrote a letter about it, and he left me his ring."

"Have you the ring still? Or the letter?"

He shook his head. "Both were stolen from me in Londinium, with all my other possessions. I'd moved there to look for my family, and I spoke too freely about…about some property that my father said he would bequeath to me. My own fault, I suppose, for opening my mouth too wide. I was left with nothing but my tunic and sandals. I managed to get to the coast, and eventually I joined Voltacos' men."

I felt so excited, I didn't know which of several questions to ask him next. But I asked none, because he was clearly getting impatient with this topic.

"Look, this is all typical stupid Roman bureaucracy, isn't it? You waste time asking about my ancestors, while that poor girl and her baby are out there on the sea."

"*What?*" we all exclaimed.

"That's the reason I fell out with Voltacos. He kidnapped a lass and a baby today and left them to die in an open boat. I was sickened by the whole thing."

Divico strode forward and reached out to seize Rollus by the throat, but Quintus pulled him aside. "All right, calmly now, everyone. I think we can all see where he's driving, and we need to be quick. Rollus, you say a girl and a baby are at sea in a boat. A *live* girl and baby?"

"That's right, in the boat that was sent out for the gods. Voltacos put them there. He really wanted some woman called Elli, but he said as long as he'd got Elli's baby, the other girl would have to do instead."

Elli gave a low moan, and Aquilo put his arm round her.

"But I was at the ceremony!" Balca spoke up. "There were no live people in the boat when it was launched. Just two dolls."

Rollus nodded. "Of course there were dolls *then*. But later Voltacos went after it in his own boat and put in the girl and the baby instead."

"Why?" Aquilo asked. "Has Voltacos some quarrel with Bodvocos?"

"Quarrel? Hardly! It was Bodvocos who ordered us to do it. Ordered Voltacos, that is, and paid him. Coriu brought the money, but it was the Chief wanted it done."

"No!" Elli shrieked. "It isn't true, it can't be. Father—where's my father? I'll fetch him, he'll tell me you're lying."

He shrugged. "Whether you believe me or not, it doesn't alter the truth."

"Elli," I said, "don't forget, some of the Gauls tried to capture you today. They took me instead, and when Voltacos found his men had brought me and not you, he was furious, and said something about the Chief being angry, but it was the baby he really wanted. He sent his men back to look for it. They must have found Illiana with your son at the feast."

"That's right," Rollus agreed. "I was with Voltacos when they brought you to him. He said Bodvocos wanted his daughter and the baby dead, on account of they'd brought disgrace on his family, but especially the baby, because being a boy it would be more of a threat if it was allowed to grow into a man. Voltacos sent his men back to the feast to find them both. He didn't think you'd survive your swim," he added, looking at me.

"I wouldn't have done, if you hadn't insisted they untie my hands before they threw me in. I owe you my thanks for that."

"Just common sense, like I said. And, well, when you mentioned your brother's name..."

But our own family concerns weren't the important issue just now. "So the raiders came back here," Aquilo said, "and saw Illiana with our baby, and made another mistake."

Rollus nodded. "That made Voltacos madder than ever, but he said they couldn't waste any more time. That was when he told us what he intended to do with the lass and the child. It disgusted me. Raiding and pirating, that's one thing, but killing an innocent girl and child...I made up my mind to leave Voltacos straight away. But I didn't dare risk an open quarrel about it. They'd have killed me on the spot. So I said I'd got a bad belly ache and lay low in one of our caves till I got the chance to sneak off. I knew the place they were going to raid, the farm where the gold was supposed to be. I went and warned the people there, and gave myself up."

Elli stepped slowly towards the prisoner. I tensed, thinking she was going to attack him, but she stopped in front of him, her face only a hand's breadth from his. "I'm Elli, daughter of Bodvocos," she growled, "and I've heard what you have to say. Do you swear it's all true? Because I shall ask my father about it, and if I find you've made it up to save your life, I'll kill you with my own hands."

"I swear. By my father's life, and by the gods of the sea, I swear it." He added after a pause, "I'm sorry, lady."

She covered her face with her hands and began to sob. "They've killed my baby! They've killed him!"

"Not necessarily," Quintus said. "The currents around the bay are strong, but they change with the tide. Surely there's a chance the boat may come back to land again while they're still alive."

"There's no chance." Elli's voice was like the cry of a tortured animal. "They're both as good as dead!"

Aquilo said, "Don't give up hope, love. The gods of the sea won't allow such an injustice. They'll let the boat come ashore again."

"The gods have no choice in the matter. They're given a little help by their priests."

"Help?" Aquilo said, and we all stared at her blankly, not understanding.

She dried her tears. " If the Mother-gift comes back to land, it brings a curse on the people. It happened once years ago, the boat came ashore after three days, and there was a drought all summer long, and a cattle-plague and a famine. So now the priests make sure the boat has a small, slow leak in it. Wherever the currents take it, it will always sink, and never return."

Quintus was the first to break the stunned silence. "How long have they got?"

"A day and a night, perhaps," Elli answered. "But this night is cold and damp. The baby won't live through it, even if the boat does."

"Then let's waste no more time. Rollus, you know these shores well enough. Can you make a guess at which way the gift-boat will drift?"

"Perhaps."

"Will you sail out tonight and try to find it?"

"What's the point? I'm an outlaw, a prisoner in chains. You hinted about sparing me, but I've no reason to trust you. Why should I risk my life out there, if all I have to come back to afterwards is death?"

"Please," Elli begged him. "Ask whatever you like, I'll give it to you, only please say you'll try to save my baby."

Quintus said, "Rollus, I'll make a bargain with you. If you'll take a boat and crew out now and look for them, I promise, before all these people, that I'll spare your life and let you sail away a free man. I, Quintus Antonius Delfinus, give you my word."

Rollus considered, then he looked at Lucius. "What about him? Will he promise too?"

"I, Lucius Aurelius Marcellus, give you my word too. Now will you try?"

"I will."

Chapter XXX

Rollus chose a hide boat, the kind the natives use, with benches for six rowers. "It'll be fast, and large enough to bring them back. I'll need five strong lads. Who'll come with me?"

A dozen volunteers stepped forward, but the most determined and persistent were Aquilo, Titch, and Brutus with his two men. Elli clung to Aquilo, but he insisted on searching for their son. Balca gave Titch a hug and a goodbye kiss. Brutus and his men dragged the frail-looking craft to the water's edge, while Rollus issued a string of instructions. "I want to take blankets for the girl and the child, and sheepskins too, anything to warm them. Also a lantern, and water and food. After we're gone, keep a big fire blazing above here to guide us back. And if the mist doesn't clear, blow a horn nice and loud now and then to give us a direction to head for, in case we can't see the fire."

It was all done remarkably quickly. As they stood ready on the sand, Rollus raised his right hand. "Gods of the sea, protect us now. Injustice and blasphemy have been committed in your name. Help us to find the girl and the baby and bring them safe home." He turned to his crew. "Let's go, lads."

We watched as they rowed out across the bay and vanished almost immediately in the darkening mist. For a little space we all stood in silence, gazing out to sea, feeling the need of quiet. I know I sent an urgent prayer to Diana and Apollo. I expect the others prayed too.

Quintus and Lucius began organising a stock of dry logs to be positioned by the nearest fire. I heard Balca suggest to Elli that the servants should use the fire to heat up some cauldrons of watered wine. Elli agreed, but she was too lost in her own despair to give the orders, so I went to help Balca, and together we got them bustling about. Everyone seemed glad to have something to do. I wondered fleetingly where Elli's mother was, but neither she nor Bodvocos were to be seen.

As the sky grew dark, especially to the east above the ocean, Lucius said he'd go and find a good lookout point near the cliff path. As he set off I fell into step beside him.

"Lucius, this man Rollus..."

"I know. That's why I asked Quintus to bring him. I think he could be our brother."

"So do I. But after being deceived once, I'm being cautious."

"I was the one deceived, not you. You were always cautious."

"But this one's story fits all the facts we know. Still...he's lost his ring, and his letter."

Lucius nodded. "But he knows that they exist. And the story of how he lost them has the feel of truth. But above all, it's his looks, isn't it?"

"As Father himself said, it's strange that his British son should be the only one to take after him in looks." Suddenly I wanted to laugh. "Gods, first we thought we had a traitor for a brother, now we find he's merely a sea-raider with a price on his head."

"Not now. He's been pardoned, because he's also a man who refused to leave a woman and child to drown. If he is our brother, that's something to be proud of."

We halted at the edge of the cliff. "This should do for keeping watch," my brother said. "There's some shelter from those trees, and it's away from the fire. I want our eyes to be adjusted to darkness when full night comes, so we don't miss anything out to sea."

"Right. I'd better stay close to Elli. She's near breaking point, poor girl. I'm afraid she may do something violent."

Even as I said the words, I heard Elli's voice raised in an angry shriek. As I hurried back to the crowd near the fire, I could hear her screaming curses and abuse, and realised that Bodvocos was approaching.

"You kidnapped my son!" she was shouting at him. "You told the raiders to put him in the mother-gift boat today, and leave him to drown. You wanted to drown me too! How could you, Father? How could you do such a dreadful thing?"

"I don't know what you're talking about, Elli." The Chief spoke slowly and patiently, as if to a disobedient child. "You should go back to the house now and lie down. You're over-excited, you've not been well. The boat had the rag dolls in it, as usual."

"Yes, when it left here. But not now. One of the sea-raiders has told us everything. Illiana and my baby were offered to the gods, *on your orders*. Do you deny it?"

"Certainly I deny it, daughter. Whoever told such a tale is lying, to try to save himself presumably." But his face had gone as white and hard as chalk. "Where is the man who accuses me of such a deed? Let him repeat his lies to my face, and I'll make him take them back."

She ignored him. "You wanted to punish me, but you should not take vengeance on an innocent child. He was mine. Mine and Aquilo's. And now he's gone!"

"So you admit that you have borne a child?"

"I have, and you have no right to touch him, let alone kill him!"

"I would have had the right," Bodvocos said calmly. "But I did not exercise it. How could I? I didn't realise you had a baby, let alone that the father might not be the man you're betrothed to." The icy scorn in his words made Elli turn pale, but she stood her ground as he went on, "I see now the meaning of your so-called illness. You weren't sick, you were carrying a bastard child, and you managed to get away from here to give it birth and keep it secret from me. As I knew nothing about it, I could not have ordered its destruction."

"You lie. You knew everything." Elli's mother stepped forward to stand next to her daughter. She looked frightened, but also very determined.

"Be quiet, woman, and get back to the house!" Bodvocos snapped. "Leave me to deal with our daughter, who has brought disgrace on us all. It's none of your concern."

"Of course it's my concern. And I've had enough of lies and deceit, my lord Bodvocos. You knew about Elli's child because I told you."

"Mother!" Elli cried. "You told him? I trusted you, and…"

"I'm sorry, Elli. He made me. If I'd realised he intended to murder you both, I'd have died before I betrayed your secret. He threatened to kill me more than once, that's why I finally gave in."

"To kill you? But surely a few angry threats…"

"Look!" She flung off her thick cloak, and then swiftly unclasped one of the twin brooches that held her tunic. The fabric fell away from her, revealing the flesh of her right breast and shoulder, discoloured by several large purple bruises and a livid red knife-cut.

"Mother!" Elli cried. "Did he do this?"

"Cover yourself!" Bodvocos roared. "You should be ashamed before all these people."

"No, the shame is yours." She began to fasten the tunic again. "You did this to your wife, before you murdered your grandson." Elli helped her put on her cloak, and the two women stood together, their arms round each other, crying as if their hearts were broken.

"So, Bodvocos," Quintus said. "Do you still deny you ordered the death of Elli's baby?"

"And my sister!" Divico exclaimed. "You've murdered my sister too, and by the gods, if Rollus doesn't find her I'll kill you."

"He won't find them," Bodvocos snapped. "Nobody will ever find them. They've gone to the gods."

"Rollus knows where to look for them," I said, expressing more confidence than I felt. "He'll bring them back safe."

Bodvocos gazed at us with malevolent snake's eyes. "You Romans can't alter the Parisi code of honour. I have the right to do what I must with my own family, by our law and by Roman law."

"But not with mine!" Divico shouted. "You've murdered my sister, an innocent girl, just to take revenge on your own daughter."

"I didn't intend to involve Illiana. I ordered Voltacos to take my own slut of a daughter and her bastard." Now that he'd admitted it, he glared round us all, defying us to say anything against him.

"You ordered Voltacos? So you admit it!" Divico shouted, and then stopped and went on in a tone that was quieter and infinitely more frightening, "You foul old man, I've just seen through you. You've been giving orders to Voltacos and the sea-raiders for months. Orders to rob and plunder. Orders to kill Belinus!"

"No, Divico, I never ordered Belinus killed, I swear it. Belinus was one of our own people, I'd never have harmed him. The Long-hairs…"

"The Long-hairs were acting on your orders. They're dead now, but you still live. I'll take a blood price for my sister and her man, and I'll take it now." He flung himself forward, his hands reaching for the old man's throat. But Bodvocos was quick, very quick for an old man, and he twisted out of Divico's reach and raced away from the circle of firelight into the near-darkness around us. Divico followed, and Quintus was close behind him.

"He's trying to get to the cliff path," Elli cried. "Head him off, don't let him escape!" We all began to run seaward, but we were too slow to be of any use. Bodvocos made a desperate run, but Divico was younger and faster, and closed in behind him, letting out an exultant cry as he caught up with his quarry. He leapt on the Chief's back and brought him crashing to the ground, and they grappled together, rolling on the short turf only a few paces from the cliff edge.

"May the gods of the Otherworld curse you!" Divico called out, and I saw a faint gleam as the firelight caught the long blade of a knife in his hand. As he plunged it into Bodvocos' body, the old man made a supreme final effort, lifting himself off the ground. Divico let go the knife and stepped back just in time. In the blink of an eye Bodvocos' body plunged over the edge of the cliff, and we heard a despairing cry, then a splash from below. After that there was only the sound of the sea.

Chapter XXXI

It was a long, long night.

If we'd had clear skies as we waited there by the shore, the moon and the planets would have reassured us that the hours were passing, however slowly. But our whole world was shrouded in fog.

Quintus led men down the cliff to look for the Chief's body, but the tide was high, and they came back empty-handed. Divico approached him as he reached the top of the path, for once without his usual air of truculence.

"I've taken my blood price, which was my right. I'm not running away, I must wait for Illiana. What are you going to do with me?"

"Nothing at all," Quintus answered. "I've no jurisdiction here. With Bodvocos dead, there isn't a local magistrate to deal with a case like this, but if there were, I imagine he'd rule that you were acting correctly under tribal custom. Don't you, Lucius?"

"Certainly," my brother agreed. "But surely the person you should be asking is Lady Elli."

Elli and her mother were clinging together, trying to comfort one another. When she heard her name, Elli looked up, and Divico walked to her and, to my astonishment, knelt down.

"Lady Elli, I've taken my blood price. I had the right to, but he was my Chief, and your father. I am in your hands."

"Please forgive my son." Old Esico limped out of the crowd. "For my sake, and for Illiana's. She has helped…will help you with your baby. And without Divico, she and I can't survive."

Elli looked at Divico for a few heartbeats. Everyone else stood silent, watching and listening intently. Then she reached down her hand and raised him to his feet. "He was no true father to me. He would have killed me, and I think he's murdered my son. So you have avenged me, Divico. I've no quarrel with you."

"Thank you, lady." The crowd relaxed, and there was a murmur of approval. She had done the right thing.

Albia went to her and spoke softly for a while, then beckoned me over. "We'll take Elli and her mother to the house, Relia. Can you help me get them to bed?"

But Elli refused absolutely to leave the cliff top. "Help my mother to her bed, please, Albia. It's what she needs. But I'll wait here for Aquilo and my son. I don't ask the rest of you to stay," she continued, raising her voice. "Go to your homes if you want to, and for our guests, my people will find you accommodation in our house."

Nobody moved, and Balca said, "We're all staying, Lady Elli. Just tell us what we can do to help."

"Thank you. Then please fetch warm cloaks for me and anyone else who needs them. Blankets too. And bring out food and drink, in case anyone's hungry."

One of the guard said, "We shan't need to eat for days," and several people laughed.

Elli turned to the man. "Galgacos, you're the senior warrior here now, so you're in charge of the guard. See that the house is properly protected tonight, will you?"

"Yes, my lady. And that seaman mentioned blowing horns in the mist. Shall I fetch a couple?"

"Yes please. Make two good men responsible for sounding them regularly, all night long if need be. Tell them to count slowly to one hundred, then give three long blasts on a horn, then count to one hundred again...and so on."

"Yes, my lady."

Elli looked round the people assembled by the fire. "We must be prepared for a long cold watch tonight. But lives depend on our being alert and vigilant, and if the gods are with us, our friends will come back safe to us, bringing Illiana and the baby. We must be ready and waiting to welcome them all."

There was another murmur of support from the crowd. The Chief's daughter was taking command, as was her right and her duty. Only a few of us saw how, when she turned her head to gaze out to sea, she was fighting back tears.

I said quietly, "I'm so sorry, Elli. For everything. Your father, and Coriu…you have deserved better from your family."

"I want no family among the Parisi," she said bitterly. "Not any more. I renounce them all, except my poor mother. I'll make my life with Aquilo now. And if they succeed in rescuing my baby…"

"Rollus has a strong crew," I said, "and a determined one. They'll succeed."

She bowed her head and whispered something in her own language. I couldn't catch the words, but it was a prayer. Then she straightened up. "I wish we'd never heard of Caratacus' gold. I still can hardly believe that Coriu made a secret ally of Ostorius Vividus, just so they could keep it all for themselves."

"Gold changes people." Quintus had come up to stand beside us. "Did you know that Coriu had dealings with the raiders?"

She shook her head. "Not Coriu. Especially after he was wounded…but one of Ostorius' men must have done that. I did suspect that father might be hiring the Gauls to look for the gold, once the Ostorii began searching for it. He was so determined to get to it first. Of course that meant he'd be turning a blind eye to whatever petty crimes Voltacos got up to in the district. I never asked, and I should have done. I was guilty of turning a blind eye myself."

"Lady Elli," Balca spoke up. She looked pale and strained, but she faced Elli squarely. "My father would never have done anything to betray the Chief. If he made a secret alliance with the Ostorii, couldn't it have been to lure Vividus into a trap at Albia's farm, pretending to meet him there as a friend, but planning to capture him when he began the raid?"

"I suppose it could," Elli conceded doubtfully. "If so, it was an extremely risky thing to do."

"Warriors have to take risks. Sometimes the risks are too great, and they must pay the price." She stalked away into the darkness, and my heart went out to her. She couldn't bear the idea that her father had acted dishonourably. She could conceivably even have been right about his supposed plan. I doubted it, but if it gave her comfort to believe Coriu was not just a greedy, treacherous treasure-hunter, it could do no harm now.

The night dragged on, punctuated by the strident horn-blasts. We waited about in small groups and didn't talk much, only enough to keep ourselves and one another awake. I remember Albia and I reminisced about father, and marvelled at the way the Fates had brought Rollus to us. Then Albia talked enthusiastically about the plans she and Candidus had for their home. "I'll have time to re-plant my garden before the new baby comes. And I must put in more new trees, which gives me the perfect excuse to visit the Oak Tree and gather some of your acorns."

"You can take down your stockade now," I said. "Can't she, Quintus? Today has seen the end of the raiders."

"I hope so. With Voltacos and their two main paymasters gone, they're finished. I suppose any that aren't dead yet will go back to Gaul, and I assume someone may have to go after them there, but I doubt if it'll be me."

At one point Elli returned briefly to her house to make sure her mother was being cared for properly, and Albia went with her to check on the twins, who were sleeping soundly, with Nasua and Taurus taking turns as their guard. Other people wandered about as the mood took them, to keep warm, or at least awake. Quintus and I walked across to Lucius' lookout point and chatted to him for a while.

We started discussing Magnus' murder, and Lucius and Albia asked me to relate in detail the events of the morning, So I described Rinacus' confession, and how I ended it by dropping a chamber-pot on his head, and Niobe's realisation that Vividus could have imitated Magnus' voice in the bath-house. "So it seems Vividus had something to do with the murder," I finished, "though now I doubt if we'll ever know the whole truth."

Quintus said, "If Vividus killed Magnus himself, he certainly had nerves of steel. I spent some time with him, you know, after their morning bugle-call, while he made his morning rounds of the guards. He seemed as calm and carefree as anyone would wish to be. Surely if he'd just stabbed his uncle he couldn't have appeared so completely at his ease. More likely he found his uncle dead—as he thought—stabbed by Rinacus earlier. He didn't want Niobe to come in and find him standing over a bloodstained body, so he pretended to be Magnus when he called out to her, and sent her away without suspecting anything was wrong. Then he left the bath-house and met me as arranged."

"Still, even if he hadn't actually done the stabbing, you'd think that finding Magnus stabbed by someone else would have upset him," Albia mused.

"The Ostorii seem a pretty tough lot," I pointed out. "Look at the way Ferox got back to work immediately after being released from a night in the lockup, and a disturbed night at that."

"What did you and Vividus talk about?" Lucius asked. "Did he mention the gold?"

"Not a word. He boasted about the Fort, how well defended it was, and he talked a lot about the plans he and his uncle had for improving the farming of the estate. And he joked about Aquilo and his new baby, rather unkindly, saying his Uncle thought the only way Aquilo would ever get a woman pregnant was…"

"Stop!" I almost yelled. "Vividus knew about the baby?"

"Yes. I was a bit surprised by that, but then later you told me Niobe overheard Aquilo talking about it, and she presumably spread the news around."

"No. She only told Magnus, very late the night before he was killed. Nobody else."

"Are you sure? Is she reliable?"

"On something like that, yes. She'd no reason not to be."

Quintus smiled. "Then that settles it."

"It does. Vividus killed Magnus."

"I don't see what you're getting at," Albia objected.

"Vividus could only have heard about Aquilo's baby from his uncle," I explained. "And since he didn't see the old boy late at night, he must have talked with him in the early morning, in the bath-house."

"And then stabbed him," Quintus finished. "Yes, that definitely settles the matter."

By then I'd lost all track of the hours, but it must have been quite close to dawn when I felt a small breeze stirring and noticed the mist was thinning, and a very few faint stars showed above us. Several other people saw the change too, and there was an excited buzz of conversation as we all prepared ourselves for the end of our long ordeal. Someone called, "Look, it's getting light," and the relief we all felt was almost tangible. As the sky brightened from black to blue, we saw that the breeze had swept the mist away at last, leaving behind only a few tiny wisps of cloud. One of these was along the eastern horizon, and the sun rose through it, making a luminous red-gold band where ocean and sky met. When it climbed high enough to shine out and make a glittering path of gold across the waves, it was breathtaking. I've always loved the dawn, and this one was beautiful.

"There's a boat!" Lucius yelled. "A boat coming in towards us from the Headland!"

Soon we could all see a dot on the shining water, which gradually took on shape and colour. "I recognise it!" Elli cried. "It must be Rollus!"

She began to run down the path to the beach, and we followed eagerly, ready to welcome them home. A few of the watchers cheered, but most of us held our peace till we knew whether Illiana and the baby were on board.

Quintus and several of the other men waded out and pulled the boat in. The rowers looked exhausted, but they smiled as they clambered stiffly out and splashed through the shallow water onto the sand. Aquilo, holding his baby in his arms, called out, "We found them! They're safe!" and then we all cheered till the cliffs echoed.

Elli ran forward and embraced Aquilo and the child, then she turned to Rollus and grasped both his hands. "Thank you, Rollus. I'm in your debt for ever."

"I'm glad we found them. They were cold and wet, but we've kept them warm and they'll be fine."

"You've all done brilliantly. Did it take you long to pick them up?"

He shook his head. "We heard the lass calling out for help, and we got them into our boat just after full dark. But by then we couldn't see the shore, so we couldn't get back to you till the mist began to clear. We were only just in time, their boat was taking in water quite fast. We left it out there to sink. The little dolls were still in it, so the gods have their gift." He paused. "Your father...did you talk to him?"

"He confirmed what you told us. Now he's dead, and he deserved it."

"I'm sorry. I never really knew my own father. It must be sad to lose yours, especially like that. But you've got a fine man there."

Aquilo placed the baby in her arms, and Rollus left them and strode up towards where Lucius, Albia and I stood together, watching the various reunions. Divico and Illiana...Balca and Titch...it was a scene of pure happiness, lighted by the bright morning sun. And I knew without any doubt that we three would have a share in the happiness now.

Rollus stopped a couple of paces away from us. "I've had time to think, while we were out there. I believe I know why you asked me all those questions about my parents. You thought...you think...I might be your brother, is that right? That means you'd heard about Mother and me. From your father?"

"In a way." Lucius took something out of his belt-pouch, something that flashed in the sunlight. "Do you recognise this ring?"

"Yes! It's like the one Father left for me."

"It *is* the one. It's yours." Rollus took the ring, and we three held out our left hands. All four identical rings glittered gold.

"But how do you come to have it?" Rollus exclaimed. "You didn't...I mean it can't have been any of you who stole it."

Lucius laughed. "No, but the man who did steal it came to me, pretending to be you. He brought me your mother's letter too. He deceived me for a while, but we realised our mistake. There's no mistake with you, though. You have the looks of Lucius Aurelius Marcellus, our father."

"Yes, he said I was the only one to take after him." He smiled. "Well then, you're Lucius, and these ladies are my sisters?"

"I'm Lucius. These are our sisters Aurelia and Albia." Suddenly we were all smiling. "Welcome into our family, brother."

"Welcome," I repeated.

"Yes, welcome indeed," Albia echoed. Then, ever practical, she added, "Now let's see if we can find you some breakfast. If you're an Aurelius, you're bound to be hungry!"

Indeed we were all hungry, and we ate a cheerful breakfast at Elli's house. Elli made a short speech thanking everyone, and Aquilo invited us all to their wedding, which would be at midsummer. After that, he said, they would set off for a tour of Italia.

It looked as if another party was likely to develop, but we didn't stay long. Albia wanted to hurry back to the farm and introduce Rollus to Candidus. They set off together, with the twins, Nasua and Taurus, and Quintus and I promised to follow on later.

Lucius and his men set off for the Headland. "We'll stay at our camp for a day or two," he told Quintus. "I want to make quite sure all the sea raiders are gone, either to the Otherworld, or at the very least back to Gaul."

"Good. Then I suppose you'll be going back to Eburacum?" Quintus asked.

"But not in any great hurry," my brother answered. "Let's try and fit in a few days' hunting at Oak Bridges first."

Titch appeared just then, looking weary and dishevelled, but smiling from ear to ear. "Sir, you won't need me today, will you? I want to spend it with Balca before we move on. I take it we are moving on?"

"I am, yes. I'm bound for Londinium, but I'll have a spot of leave at the Oak Tree before I go. How about you?"

"Me? Am I not coming with you?"

"That's what I'm asking. This was a trial assignment, remember. If you don't want to continue as my assistant, now's the time to say so."

The lad looked crestfallen. "I thought you...I mean, I didn't think I was doing too badly. Are you saying you don't want me to work for you any more?"

Quintus smiled. "I'm saying I'd like you to. But it's your choice."

"I'd like it too. Is it a bargain then?"

"It's a bargain. You can have today to enjoy yourself with your shepherdess. Come to me at Albia's tomorrow morning."

"I will. And you two can enjoy yourselves too, now the job's finished." He winked and strode off, whistling.

"Cheeky little tyke," I said, but Quintus was still smiling.

"He's got a point. We have time to ourselves today." He put his arm round me. "Or have you something else in mind?"

"Well...He said our job's finished, but it's not quite done yet."

"What's left?" But the flash in his purple eyes told me he knew the answer.

"We still have to find Caratacus' gold. And I know where it is."

Chapter XXXII

Candidus and Albia weren't sceptical when I told them I could find the gold. They were downright disbelieving.

Albia just said, "Oh really, Relia, do be serious," and handed me a beaker of wine.

"I'm afraid she is serious," Quintus smiled, accepting a wine-mug for himself. "That's the worrying thing."

Candidus said, "But Aurelia, our boys and Brutus' men have dug over every inch of this farm—well, every inch that fits the description. A pit north of a tall tree, within sight of the sea from the top of it. We've sixteen trees on the farm that are tall enough to give a view of the sea if you climb right up. We've looked under them all."

"But," I asked, "have you checked the trees that were here thirty years ago, when the gold was buried?"

Candidus looked at me as if I were mad. "How can we?"

Quintus gave me a sudden smile. Albia leapt to her feet, almost dropping her wine-beaker. "The tree stumps!" she exclaimed. "Where the big old ash trees were cut down. No, we haven't looked near those."

Candidus, Rollus and Taurus ran for spades, while Albia led Quintus and me behind the house and through the new stockade to the field where the ashes had once made a windbreak. Three wide stumps were all that was left of them now. They'd been cut down to within a hand-span of the ground, but their girth showed that they were the remains of huge, lofty trees.

"These are the largest," Albia said. "We'll begin here." She glanced up at the sun, which was almost at its zenith. "I never thought about it before, but they're in a row from east to west. So if you dig a trench there," she pointed beyond the tiny stump-shadows on the grass," you'll cover the north side of all of them." She giggled. "I think at last you may have found the right road, Relia. Come along, you boys. And I promise you, when you've found the gold, we'll have the best party this province has ever seen!"

"We'll each dig near a different tree," Candidus said. "We'll join the pits up later if we need to."

"Before we begin," Rollus said, "I'd like to say something. I've always assumed that Father's letter meant his hoard of gold was for my mother and me."

We all stopped dead and stared at him. Was he laying claim to the whole hoard? After everything that had happened?

"Not necessarily," Lucius said.

"And you said you wanted to share it," Albia objected, and then caught her breath. "No, of course, that was the man in Londinium pretending to be you."

"Are you saying you intend to keep it all for yourself?" Lucius asked, in a dangerously calm voice.

"I'm saying I could if I chose." Rollus looked at each of us in turn. None of us contradicted him, because in our hearts we knew he was right. "But I don't choose. This is a gift from our father, and I want the four of us to share it. It may be a fortune, or just a few coins or some jewellery. Whatever it is, we divide it equally. I'd like us all to shake hands on that now, before we start."

"Thank you, Rollus," Lucius said. "That's very fair, and we accept. Don't we?"

Albia and I agreed, and we all three shook hands with Rollus. But this touch of formality, necessary as it probably was, had made us all self-conscious and slightly wary. Then Taurus announced, "Don't forget I'll expect at least one gold piece for helping you dig it out."

Everyone laughed, and the men set to with a will. Taurus, with his huge strength, dug his pit faster than the others, and before long he'd gone so far down that only his head and shoulders were above ground. Then even these disappeared as he knelt down at the bottom of the hole. "I've found something," he called. "It looks like the lid of a basket. A bit tattered, but still in one piece."

Everybody stopped what they were doing. I said, "Can you see what's inside?"

"No." His voice sounded slightly muffled. "The lid's attached to something underneath, I suppose it's the rest of the basket, which is still buried. Just wait while I uncover it. I don't want to be too rough."

We crowded round and peered over. All we could see was Taurus' broad back, and the powerful movements of his shoulders and arms as he scraped soil away from him with his bare hands.

"That's cleared it." He stood up and faced us. "It's a complete basket, but it's in a bad way. All the canes are cracked and rotten. If I lift it up as it is, it'll break."

"I'll go down and help," Rollus offered.

"No, I'll go," Lucius answered.

Quintus said, "I'll go, if anyone needs to. You Aurelii stay together up here."

"It'll be easier with two," Taurus said, "but first we've got to find a way of lifting it."

"We'll lay it on a blanket, or a sack," Quintus suggested. "Anything strong enough to take the weight, then we can heave it up by the corners."

"That's easy, I'll use my tunic." Taurus stripped off his brown wool tunic, and Quintus jumped down into the hole beside him. There wasn't much room, but together they managed to move the basket onto the tunic, and then lift both tunic and basket up and up, till Lucius and Rollus were able to take the strain and haul the heavy burden out.

"By the gods," Lucius said, "if that's all gold…"

Taurus and Quintus scrambled out as my two brothers put their load quite gently onto the ground. There was a creaking, tearing sound, and the worn basket split open like an eggshell.

A cascade of small blue-grey pebbles poured out onto the grass. Lucius seized the lid and wrenched it off, and as the basket collapsed completely we could see nothing but stones.

There was a stunned silence, and then we all started to laugh. It seemed the final absurdity. After everything we'd gone through, our hopes, our fears, our efforts, this was the legendary gold of Caratacus.

Quintus, laughing like the rest of us, dug both hands into the heap of stones and scattered them. "May as well make sure," he said, and we all bent down to help him. Near the bottom of the pile my fingers touched something larger than a pebble, and as I pulled at it, the sun sparkled on shiny metal—not gold, but a silver-grey box.

I stood up and held it aloft. The box was intact, its lid secured all round with wax, and in two places there was the imprint of our father's seal. "Well, Father left us something, after all. It's too light to contain gold though. A letter, I expect."

Lucius reached out his hand to take it. "Let's have a look, Sis."

"I'll open it," Rollus said, moving towards me. "I'm the oldest."

"But I'm the head of the family."

"If it's a letter, it's likely to be for me, though, isn't it?"

I kept hold of the box. "I found it, I may as well open it."

Quintus stepped forward. "*I'll* open it, and read whatever's in there out to all of you. Will that do?"

Everyone nodded, and I handed it over to him. He broke the wax seals and pulled back the hinged lid. Inside was a folded piece of papyrus. It was bone dry, and when he unfolded it, the ink on it stood out clear and black. He held it up so that we could all see it. "Does anyone recognise the handwriting?"

"It's father's," Lucius said.

"Father's," Albia and I agreed.

"Yes. It's the same as my mother's letter," Rollus said.

"Good." Quintus began to read:

To Rollus, Lucius, Aurelia and Albia, my dear children, from your father, Lucius Aurelius Marcellus, greetings.

I hope you never read this. If you do, it will mean I have not been able to tell you certain things that I always intended to share with you. But it will also mean that some or all of you have been resourceful and determined enough to find out my secret. Resourcefulness and determination are two traits of character we Aurelii have. So is another quality you will need now: the toughness to accept a disappointment.

No doubt you were expecting a basket of Caratacus' gold. A large hoard of gold coin was indeed here for a while. Years ago I found it. I gave half to my friend and blood brother Nertacos, and with my permission, he buried the other half here. I was a soldier then, I could not take it with me on the march. Now I've left the army and come back to Britannia to settle with three of my children. I've returned to fetch my share of the gold, and it amuses me to replace the coins with something just as heavy, but rather less valuable. If strangers dig up this basket, which they have no right to do, they will have found what they deserve.

But there will be no gold pieces to share out among the family. I need it all to complete the building of our new mansio and to buy the land that must go with it to ensure its success. It has cost more than I expected, more than I had, even though that was a considerable sum. Several officials and local men of influence have charged a high price for helping me. I don't resent that, it's the way the world is. With Caratacus' gold I have enough. I hope that the mansio proves to be the success I dream of. I hope too that the Fates have allowed you four, my children, to come together as I always intended. You are all my family, and my love and duty are yours in equal measure. Farewell.

It took time to absorb the contents of the letter, to read it through again, as we all did for ourselves, and realise fully that our dreams of family wealth would never be fulfilled. I felt a mixture of emotions, and didn't want to talk about any of them, even to Lucius. So I wandered off into the little patch of woodland behind the house. Soon I heard footsteps on the soft soil, and Quintus came to stand beside me. "Are you very disappointed, Aurelia?"

"A little, I suppose. But oddly enough I'm relieved too. Doesn't that sound stupid? Relieved not to find a consul's ransom in gold?"

"I understand. Gold can bring out the worst in us sometimes."

I nodded, remembering the way Lucius and Rollus had been squabbling like half-grown pups. "Having two brothers will take some getting used to, for all of us. We'll do it more successfully without any added complications."

"Lucius will always be head of the family," Quintus said. "Rollus doesn't want to challenge that."

"You've been talking to him about it?"

"He's begun to talk about it himself, to Lucius and Albia. I said I'd find you. If there's to be a family council, you should be there."

"Yes, I should. I'll come."

We did talk about it, seriously and at some length, and without any silly bickering or point-scoring. We three were happy to accept Rollus as our brother, and we all agreed that Lucius remained head of the Aurelius family. We were willing to offer our new brother a place at the mansio, if he wanted a job there. It seemed only fair, and we were sure father would have done this himself eventually. Rollus was grateful, but admitted he couldn't decide about his future yet, everything was too new and strange now. He said he might go back to sea, but not, he promised, as a raider. We agreed that if he did, we'd set him up with a boat of his own.

Our sober discussions ended abruptly when the twins came racing out of the house, followed by Nasua and Taurus. "We couldn't keep them quiet any longer," Taurus said. "They want to know when the party will start. So do I."

"The party?" Albia looked doubtful.

"Taurus says you p-promised us," Nasua put in, and the children ran round us, yelling "Promise! Promise! A party! A party!"

My sister shook her head. "The party was going to be to celebrate finding the gold. But now we've lost a fortune, it doesn't seem such a good idea."

Taurus said, "But you haven't lost it, because you never had it. And you've got a new brother, and *you,*" he smiled at Rollus, "have got a whole new family. I think those are good enough reasons for a party. Don't you?"

Of course he was right. The reasons were good enough. The party was spectacular.

About the History

It's hardly surprising that we know far more about the Romans of Britannia than about the native Celts. The conquerors have left us a much greater wealth of material remains, from buildings to beakers, than the Britons did. And they left us contemporary accounts of the province, which the Celts have not. This wasn't just because the winners' versions of wars tend to prevail, but because the native Britons hardly used writing at all, and certainly not for recording history.

Once they controlled a province, the Romans encouraged its inhabitants to adopt Roman education and ways of thought. Many natives undoubtedly did this, especially among the old tribal elite who were used to power and wanted to retain it. They became Roman citizens, spoke Latin, and enjoyed the lifestyle of their conquerors. How far the poorer people did this too is harder to say for sure. Nor can we tell whether the Romanised part of the population abandoned their Celtic culture completely; it seems unlikely, given the importance of family and tribal ties.

One important thing we don't know about the British Celts is how they spoke. Their language died out after the Empire fell, though Welsh and Cornish, two quite similar Celtic languages, did persist and develop, and they give us clues about ancient British speech. What little survives, such as people's names, tended to be "Latinised" by the Romans. For instance many Celtic men's names ended in –os, but have come down to us with the more familiar –us ending, either because their owners wanted to make themselves sound more Roman, or, more likely, because the Latin-writing historians wrote them in a way their Latin-speaking readers would find familiar.

Caratacus (whose name should only include two c's, not three), was a real war leader who opposed the Roman invasion and was finally betrayed by the Queen of Brigantia. But don't come searching for his gold; that part is pure fiction.

We can't say exactly what the coastline around the Headland—modern-day Flamborough Head—would have looked like to Aurelia. The North Sea has steadily eroded away the land over the past two millennia, especially to the south in Bridlington Bay. There is evidence that both Romans and Celts lived in the area, but their harbours and seaside dwellings are under the water now. We must look to modern archaeological techniques to tell us more about them some day.

Most other geographical features in the book are recognisably still here: the Headland itself, the wolds, and the Roman roads that Aurelia travelled. The Oak Tree Mansio is fictitious, but its location is real, at the bottom of a steep hill on a main Roman road that still carries traffic between Eburacum and the coast.

We know quite a bit about Roman medicine, (which was Greek in origin) thanks to doctors like Celsus and Galen who were also prolific writers. It was sophisticated and in many ways impressive and successful, especially given the gaps in classical knowledge: they knew nothing of how germs cause infection, or of the circulation of blood through the heart. But in practise much of it worked, and was the basis of European medicine for many centuries.

I read stacks of books about Roman times. For me researching is as much of a pleasure as writing. These days I also use the Internet—with caution, because some so-called "history" out there is incomplete, biased, or just plain wrong. But you'll find many useful translations of Latin texts, and photos of Roman sites and archaeological finds from all over the Empire. There are also knowledgeable folk in cyberspace who are generous with high-quality advice on historical matters. One group of academics, the brittonica mailing list, specialises in ancient British-Celtic matters, especially linguistics, and has given me invaluable help with sorting out some characters' names. Find more about it at http://tech.groups.yahoo.com/group/brittonica/

I'll end with a list of some of the books I've found useful. I wish there was space for all of them.

Roman authors:

Agricola: Tacitus. Tacitus' account of a general and Governor who spent much of his career in Britannia

The Twelve Caesars: Suetonius. A wonderfully gossipy account of Roman court and political life

De Medicina: Celsus. Not for the squeamish, but fascinating. Print editions are expensive; you can find translations on the Internet

Letters of the Younger Pliny. Not about Britannia, but very much about the Roman mindset

Modern authors:

A History of Roman Britain: Peter Salway

Life and Letters on the Roman Frontier (Vindolanda and its people): Alan K. Bowman

Women in Roman Britain: Lindsay Allason-Jones

Iron Age Britain: Barry Cunliffe

The Finds of Roman Britain: Guy de la Bédoyère

Greek and Roman Medicine: Helen King

The Classical Cookbook: Andrew Dalby and Sally Grainger

What the Romans Did For Us: Philip Wilkinson

To receive a free catalog of Poisoned Pen Press titles, please contact us in one of the following ways:

Phone: 1-800-421-3976
Facsimile: 1-480-949-1707
Email: info@poisonedpenpress.com
Website: www.poisonedpenpress.com

Poisoned Pen Press
6962 E. First Ave. Ste. 103
Scottsdale, AZ 85251

CPSIA information can be obtained at www.ICGtesting.com
Printed in the USA
BVOW05s1532011115

425147BV00001B/56/P